D1715428

To Mackenzie—for helping me make Noble House the best geeky kink club I could imagine.

IN THE ROUGH

SARA BROOKES

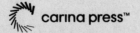 carina press™

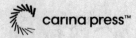

ISBN-13: 978-1-335-01313-2

In the Rough

Recycling programs for this product may not exist in your area.

www.CarinaPress.com

Printed in U.S.A.

IN THE ROUGH

Chapter One

"What the hell am I, the bag lady?" Enver scowled at the bundle of colorful plastic bags Saint handed him.

"Just smile and look pretty," Saint offered. "It's what you do best."

Enver's eyes narrowed. He knew his buddy Ford "Saint" Templar was a lot of things, but a swindler wasn't one of them. "Cut it with the crap, asshole. I'm not some fresh-faced subbie at the club you're trying to charm. You didn't drag me all the way to Vegas to juggle these useless pamphlets."

"I already told you I need you to dazzle the masses with your bright wit and shining sense of humor." Saint laughed as Enver gave him the middle finger. "Because, you ass, you're part owner of a club known for cutting-edge technology." He slapped a flyer against Enver's palm. "You're interested and being responsible with your investment."

Enver scowled as Saint smiled widely. "Yeah, yeah. I know I get a say in the money, but I'm still not sure how you roped me into attending a trade show about geek shit I know nothing about. Kochran usually handles this kind of crap. Or Ezra. Or any of a dozen other employees who have more brains than I do about computers."

"You know as well as I do you can sniff out the bullshit better than anyone."

Saint wandered off to a nearby booth, leaving Enver alone. Yeah, he owned one third of Noble House, a hybrid kink club that specialized in getting members off through computers, games and live-action play, but he still wasn't clear how that qualified him for this kind of work. Supervise was more like it. He suspected that was the true reason Kochran had suggested—voluntold—Enver accompany Saint to Las Vegas for the show. A fucking desert. The least these geeks could have done was to have had their dog and pony demonstration in Hawaii. That sand gave way to the ocean. Palm trees. Water. Tiny bathing suits.

His sour mood wasn't helped by the fact he'd recently had to break things off with his long-term submissive. Bracey had wanted him to be something he wasn't. Wanted a relationship he wasn't equipped to give. Though she'd promised she understood, he'd recognized the disappointment in her eyes as they'd come to a solution.

Nothing he hated more than disappointing a subbie.

A sudden slap of pain jolted him out of his thoughts. A blur of color dropped to the ground a few feet away as Enver's shoulder throbbed from the hard contact. "What the hell?"

"Fuck, sorry, I'm late. Fucking shit." The harried man unleashed a waterfall of curses as the papers he'd been carrying spilled to the ground. "Shit it all to shitty, shitty hell."

Despite his annoyance at being slammed into, Enver bit back a smile as the man's tirade continued while he collected a few sheets within easy reach.

"Need a hand?" Enver crouched without waiting for an answer, scooping up a handful of papers covered with indecipherable numbers and letters.

"Know the location of the closest Tardis?" The frazzled man snatched a bundle of paper closer, rescuing it from being embossed with a footprint watermark from a passing attendee. Absently, he tunneled his auburn hair into total disarray. "Christ, people have no respect for someone else's work."

As the man continued to gather his scattered paperwork, Enver regarded him with a keen eye. He was male enough to appreciate the man's overall physique, but the scars marring one side of the man's face were more intriguing. The discoloration along his cheek and jaw and neck was splotchy, dark red in some places while a light pink on others. The marks dotted the skin all the way to his ear and disappeared under the collar of his polo shirt, an indication the scars went farther. His gut clenched as he discovered he wanted to know more.

"I'm sure you'll be able to put everything back in order."

As though a geyser had exploded, the man suddenly burst into animation. He stood, waving the papers wildly around. "No, I can't! It took me all fucking night to get everything straight. Do you have any idea how much this whole stupid thing is costing me?" The guy swung his arms wildly nearly taking out someone trying to pass. "If I don't get this shit together, I can't make a sale. I can't pay for food. Or a place to live. I'll be homeless and living in my car. Again."

"Whoa, whoa." Enver intercepted the man when he lost his balance as he tried to turn around. "Breathe, man. Take a couple of deep breaths or you're going to hyperventilate." He squeezed the man's shoulders in encouragement as his chest expanded and contracted with each breath. A full minute later, things appeared to be returning to normal. "Nice and easy. There you go."

"Sorry." The man's gaze finally lifted, the dark circles under his brown eyes indicating just how stressed out he was. He froze for a second, startled, as though he'd finally seen Enver for the first time. As he blinked, one side of his mouth lifted. "You must think I'm some wacked out nut job."

The genuine embarrassment and half smile aimed Enver's way caused a vicious tightness in his chest and nearly knocked him off his feet. Shit. He took a few breaths himself before responding with measured tones. "No, I think you're overstressed about something you don't have control over."

The man ran his hands over his face. "You could say that."

"Okay. First things first—let's get this all picked up and get out of the main thoroughfare before we both get run over." Enver crouched with the man, assisting in gathering the loose papers. It took them both a few minutes, but the simple process appeared to bleed off the visible tension from the guy's shoulders.

"Thanks again." The man held out his hand to take the paperwork Enver had collected and flashed a genuine smile. "I can get it from here."

Enver realized he wasn't ready to separate. Though he wasn't certain if it was because he was interested to learn more or was still concerned after the panic attack. "I can give you a hand getting this stuff back to wherever you were headed."

"You sure? Look like you've got your hands full already."

Enver glanced to the bags he'd set down. "Nothing I can't handle."

"Great. Should only take a few minutes." The man gestured with his chin. "I've got a booth a few aisles down."

"Got all the time in the world. Lead the way."

As they walked, Enver looked around the long aisles of company displays, a dizzying array of lights and sounds he likened to casinos or strip clubs. Everybody had their thing. For the people surrounding him, it was computers and smartphones and whatever the hell else sort of technology Enver didn't give a shit about. The chaos of it all blurred together. Give him a set of ropes, carabiners and a handful of panic snaps any day over this jumbled mess of electronics.

"This is me. Thanks again."

"No problem." Enver glanced around the booth as he handed over the papers he'd carried. A few piles of open boxes were scattered near the separator curtain, but there was nothing that stood out about the booth. The vendors on either side had gone over the top with their displays, which made the bare bones area in front of him seem even more underserved. "So...ah."

The man grimaced as he followed Enver's gaze. "It's not much, I know. Certainly not as elaborate as those weaselhead fucknuggets over there." He glared at a nearby booth.

Enver burst out laughing as he leaned his hip against the table. "That is some inventive schoolyard name-calling."

"What else do you call a bunch of losers hawking burned-out motherboards and faulty RAM sticks to companies needing a hand?"

"Speaking from experience, I take it?" Enver asked as he eyed the burned cuff of the man's shirt.

"Just my annoyance talking." The man rolled his eyes. "Not all of my equipment made it in time. Airline lost half my shit. My amped-up power supplies didn't make it either, which is why I was trying to science the hell out of this piece of crap so I'd have something to display." He tapped the edge of a burned circuit board.

"And the weaselhead fucknuggets sold you something subpar. Hope you got your money back." Enver juggled his bags as he picked up a colorful pamphlet that looked exactly like the other hundred or so flyers Saint kept bringing him. So far, nothing set this guy's company apart from the thousands of businesses trying to hawk their wares.

"BLINC." Enver turned the nondescript advertisement over, frowning at the lack of explanation. "What does that mean?"

"Bio-Linked Inter-Neural Client." The man gestured to pieces of equipment scattered around the booth. "All of this."

"Clever." Though Enver had no idea what any of it meant, he was enough of a businessman to recognize the man was trying.

"Don't happen to work for the government, do you? Looking to offer a multimillion-dollar contract to the underdog?" the man asked hopefully.

"Alas, no." Though Enver had no idea exactly what he was looking at on the shiny card stock, something told him this was the kind of stuff Saint and Ezra would salivate over. He still didn't know why he'd been strong-armed into the trip, he could at least take the pamphlet and add it to the pile. "Have you got a card? This looks like something my partners might be interested in."

The man grimaced.

Jesus, this guy was so all over the map it was ridiculous. "Let me guess…airline?"

"Would you believe the printer forgot to mail the box?" He barked out a hard laugh. "Nothing about this trip has gone right, but things are looking up." He gave Enver a lingering once-over that signaled his meaning, his gaze almost feral. That heated glance continued as he licked his lips. "The website listed on the bottom has my contact info." He plucked the pamphlet from Enver's hand, wrote something in the top corner and handed it back.

Marcus Holly. And a phone number.

"That's my direct line. Just give me a call if you have any questions or want a full demo." Marcus pulled out a cell phone and snapped a pic. "Don't worry, I'm not going to plaster your pic all over social media or anything. I'll forget we talked later. Name to face sort of deal."

"Enver Furst." Enver hesitantly extended his hand, hoping Marcus wouldn't be able to tell how heated his skin had gotten. As their hands connected, a buzz vibrated down his spine and collected at the base. That heady sensation was going to follow him for the rest of the day. Way more pleasant to think about than the torture Saint was putting him through. Maybe something interesting would come out of this trip after all. "I'm sure I'll be in contact."

"I look forward to hearing from you."

He must think I'm a wreck.

Marcus watched Enver walk away, just like all the

rest of his potential customers. At least this one had a mighty fine ass. The black jeans he wore enhanced his assets, lifting and separating them in perfect alignment. Marcus didn't need to see to know the skin under those jeans was just as taut. Men with asses like that didn't wear tight jeans without intending to show off.

His body had never reacted so quickly to another person. Watching Enver walk away left Marcus with a dick thickening in the confines of his pants and his pulse racing so violently his head felt like it was going to explode.

The harsh convention hall lighting had made it hard to judge the man's age, but the touch of gray at his temples and the lines around his eyes indicated he was more than Marcus's thirty-three years. Didn't matter. Whatever the guy's age—he wore it well. Damn well.

Older men didn't usually do it for him, but there was something about the guy's smile that had compelled Marcus to offer up his private number. Yeah, he'd been purposefully obtuse about what kind of business he was in, but Marcus wasn't interested in just a contract. He really needed a job, but those were as hard to come by as fulfilling his other…requirements.

He didn't believe in fated souls, but when he spent as much time as he did inside virtual reality, it was easy to trick himself into thinking such a thing was possible. That spark of connection caused all rational thought to flee.

And then reality set in.

It didn't matter how much flirting or how many hot glances they shared. Not as though someone like Enver would be interested in someone like Marcus. No one had ever gotten past the damn scars he was forced to look at every morning.

A steady buzzing sounded overhead. He looked up to see a drone hovering over the area, a camera mounted on the underbelly scanning the vast crowd. There was nothing extraordinary about the quadcopter, and its presence wasn't unusual during a convention, but something about it raised the hairs on the back of his neck.

"Overreacting, Holly." He scowled at the meager display he'd scraped together and realized his lack of setup was going to be displayed on YouTube for all the world to see. "Great way to make a first impression."

His gaze fell to the next booth and saw the guys waving at the drone to get its attention. "Fucknuggets," he muttered under his breath as he grimaced. The absurd curse had sounded completely different tripping off Enver's tongue, that whiskey and smoke voice caressing each vowel and consonant like a lover instead of a disgruntled business owner.

He brushed off thoughts of the man and settled down to try to salvage what he could of the disastrous weekend.

Chapter Two

Enver sat in a chair with his legs crossed, feet tapping with the beat of the soft music filtering through hidden speakers. Though this area of Noble House was mainly used for aftercare, it wasn't currently being utilized for that purpose. Instead, it served as his office. Of the three men who owned a stake in the club, Enver was the only one who didn't have a designated space.

In truth, he didn't need one. Why would he? He left the daily running of the business to Kochran and Saint. Besides, neither of them had this view. The oversized and overstuffed chairs were positioned directly across from what most members referred to as the club's art gallery.

Boyce Denali, Saint's husband, was also the club's official photographer. Whenever he wasn't serving as DM or participating in a scene with Saint and Grae, their wife, Boyce could be found documenting the club with the camera strapped to his neck. Enver not only admired Boyce's work, he'd served as a model for him on more than one occasion.

The results of one of those photo shoots had been blown up and laid onto a canvas that stretched from floor to ceiling. Done in soft, muted colors, the picture depicted a submissive's aftercare. Enver sat cross-legged on the floor, a satisfied sub cradled in his arms. Pink and red rope marks showed on her thighs and hips where she'd been suspended in Enver's rigging. The shot had been difficult, both for the subjects and the photographer, only because Boyce had been struggling with personal demons. But they had been shed away long enough for him to capture the stunning image on the wall.

Too bad Enver hated the picture.

His shields had been stripped away, showing him at his most vulnerable. He refused to ask Boyce to remove it because Enver had recognized the glint in Boyce's eyes when he'd snapped the last frame. If his weakness had allowed a good friend to heal, then so be it.

"Sorry, I didn't realize anyone was here."

Enver looked up, recognizing Marcus from the convention. A rush of intense arousal crashed through his system, his cock instantly hardening. Marcus's disheveled appearance on the trade show floor had been replaced with tall, not so dark, but still deliciously dangerous. His mop of auburn hair had been tamed into a sleek cascade that almost brushed the collar of his shirt. Brown eyes peered out from behind matching tortoise frames. The burned lab coat had given way to tan slacks, a denim-blue oxford shirt and an ivory sweater vest.

Dear god. Enver'd gotten hard over a guy wearing a *sweater vest*.

The scars that had fascinated Enver at the convention were still just as intriguing.

Enver cleared his throat and stood, offering his hand. "Kochran said he'd added a new geek to his stable of experts. Glad to see it worked out so well for you." In fact, soon after he'd left Marcus's booth, he'd trashed all the bags he'd been loaded down with and given Marcus's flyer to Saint. The instant spark that had lit Saint's eyes when he'd read the information confirmed Marcus had something the club would be interested in, so it wasn't much of a shock to see him standing there.

When Marcus touched his hand, Enver did his best to ignore the clench of his stomach and the immediate rigidity of his dick. Such a simple expression shouldn't affect him that way. Shouldn't make him feel as though his world had fallen off its axis.

The handshake was solid and friendly without all that stupid posturing some men used to assert their position. It was safer to chalk up the reactions to his thoughts about the photo and the recent upheaval of his separation from Bracey. Too much unresolved emotional turmoil still clawing at him even though he knew their separation had been for the best.

"Just getting started?" Enver asked as he pulled his hand away. He fought the urge to dig his fingers into his palm to erase the residual tingle.

"I moved in my equipment last week, but I just got everything set up and ready to start the other night."

"Airline lose your stuff again?" Enver prayed the inflection in his voice didn't give away the heat winding down his spine.

Luckily, Marcus laughed at his comment. "No. Just took me a bit to find somewhere to live while I'm here. Guess this is my new home away from home." He looked around, taking everything in. "Brighter than I expected."

Enver watched him for a few minutes, enjoying the

expressions on Marcus's face as he took in the club from a newcomer's viewpoint. "Imagine the stereo-typical ominous darkness? Basement has some of that."

"Nothing about an online BDSM club is typical. The fact there's also a physical location built from a former military armory is unusual as well. I've visited plenty of clubs, but this is…entirely off the rails. Never imagined this kind of place existed for me to even consider working at. Kochran is a genius."

"For opening the club or for hiring you?" Enver asked, genuinely interested in the answer.

Marcus smirked. "Both, of course."

Enver watched Marcus with a more critical eye as the man continued to explore. He was an enigma. Most people were an easy read. Enver could usually figure out pertinent details within a few minutes of meeting someone for the first time, but Marcus was proving dif-ficult to pin down.

He never would have pegged Marcus as someone with an interest in BDSM. Just like he couldn't get a read if Marcus was dominant or submissive. Switch, possibly? There certainly seemed to be enough of that going around lately. But no, something told Enver what-ever side of the fence Marcus stood on, he was that all the way.

Marcus's posture changed visibly as he turned and spotted the photo. "Oh, wow."

Enver had stopped trying to look at the photo from an outsider's prospective months ago. No matter how hard he tried, he'd never saw what everyone else raved about. He only saw the flaws. The unvarnished vulner-ability of a Dominant and submissive.

"This is extraordinary," Marcus continued. "I'm not

much of a photographer, just the everyday stuff with my smartphone, but whoever did this has a shit ton of talent."

Boyce would appreciate that. "I'll be sure to let the photographer know."

Marcus touched the canvas.

Boyce would *not* appreciate that.

Marcus faced him. "How long have you been with her?"

Enver winced, then covered it by shifting in the chair. "We're not. Bracey and I were just helping out a friend. Saint's husband was the photographer."

"Jesus on hot buttered ass, he knows his stuff. The connection between the two of you is remarkable. The comfort you're giving her after the scene. The gentle way you're giving her the support she needs after an intense session."

Any arousal Enver had toward Marcus evaporated as he broke down every reason Enver hated the photograph. The sort of exposure and vulnerability wasn't what he was looking for out of sessions. He'd been that once, long ago when he'd thought his life had been heading a different direction. Because of that, he'd made a promise to himself never to allow it again.

Sessions with submissives fulfilled his need for duty. Helped him patch over the holes living inside him for a few hours before the cement cracked and broke away. He was always safe in the confines of the sanctuary he used to shield himself from the outside world when those breaks finally happened.

This moment, though...this one had slipped by his shields.

Enver snipped the threads on the reminder of his

weakness. "If you're looking for the offices, they're up on the third floor. Except for Kochran's. His is in the lounge back down on the first floor."

"Actually, I was looking for you." Marcus bounced up onto the balls of his feet, anxious as any schoolboy waiting for summer vacation. "Kochran said you were around when I mentioned needing a hand."

Work. Something that would take his mind off all this emotional shit he didn't have time for or want. Enver unbuttoned one of his shirtsleeves and rolled it once. "Airline finally find your stuff?"

Marcus pointed to the stairwell. "My equipment is already set up in one of the auxiliary rooms downstairs."

"So what do you need from me?" Enver asked, confused.

"I need you naked."

Marcus smothered a laugh at the abject horror darkening Enver's stunning eyes.

"Excuse me?" Yeah, the tone of that husky voice got better every time the man spoke.

Marcus gestured for Enver to follow him down the stairs, but Enver remained stubbornly in place. Marcus knew he was going to have to do something to convince the other man before he bolted. "Bear with me for a moment, Enver."

Marcus pulled out his cell phone, swiped to his notes and located the one that would help him plead his case. He shifted closer to Enver, angling his phone so the other man could see. "To get the most out of the virtual experience, it helps to have a visual aid. The idea is members will come in to see me and get a full body scan."

Marcus started the crude animation he'd worked up to help illustrate the idea. He was a bit-banger, not an artist. "That way, when they're plugged in with their chosen partner, the visual is more realistic. Personal. It's one of the few things I have that sets my program apart from all the other jerkoffs out there."

One of Enver's eyebrows lifted. "And how long will I need to be sans clothing?"

"An hour, tops. Two at the most depending on how temperamental the scanners are being." Marcus locked his phone and shoved it into his pocket. "Kochran said he would help, but he's tied up for the rest of the day."

"Of course he is," Enver muttered.

It truth, Marcus had suggested Enver as the perfect model. Not only because he was one of the club owners—helpful to have a familiar face when they opened it up to the members—but also for entirely selfish reasons. Marcus wanted to see the man nude. He had a feeling Enver was hiding a sinfully decadent body that would make even the staunchest conservative blush.

Bottom line, too…it had been a damn long time since Marcus had seen another human in the flesh. The virtual world he'd begun to develop years ago had eaten away at his personal time. And the few attempts Marcus had made toward a sexual connection with anyone had ended disastrously. No one wanted a submissive who wore the kind of scars he did.

He flashed Enver his friendliest smile. "It won't hurt, promise."

"If that's the case"—Enver smirked—"you've come to work at the wrong place." He waved him on. "Two hours. Let's go."

Chapter Three

Two minutes later, Marcus extracted the key Kochran had given him to keep his equipment secure. No doubt this wouldn't be his permanent home, but he didn't expect to spend much time in the area after things were up and working. The system was self-sufficient. Brief meetings with Saint, Maddy and Ezra had given Marcus the impression they could competently handle any issues once he got them trained. He could drop by once or twice a year for a tune-up on the virtual reality system he would develop for them, and move along.

Marcus Holly never stayed in one place longer than necessary. Not since the parole letters had started arriving. The latest had been the most worrisome as the impending date closed in.

"So where do you want me?"

Marcus shook off the threads of his past that had shaped him. "By the desk is fine. I need to get some extra electrodes." The case with the small disks was positioned about ten feet away, but still within eyeshot of Enver. Which meant Marcus could see Enver clearly in his peripheral vision while he collected the items. He paused when Enver grabbed the bottom edge of his shirt and lifted. Delicious lines and planes were revealed as the fabric rose to reveal perfectly chiseled and…lickable abs.

Real men didn't have those kind of abs. Gods did.

"Tell me again why I have to be entirely nude? Why I can't keep my underwear on until it's time for you to do whatever you need to do then?"

Marcus swallowed as he dug through the pile of electronics. "You could, but you'll risk popping off one of the receivers when you try to remove your underwear. Safer just to start without clothing. Eliminates the risk. And let's face it, this is a sex club. What would be the point of a virtual model where you don't get to see the goods?"

When Marcus turned, he got his first head-on encounter with the full beauty of Enver Furst. He dropped the entire collection of diodes as he sucked in a breath. Enver's chest had a fine layer of hair across the pecs, the light of the room catching the glimmering strands of gray sprinkled throughout. The last Dom Marcus had been with had chosen to keep his body void of any hair. Though Marcus had no preference either way, he found he liked seeing the natural beauty that made him want to reach out and touch what had been trapped beneath the shirt. The fabric had also hidden a large tattoo inked down the right side of Enver's torso.

Marcus recognized the pattern as the same one painted on the wall of the club lounge. Three lions surrounding some kind of shield crest. The emblem was also splashed on one corner of the club's website that Marcus had perused seconds after ending the phone call that had brought him to the club.

He studied all that mouth-watering skin. That fine slope of chest and the taper to the abdomen that disappeared under the waistband of a pair of well-fitted jeans. He wanted to take a bite. A great big one that would allow him to experience all the flavors Enver had to offer.

Enver eyed him. "Anything I can help with?"

Marcus shook his head, licking his lips as he turned his attention back to the task. Yeah, he'd fully intended to ogle the hell out of the man, but he hadn't expected Enver to be so…large. The relaxed tee had masked the expansive build. Big physique meant tiny dick, right? Enver had to be packing something that rivaled a Vienna sausage that would shatter the lust coiling through Marcus.

Yup. Tiny, tiny penis. Muscles for miles to compensate. Yeah. Perfect.

Hands full of diodes, Marcus turned and saw that he'd been so focused on wishing what Enver had, he'd missed the fact Enver had stripped down completely. *Don't look. Don't look. Don't…*

The tiny plastic circles in his hands fell to the ground in a cascade and scattered when they hit the concrete.

It was more like a salami.

Fuck me.

The twitch of a smile turned up one corner of Enver's lips. "Need a hand?"

"I've got it." *Don't come over and…*shit.

Enver didn't listen. He crossed the space between them, his flaccid penis bouncing between his muscular thighs as he approached. "What are these things anyway?"

Marcus focused on collecting the pieces and not the naked man just inches away. "Receivers. They light up when the beam contacts them. In return, they'll send the information to my machine, and then the computer generates a three-dimensional rendering of the subject that will be loaded into the virtual environment. From there, users can manipulate the avatar however they'd like."

"Sorry I asked." Enver used his wide hands to scoop up most of the fallen items and deposited them into the bucket Marcus normally used for transport.

Marcus focused on gathering the rest of them and not on Enver's body as he walked back over to the desk. He had already gotten an eyeful of the front. He'd probably keel over if he saw Enver's ass.

"Never seen this room so bare," Enver said conversationally. "Usually a bunch of equipment here."

I have chats with naked men all the time. No big deal. "Not computer equipment, I take it?"

"This past summer, it was a torture chamber. One of our regulars liked torment scenes and kept a cage over in that corner." He pointed to that corner first, then the opposite. "Relief area over there. Chair here in the center where your desk is set up. A chest back by the door full of all the usual equipment."

Marcus had competent enough visualization skills to imagine this room full of those things. That level of play was well beyond his interests, but the idea of it intrigued him. One of the perks of his work was helping others live out their wildest fantasies. He'd seen more than his fair share of intense scenes during his research to perfect the program for potential customers.

Enver watched him for a time before asking, "How did you get into something like this?"

Marcus busied himself with connecting the diodes on top of Enver's feet. Eventually he'd have to face the inevitable, but for now he would at least focus on the task and the conversation. "By accident. I was always interested in computers, even as a kid. I changed careers around ten years ago and during the transition, I learned about the VR technology."

"Hooked from then on, huh?"

Marcus shrugged, dislodging one of the diodes. He adjusted it and moved on. "Pretty much."

"What did you do before this?"

He didn't mind Enver's questions. It kept his mind off the fact a virile man stood just inches away. Under different circumstances, Marcus may have flirted with Enver even more than he had during the convention. "I used to teach high school."

"So you're a masochist too."

Marcus chuckled as he painted a swath of spirit gum on the back of the diode. "Evidently." He had to shake off the phantom threads of a past he would never be able to move away from. Not when he had a constant reminder of it that looked back at him in the mirror every morning. "What about you? What do you do when you're not attending trade shows you have no interest in?" Silence met Marcus's questions. He glanced up, worried he'd said something offensive. "Sorry, I didn't mean—"

"It's all right," Enver interrupted. "I don't talk about my life away from the club while I'm here. To be honest, not used to people asking. Too wrapped up in their own shit to worry much about mine. Which is how it should be, to be honest—keeping the personal and private separated from one another."

Marcus felt his stomach clench. This was a very disjointed man. Kept to himself. Came to the club, did his job and left. Marcus had noticed the distance earlier when he'd commented on the photo. Though Enver had been the subject—was a Dom at the club—Marcus suspected he didn't relish the spotlight. Odd, given the nature of activities that went on there.

Marcus focused on aligning the markers around Enver's knees. "Once I get these in place, I'm going to do a test scan to see where there are gaps. Probably take a few adjustments as I'm not one hundred percent efficient yet. Going to take a few more trial cases before I perfect the locations."

"Have you done this before? Or am I really a guinea pig?"

"Only once or twice." He continued working, placing the little electronic receivers at even intervals. "Mostly on myself."

"A virtual Marcus," Enver said quietly. "Interesting."

Marcus had no idea why, but the earnest tone of Enver's statement made him warm all over. As though having Enver's approval meant something. Special. Important. Whatever it was, he needed to nip it in the bud. Men like Enver didn't go for guys like Marcus who were damaged on the inside was well as the outside. Not when Enver could have his pick of the club's membership roster.

Besides, given that enlarged photo Marcus had seen earlier, it was pretty damn clear which side of the fence Enver stood on in the sexuality department. He'd also made it clear he wasn't interested in talking about himself, so it wasn't as though Marcus could come out and ask him about his orientation.

"Don't mean to rush you, but the temp in here isn't exactly comfortable."

"Shit, sorry." Marcus set the adhesive to the side and

went to adjust the thermostat. "Gets too hot, just let me know. I need to keep it cooler in here because of the equipment, but for a short period of time, it should be okay. I got used to the cold years ago, forget not everyone else has."

He sat again, picked up the container of glue and realized with a start that Enver's body was covered with the diodes except for one swath of skin low on Enver's abdomen. No help for it now—Marcus needed to finish.

"Just…ah, let me know if you get too uncomfortable." He reminded himself that he was going to have to remove each and every one of these damn things with as much care as he took placing them. Each one was expensive to replace and funds were low as it was.

In truth, he hated to mar the beautiful line Enver's impressive cock made between his legs. He needed to focus on the task at hand, at the science he was trying to make and not on how much he longed to cup the length, worship the ridges and smooth skin of the thickly veined shaft. How the heavy weight of Enver's testicles begged for Marcus to run his thumb slowly over them, exploring as he wrapped his lips around the wide width of the crown.

Marcus's cock pressed against the restraint of his fitted boxer briefs, eager for attention. The energy of the moment, of the prospect of having a scan of someone else besides himself in the program, should have propelled him to finish. Instead, he sat there staring dumbfounded at the spectacularly fine specimen of nude male before him. He'd have to take an icy shower later. Or beat a desperate, over-too-quickly orgasm out in one of the bathrooms in order to have the capacity to think.

"Just as embarrassing for me as it is you, man," Enver grumbled. "Get it over with."

The growly tone of Enver's words did nothing to calm the tempest. Marcus bit down on the inside of his cheek, trying to hold on to his control as that whiskey and smoke voice wrapped around the base of his dick and squeezed. Except the pain had the opposite effect, ratcheting his arousal up exponentially. Heat and tension flooded his loins, his chest, tightening every muscle in his body so that thinking became incredibly difficult. He'd heard of suffering for work, but God help him, this was ridiculous.

"Fuck it all to fucking fuckery," he muttered as he set to work.

Chapter Four

Two hours later, Marcus had a perfect digital rendering. Pleased with the results, he'd removed the receptors from Enver's body and settled down in front of his equipment.

"How does it look?"

"Pull up a chair if you'd like." Marcus glanced over cautiously, grateful Enver was clothed once again. Though the arousal threading through him had muted while he'd directed Enver to stand and move and bend in different ways, the press of his dick against his pants was still evident.

The thought of the oversensitive body part reminded him of something else. He opened a nearby drawer and set a small vial on the desk. "Mineral oil to remove any residual spirit gum."

"Thanks." As Enver grabbed a chair and dragged it over to the table, Marcus sat up, draping his arm across his lap to hide his lingering reaction. Enver had been nothing but professional throughout, and Marcus had gotten a woody like some eager teenage boy who didn't know the definition of control. "So how long do I have to wait in exchange for embarrassing myself for the past few hours with your little…whatever you called them?"

"The system will continue rendering details of the three-dimensional images in the background, but I can start testing without waiting." Marcus doubted Enver had a clue what he was talking about. A glance over at Enver's glazed look confirmed his hunch. He truly forgot not everyone shared his passion for technology and that he needed to put things into layman's terms.

"Basically, each bit of information the diodes feed into the system has to pass through this program and get assigned a place marker. Then they all piece themselves together in the assigned order, and voilà." Marcus tapped the mouse on the large monitor mounted on a support bracket. When the screen came to life, he gestured to it. "We get a digital copy of you. Or your foot, at least, for the time being." Marcus used a special mouse shaped like a dial and tilted and turned the graphic so Enver could see. "Once this is all done, I'll take the fully rendered image and drop it on this machine here."

Marcus spun in his chair to face his other workstation, a more powerful computer that handled the main program for BLINC. Instead of a monitor, he used a sixty-inch widescreen television so others could watch while a user interfaced with the program. In time, he hoped to have larger displays for businesses that wanted observers to be just as much a part of the program. Someday, he'd like to have a fully immersive room. Right now such tech was the stuff of the Holodeck on the starship USS *Enterprise*.

No reason not to dream big.

"What's all that?" Enver gestured to the green lines filling the black background.

"The club. Or at least a rudimentary outline of a

few rooms I've had a chance to measure off. This one. Court. The lounge." Marcus glanced around, but didn't immediately locate what he was looking for. He needed better organization. "I have the headset somewhere around here."

Enver stood, pushing the chair back against the wall. "That's all right. I need to get going. Stuck around a little longer than I meant to."

"Sorry." Though Marcus wasn't too remorseful. He'd gotten to admire Enver in his full glory for more than an hour. Hard to complain about work when it came with that kind of benefit.

"No worries." Enver gestured to Marcus's setup. "Mind if I take a look when that's done? See what kind of sacrifice I've made by agreeing to have my body scanned?"

Marcus smiled. "The rendering should be finished up by tomorrow if you want to come back. Just let me know beforehand and I'll make sure I have it loaded before you get here."

"May be a few days before you hear from me since I have some work of my own to take care of, but yeah, I'll let you know. I'd be interested to see the final product just from a curiosity standpoint. Thanks." Enver paused as he glanced to the equipment again. "It was… enlightening."

Marcus sagged as Enver left, breathing deep for the first time since he'd requested the scan. He hadn't been this on edge in a long time, this at odds with his brain and his body. He was aroused by the prospect of his work finally moving forward and aware of the tension radiating from his abdomen.

His cock twitched, reminding him it was still there

and still very much in need of attention. But each soft beep of confirmation from his program drowned out the demand, and allowed him to push the arousal down deep. The amount of work he had before him was enough for him to keep fully focused, though he doubted he was going to be able to forget the bliss of the past two hours with a gorgeous naked man.

As his gaze slid back to the screen, he caught sight of the mineral oil vial still sitting where he'd set it earlier. Hopefully he could track down Enver before he left. Removing any traces of the skin glue would be almost impossible without it. He'd likely scrape his skin raw if he tried.

He scooped it up, locked his terminal and stepped out of the room. Thanks to the network of televisions mounted in the hallways, he saw Enver exit through the front door. If he hurried, he could catch him before he left.

In the parking lot of Noble House five minutes later, Enver sat in the '74 Dodge Charger he'd purchased with his own money as a teen. He used it as a shield against the power that had followed him out of the club, gripping the steering wheel until his knuckles turned white.

It had taken every ounce of control to keep himself from reacting to Marcus's touch. Several times he'd been thankful Marcus had gone to retrieve more of those damn electronic gadgets, as it had allowed him to take a deep breath, collect his thoughts and get himself under control again. He hadn't missed the few lingering glances either, which had made his predicament all the more excruciating.

And precarious.

His reaction to Marcus had been visceral from the beginning, but standing there nude before him had forced Enver to put every restraint trick he knew into play. Remember every promise he'd made to himself. At some point during the process, the ache in his gut had become an edgy throb.

He'd used that energy to focus, to give himself something else to think of instead of how goddamn *good* Marcus's hands felt moving over his body. Those hands. Those fucking hands he couldn't stop thinking about even now as he trembled with need within the privacy of his car.

When Marcus had turned his focus to the final area not covered with the small diodes, a single brush of knuckles against his shaft had made Enver want to bury every last inch of his cock deep inside Marcus's mouth.

The image of doing just that flashed behind Enver's eyes. His cock throbbed so hard, he growled as he saw himself roughly fucking Marcus's mouth, coming on his tongue and down his throat. The man reveled in the treatment, his grunts of pleasure filling the air around them.

He always managed to keep his needs under wraps, not because he wanted to—but because he *had* to. He hadn't been this excited in forever. This desperate for relief, his body all but vibrating with a savagery he hadn't experienced in quite some time. He wanted to weep from the power of it. Wanted to roar. Storm back into the club, fold Marcus over one of those damn computer tables and shove inside him to unleash all the raw, pent-up possession burning through them both like wildfire.

Ah, God, this is madness. Enver slapped his hand

against the steering wheel. Again. *Sheer fucking madness.* The pain did nothing to dull the blinding ache. Working with the subbies at the club more than fulfilled his sexual desires, even if it never—*could never*—result in his climax. The subs were the focus, seeing to their needs of the upmost importance to him. To see them content gave him all the satisfaction he longed for.

What a crock of shit.

The desire—the need—tore at him because the last time he'd come was nothing more than the ghost of a memory. Not that he hadn't been tempted, especially when he'd worked with Bracey. She'd been exactly the kind of submissive he would have gone for if he'd been interested in participating fully in the scene. He'd been there for her. God, had he. Over and over without fail, he'd given her the kind of loving attention and support she'd deserved until it had nearly broken him.

With Marcus, he wanted to be broken.

He lifted the lever on the seat, angling the back so he was at a sharp angle and well below the level of the windows. The parking lot was filled with cars of members already inside the club, and Enver had parked in his usual spot at the dark corner at the far end, so the danger of getting caught was minimal.

In the space of a breath, he had his zipper open and freed himself from the confines of his underwear. His sharp hiss filled the car as he wrapped his fingers around his erection. The relief was short-lived as the image of Marcus on his knees, looking up and offering himself slammed back into him, assaulting him with the ferocity of his desires. Oh God…he didn't know why he was so taken by the thought of the man, but he couldn't stop using him as masturbation fodder. Didn't want to stop. *Feels too damn spectacular.*

He dragged his fist over his cock, pulling his hips back to heighten the sensation of friction. He tightened the grip, a strangled gasp ripping from his throat as the tight clasp reminded him what it felt like to be buried deep inside a lover's mouth. As he imagined Marcus on his knees again, looking up with those haunted eyes that had experienced too much pain, Enver swiped his thumb over the tip, using the drops of precome to lubricate his path. Marcus drew him in, taking him to the back of his throat in a single swallow.

Holy God, he was a beautiful specimen of male.

"Fuck," Enver muttered into the quiet of his car.

He splayed his free hand on the cushion beneath his thighs, using it as leverage to angle higher into his own grip. Marcus licked and sucked and worked without reprieve. He entered a trancelike state, arching his back off the seat as he jacked himself harder and faster. A familiar desperate yearning had taken up residence in his gut, surging through him as his balls drew up, his body quivering intensely as he worked himself closer to the edge.

He thrust his hips upward as he dragged his fist down in rough, uncoordinated jerks. Again. And again. Fast, then slowing a few seconds before returning to the same brutal pace. Drawing it out, working his hand up and down his shaft, as agony filled his testicles. Delicious pain that made him feel as though he was going to die right there in his vehicle.

He continued working, feeling his cock thicken and lengthen as orgasm drew closer, knowing the release was going to feel glorious when he finally allowed it.

Details blurred and nothing filled Enver's mind but the desperate urgency to get off. He snarled loudly as he bucked against the seat, his movement growing jerky and frantic. He called the insatiable storm forth, letting it flood his senses as he started to come in a sudden explosion of light and heat.

Un-fucking-believable.

Fire flashed hot through Marcus's palm as the vial of oil he'd been clutching shattered in his grip. As Enver came, a blinding, desperate urgency roped through Marcus. A primal need to yank open the door and share in Enver's climax.

He felt like he'd been hit in the solar plexus with a head-butt. Common sense had told him to turn tail and leave Enver alone, but how could he not watch such a beautiful thing? Instead of listening to his brain, he listened to other parts. The quadruple stack of opera windows allowed him to find the right vantage point while standing near the passenger side of Enver's classic muscle car. The slender porthole windows helped overcome the two-door car's blind spot, but allowed him to watch. Of course, if Enver opened his eyes, he would instantly spot Marcus but the risk was worth the reward of watching at the perfect angle to see the man in all his glory.

Hard, deep, mind-blowing, commanding sexual glory.

Enver's muted growls grew sharper, deeper as he continued to milk his shaft, pumping until a thick pearl of moisture beaded at the tip. His thighs bunched under his jeans, his breath coming in fast pants as he jacked himself with short, rapid strokes. A man desperate for respite, but fighting back the onslaught, his mouth twisting in a grimace as animalistic need captured him.

Marcus had never seen a man wear his agony so beautifully.

A second later, Enver came again, a thick burst of semen spurting from him as his deep roar wrapped around the base of Marcus's cock. His body trembled furiously like an oak recovering from a close proximity lightning strike, the power of his climax rippling through his formidable frame. The scent of viciously aroused male slammed into Marcus. It called to him, releasing an unexpected flood of his own arousal when he thought he was as excited as he could possibly be.

"Holy shit," Marcus muttered softly as he watched stark relief wash over Enver's face. The older man continued to hold his amazingly semi-erect dick, slowly moving his fingers as though two climaxes weren't enough to satisfy whatever need had driven him to masturbate in the club's parking lot.

Marcus recognized the struggle, had seen more than a few submissives—and a few Dominants—go through the same thing. Mentally ready to experience more pleasure, but physically unable to perform because the body was too exhausted. But it was more than the violent power of the two releases.

Marcus inexplicably felt lingering emotions he couldn't identify, sharp and as powerful as the residue of a gunshot despite the glass separating them. Enver hadn't been absently trying to jack himself off—he'd been thinking about someone in particular.

Enver's hand movements quickened, going from lazy enjoyment to single-minded purpose. Within a few strokes, Enver had brought himself back to full staff. Marcus's heart started to pound as he realized Enver didn't intend to stop until he'd satisfied himself to the point of real exhaustion.

He'd been wrong earlier. There had been no struggle. Only a few moments of respite as Enver luxuriated in his pleasure until he was ready to go again. This was a man who had uncompromising control and could go all night.

All fucking night.

The need to serve the insatiable man slammed into Marcus so hard, he nearly dropped to his knees to worship at the altar of Enver Furst. Instead, he angled back and away from the car, moving as quickly and as quietly as he could so as not to disturb Enver.

He finally noticed his hands were shaking as he stepped back into his makeshift office. It took him a few more lengthy seconds to realize blood stained his right palm from the splintered glass. He grabbed the first aid kit he stowed for emergencies, patching up his sliced palm with trembling fingers and not even feeling the sting of the antiseptic gel.

For long moments, he was too stunned to focus on the pile of work he faced. He simply stared off into space, the explicit images of that exquisite, beautiful man fucking his fist playing over and over in his mind on an endless loop. If there had ever been a shadow of a doubt to his attraction to Enver, what he'd just seen had shattered it into a million tiny shards.

Chapter Five

Enver slammed the hammer down onto the glowing hot piece of steel. Then did it again. And again. He usually gained a measure of satisfaction from pounding metal into shape, but not today. Too many things on his mind. Too many distractions. Too much pent-up frustration.

He typically came to the forge to forget or to clear his mind. The juxtaposition of the simplicity of the work and the complexity of bringing pieces to life usually brought him some clarity. It was the same kind of headspace he often found during a scene at Noble House, but he couldn't seem to shut down the shit whirling through him like a tornado since the scanning session with Marcus three days ago.

Even taking care of himself in the parking lot of Noble House hadn't been enough. Release had come a few times, but never fully dulled the edge of need. He'd finally given up when he realized he could have fucked his hand all night and it would never be enough. Escaping to the solitude of his mountain, to his forge, had seemed like a good alternative to burn away the energy. Give him the clarity he needed. Remind him how much he'd risked with that jackoff session. How many steps back he'd taken in his recovery.

"Hope you're just practicing."

Enver glanced up to see Oz standing in the doorway. "What?" He looked down and scowled. He'd gotten so caught up in his thoughts, he'd taken the piece past the point of use. "Shit." He dumped the rounded blob of metal into a nearby bucket of water, avoiding the plume of steam as he tossed the hammer to a nearby table.

"Think the pictures you've shown me of your first pieces as an apprentice were better than that." Oz eyed him as he stepped inside the workshop. "You all right, buddy?"

Enver stripped away his safety goggles and rubbed at the pressure stacking up behind his eyes. "Metal got away from me."

"It never gets away from you." Oscar Nakamura scooted onto the table filled with Enver's tools, wiggling back against the pile of tools to make room. Oz was a short man, so his scarred and dirty boots dangled several inches from the ground.

"You've been working too." Enver pointed to the thick layer of rubber sole that protected Oz when he chose to play around with electricity. He removed his protective glove and shoved it into his back pocket as he straddled the anvil. "Looking for something new?"

"Aren't I always?"

Enver thought about the wide assortment of metal he'd already made for his friend. "Don't you have enough toys already?"

"Are you trying to talk me out of placing an order?" Oz slapped his palm against the center of his chest, his thermal shirt wrinkling as he clenched the fabric. "That hurts, man. If you don't want my money, I can take my business elsewhere."

"Go right ahead." Enver folded his arms. "Who else gives you the same kind of quality I do at the price I charge? No one."

"Fuck you." Oz flipped his middle finger up.

Enver chuckled as he crossed the workshop to draw off two feet of brown craft paper from a roll and retrieved a black grease pencil from his nearly bare desk. "What are your specs?"

"Looking for a new plug. Nothing too unusual, but something that would definitely catch attention. Curvy, but has a sturdy handle. Five or six sections." Enver noticed the glassy cast that had glazed over Oz's eyes as he'd been describing his wish list. Oz took delight in metal toys the same way some men lusted after their lovers. "Can be graduated or equally sized. I'll leave that up to you." He paused, his brow wrinkling as he dropped into deep thought. "Scratch the handle."

"Gonna need something to retrieve it, my friend. Or you're going to be paying a hefty hospital bill."

"I'm not an idiot." Oz scowled. "Been playing with asses for as long as I remember and haven't lost a piece yet. I need something that is versatile enough for long-term wear, like a flared plug end. But gives me something to grip on to when things get intense. Needs space for me to add power to it." He extracted his phone and fell silent as he searched for something. "Like this, but…not."

He handed the phone to Enver, who glanced at the screen and saw a mass-produced butt plug with a jewel-encrusted base that had a connection for a TENS unit. Though he was used to Oz's kink for electricity play being added to his toys, this wasn't the typical piece Oz usually asked for. He usually went for larger plugs that were straightforward. Cock rings that did the job denying orgasm. No flash or flare. Just an implement that prepped a submissive for the eventual fucking of a lifetime.

What Oz was describing was something long-term lovers would exchange.

Enver thought about the specifications carefully, an idea forming in his mind based on his previous work for Oz. He worked quietly for a few minutes making adjustments. In the end, he had a plug with a jewel-encrusted base that would be comfortable for long- or short-term wear. On one side of the bottom was a receptacle to allow the plug to be connected to a TENS unit.

He stood, staring down at the sketch and already seeing where he would make adjustments. This would give Oz a foundation Enver could build off of. "Looking for any color out of this or just the usual?"

"It's scary how you can pluck ideas out of my head and bring them to life." Oz stroked his fingers over the rough sketch and whistled. "Add some red, if you don't mind, and then it's perfect."

Enver made note of the request, jotting his initials in the corner of the paper as his acceptance as the metal-smith. "Anyone in mind for this beauty?"

"Just an idea I had." Oz's eyes clouded again for a moment before clearing.

They'd been friends long enough for Enver to know the man didn't lie often, but he also knew him well enough to know that statement had been a total fabrication. But Enver's job wasn't to question his friend's motives. He had a service to provide. He jotted down a price by his initials, knocking some off his usual fee because Oz was one of his best customers and a fellow Dom at Noble House.

Oz took the grease pencil and signed his name. "You should really get a computer instead of this rudimentary system you've got going."

"Have one." Enver pointed to the entrance where he'd used a battered and dusty tower to prop open the door of the workshop when he needed extra ventilation. He rolled up the sketch, carrying it with him to the corner where he kept his bar stock. He took down a few strips of metal, his mind already formulating how to shape the piece into the desired shape.

"Normal people don't use those things as a doorstop."

He glanced over his shoulder and gave Oz a sly smile. "Normal people don't commission custom butt plugs to be used in a power exchange scene. Or cock rings. Or nipple clamps. Or—"

"All right, all right. I'll shut up about your lazy accounting practices and you'll make my order without any more questions." Oz jumped off the table, a puff of dust rising as he landed. "You going to be at the club tonight?"

Enver dropped the pieces back into their storage spots. The metal wasn't ideal for his use this time. Of course, what he did want, he didn't have on hand. "I can be if you need something."

"Jesse has been hinting at some rope play. I've been working on it, but could really use some assistance." Oz held up a hand. "I know, I know. No sex. Not asking for you to join in. Just need a pair of experienced eyes."

Maybe that work would distract him enough to keep him in the right frame of mind. To keep from chastising himself for unleashing the caged beast inside him. He hated the idea of returning to the club again so soon, but Oz wouldn't have asked if he didn't truly need help. Distance was usually the only thing that kept the lock engaged, spreading out the days so he could get into the right headspace again before returning. He'd just have to keep his head down and focus on whatever Oz needed.

"Sure."

"Thanks. Jesse's supposed to be there around ten. Meet me in Court around nine-thirty for some setup? No delivery date on that, by the way." Oz gestured to the sketch.

If Enver were a betting man, he guessed the man Oz was fascinated with was someone who was already a part of his life. Not a member of Noble House, obviously, because Oz wouldn't have restrained his desires if that was the case. That wasn't his nature.

After Oz left, Enver tidied his workshop. If he was going to be at Noble House by nine, and pick up the metal for the plug he'd just been commissioned to make, he'd need to leave soon. The drive would give him plenty of time to map out a way to avoid Marcus.

Something told him he'd already lost that battle.

Chapter Six

Marcus leaned back in his chair and stretched. He'd been hard at work for the past eight hours, immersing himself in smoothing the last few details on the computer model of Enver. Which meant he was in desperate need of a break. He shut the system down for the night, and locked the room as he left.

Loud music filtered through speakers as he stepped out into the hall, signaling that club action was in full swing. He angled toward Court. Real live action would be a nice and well-deserved change of pace. Not to mention it kept him from reliving the moment he'd caught Enver jacking off in his car. It certainly hadn't been the first time he'd watched someone pleasure themselves, but that level of desperation... Nothing short of spectacular.

The throbbing music of Court pressed against him as he stepped through the room's double doors. The dim lighting should have given privacy, but instead it somehow enhanced it. This was further highlighted by the strategically placed spotlights aimed at the more shadowy corners of the large space.

He'd measured off the room before and taken copious notes about the décor, but he'd been the only one there

at the time. Now, it was teeming with energy and life.
The concrete floor that had been bare now had plush,
heavy pile area rugs to further delineate scene areas.
The exposed structural supports for the second floor
he'd dimensioned were now camouflaged behind ornate
maroon drapery printed with the club's herald in gold.
Eyebolts had been embedded in a handful left bare to
be used as anchors for rope or chain play.

The roped-off scene areas were full, with an assortment of activities occurring that anyone was free
to observe. Pony play. Knife play. Extreme bondage.
Though they were all interesting enough to compel him
to watch, he stopped looking when he spotted Enver in
a scene area in the far corner.

The man he stood with was far shorter and younger.
For a split-second Marcus thought he was watching a
Dom negotiating a scene with his submissive. But after
a few moments, he noticed interesting things about their
body language. They didn't touch or look at one another except to acknowledge an understanding or ask
a question. Their postures were relaxed as they moved
around the area, but it was more in line with two men
who were good friends than sexual partners. As Enver
tied off a length of rope, then unknotted it and offered
it to the man, it was clear Enver was instructing the
other man in the art of shibari. Though Marcus had no
experience with the ancient Japanese artistic form of
rope bondage himself, he'd seen the practice used a few
times at other clubs.

As Marcus drew closer, the music faded and allowed
him to hear the conversation between the two Doms.

"Most important thing to remember is to keep the
weight on the rope and the wood. Keep checking the

pressure points we talked about." Enver looped a strip of rope around his own wrist, yanking on it so the skin underneath visibly turned white. He held it in place as he used the opposite hand to try to wiggle his forefinger under. "You see any discoloration of the skin, readjust or stop the scene entirely to re-tie. Nine times out of ten, it's better to be safe than sorry."

"Good rule of thumb is you need to be able to comfortably get a finger between the rope and the skin, right?" The other Dom demonstrated this as he asked.

"Exactly," Enver said with a nod as he slipped the rope off his wrist. "In this instance, you're going to want to use a knot that will allow your sub to struggle as much as he wants, but won't slip out of place."

While they continued to talk, another man crossed the scene barrier, placed a small bag next to the swing rig and went to the corner of the area. There, he stripped off his white shirt and pants, exposing dark skin that had been honed and chiseled into a decadent display of masculinity. As he added his underwear to the clothing pile, Marcus caught the glint of metal. When the sub shifted, Marcus noticed he had a barbell piercing running horizontally through the tip of his penis.

As the sub kneeled on the large pillow, he fit a circle of metal just beneath the crown. Within the space of a few breaths, the man's cock hardened, jutting from between his thighs in a rigid arc.

Neither Dom acknowledged his presence, continuing their discussion as the sub's hands came to rest palm-up on the tops of his thighs and he bowed his head in a brilliant display of surrender.

Enver made eye contact with Marcus as he turned. He acknowledged him with a silent nod, but stayed

within the roped off area. Not dismissal, but not encouragement to come closer either. Enver stepped back, as
though he intended to remain to provide guidance and
suggestion but intent on giving the Dom a wide berth.

Enver's companion now stood in front of the kneeling submissive. The Dom crouched, speaking quietly as
they discussed the parameters of the scene. The longer
they talked, the more tension bled from the sub's rigid
shoulders. His head sagged low, his chin nearly touching his chest. The visual surrender was as humbling as
it was beautiful.

A true connection between a Dom and a sub who
trusted one another.

He'd witnessed interactions between subs and absolute Masters like Enver. Watching them had made
him weak-kneed, aching to experience the supreme
nirvana where the will of a Dom and the desire of the
sub melded into a magical synergy. The reminder the
careful back and forth still took place told Marcus this
was the kind of club he would like to be a member of.
But he couldn't afford such a personal luxury since
he'd sunk all of his savings into the tech he was developing. He'd rented a tiny house nearby that he could
barely afford and missed the normalcy of owning his
own home. Tending the lawn. Cooking a meal. Looking at the same view out his kitchen window while he
washed dishes for years and years.

The clink of metal pulled Marcus out of his musings.
The Dom had positioned the sub against a thick length
of wood that had been suspended horizontally from the
ceiling. Though the submissive stood, he was bent forward slightly so his chin rested against the top side of
the beam, his arms spread wide. The Dom took his time

wrapping segmented lengths of rope around his partner's wrists, biceps and shoulders. Satisfied, he stepped back, pulling on the loose end to lift the beam higher and forcing the submissive onto the balls of his feet.

The Dom lifted the sub's feet, angling the man's legs back so his entire weight was supported by the beam. He tied the man's ankles to a stout length of metal pipe jutting from the floor, ensuring the man's toes were the only things touching the ground. The network of ropes and heavy-duty panic snaps secured the man.

Enver moved in to offer advice, but pulled back into the shadows when the Dom grew more confident with the equipment. After another few long minutes, Enver stepped over the rope barrier and flagged Marcus.

"Is he your apprentice?" Marcus leaned closer as he admired the Dom's attentiveness.

Enver shook his head. "Oz is one of the more well-established Doms here. He just needed guidance on equipment he wasn't familiar with."

"Yours?" Marcus asked in surprise. "Not the sub, I mean the equipment. The ropes and the rigging?"

"I made most of that, yes. Not the rope, though I do have a supplier for those." He gestured to Oz, who was using a flogger on the man's backside. Though Enver conversed with Marcus, his hawk-like gaze remained honed on the scene area. It pleased Marcus to see such a level of dedication. People didn't take that kind of pride in their work anymore. Even he wasn't that judicious.

"The cock ring and plug are mine as well," Enver added.

"Wait…what? Did you just say you *made* it all?"

Enver's gaze slid over to him. "The panic snaps are

a new design and I wanted to be sure he understood how they worked."

"I didn't realize people *made* them." The idea that Enver had taken the time to craft metal into that form pleased him, though he couldn't put his finger on why.

Enver turned his attention back to the scene. "It's easier to go to the hardware store and pick up a handful, but you need to be confident some unknown robotic machine is responsible for either your sub or yourself depending on which side of the fence you're stationed on. Most people don't give it a second thought."

It occurred to Marcus that Enver's reach wasn't confined to only the scene. "You provide all the rigging equipment for the club, don't you?"

"Yes," Enver stated simply.

The admission wasn't surprising when Marcus thought hard about it. Enver came across as the guy who took that level of responsibility seriously. It was his way of caring for each and every member at the club. He wouldn't accept anything less and would probably lecture anyone who questioned his authority.

"Have to admit, for a second I thought maybe you were going to join in."

"No." Enver's gaze darkened. "Split with my sub a few weeks ago."

"Not ready?"

"That and I don't want things to be uncomfortable for her," Enver said slowly. "It was a mutual breakup, but it can be jarring to see your former Dominant engaging in a scene with someone else. Seems best to relegate my involvement to instruction…and helping you."

Marcus immediately felt guilty. "If you need to focus on something else, I get it."

"No, it's all right." Enver held up a hand to stop him. "Keeps my mind occupied. Bracey is smart and resilient. She'll find someone much better suited for her eventually."

Marcus watched Enver examine everything and everyone in Court with a critical eye. "You did a good thing, you know. Not a lot of Doms would recognize the incompatibility and know it wasn't working out for either of them. Takes a lot of strength to walk away instead of causing damage down the line."

"Doesn't feel like it sometimes, but yeah, it's for the best for both of us."

A realization washed over Marcus as he continued to watch Enver. "You're not going to scene at the club until you're sure she's okay."

Enver sighed. "Not until I'm sure she's truly all right."

Marcus wasn't sure why, but he was suddenly struck with the overwhelming need to do something for Enver to take his mind off his troubles. "Busy later?"

He regretted the question as soon as he asked. *Great segue, man.* Too late to take it back now. Silence stretched out, and for a long time Marcus thought Enver hadn't heard him.

"Once I'm finished up here, I'm done for the night. Need more scans?"

Though it was the perfect excuse, Marcus bucked his courage. "I haven't eaten all day because I've been focused on work. Could use some company. If you're up for it."

"Yeah." Enver glanced to the scene. "Around eleven all right? Been a while since Jesse has scened, and even with the cock ring he'll blow sooner than later. Excuse me," he said, leaving without waiting for a response and stepping back into the scene area to offer a correction to Oz.

As Marcus watched, it was easy to imagine Enver tending to his own submissive in the ropes. Binding his chosen partner for both their pleasure. Making trinkets specifically designed to torment and tease. Maybe a little too easy, especially after stumbling upon Enver pleasuring himself in the car. That kind of furiousness wasn't something easily forgotten.

Marcus's cell phone vibrated in his pocket to signal an incoming text message. With his thoughts still tangled around that salaciously hot moment, he extracted his phone and swiped the screen without looking. When he finally shifted his focus to the device, he fumbled it, startled by the message.

Ready for our next lesson, Mr. Holly?

A picture arrived seconds later, the familiar face of one of his former students glaring at him through the screen. Ten years since the attack and eight years of prison had eroded Davis's boyish features. The lean, sinewy high school senior had been replaced by wide shoulders and a thick bulk of someone who spent most of his time lifting weights. One thing hadn't changed: the malevolent grin that reminded him of something out of a comic book.

Marcus's hands started to shake as bile churned in his stomach. He knew the day would arrive when he'd have to face Davis's inevitable release, he just hadn't expected it to arrive so soon. Then again, his time served was up.

Marcus glanced longingly at Enver, who stood discussing a tie with Oz, helping the Dom with an adjustment. The compulsion to run zipped through his veins. He reminded himself that Davis had no way of knowing exactly where he was. Then again, he'd somehow gotten ahold of his phone number. Marcus suspected there was a bribe involved in that information.

He dismissed the message, keying in his best friend's contact information. "Davis is out of prison," he said as soon as she answered. "He messaged me, Zoie."

"Are you kidding? Forward it to me," she demanded, the sound of her fingers flying over a keyboard sounding through the connection. "I'll try to find out how he got your number. Don't do anything drastic right now. Promise me that much." When he remained silent, she sighed. "Don't give him the power, Marcus. Just keep living your normal life."

"Right." His life hadn't been normal since one of his students had attacked him with a container full of acid.

Chapter Seven

Enver expected to see Marcus waiting for him in the lounge. What he didn't expect was to find Marcus beating his head lightly against one of the tables. He frowned as he slipped his hand in place so Marcus's forehead connected with the back of his hand instead of the table. A tremble shook Marcus hard—almost violently—before his shoulders dropped, clearly in no rush to sit up.

Enver's heart leapt into his throat. Marcus looked like he was ready to crumble.

The urge to flip his hand over to cradle Marcus's face raced through his veins. Especially after assisting Oz with his scene. The residual traces of the power exchange weren't new to Enver, but the overwhelming desire focused toward Marcus was. Funny thing was, he wasn't interested in spending less time with Marcus in order to have it dissipate.

"Long night?"

"Long life," Marcus said after finally lifting his head.

Enver was startled by the dark shadows smudged under Marcus's bloodshot eyes. The wet lashes that indicated he'd been crying. He pressed his lips together as though he was restraining a second flood. A moment later, he opened his mouth and released a low, frustrated sound.

Enver couldn't let him crumble, not like this. "Need to talk?"

"Need a drink. Or seven," Marcus muttered as he glanced toward the serving area.

Enver had started to slide into the booth, but stopped. "That can be arranged." He shoved his hands into his pockets to keep from reaching out to Marcus again, his skin tingling where he'd touched him earlier. The way Marcus's gaze kept darting around the lounge and the way he flinched whenever someone new walked through the doorway signaled something was truly wrong.

"Let's get out of here."

"Can't I find something here that will work?"

"You're about ready to jump out of your skin. Drinks from the Noble House bar aren't going to cut through the nerves." He continued at Marcus's puzzled expression, wondering if this was the proper approach. If he was somehow making things worse. "We don't serve anything near the strength you need. Just a bunch of fruit juices and energy drinks. You're wired up enough as it is, don't think you want to make it worse."

He gestured for Marcus to follow when one of the Noble House slaves appeared and dropped to her knees, blocking his path.

"Master Enver. Permission to speak."

"Granted." The response came without thinking due to years of play.

Asha had gone for a glam look for the night. Her normally cotton-candy-pink hair had been stripped to blonde and was spun up into a fancy arrangement that had probably taken her a few hours to perfect just so a Dom could muss it. Her dress belled out as she knelt, and though he couldn't see, he suspected she had on heels as high as skyscrapers.

Under different circumstances, he would have made her stand, left her fully dressed in her vintage glam, adorned her body with an intricate network of his ropes and had her kneel again right there in the lounge while he enjoyed a drink.

"I saw you with Oz and Jesse earlier and know you're without a submissive right now." Her voice took on a breathy quality. "I would like to offer myself if you're available."

For the first time in a long time, he wasn't tempted to enter negotiations with a willing submissive. "Though I appreciate the sentiment, I'm going to pass tonight, Asha. One of our resident geeks needs to forget whatever is bothering him."

"I would be happy to share you with him, Master Enver." Her face lifted, her cheeks flushed as her enthusiasm poured forth. "I haven't been with two Doms since Kochran decided I needed a behavior lesson." Her gaze landed on a spot between his feet.

The scene she'd mentioned was one of the most talked-about sessions amongst the Noble House membership. Saint and Boyce had spread Asha out on a table right in the center of Court and utilized one of Saint's fucking machines. Everything had been going well until someone had set off a flash which had triggered Boyce's PTSD. Feeds had been cut and Kochran had offered a lengthy explanation to members along with his apology.

Though Asha had been genuinely worried about Boyce's state, even this long after the incident, Enver

could tell she had been disappointed the triad scene
hadn't been able to continue. He didn't get the Dom
vibe from Marcus, but Enver did get a sense he would
follow clear instructions that would allow Asha to have
that kind of scene. Under different circumstances, he
may have considered it.

"Copious amounts of alcohol and pretty slaves don't
mix, Asha. You know that." He crouched, tracing one of
the frown lines bracketing her lips. "Don't look so sad,
kitten. I saw Jannik hanging around the semi-private
rooms earlier, dropping hints he was looking for a sub
to play with in the garden room for a capture fantasy."

Her face lit up at the mention of the single Dom, her
dress swinging around her knees as she stood. "Thank
you, Sir!" she exclaimed before rushing off, almost
crashing into a couple coming through the lounge doorway.

"Anxious as ever," he said with a laugh. "Ready to
head out?" He gestured for Marcus and left the lounge
without waiting to see if he followed. The drive to get
out of the club was a powerful throb in his veins. While
he wasn't interested in dismissing the obvious energy
that kept arcing through him whenever Marcus was
near, he decided not to tempt fate either.

"That happen a lot?" Marcus asked when he caught
up. "Subs throwing themselves at your feet?"

"No. Asha was recently granted the position of
House Slave. There are only a few of them, so I typically handle their initiation in one of the private areas.
For hers, I was at the trade show playing pickup with a
certain virtual reality tech."

Marcus's eyes went wide as the implication sank in.
"You don't have to babysit me if you have other plans."

"My car or yours?" Enver swore he saw a flush creep over Marcus's cheeks, but it was gone just as quickly as it appeared. Maybe he'd just imagined it. Wanted it to be there because it would be a telltale sign he was interested. "Tell you what—since you want to drink, we'll take mine. Just changed the brakes and gave her a tune up, so she should purr real nice. We'll figure out the logistics of getting you home later."

Marcus cleared his throat. "I don't know if this is a good idea."

Enver glanced over his shoulder, noticing that Marcus hung back even though he was still following him. "Everything all right?"

"We can...do this another time."

"Why? I could use a drink or two myself." Enver unlocked his car and slid behind the wheel. Marcus remained outside, his hands shoved into his pockets. Glancing over, he noticed the window framed the crotch of Marcus's jeans. He also noticed Marcus had left the zipper down the last time he'd used the restroom. The gap in the fabric allowed him to see the telling ridge of a semi-erect dick. Looked like someone else had a little residual energy they needed to burn away as well.

Hard to tell if it was from Oz's scene or Asha's offering.

Enver leaned over, stretching out to reach the door and shoved it open enough to tap Marcus's thigh. "You actually need to get in if we're going to get anywhere. Unless you've got some *Dukes of Hazzard* fetish and want to climb through the window? This baby is the wrong year Charger, but she'd give that '69 a run for her money."

Another few seconds passed before Marcus slid into

the passenger seat. His gaze darted around the interior, just like inside the club. Enver thought he caught another flash of pink to his cheeks, but Marcus turned his face when he reached for the seatbelt. When he turned back, his expression was blank.

As Marcus buckled in, Enver fired up the engine. The eight-cylinder motor roared to life, emitting a deep, rumbling growl that clearly announced it was ready to chew up the miles. He never got tired of that sound and worked hard to maintain the quality.

Enver focused on maneuvering out of the narrow spot. "Most of us normally hang out at Screwdriver, but the owner and head bartender is currently tending to his submissive at the moment. Oz owns the bar," he offered even though Marcus hadn't asked.

"He shuts down the bar when he's here?"

"Nah, just a different vibe when he's not working. Anywhere in particular?"

"I live in Ashes Fork. There's an okay place on Main."

"The Gullible Octopus?" The low-key bar wasn't the environment Enver suspected Marcus needed. Not only was it known for its vast selection of local brews on tap, it was also the kind of establishment known for random, anonymous hookups. Hence the apt name.

"You're familiar with it?"

"Yeah, that's the kind of place you go to in order to drink yourself stupid when you're broken up over a lost love, not when you're so stressed out you can't remember to zip your fly."

Marcus hastily corrected the issue. "Thanks."

Enver chuckled. "Happens to the best of us, man. Don't sweat it." He dropped the car into gear and glided it through the parking lot. "The bar is also right next door to Vanilla."

"Their pastries are to die for." Marcus's face lit up in the first genuine spark of interest for the night. "Been almost every day since I moved in."

"Charlie would love to hear about a new regular."

Marcus's gaze flicked toward the club as they passed the front entrance. "Is that one of your regulars?"

Enver laughed as he guided the car down the lane toward the exit. "Charlie would never be caught dead in a place like Noble House. Let's just say she lives up to her bakery's name." He gunned the engine after he turned the car down the narrow two-lane road leading away from the club. "How do you like what you've seen so far?"

"Of the club?"

"Everything."

Marcus stared out the window for a bit before answering. "Ashes Fork reminds me of home. Small enough to be quaint, but large enough still not everyone is all up in your shit."

Enver had grown up in a big city, so the feeling of small and quaint hadn't taken hold of him until later in life. Since he'd bought the land up on the mountain he'd turned into his workshop, he couldn't imagine returning to the noise and bustle he'd left behind.

"Couple of regulars of the club live there. Ezra had a place nearby, I think, before he moved in with Kochran last month."

"We met a few days after I started. Met most of the tech employees, actually. No one beyond that, though."

The unique aspect of the club that allowed members from all corners of the globe to belong was also the drawback. It made Noble House seem so large. With the recent expansion of the online component that allowed members to play in a simulated replica of the club, Ezra was probably buried under a ton of work and hadn't taken the time to make the rounds with Marcus.

"I'll take you around when you have some time. Let you at least meet some of the other staff. Have you made good progress?"

"Better than expected." Marcus turned slightly to face him, the lap belt allowing the freedom of movement. "I finished the model you helped me with, so you're welcome to come see it anytime. Next few days, I'll have a good working mock-up."

Enver noticed the relaxed posture and the rambling about the program. Whatever agitation Marcus had been experiencing earlier seemed to have evaporated. Good. He didn't like seeing Marcus get so spun up. There wasn't much Enver had to offer, but a night out bookended with conversation and drinking to forget he could deliver.

"Mind if I ask you something personal?" He paused to offer Marcus an easy smile. "You've seen me naked, after all. Seems only fair."

Marcus eyed him as he gestured to the marks on his face. "These? Most people ask at some point." He shrugged off the inquiry. "Not really much to talk about, to be honest. Just an accident a while ago. Me being my usual clumsy self."

The tone of the statement led Enver to believe there was more Marcus wasn't disclosing. A story behind the scars that he wasn't willing to talk about. Perhaps it was because they didn't know each other well, or maybe

Marcus was more sensitive about the injury than he wanted to admit.

"They don't hurt or anything. Haven't for years. Only reason I remember they're there is the odd looks I get when I'm out in public. Most people don't pay them any attention, but a few people openly stare." Marcus's rambling abruptly stopped when Enver merged onto a four-lane highway. "I thought we were going to Ashes Fork."

"I know somewhere better," Enver finally answered after a time, glancing at the clock and thinking they would arrive for the main performance. "Livelier."

"Let me guess—a shuffle board league tournament?"

Enver gave him the side-eye and didn't say anything for a long time. He finally spoke as he turned off the main road. "Keep it up and I'll put your name on the list of performers where we're going."

Marcus look horrified. "For fuck's sake. If you're taking me to a karaoke bar—"

Enver killed the engine and pointed to the building over Marcus's shoulder. "Better."

Marcus turned, spotting a one-story concrete building across the parking lot. Teal and purple lights shined down in vees that were reflected off the blinding white paint job that could probably be seen for miles. If that wasn't enough, a wild array of vibrant colors flashed on the LED screen perched over the top of a sweeping arched steel awning that was like a beacon in the night.

"Boylesque." Puzzled, he slipped out of the car and looked at the line of people filling in all the space behind the barrier waiting to get in. "A drag club?"

"Why not? Impossible to be sad around drag

queens." Enver waved at the bouncer as he gestured them through the set of double doors at the club's entrance and right past the line of hopefuls eager to gain admittance. Lots of attitude was slung their way, which Enver just ignored. Not surprising, given the fact Enver didn't seem to give a shit about what others thought.

If there was ever a man who had no fucks to give, it was Enver Furst.

"Come here a lot?" Marcus eyed Enver, curious about the ease with which he guided him through the front entrance and directly to the bar to order drinks. His familiarity with the establishment and those working behind the bar signaled he was more than a casual visitor. "I know, you're secretly one of the performers."

"Watch it, kid." Enver's words lacked heat, further offset by the half grin he shot Marcus's way as he shouldered his way to the front of the line. "One of the performers is a customer. She should be on in a few minutes, so we should grab a seat as soon as we can." He gestured to the bartender then glanced at Marcus. He looked like he was going to ask something, but had changed his mind.

Marcus barely listened to the drink order because he was too busy taking in the lights and sounds and smells of the club. The same color scheme on the outside of the club was reflected in the interior with a similar teal and purple lighting package.

Two lengthy couches had been placed perpendicular to the stage, their thinly padded seats and puckered backs clearly not meant for long-term viewing. A large u-shaped couch upholstered with deep purple leather was positioned a few steps away in a roped-off area clearly meant for VIPs. He thought Enver would lead

him there, given the way he'd barged right in with barely
a glance to the line, but instead, Enver handed him a
martini glass and led him to a semi-circular shaped
booth off to the side. Marcus had a few more minutes
to take in the twin fairy-light disco balls hanging from
the ceiling, the herringbone pattern of rectangular tiles
in various shades of purple on the walls and the con-
trasting utilitarian gray concrete floor. Somehow, the
club managed to be outrageous and functional at the
same time.

"Show's starting back up," Enver murmured as he
tapped him on the shoulder.

Marcus turned to face the stage just as the master of
ceremonies stepped out with a flourish, tilting his top hat
toward the crowd. His outfit was better suited for some
macabre three-ring circus, but it somehow worked for
the club. "Put your overpriced, over-polished manicures
together for our headliner tonight, Ms. Kiki Fontana!"

A tall performer in a neon green skin-tight bodysuit
walked onto the stage as the crowd erupted into loud
cheers. She played it up for the audience, flipping her
long cascade of auburn hair over one shoulder, clearly at
ease with being the center of attention, as a song started.
The singer's husky voice filled the club, the lyrics immediately telling the story about being a bad, bad girl
because she'd been careless with a delicate man.

As she angled her hip out, she held the exaggerated
pose while a length of rope descended from the overhead. It coiled on the stage, the vibrant pink color offset-
ting the glittering white crystals of the stage's backdrop
and the performer's bright green outfit. The audience's
clapping died off as Kiki crouched to skim her fingers
against the rope. When she wrapped her hand around it

as though measuring the diameter, she gave the crowd a sly, sexy smile. She dropped to her knees, crouched over the rope and pantomimed licking it. The noise level of the room suddenly became deafening, drowning out the song.

She stood, wrapping a section of the rope around her forearm and calf to support her weight, and the rig lifted her into the air as the noise level returned to normal. The reason Enver had a connection to the club, and Kiki in particular, finally clicked.

"You made that, didn't you?"

Enver smiled, then set his finger to his lips before pointing to the stage. "Relax and watch the show."

For the next fifteen minutes, Marcus was swept away by the sensual display of athleticism as Kiki wound the rope around her body, posing in different configurations that displayed her body perfectly. The performance was as mesmerizing as it was incredible, further reinforced by the knowledge Enver had had a hand in the safety of the performance.

He'd never seen anything like it. Kiki was a natural performer, expertly balancing sultry with innocence. At one point, she drew the rope between her legs, gripping it like a penis as she set her hand over her open mouth as though in shock.

The show ended a few minutes later. Marcus joined the rest of the crowd, clapping as she held her arms up and curtsied while the curtain dropped. He turned back to Enver. "That was fucking amazing."

"She gives a good show."

Marcus finished off the last of his drink, which was now warm thanks to his full attention being on the stage. The lights came up to full and the patrons were still talking about Kiki and her performance. It definitely had been the kind of performance that would draw in curious onlookers and regulars alike.

"Ever think to talk to Kochran to bring something like this to the club? The members would eat it up. I realize the club relies heavily on an online presence, but he could treat it just like a live scene that gets uploaded. Like some kind of theme night." When Enver stared at him without saying a word, Marcus's cheeks heated. "Sorry. Just a suggestion."

"You've got good business sense, Marcus. Stop doubting yourself so much." Enver leaned forward, setting a bag on the table. "New rig. She likes to replace the mechanics every few months to keep everything in working order. I take the old ones, re-machine any parts, if necessary, to fix any surface damage, or replace them entirely for when she's ready for a new set."

"So our visit isn't entirely for pleasure." Marcus's sprits waned.

"Done right, business *is* pleasure." Enver signaled a wandering waiter and ordered a glass of water for himself and another round for Marcus. "You looked like you needed a friend tonight, Marcus. I would have brought you here regardless."

Applause erupted from one corner of the club, drowning out anything else Enver had been about to say. Marcus glanced over his shoulder. Kiki Fontana was weaving her way through the crowd, pausing every once in a while to accept a hug or brush a kiss against an audience member's cheek. She was very much at home and very much in her element as she accepted the accolades.

Her gaze landed on their table, and she immediately

detoured to them. The few minutes it took for her to wade through the crowd gave Marcus a chance to notice she'd exchanged the formfitting bodysuit for a sheer black and nude dress embellished with glittering stones that caught in the club's lighting. The see-through skirt swept the floor as she approached, drifting with her movements to give the appearance she was gliding toward them.

As she drew closer, Marcus spotted the ultra-short nude miniskirt beneath that exposed the long line of her legs. Though her hair was still the same auburn as during her performance, the style was slicked away from her face to play up the severe cut of her nose and jaw. She wore no jewelry, allowing the glitzy dress to speak for itself.

"Well, look at you, Mr. Studmuffin." She swept in, going right for Enver to embrace him. Enver laughed, returning the big hug with equal enthusiasm. "You've been hiding in the not-so-secret workshop of yours too much. But you brought me presents!" She wiggled her hips as she fingered Enver's bag, the gauzy fabric drifting around her legs as she moved.

"Hot out of the fire, just for you."

"You are too good to me, Mr. Studmuffin." She bent over, brushing her lips against Enver's cheek. "Too, too good." Emotion rang through her voice, which had dropped a few octaves to give Marcus an idea of how she sounded naturally.

It twisted Marcus's heart to see such unequivocal acceptance between two friends. He'd only ever had that with one person in his life. Knowing Enver had someone like that in his life as well made him smile. That smile vanished when Kiki turned her attention on him.

"This your latest conquest?" She gestured toward Marcus as she ran her assessing gaze over him. "Go on and stand up for Momma Fontana. Let's have a look at you."

Marcus eyed Enver, feeling instantly on the spot as he stayed in his seat. "We're just coworkers."

"So what? Just 'cause you work together doesn't mean you can't still blow that fabulous dick of his."

"Still haven't learned tact, I see," Enver said dryly.

"Mammie tried to wash the garbage out of my mouth with a bar of Ivory soap when I was five." She wrapped her hand around Marcus's elbow and forced him to stand. "Only thing that did was teach me I was born to have large objects in my mouth. Mmm-mmm. Aren't you cute? Bit young for you, don't you think, Mr. Studmuffin?"

Enver gave her a half smile. "Great show as always, Kiki."

She waved to someone a few tables away and held up a finger, indicating she would be there in a moment. "We need to talk. I've got an idea for a new show and need your help—as always. I'll give you a call tomorrow." She turned to Marcus, eyed him one more time before she winked. "Watch out for him, cutie. There's a teddy bear under his gruff exterior." She flounced off in a blur of sequins.

When he looked back, Enver was smiling. "This better than moping over a parade of beers in a dark bar by yourself?"

"It is. Thanks." Marcus realized with a start he hadn't thought about Davis's text message for the past hour. Hadn't thought about the emotions tugging on his heart at the reminder his attacker was free on the streets again. Somehow Enver had miraculously made him forget about all the shit that existed in his life and given him a few moments of escapism. He'd intended to take Enver's mind off things and the tables had turned. "She, ah, likes you."

"As the man who keeps her safe, yes, she does." Enver pointed to where Kiki stood with a crowd, occasionally flipping her hair over her shoulder. "Kiki Fontana is a born performer who needs the roar of the crowd to exist." Enver dug his phone out of his pocket, coded it open and pulled up a video he showed to Marcus.

There was no audience, no bedazzled bodysuit or teased wig on the barren stage. There was only an athletically built man in a pair of form-fitting shorts and a sweat-saturated tee, who listened attentively while Enver explained a rig. "Kai McKinnon is an insecure gay man who used to jump at the sight of his own shadow. Still does from time to time on a bad day."

"I know him." Marcus paused, trying to remember where he'd seen him. He wasn't the greatest when it came to remembering faces, but he'd seen this man's enough that it stuck out. The alcohol buzzing his system wasn't helping his mental state. "Vanilla," he said suddenly. "He works behind the counter at the bakery." Marcus recalled the polite though shy man who had taken his order. He'd always been courteous and helpful with customers, but Marcus would have never guessed Kiki and Kai were the same person.

He finished off the last of his drink and propped his head up on his hands. Warmth had started to creep into his veins a few minutes ago and a nice fuzz had taken up residence in his brain. The already glittering lights inside the club were starting to draw to long points. "You ever want to get up on the stage and just let it all loose?"

"Think we've reached your saturation limit." Enver stood and offered his hand. "Come on, let's get you home."

Marcus swayed as he stood, grabbing the table for support.

Enver snagged his elbow, pulling him against his body. "Come on, lightweight."

"I can't walk. Wait. Can. I *can* walk." Marcus giggled as the feathers from a passing performer's elaborate headpiece tickled his face. "Shiny."

"C'mon, twinkle toes."

Marcus allowed Enver to drag him out, the warm buzz causing him to lean against the man. By the time they reached the car, he was nestled against Enver's firm body and thinking about what he'd like to do if their clothes weren't creating a barrier between them. Without thinking, he wrapped his arm around Enver's waist.

When Enver reached around him, Marcus turned his head, pressing his mouth against Enver's. Enver immediately stiffened, jerking back as he blinked at Marcus. The horrified look in his eyes sobered Marcus instantly.

"Sorry. Sorry. I—shit. Alcohol is making me... Forget it. Stupid mistake." Marcus ducked under Enver's arm, slid into the passenger seat and reached for the seat belt. He fumbled it a few times, his fingers shaking from the surge of adrenaline.

"Here, let me help." Enver grabbed his hand, holding it as he secured the belt in place across Marcus's lap. He shut the door without a word. Marcus kept his head down as Enver walked around the car. How could he have been so damn stupid? So fucking predictable? Couple of drinks in his stomach and he put the moves on someone who was clearly not interested in him.

Too much stress. Too many things on his mind. For a few hours, Enver had taken him out of his head and allowed him to think about something else. Why the hell had he thought Enver would be interested in someone like him? And getting drunk, trying to kiss him... Jesus fucknuts. He was acting like a lust-drunk teenager who thought he had a chance with the teacher.

The thought further sobered Marcus. He noticed Enver had pointed the car toward Ashes Fork. "I'm on Central. Small row of cottages at the end in the cul-de-sac."

Enver nodded as he entered the main part of town, saying nothing as he followed Marcus's directions. A few minutes later, they'd pulled up in front of the row of charming houses.

"Shit. My keys are back at Noble House—you know what, never mind. I'll break a window or something." He snapped open the belt and stepped out. Before closing the door, he ducked his head, fighting against the wave of nausea that came with the angle. "Thanks for taking me to the club. For...for looking out for me." He stepped to the curb, shutting the door without waiting for Enver to respond.

The engine roared as the car pulled away, the rectangle taillights of the vintage automobile fading fast in the dimly lit street. Marcus wasn't surprised. He would have sped away from him as fast as possible as well.

Chapter Eight

Enver leaned against the outside wall of Noble House. He expelled a stream of smoke, and kicked up the collar of his jacket against the unseasonably cool air. Once upon a time, he hadn't minded standing out in the chill for a few pulls on a cigarette, but after he'd turned forty, the annoyance of the act perturbed him.

Not enough to quit, though.

Headlights splashed on the wall beside him as a car parked in the lot. He only half paid attention to the new arrival until the driver stepped out. A surge of annoyance jabbed at Enver's gut. His irritation wasn't with Marcus. He was simply bitter about his reaction.

Three days had passed since Marcus had drunkenly kissed him in the parking lot of Boylesque. Seventy-two excruciating hours Enver had battled his desires for the man. To make the situation more complicated, Marcus appeared to be doing everything and anything he could to avoid Enver. Who could blame him? It wasn't as though Enver had welcomed the kiss with open arms. Or even explained he wasn't interested and laughed off the gesture. He'd dropped Marcus off at the curb and vanished without explanation.

Problem was—he *was* interested.

Dominating a man like Marcus Holly would be fucking fun.

He'd never had a problem expressing his desires about someone before, but Marcus was a different breed. Not because he was a man. Enver wasn't choosy when it came to the gender of his partner. But because Enver was experiencing thoughts and desires so strong, most of the time he couldn't think about anything else.

He'd done a bit of his own avoiding because of that.

Hell, he'd tried to do everything he could to forget about the man. But the plan always backfired, his thoughts veering right back to how Marcus's hands had felt on his body during the initial scan. How right it had been for Marcus to be in the front seat of his car. How damn much he wanted more of those sloppy kisses.

Enver took another drag of his cigarette as Marcus crossed the parking lot. He'd pulled up the collar of his coat as well, fast-walking toward the entrance. Rosen, a well-muscled Spaniard who was the bouncer for the night, waved him in without asking for identification. Sloppy. Kochran wouldn't like that at all. Hell, Rosen usually made the owners show their credentials on most nights.

Enver pulled the glowing cherry out of the cigarette and stomped on it a few times to extinguish the embers. He pocketed the discarded filter to dispose of later and pulled out a mint from the tin he habitually kept in his pocket.

Rosen blew into his clenched hands as Enver approached. "Chilly night."

"Gonna be even more so when Kochran finds out you're potentially opening up the club to non-members. Hell of a lawsuit just waiting to happen."

Rosen's shoulders stiffened as his head dropped. "Hands got cold."

"Know this whole deal with kink really isn't your thing, Rosen, but at least show some respect for the rules no matter what the fucking temperature is." Enver shoved his hands into his pockets to keep from slapping the bouncer upside the head. "We'll keep this between us, but I see it again, I'll personally drag your over-muscled ass into the club, tie you up in a rig in Court and make an example out of you. Several times over."

Rosen muttered his apology, extracting the tablet he should have been using to scan membership identification from his back pocket. Satisfied he'd gotten the message, Enver displayed his own membership card. Rosen snorted, shaking his head as the tablet beeped.

Fired up now, Enver headed straight for the room Marcus had set his equipment up in and found him hunched over the makeshift table. He made himself stop when he noticed the tension gripping those shoulders. As though Marcus would break if touched. Had to be more there than annoyance at his drunken actions, or Enver's avoidance.

Something else was going on.

The instant Enver set his hand on Marcus's shoulder, the tension holding those muscles tight snapped. In the space of a few heartbeats, it returned. Marcus shook off Enver's hand and continued working.

Irritation gnawed at Enver's gut, raising traces of that same uneasiness he'd been juggling since they'd met. From the start he'd known Marcus had the power to destroy him. Every minute they were together seemed to fortify that summation.

"You got a problem with me, at least have the decency to tell me to fuck off, Marcus. Pretty damn sure you're familiar with the word."

Marcus cast him a sidelong glance. "I quit. There are hundreds of other reputable companies you can hire to do this job. Get them."

Enver stepped closer, blocking Marcus's path. "You talking about those weaselhead fucknuggets who you said just sell customers a bunch of spare parts?"

Marcus's eyes flashed. "They're more experienced than I'll ever hope to be." He slammed the lid shut but made no effort to leave. "Their equipment is top of the line too. Better than my cobbled together pieces of useless trash."

Enver knew it was all just idle threats. Marcus had too much passion for the project to abandon it so easily. He had no idea what was going on inside Marcus's head, but he knew exactly how to silence all that noise. Knew how to fix the folly of the other night when he should have returned Marcus's kiss even though it could cost him years of hard work.

He leaned in, not stopping until his lips connected with Marcus's. The explosion of heat almost knocked him off his feet. He stepped closer, fitting their bodies together. Marcus growled softly. Enver tilted his head, deepening the kiss. This wasn't foreplay. This was the main fucking event.

As Enver pulled away, Marcus slowly opened his eyes. Glassy now, any trace of the tension clouding them had vanished. "Guess that answers that question," he said quietly.

"What question?"

"Which way you swing."

"I swing any goddamn way I choose." Enver wanted

nothing more than to see those kiss-swollen lips wrapped securely around his cock. But he wouldn't—couldn't. He had too much to lose if he gave into that impulse. Instead, for the sake of his sanity, he took a breath, settled his libido and slowed down. "Sorry for taking off the other night. You took me by surprise."

"Sorry for getting drunk." Marcus shrugged. "And for trying to make a stupid move on you."

Enver snorted softly. "Yeah, you had a lot to drink, but you know as well as I do that it wasn't stupid. How about we call it even and you show me what you've been working on?"

Marcus blinked. The past few days had been a confusing, chaotic jumble of emotions and somehow, Enver made everything settle in an instant by asking to see his work. And kissing him. His mind was still reeling from how that kiss had made him feel and want something he'd been longing for since the instant they'd met in the crowded convention hall. He'd thought he screwed up with that embarrassment in the drag club parking lot. He wanted to thank Enver for resurrecting those feelings because he'd been so focused on work, he'd forgotten the beauty of human interaction.

He licked his lips as he stepped back, tasting peppermint with an undercurrent of smoky muskiness as he watched Enver track the movement of his tongue. It had been a long time since he'd kissed a smoker. Never felt the compulsion to pick up the habit, but it felt right for Enver somehow.

Marcus turned, praying his fingers wouldn't shake as he pulled the case containing the viewing lenses closer. The pop of the lock echoed through the nearly empty room. "These are the receivers the user wears. Sort of like a pair of glasses."

"Lots of wires for glasses."

Marcus had thought the same thing since day one. "I'm working to eliminate them completely. The wireless tests haven't panned out like I'd hoped, so it is what it is for the time being. The wires plug into the processor." He grew more confident as he explained his setup, his familiarity with the equipment soothing him and focusing his mind on the task at hand. Enver would have no idea what Marcus was talking about, but he was committed to listening and that was enough. "Put these on."

Though Enver's eyebrows lifted at the order, he took the glasses from Marcus. He grunted as he slipped them into place. "Lighter than I expected."

"Most people I've demo'd this to say the same thing. Eventually I want to strip away this kind of interface entirely. Remove anything that distracts the user from the program itself."

"How would you do that?" Enver shrugged off his jacket and draped it over the back of a nearby chair.

"There are a few theories. It's the same problem everyone else is working on, so at least I'm not alone there. One thought is injecting some kind of receiver underneath the user's skin. Less invasive would be some kind of silicon patch. I'm leaning toward special contacts that could be worn and triggered when a user logs into the system. They could either wear them all the time or only when they want to interact with the tech. The possibilities are endless. The program just needs to be nailed down first and then all the fancy gadgets can follow. I'd also need more employees. I don't have the expertise to be able to do all of that myself."

"The contacts would be more appealing to a larger group of individuals." Enver took the lenses off to look them over. As he fingered the stems, Marcus forced himself to focus on what he was saying. "These would too. Sliding something under the skin... Too many people may not like such an invasion."

"That's why I'm leaning toward the contacts. I have a few feelers out about that since that is a few levels above my skill set, like I said." Marcus looked over Enver, carefully studying the way Enver was methodically breaking down the process with him. It aligned with the way he'd talked at the convention. "You know more about business than you're letting on."

Enver set down the glasses, shoved his hands into his pockets. "I own a stake in the club."

"Okay," Marcus said deliberately. "But it's more than that. I've seen you interact with the members. You guard them as though you are personally responsible for each one. Kochran may have that same drive, but not to the level you do. He's got a business to run and that's always at the forefront of his mind. Your business savvy is due in part to something else." Marcus just wished he could put his finger on it.

"Like I told you at Boylesque, I make a lot of items the members use here. It's a good idea to know your demographic." Enver picked up the viewing unit again, this time handling it as though he was measuring the weight. "The glasses are a good start to your plan. It will make the transition to the contacts easier."

Marcus logged into the system and pulled up the

beta program. He tested the view before pulling up the interface that would allow him to add additional users.

"I'm going to need a trigger." When Enver just stared at him, Marcus continued. "A safe word for the virtual world, so to speak. If you're uncomfortable, can't end your session through the usual means, I can program in a gesture, a word, anything that would immediately end the session. Same as during a play scene."

"Monster," Enver said without further hesitation. "My safe word is, and always has been, *monster*. Use that." He set the glasses in place, his lips forming a tight line as he waited.

Marcus withheld a scowl, unsure what to say. He thought he was fucked up, but Enver was giving him a run for his money. He pressed on doling out instructions. "The switch to the virtual reality world can be jarring and you may feel a little sick for the first few minutes until your brain and body adjust to the change."

When Enver nodded, Marcus tapped the control button. In Marcus's headset, a computer-generated rendering of Enver appeared out of thin air. He mentally made a note of the gaps in his work, but otherwise, he was pleased with the results of the scan. Thankfully, he'd had the foresight to add clothing to the model he'd been working on before Enver had donned the glasses. He'd already embarrassed himself in real life. No reason for the trend to continue inside a world he'd created.

"Can you hear me?"

Enver's computer doppelgänger blinked. "Yeah." He blinked again. "Whoa."

"Strange, isn't it? I'll give you a couple of minutes to acclimate while I make a few adjustments."

Chapter Nine

Enver couldn't believe what he was seeing. This digitally rendered world was…gorgeous.

And familiar. As he turned, the view changed, providing him with a 360-degree view. Directly in front of him was the club. Or at least a duplicate of it. He took a few tentative steps forward, amazed at the swish of grass under his shoes. The gentle breeze swaying the trees. The warmth of the sun on his face.

When he reached the large structure, he reached out and touched it, snatching his hand back when he connected with rough stone. It was as though he was actually touching the building. The cracks and crevices that gave the old structure character and life. But he knew he was tucked away inside a room of that building, hooked to a machine that was duplicating reality.

He didn't understand the hows or whys, but he certainly wanted to know more. What started as a way to distract Marcus from whatever was bothering him had turned into an education for Enver. He wanted to find out just how realistic this place was. How skilled Marcus was despite his assurance otherwise.

He turned to find Marcus standing a few feet away. In this virtual rendition, Marcus wore the exact same clothes he'd been wearing in the real world, but something had changed. As Enver drew closer, he realized the difference. The scars weren't there. Enver didn't know whether to be angry or disappointed. He'd never got a sense Marcus was ashamed of the permanent markings, but he never would have guessed Marcus would use the virtual platform to hide them either.

"Impressive place you have here."

"It could be smoother."

"Says every perfectionist alive." Kochran and Saint were the same. Always striving for goals impossible to achieve. Enver had abandoned that futile hunt years ago about the same time he'd changed the path of his life. "Life would be easier if you didn't give a fuck."

"Oh, I stopped giving a fuck a long time ago." Marcus licked his lips. "All the shit I've been through? Makes it so I reserve my fucks for only the most fuck-worthy situations. I'm not afraid to fail. Rejection rolls right off me. All those unpleasant things humans have to endure are a hell of a lot easier and more pleasant 'cause I just don't care what people think about me or these scars I stopped trying to hide a long fucking time ago. They don't like 'em? Get over it or don't look. Makes those unsavory shit sandwiches life doles up a little more palatable. Give a few less fucks and life is pretty fucking easy."

"Yet you used this simulation to alter your scars. That tells me you do give a fuck."

"I… There are other reasons." Marcus turned on his heel and disappeared into the club. Enver followed, noting how similar the artificial structure was to the real one. There were subtle differences, but the layout and overall appearance was the same. He was torn between tracking

Marcus down immediately, and exploring to see just how much of the club had been mapped out in the program.

After a quick check of the replica of Court and the row of semi-private rooms lining the hallway leading to the second floor, Enver found Marcus standing at the top of the stairs. Somehow, he shouldn't have been surprised to find Boyce's photographs replicated in the virtual world. Marcus had appeared just as fascinated as the rest of the membership.

Marcus gestured for him to follow, and they ducked into a room Enver hadn't been in for quite some time.

"Kochran said this is one of the most requested rooms at the club, second to Court. Thought it was only appropriate to immortalize in pixels early on."

"It is," Enver said as he tipped his head back to look at the soaring ceiling of exposed wood beams. Dream Within a Dream had been designed to replicate a small house nestled among the sturdy branches of a soaring tree. Which mean it was essentially an adult treehouse with all the BDSM trimmings. It was also one of the few rooms at the club that spanned two stories.

"The details on the walls are so intricate, I wasn't sure I was going to be able to replicate them effectively. You're the expert—what are your thoughts?"

The room was a lot to take it all at once, but Marcus had managed to capture the character of the space. Even down to the loose nails on the planks of the short staircase that led to a loft area. Ideas were already starting to form in Enver's mind about the kinds of things he'd like to do in that particular part of the room.

"It's remarkable." So much so, Enver wanted to reach out and touch everything. The soft blanket draped over the back of an overstuffed couch. The dull metal of the cast-iron stove. Even the pile of the area rug tucked into one corner.

Enver crossed the room, touching everything he could just to see if it was as realistic as it appeared. When he reached the other side, he stood in front of a large panoramic window and gazed out. Boyce would be pleased to see the photographs he'd mounted outside the windows to further add to the illusion had been perfectly replicated. Enver had always felt as though he'd been transported to another world inside the room and Marcus had managed to expertly duplicate that magic.

"It's like you've built your own personal Room of Requirement," Enver said.

Marcus stared, clearly stunned by the reference.

Enver grinned. "I've got a niece and nephew who are big Harry Potter fans."

"Oh. Thought you were going to tell me you had a sub who was."

After making a slow circuit of the room, Enver came to stand directly in front of Marcus. "You said you had reasons. I'd be interested in hearing more." Enver had his suspicions, but he wanted to hear them directly from him. When Marcus remained quiet, Enver knew it wasn't the time to dig deeper. "How did you create all this? The work you've done in such a short time is amazing. With the right amount of help, I bet you'd have a working prototype inside a month."

"Ezra and Maddy did a lot of the work in the simulation they have. I used their stuff as a jumping off point, merging it with my programs and created my augmentation off of that. We're going to keep both worlds because everyone has a preference for how they'd like to play, but the idea is to get members to come over to the dark side."

"Why do I get the feeling I'm supposed to know what that means?"

"Really? You don't know that's from *Star Wars*? Aren't you old enough—never mind."

Enver enjoyed the alluring flush that tinted Marcus's cheeks a little too much. "I was two when *Star Wars* came out. My sister took me on a Saturday afternoon and couldn't stop talking about it as we left. Neither could anyone else. I was too young to understand it then. I know what it means. Just wanted to give you a hard time." He enjoyed teasing Marcus probably more than he should have. "Go on, talk geek to me."

Fuck if he knew why he didn't mind hearing it from Marcus when he tuned Ezra and Saint out every damn time they spouted movie lines. His sister had long ago stopped trying to explain it to him because she was convinced he was hopeless. Something told Enver he just hadn't found the right incentive.

"You've already experienced touch. Smell is another feature. Though it still needs tweaking." Marcus gestured toward the tiny kitchen area of the treehouse. "Take a whiff."

Enver inhaled a rich, decadent aroma that almost made his stomach growl. "Brownies."

"Excellent. It hasn't worked every time. You'd think a hundred lines of code wouldn't be giving me such a hassle."

Enver had no idea what the number of code lines had to do with any of this, but he wanted to know just how far the world had been expanded. "What about taste?"

"Hold out your hand."

Enver did as instructed, and a dark brown square appeared on his palm. The heat of the dessert radiated against his hands and his lips as he opened his mouth to give it a taste. Rich chocolate fudge slipped over his tongue, the flavor exploding through his senses. "Jesus. These are worthy of the dark side."

Marcus blinked. "Wow. He can make a joke."

"Rare 'cause I save them for worthy adversaries." He examined the treat in his hand after taking another bite. "How is this even possible?"

"There's an embedded code your brain picks up, tricking your brain into scent, feel and taste."

"Impressive." He was certain the cheeks of Marcus's avatar flushed a little. The same sensations that compelled him earlier made him move forward again. "So all five senses are in use. Given the idea is for members of a fetish club to engage in something other than baked goods, have you tested that aspect out yet?"

Marcus's throat worked as he swallowed, averting his gaze to everywhere but Enver. "No. Haven't been able to find anyone willing."

Good to know that bullshit meter of Enver's worked even in virtual reality. Something told him Marcus hadn't even tried.

He spread his arms, gesturing to the room. "Plenty of test subjects around Noble House who will be more than accommodating."

Marcus met Enver's glaze. "The one right in front of me would be a perfect candidate."

Enver admired his boldness. While he didn't mind the docile sub, he preferred one with enough balls to ask for exactly what they wanted. "I'm probably the last one you should use."

"Best, actually," Marcus countered. "You're someone who isn't familiar with the system. Won't pick apart the technology and simply use the product as it was meant to be utilized. Since you shun tech like you do, that makes you the perfect candidate. You'll ask the most questions. Just like your business partner said when he sent me to you."

Damn Kochran and his method of madness. He would have known Enver would make the best candidate to play guinea pig. But the fact of the matter was that Enver couldn't participate no matter how much he longed to. He'd already fallen back into old habits.

"You really want someone else. I can't give you what you want."

"Thought I was supposed to be the judge of that." Marcus titled his head. "I haven't been out of the loop so long that I don't remember who has the fucking power."

"Really," Enver said calmly, despite Marcus's ire. "I can't give you the full package."

"I've already seen that."

Enver smirked. "Fine. Let me spell it out. My hard limit is sex."

"You're celibate?"

"Didn't say that. No intercourse during a session. Virtual. Or real," he added as a caveat.

"Why?" Marcus fired back.

Enver had gotten used to people being curious about his life. Knew how to deflect it. "You want my help or not?"

Marcus's mouth twisted for a moment. "Yeah. Intercourse doesn't truly matter, to be honest. Not at this stage. Though I would like to test that component of the program before unleashing it on the members." He paused, his gaze flashing as it became clear who he'd like for the test subject to be. "Sex isn't off the table for me, just so you know. Blood is. That's about my only hard limit. I can take all the rest."

Enver grinned. "We'll see about that. Need a few things. Care to fix me up before we get started?" He rattled off a list of items he'd like to have, and a few moments later they appeared on top of a long table pushed against the wall. He stepped over, brushing his fingers against the array of items, as though testing their authenticity.

The rope felt strange in Enver's hand. He knew logically he was in a room on the first floor of Noble House wearing a crazy setup Marcus had given him. But because of Marcus's program, Enver also knew he was standing in a replica of the room where reality was augmented. He saw the rope in his hand, felt the uneven texture in his palm, but he was also aware of the fact it wasn't actually there.

Truly a dream within a dream.

"It's better if you relax and just let instinct guide you," Marcus offered.

"Is my nervousness that easy to see?"

Marcus tapped the side of his forehead. "I have a transparent display in my set that relays data as we're inside. The heads-up display is admin level so I can monitor all your vitals. Your pulse has been elevated since I dropped you into the program, but even more so since you picked up the rope."

Which meant he couldn't hide anything. Since he'd volunteered to play guinea pig for Marcus, he owed it to the man to give him full attention. And his expertise. He clutched the rope in his hand, trying to think about all the reasons this was a bad idea—and couldn't come up with a single one.

"Let's do this."

Chapter Ten

Marcus didn't need his HUD in his unit to know Enver was operating well out of his comfort zone. He'd have to figure out some way to make this up to Enver when they were outside again. A round of drinks or something. It wasn't often people went so against their comfort zone for Marcus. Usually, it was the other way around.

"Same rules of physics apply in here as in the real world," he told Enver. "Of course, that can be adjusted depending on the user preference, but the idea is to simulate reality with some enhancements. We can test out the range, but for now I've got it set to normal."

"So no leaping tall buildings in single bound?" Enver cracked a smile that clenched Marcus's gut. "You going to keep your clothes on for this?"

That raised eyebrow nearly brought Marcus to his knees. After that kiss, his system was more unsettled than he'd expected. Good thing Enver couldn't see his vitals.

"I mean, it's only fair," Enver said conversationally. "Though you could have altered a few more things when you've had the pleasure of seeing me nude in real life. Or maybe you really want the full experience?" He stepped back, a change darkening his eyes.

Even though Marcus was the programmer, it was a thing of beauty to watch Enver slip into a different mindset. He'd been wanting to see it since he learned Enver would be the one assisting him, and now he was finally going to get the chance up close and personal.

"Strip," Enver ordered in a voice that spoke of sin and command.

Marcus swallowed. He didn't have to be physically nude to accommodate the order, but the imposing tone certainly made him want to peel away every stitch of clothing. He could have quickened the process by simply coding in the correct sequence, but if he wanted to fully test the capabilities of the program, he was going to make the experience as authentic as possible.

Thanks to his foresight to match the temperature of the real and virtual worlds, the chilly air caused a ripple of gooseflesh along his forearms. He did take advantage of the program by having the clothes fade away as he removed each item so there wasn't a pile nearby.

"Sometimes it's good to break the rules." Marcus winked as he responded to Enver's curious look and tried not to fidget. Standing naked before someone new was a nerve-racking affair even in virtual reality. He'd made some peace with his scars some time ago, but not everyone had the same casual attitude he did. Sharing such an intimate thing with someone was already discomforting, but even more so because Enver had wanted to see the full package. It was only fair, after all, since Marcus had kept Enver nude for the initial scan.

"Any enhancements?"

Marcus lifted his gaze. Fuck, Enver's beautiful multicolored eyes held him captive, stripped him to the core even in the virtual world. He licked his lips, trying to soothe his overanxious nerves. "No."

"Fucking incredible." Enver moved in close, curling his hand around Marcus's neck to pull him closer. He licked Marcus's bottom lip, the contact shooting tingles all the way to his toes. He continued to kiss him as he swept his hand over the hills of Marcus's buttocks.

"Christ, you are a fucking temptation even inside a computer program," Enver murmured before licking Marcus's mouth again, then feathering his lips back and forth. The contact drew a needful little noise out of Marcus.

He trembled as Enver's quiet curses washed over him, revealing at the feel of the clothed body against his naked one. When Enver closed his mouth over Marcus's, Enver went light-headed as the power of the moment hit him full force.

"Mmm, there you go, subbie." That smooth, deep voice wrapped around Marcus, dragging him further down. Enver fused his mouth to Marcus's again as he dug his fingers into Marcus's hip, gripping with a brutal strength. He followed the curve of one cheek, delving deep to finger Marcus's asshole. The blunt tip of his finger circled the entrance, his hum vibrating Marcus's nerves.

"Taking this ass is going to be a damn fine pleasure."

Marcus sucked in an unsteady breath. Enver broke the kiss. "I thought you said no sex."

Enver's eyes glimmered. "I said no intercourse, but that doesn't mean I'm not going to get you off. Best way to test the system, right?"

Marcus watched him gather up a handful of ropes and cross the room again. The beauty and power of

Enver emanated through the millions of pixels so that Marcus could feel his presence pressing against his back. He also felt the telling press of that very impressive cock against his electrified skin.

He needed some levity to break the atmosphere. "So, what, are you the forty-three-year-old virgin of the club?"

Enver pressed closer. "I said I don't have sex *here*, not that I don't have sex at all. So fucking literal," he swore under his breath again as he stepped back. "Time to get you trussed up."

Twenty minutes later, since Enver hadn't been interested in taking any shortcuts during his process, Marcus was suspended from the framework of the loft, one leg perpendicular to the floor, the other bent so his ankle was against his butt. His wrists had been secured to the ropes that tied his ankles to his backside. An interlocking network of knots and weaves formed a harness that not only decorated his torso, but also kept his weight evenly distributed.

The entire setup was suspended by a single point that hung down from a support beam. Some of the detailing was off on the equipment, but inside the virtual world, the imperfections wouldn't matter. He made a note to tell Marcus later when they were finished so he could work on the surface marks. Breaking into his opinion about the program would shatter the state Enver had spent so much time working Marcus into.

Guy just did *not* know when to shut it down.

"How's that feel?"

"Like I'm floating," Marcus responded with a lazy drawl.

Given the hazy cast of Marcus's eyes, Enver didn't have to guess he meant literally and figuratively. He checked over Marcus's form, inspecting for pressure points that could cause nerve damage. It was a step he could have skipped given the fact they were in virtual reality, but Marcus had insisted on having the full experience. Enver took his time at the task, falling into a state he normally only connected with during more intense scenes, and was pleasantly surprised by the tingling buzz across the expanse of his shoulders.

Enver set his hand on Marcus's knee, happy with the normal body temperature that indicated there was no restriction in blood flow. "Safe word?"

"Fucknuggets."

Enver smothered a snort at the word. "Have a hard time believing you'd never say that during a scene."

"Sounds like a challenge to me."

Enver pushed on Marcus's knee, taking a step back to remain close at hand, but far enough away Marcus would get the sensation he was alone in the suspension.

"Good Christ."

Alarm bells would have sounded in Enver's head if he hadn't heard the needy undercurrent of the words, but he was ready to cut the ties if needed. "You all right, Marcus?"

"I'm okay." Marcus closed his eyes and allowed his head to angle back as he rotated in a slow circle. "Damn, this is good. You're good."

The slurred tone of Marcus's words signaled he was slipping deep into subspace. Enver set his hand against Marcus's head, slowly bringing him to a stop by walking around in a circle instead of abruptly halting him.

Enver wasn't interested in jolting him out the state. "Ready for more?"

Marcus hummed instead of answering, his eyes still clouded as he basked on the endorphins flooding his system. Good to know those were just as effective in this constructed world. Unable to stop himself again, Enver leaned over. He pressed his lips to Marcus's throat right against the place where his pulse was the strongest. Marcus groaned softly as Enver dragged his lips up, following the strong line of the jaw until Marcus was all but vibrating against his bonds. He made a soft noise when Enver captured those lips, a breath of sound that almost sounded like a whimper. Everything inside him strained toward the man in his ropes.

Damn if he couldn't stop kissing this man.

He couldn't afford to let himself get tangled with Marcus. Instead, he severed the connection and moved to retrieve a glove and a tube of lubricant from the nearby table Marcus had included in the computer-generated world.

He wiggled his fingers, pulling the latex over his hand. "How long has it been since you surrendered to someone?"

"A while," Marcus answered simply.

Enver itched to have a cane or a whip to show Marcus he didn't want ambiguous answers to direct questions. He'd have to get Marcus to show him how to request an item once they were out of BLINC again. For now, he'd have to make due with other attention-getting methods.

He retrieved a short strip of leather he'd seen sitting on the table with the rope, and wrapped it around the base of Marcus's cock, pulling up his testicles to include them in the bundle. Marcus's flesh flushed red, and after an initial check, Enver was pleased to note the reaction was because of arousal and not because he'd fastened it too tightly around the shaft.

"Now, I'm going to ask you again. How long has it been?"

"Couple of years since I participated in a scene." Marcus paused for a moment, breathing in and out slowly before he continued. "About nine months since the last time I had sex."

"You give or take?" Enver asked, though he already knew the answer based on the reactions he'd seen so far. This virtual world wasn't exempt from the usual formalities of power exchange play.

"I'm a bottom," Marcus replied. "Since I was sixteen."

The weight of the admission signaled that statement hadn't come easily. Enver suspected it wasn't because Marcus was ashamed of his sexuality, but because it somehow connected to those scars winding their way across his face, down his neck and across his shoulder out in the real world.

Enver skimmed his gloved fingers against Marcus's butt, noting the way the muscles flexed against his touch. Though this was different than any experience he'd been through before, he could get used to this computer-generated world. It certainly wouldn't replace truly feeling a submissive in his ropes, bucking and screaming when he allowed them to orgasm, but it was interesting enough to continue.

Marcus didn't tense as Enver slipped his finger deeper. He did jerk in the rig as Enver touched the sensitive bundle of nerves. He let out a soft groan as Enver swept his finger against it each time he slid back inside, manipulating his prostate.

Pleased with the reaction, Enver settled in for a long session.

Marcus was flying, soaring higher than he'd ever had during a session with a Dom. His body was wired, in tune to Enver. The slick slide of thick fingers slowly dragging in and out were enough to make him blow. But he forced himself to calm down. Too quick and he wouldn't get a good read on how the program operated.

"Always thinking about work and never about relaxing even with my fingers shoved deep in your ass."

"Can't stop." Marcus wasn't embarrassed to admit it. That was why he was in this precarious position in the first place.

"Can't or don't want to?" Enver countered.

"Can't," Marcus repeated firmly.

Enver twisted his fingers, and Marcus felt as though his head were going to explode with needy desperation. "Then stop right now, Marcus. Geek thinking doesn't have a place in my scene. You need to focus on me and how I'm going to shove my dick down your throat if you don't get back into the moment with me."

As appealing as the idea sounded, Marcus nodded. "No work." He groaned when Enver slid out and then pushed a third finger inside. Jesus, he'd forgotten how exquisite it was to be stretched and filled.

"Greedy little asshole you've got here." A few more stokes and Enver added another finger. He thrust deep, all the way to the knuckles, withdrew and thrust deep again. Again. And again. Full penetration each time that left a clawing trail of need spiraling up the shaft of Marcus's cock. He balled his hands into tight fists, wishing he could open himself more to Enver. Feel the delectable length of Enver's dick buried deep inside him, shoving him through climax after climax.

"Very greedy." Another few full strokes and Enver teased the rim with his thumb, Marcus's need bursting with the undeniable urge to just let it all ago. To give everything of himself to the other man. "Ever take it all for your Dom?"

It took a few minutes for Marcus to focus enough to answer. "Once. Wasn't in a club, though. Just my boyfriend and I fooling around."

Enver clicked his tongue against the roof of his mouth. "Sounds like a good test of your system."

Fuck. Right. This wasn't really happening. They were both inside a program, millions of pixels rearranging themselves to accommodate their choices. Out in the real world, Marcus would never even think about such an act during the first scene with a Dom. Here, suspended in virtual reality, rules could be accommodated.

"Sure." Marcus closed his eyes for a second, breathing deep and slow, as though he truly was going to take Enver's fist. It was a testament to his programming skills that this all felt so real.

"Place may not be real, but I'm working up a sweat." Enver's touch disappeared. He moved around to Marcus's line of sight and stripped away his shirt.

Marcus wasn't going to complain, pleased the program was making the right atmospheric adjustments and the hours upon hours of work he'd put in on the virtual model was paying off.

As Enver dropped his shirt to the floor, he shot Marcus a narrow glare. "You're geeking out again."

Marcus felt his cheeks heat, then heat some more when he realized he was also thinking about how Enver's skin would taste.

"It works, Marcus." Enver peeled open the fly of his pants, exposing his erection. He crouched, touching Marcus's chin to lift his face. "I'm sitting in that room in the club with you, wearing silly headgear and sporting a hard-on just like this. Stop doubting your skills and let me use mine. Agreed?"

Marcus licked his dry lips. "Yeah."

Enver stood again, tugging his pants back up but leaving the zipper partially down to expose the top quarter of his dick. "No reason I can't keep this as a handy reminder for you if you keep refusing to let everything go." Enver winked as he moved back between Marcus's spread legs. "Don't doubt I won't hesitate to bring you in line."

The stern tone of Enver's implacable voice flashed through Marcus's veins.

Enver slid two slick fingers into Marcus's ass again, the heated caress smoothed by the cool touch of the lubrication he'd added. It only took a few moments before he added the third, and the fourth, teasing the opening with his thumb again. The layer of lube allowed Enver to move his fingers in the tight channel of Marcus's ass using unhurried and steady strokes.

"You'd go off if I commanded you to, wouldn't you?"

"Yes," Marcus bit out, knowing he was perilously close to coming right now as those long, slow glides continued. So much pressure and not enough at the same time. The rope kept him restricted, preventing him from rocking back against Enver's electrifying touch.

Enver withdrew his fingers completely then nudged

them forward. Marcus felt the burn as he pushed against the resistance of all five digits. The stretch wasn't painful as overwhelming pleasure swamped his system. He took a deep breath and fully surrendered as Enver worked his hand deeper.

They both sighed as Marcus's body accepted Enver's fist, his wrist stretching him open as Enver's fingers curled, nestling into place. He found himself fuller than ever before, a feeling he would never be able to describe to anyone verbally. Not that he'd want to. The intense connection arcing between the men was too intimate to share with another person. He wanted to keep this all to himself.

Keep Enver all to himself.

When Enver twisted his wrist, Marcus shouted. That shout became a scream when Enver wrapped his other hand around Marcus's throbbing dick. A few strokes against his oversensitive skin and the universe ceased to exist as Marcus exploded, convulsing in the ropes as he jetted hot come everywhere. Enver ruthlessly worked him, as though determined to wring every ounce of semen from Marcus that he possibly could.

Back in the real world, Marcus stripped away his headset, blinking a few times to readjust to real life. The first thing he noticed was the wet, hot liquid soaking the front of his pants. The second was that his fingers were shaking, his heart racing as he looked over to where Enver sat, his own headset dangling from one of his fingers.

Marcus forced out a breath. "Holy shit."

Enver's gaze met his, a sly smile turning up one corner. "Think you've got a hit on your hands, kid."

Chapter Eleven

The next three weeks passed in a blur for Marcus as he worked through his lengthy to-do list. He'd been so focused, he almost forgot about the text from Davis.

As he worked on cleaning up some of the code, a reminder notification chimed on his phone. Immediately, his heart gave a few hard thumps. The cheerful tone was different from his text messages, but there was still a bit of residual trepidation he couldn't shake whenever his phone made a noise.

Luckily it was just a memo to call Zoie. He pulled up her contact info, activated his Bluetooth and dialed her number. A broken line of code on his computer screen caught his attention, and he focused on fixing it while he waited.

"Pinky's Porno Palace...what's your pleasure?" Zoie asked when the line connected.

"Hey, cupcake." He paused for a moment as he adjusted a few characters to smooth movements and then set the program to run. On the screen the faceless avatar he used for testing did several jumping jacks. "Thought I'd see how you were doing since we've both been busy."

"Sorry, yeah. I've been meaning to catch up with you, but things are a little crazy right now and I'm trying to stay on top of things. Failing miserably, so I'm glad you called. Just got off the phone with Davis's parole officer. Jerk took forever to get back to me."

Marcus stopped typing as pain constricted his chest. "Any news?"

"They're keeping close tabs on his whereabouts and cell phone usage. No more activity since that night, other than he's trying to find a job and a place to live. I just can't for the life of me figure out how he was able to get your phone number. The cell he used was a burner, so dead end before we even get started."

Though Marcus couldn't relax his guard entirely, it soothed him to know Zoie was on the case. "Thanks for the update."

"Always. So are you hard at work or hardly working? Hang on a sec." Her voice came across as muted for a few seconds. "Okay, I'm back."

"Sounds like you're busy."

"Just another day in the pen. How about you?"

Marcus thought about the past week. "Have an assistant helping with my latest project. He's been invaluable. Even more of a workhorse than I am."

Enver had walked through the video frame by frame, methodically pointing out things Marcus had thought could be adjusted. Where a binding could be tightened to feel more realistic for the submissive. The surface of a latch could be smoothed so it caught the light better. All excellent suggestions that would add minute details to enhance the user experience. For the most part, Marcus had been able to distance himself from the subject matter and simply focus on the work at hand. Enver appeared to have taken the same approach as he tended to be all business inside the room.

Too bad they'd been so focused on the intricate, and necessary, details to replicate the powerful moment. Marcus couldn't work up the courage to mention it to Enver and wasn't sure he ever would. Better to keep things level between them by keeping focused on the program.

The previous evening, the intensity had finally gotten to him, and for the first time, he'd strapped on the headset, set the video to observer mode and simply sat back to watch the brilliantly captured scene. Though he knew it was physically impossible, the erection he'd had when the video had ended felt like it hadn't flagged almost twenty-four hours later.

Taking care of himself was an option, but it would only lead to immense frustration. His hand was a poor substitute after the mind-blowing orgasm Enver had given him during their test run. Yeah, he'd only been in a computer simulation, but the stain soaking his pants had been real.

That kind of reaction was the one thing he knew that gave him a leg up on the competition. As far as he knew, no one else had been able to replicate that from their test subjects. Their simulations weren't as consuming or realistic.

"Sounds like you've got your hands full. Good. Been a while since you've been that busy."

"Yeah." Sighing heavily, he pulled up Enver's avatar, frowning at the gaps in the code he hadn't been able to smooth over through usual methods. The fixes he normally employed weren't behaving as they should have. So far, every attempt had brought nothing but frustration. As rewarding as this job was sometimes, it was also equally exasperating.

"You also sound defeated."

He laughed lightly at her comment. "That too. Some code that is giving me some trouble. Every time I take a step forward…"

"You take three back. I get it. Listen, I gotta run. Give me a call later if you have some time to get together."

He sat back as he disconnected the call, folding his arms across his chest while he stared at the nude computer generated avatar he'd created from the scan. His aggravation at his work was only eclipsed by his sexual frustration.

Caught up in thoughts of how it would be to experience that scene in real life, Marcus jumped when he heard a soft tap on the door. He killed the program before turning around. "Come on in."

"Heard you could use some help." A petite redhead stepped into the room with a widescreen laptop in her hand. "Grae Burrows—sorry, Templar-Denali now. Still getting used to the new name."

He accepted the hand she offered. "Marcus. Kochran send you?"

"Ezra."

"Oh, right." The Noble House webmaster had stopped by earlier in the week to see if he or a member of his staff could provide some assistance to help Marcus work out any remaining bugs. Every time he checked one item off, ten more appeared. At this rate, he'd have the program ready to go in five years.

She set her computer down on the table and bundled her hair up into a high ponytail. "I'm a graphic artist. Usually spend my time working on trailers for movies, but I'm between projects at the moment, so I thought I could lend a hand."

"The graphic problem I talked about with Ezra," Marcus said with a snap of his fingers. "I figured he thought I was just rambling on and needed to vent."

"I'm your girl. Let's see what you have."

He gave her a brief rundown, grateful she understood the programming language so he wouldn't have to break down the terms. He didn't mind the task for Enver, but it was a relief to not have to think about carefully breaking down each thing in more simple terms.

She popped open her laptop and logged in. "I ran into something similar a few months back with Ezra's simulation program. Problem was in the source code. They missed a line that elevated what you're talking about and glitched the whole system. Doesn't sound like your problem is as widespread, but it could be the same thing. Maddy, one of our programmers, would know for sure, though. Here, take a look at this."

She tapped *play* on a video and he watched in fascination as a computer simulation unfolded. Though the graphics weren't as sophisticated as BLINC, the simulation was imaginative enough to satisfy a gamer looking to add a little kink to their sex life. If he wasn't so caught up in developing his system, he could certainly see himself losing many hours in the Noble House sim world.

"There." She paused it, gesturing to the center of the scene. "See those missing pixels right there? There's a gap the average person wouldn't pick up on."

"That's exactly the problem I'm having. I think. I don't know, really, since graphics aren't my strong point."

"Good thing you have me then." She gave him a wide smile as she dragged a chair beside him and sat, wiggling her fingers toward him. "Let's have a look."

He offered her the lenses, giving her the exact spiel he'd given Enver to explain how they worked as he pulled up the program: "Same warning I give everyone else the first time they go in. May feel a little nauseous for a few seconds while your brain and eyes adjust to the change." When she nodded, he triggered the interface.

"Whoa," she said suddenly, lifting the lenses to peer out from under them at him. "That is a little more of Enver than I expected to see."

"Fucknuts." He'd forgotten he'd left the avatar nude while he'd tried to solve the problem hanging him up. "Sorry. Only have two full-sized scans right now. Easier to try to solve the bugs before I do more."

"That's all right. Not like I haven't seen him nude before. Just under different circumstances." She fell silent as she dropped the glasses into place again and directed him to turn and bend the avatar so she could get a better idea. When she started firing off coding language, he had a hard time keeping up.

Before long, he saw the path she was heading down, and he was able to anticipate her instructions. They continued to work so seamlessly, Marcus lost track of time. He realized belatedly that Grae had stopped helping and he had closed up the hole on his own. He tapped out a few strings of code and ran it, laughing softly when Grae giggled as Enver's avatar executed a perfect cartwheel.

Not a gap to be found in the programming.

"That should solve your problem." She dangled the glasses off her finger as she gestured to his equipment. "Sweet program you have. When do you think it will be ready?"

"Too early to tell. Kochran was pretty generous with

the contract terms, so if I see something getting screwed up, I can renegotiate."

"Know how that goes, though I don't work as many contracts as I used to since I relocated. But the bright side is that I get to be more choosy when it comes to work." She looked over the setup before turning her gaze to Marcus, her mouth curving on one side. "I'd love to get a full demo when you're ready for beta testing. Maybe talk Saint and Boyce into giving it a whirl. They're always up for anything new."

Marcus eyed her as she closed her laptop with a snap. He knew she was married to both men, and the way her face lit when she mentioned them clearly indicated the depth of her love, but something she'd said earlier made him wonder.

"You said you've seen Enver naked. Have you shared a scene with him before?" When she eyed him, he rushed on. "Sorry, I'm not trying to pry or anything. Feel free to forget what I asked. It's really none of my business."

"It's all right." As she shook her head, her ponytail brushed against her shoulders. "I've been a virtual member of the club for a while, but I worked up the courage to visit in person a few years ago. First time I came, I was extended an invitation to the Keep, which is Kochran's private play area. I unknowingly walked into an initiation ceremony for Bracey and Dahlia. Gorgeous group session with two submissives and three Doms. But then my husbands showed up and I got a little distracted." As she leaned back in the chair, her eyes lost focus for a moment as she clearly got caught up in the memory. "Anyhow, Enver did the rigging for the scene and then kind of oversaw everything. Wish

I had a video to show, but Kochran doesn't allow cameras or even cell phones in the Keep."

"Does he do that a lot?"

"Kochran hasn't done a lot of things since he started seeing Ezra and Maddy." She lowered her voice, even though they were the only occupants of the room. "They're still keeping things kind of quiet, but I suspect most of the membership already knows. They're always together. Not hard to see the signs or the way they all keep making googly eyes at each other."

"I meant Enver."

Grae tilted her head. "It was his submissive in the ceremony, so he was the lead Dom."

"Oh."

Her eyes widened as she leaned toward him and set her hand on his knee. "You have a crush."

"What? No!" Marcus spat out in horror as he waved off her statement. "He's working with me on this project and he's very private."

She tapped her lip as she opened her laptop again, eying him as though she clearly didn't believe his non-interest interest. "There are a few videos of him on the site if you search his name. Last one was a few months ago, when he did some ropework for Kochran and Maddy in one of their first scenes. Won't find any of him doing much more than that, I'm afraid." She pulled up the club's website and gestured to the screen. "He doesn't participate full tilt like most of us do, but he's still one of the more popular Doms at the club."

"People are drawn to the enigmatic." Marcus glanced at the screen, swallowing when he saw there were only a handful of videos. He'd expected more, given the comments about Enver he'd seen on the message boards on the club's website. "I'll take a look through these later."

Grae touched his shoulder, shaking him gently. "You really do like him."

"I'm just trying to find out anything that will help me with the virtual model," he lied. Getting attached to Enver had *bad idea* written all over it, even though he hadn't been able to stop thinking about him since the convention. Even more so since he'd watched him masturbate in the car. And that test scene in BLINC…

"The important parts, right?"

Marcus was horrified to feel his cheeks heat. "Don't think I'm really his type."

Her eyebrows lifted. "Are you breathing?" He didn't respond as she set her hand on his shoulder. "I'm kidding. Enver is a special kind of breed that doesn't come along often. Don't let his gruff exterior deter you. Underneath, he's an old softie."

He thought about the picture hanging on the wall of the second floor. The indentations of rope temporarily marking the woman's skin while she was cradled in the arms of her Dom. He knew they were no longer together, but a stab of jealousy exploded through his chest. Foolish, of course, because she'd done nothing to earn the green-eyed monster. But he couldn't help but feel a little envious of the woman who had worked with Enver for an extended length of time. Who had obviously captured his attention enough to work with her and train her. She was the kind of submissive Enver deserved, beautiful and curvy.

Not some fucked up, scarred man who was sometimes scared of his own shadow.

"Hey, Marcus, you sure you're all right?"

He glanced over, plastering on his best fake smile. "Been working too much."

"Please don't sell yourself short, all right?" Her expression softened. "He would be lucky to have you." When he remained silent, she sighed. "Just try. Once."

He wasn't sure if it was her pleading look or the touch of sadness in her voice that made him say, "Yes."

Chapter Twelve

Enver wiped at the sweat coating his forehead as he stripped off the visor. He blinked a few times as his eyes readjusted to the difference between reality and the virtual machine. The room full of electronic equipment took shape around him.

"Think my brain is going to leak out of my ears." He handed Marcus the set and rubbed his burning eyes. "Jesus, that was intense."

"Didn't expect us to be in there for that long," Marcus said apologetically. "You're not late for anything are you?"

"Nah." Enver stood, setting his hand on the nearby desk for a few seconds until his balance was under control. "Think I'd get used to this by now. Want something to drink?"

Marcus wiped at the sweat dotting his own brow as he continued studying the data scrolling on the screen. "That'd be great."

Enver retrieved two bottles of water, handing one to Marcus as he sat again. "Hope I was able to give you some good data in there. Half the time I'm not even sure what I'm saying."

Marcus leaned back in his chair as he took a few large gulps of water. "It was perfect."

Much to Enver's surprise, each time he disconnected from BLINC, he found his system was overcharged and revved. Like he'd touched a live wire. Sitting there, staring into Marcus's sincere, dark eyes, an ember began to burn in his gut.

A long stretch of silence filled the air between them.

Each time he left one of these sessions, Enver felt as though something hung in the air between them. An unspoken tension neither man was willing to acknowledge. He chalked it up to the desire to keep everything all-business.

"I've been meaning to tell you of a side effect I've been noticing whenever I come out of the machine," Enver said slowly, measuring his words and tone so it didn't seem he was accusing Marcus of manipulating his brain waves, even though that was exactly what he was doing. "Nothing bad, just…"

"Different," Marcus finished, sitting forward to rest his elbows on his knees. "Like everything around you is heightened. Yeah, I've noticed it too."

"Is that normal?"

Marcus shrugged. "If it's happened before, I never paid attention. I don't think it's anything to be worried about, if you're concerned. Or if you feel you need to stop, I understand."

The time they'd been spending together, both in and outside of the club, had been enjoyable. But Enver wanted a real, honest evening out with Marcus, something he hadn't wanted in as long as he could remember. Everything had been about getting people off for so long, he'd forgotten the simple joy of spending time with someone in a non-power exchange level. He wanted to know the ins and outs, the stuff that made Marcus's brilliant mind tick. What kind of movies he liked. His favorite food.

If he snored.

Enver pushed up out of the chair, fighting the urge to escape. Jesus. He'd brought the brattiest submissives to their knees with nothing more than a glare, and here he was breaking into a cold sweat at the thought of something so…ordinary.

"Do you—" Huskiness suddenly coated his voice, a thickness he hadn't felt in years. He cleared his throat and tried again. "Do you have any plans on Friday?"

"Same thing I do every night." Marcus gestured to his equipment. "Hanging out with these babies."

"Want to do something? Away from here, I mean. The club." Shit. Could this be any more awkward? "Just get away from all of this for the night and hang out."

Marcus stood. "Like a date?"

"Yeah." Enver swallowed, feeling like a desperate teenager waiting for his prospective prom date to accept. "Exactly like that."

"Best offer I've had in weeks."

"Since you're not talking, I'm going to assume your thoughts are hung up on whoever you fucked last night."

Enver snapped out of his daydream with a jerk and earned a narrow-eyed gaze from the woman sitting across from him. The vulgar words made him wince. Sure, his older sister Lucille had two kids in college and was still madly in love with her husband of twenty-five years, but in his mind, she was the epitome of innocence.

He'd like to keep it that way. While he'd always had a challenging relationship with his parents thanks to a tumultuous childhood filled with divorce and abuse, Lucille and her two kids were his everything.

"Thought we promised not to talk about my sex life, Lucy."

She smirked as she pushed her dark hair behind her ear. "Nice to have your attention again." Blue-green eyes that matched his twinkled as she sipped her wine. "You're allowed to be all broody and silent except for when we're out for a late lunch."

He hadn't meant to get caught up in his head, but he'd been doing that a lot lately thanks to his interactions with Marcus. He hadn't been this antsy in years. Whenever he'd agreed to a session with a sub, he knew everything going in, even down to what kind of aftercare would be needed once the scene was over. He usually knew the submissives better than they knew themselves. There was a genuine comfort in that knowledge that kept him participating in scenes time and time again.

With Marcus and his contraption, everything Enver knew was reset. Too many unknowns about how the machine would react to changes. And there were always changes. Marcus had been working with him, showing him how to tailor the program to his needs and desires when it came to equipment.

Much to Enver's chagrin, he was figuring out the nuances of the system more quickly than he'd expected. Technology made his skin crawl, but the promise of playing with Marcus outweighed that huge detail. They'd had several more sessions inside BLINC, these far more instructional than the first encounter. But the sexual undercurrent was still prevalent between the men, and Enver found Marcus on his mind almost constantly.

He also couldn't stop thinking about the times Marcus had seemed distant on a few occasions. Whenever he'd asked, Marcus had always snapped out of it, brushing off his distraction as nothing more than thinking about what needed to be fixed on the program. But Enver suspected that wasn't entirely the case.

Even at the club, in a secure and safe environment, Enver had noted Marcus looking over his shoulder at the entrance as though he was expecting someone to appear. Every time Enver prodded further, Marcus apologized and returned to his normal self.

"Consider me properly scolded, Lucy." Enver crossed his arms. "Just been busy with stuff at the forge."

"Ah." She gave him the stink-eye. "Making your elaborate toys for the sex life we're not allowed to talk about."

He held up his hands in surrender. "Please, stop it with the sex talk already. My virgin ears can't take it. Not all of us are as disgustingly happy as you guys are." Despite his statement, he was genuinely happy his sister and Campbell were still together. Their successful partnership had always been Enver's model of how loving, committed relationships functioned.

When he thought about what they had, a tightness constricted his chest. Longing washed over him as he thought about the connection he shared with Marcus. A connection built with wires and computers and an artificial world he didn't understand.

Another flood of memories washed over him, that handsome face relaxed in ecstasy while Enver had played with his ass, stroked the length of his body. That same face now focused and determined as he hunched over a computer making adjustments as Enver described what he was seeing. The confusing mix of reality and computer-generated play wasn't something Enver thought he'd ever get caught up in. But sometimes he swore he felt Marcus's body against his. His lips. His...

"Enver." Lucy snapped her fingers. "Do *not* make me say *fuck* again."

He pointed to her, smirking as he reached for his water glass. "You just did."

"Obviously some hot thing has you wrapped around the axle to keep you distracted instead of listening to my boring stories about work."

"I may not know what the hell you're talking about, but your life is never boring." He waved off the waiter's offer to refill his glass. "I was listening, I swear."

She waggled her fingers. "You haven't heard a word I've said today. You are seriously hung up on someone." She sobered when he shot her a stern glare. "Fine. Campbell and I are working on a prototype that will help photopigment defects in his patients. We've conquered red-green and blue-yellow and are in talks with a few pharmaceutical companies to start trials. Total color blindness is rare, so we're having issues finding good candidates. The eventual goal is a lens that will help the blind process signals to the brain to help them see. We're still a long way off, but we're making progress every—"

"What kind of lenses?" He leaned forward, pushing his unfinished lunch to the side.

She gave him a quizzical look, but continued, "Contact lenses to start. A patient could order them from the local optometrist. A permanent solution, and our eventual goal, is for an intraocular lens placement behind the iris and pupil, just like cataract lens replacement.

It would send signals to the brain to help someone see who may otherwise be facing a life in the dark." Her gaze narrowed, her mouth pursing. "Why are you suddenly so interested in our work?"

He tapped the table, biting his lip to contain his grin. "I know someone who is exploring virtual reality and is looking into using lenses to help with his interface."

"Someone, huh?" She sat back, drumming her fingers against the table. "This *someone* wouldn't happen to be the same person who has had you so occupied lately?"

"What makes you say that?"

"You've never been this interested in my work, Ennie." Her voice was laced with that knowing tone she pulled out whenever she had the upper hand.

"Good God, don't call me that." He tapped the edge of his fork, tracing the flowered pattern as he stalled because he still couldn't believe what he was about to say. "I have a date in a few hours."

"Oh, sweetie, that's wonderful." Her face lit as she waved her hands in air.

"He's working on a program for the club to blend reality with computer programs that I don't even pretend to understand." He paused, allowing the image of Marcus that formed in his mind. Interestingly, he didn't think about the computer-generated version of the man blissed out in subspace. Or the one who spent hours hunched over the keyboard until his fingers bled as he worked to make BLINC perfect. Instead, it was the geek tornado version he'd first met at the convention. It seemed so long ago when they'd first met. "He has some really first-rate nerd-level stuff you and Campbell would appreciate."

"I'd love to meet him."

"Back off, tiger." He counted out enough cash to pay their bill and signaled for her to follow. When she joined him in the sidewalk, he pulled out his lighter and a cigarette. After inhaling a few times, he finally spoke. "It's just a date."

"Oh yeah?" She gestured to the pack, waiting while he shook out one, lit it with his own cigarette and handed it to her. She blew out a stream of smoke before continuing. "When was the last time you went on an honest-to-God date that didn't involve the club?"

The answer to that question scared him most of all. "You worry about changing the world, okay, Lucy? I'll worry about my dating life." He pulled her into a hug, breathing in her familiar scent as she wrapped her arms around his waist. "Take care of the rug rats."

"Ha. The beauty of being a parent—soon they'll be taking care of me."

Two hours later, as he headed east, he was still thinking about Lucille's question. He couldn't remember the last time he'd been on a date where the goal wasn't to spend time getting to know a submissive. There was always a method to the madness. Learn their interests. Hear their hard and soft limits.

Negotiate.

He still wasn't sure what had convinced him to ask Marcus out in the first place. Some part of him had hoped the guy would laugh off the invitation. Then he could banish all the residual crap that kept plaguing him and move on with his life. Maybe take a new sub at the club and pour all of his effort into their training. But he'd accepted, and Enver would be damned if he'd cancel.

When he pulled into the parking lot, he noticed Marcus had already arrived. He parked, cutting the engine and pocketing the key ring, but he didn't exit the vehicle. Instead, he went light-headed and gripped the steering wheel as he stared at Marcus leaning against the hood of his '77 Trans Am. Something was different. A sucker punch to Enver's gut that made his breath short and his thoughts fracture.

Marcus had always been dressed business casual. Khakis. Slacks. Over-pressed and over-starched collared shirts. Hair perfectly arranged. Glasses void of a single fingerprint. Hell, his loafers usually gleamed with a shine that made the club's boot blackers envious.

Tonight he'd selected obscenely tight denim, a faded tee that was riding up one side to expose a strip of tantalizing skin, and sneakers. Hair that looked as though it hadn't seen the business end of a comb in three days, and no glasses. Humor and intelligence sparked in those eyes, his smile an invitation to come closer.

Enver's body hummed in response. On a virtual level, he knew every inch of Marcus's body. Knew the length and shape of his cock. Knew what it was like to have his fist shoved deep inside Marcus's ass, muscles clenching as he came, thanks to the computer simulation. This version of Marcus was relaxed and at ease, with himself and the environment around him. He was masculine as hell, with an insanely sexy body, but also…beautiful. The scars lining one side of his face gave him a haunting edge that only added to his mysterious air.

Seeing Marcus in the rough excited and settled Enver at the same time.

His stomach flipped over when he realized he was being rude and ogling. He rubbed his forearms, hoping to dispel the persistent goose bumps that had erupted as Marcus watched him slide out of his car. For a split second, he'd felt naked. A sensation Enver was used to forcing other people to feel, not himself.

He reached back into his car, snagging the jacket he'd tossed in the backseat. The higher elevation accounted for the temperature change, but Enver scented a variation in the atmosphere that signaled the mountains were going to get their fair share of snow soon.

"Surprised that death trap made it up this high," Enver said.

"She's a trooper." Marcus traced the lower corner of the firebird insignia.

The slow drag of his finger over the worn and cracked paint clenched a tight fist around Enver's cock. If he didn't calm down, he wasn't going to make it through the two-hour tour he'd booked them on.

"Ever thought about restoring her?" He fell in step beside Marcus as they made their way across the parking lot that was quickly filling up with other visitors. "I could give you a few pointers, get you in contact with some good sources for parts."

"You're really into that kind of thing, aren't you?"

Enver gestured toward his car with his chin. "Rescued her from a junkyard. She was the first thing I bought with my own money and it took a hell of a lot of hours bagging groceries and mowing lawns to fix her up. Had her ever since."

"Someday I'd like to do the same for mine. Every

time I have some extra funds, I sink it into BLINC. Priorities, I suppose." Marcus gestured to a cluster of buildings with his chin as he shoved his hands into his pockets. "Have to say, I was curious where we were going. You were pretty vague on the details. Thought we were just going to go to the drag club again."

"The observatory certainly isn't a drag club," Enver said with a laugh. "But you will get to see a lot of glittering stars."

They checked in for the tour and went to stand in the waiting area. Illuminated globes in several different sizes huge from the ceiling, replicating the various planets. Different educational stations were inset into the walls, providing information about the closest display. Marcus wandered over to a large sculpture in the center of the room that was composed of hundreds of metal rods that were twisted into a pedestal that supported a large glass model of Earth. It was lit from the inside, a sparkling display of the major cities around the world.

"You do any of the metalwork for the observatory?"

Enver winced at the heat ribboning through his system as he watched Marcus admire the architecture. *Christ.* "Not a thing. Here as a plain old tourist just like you."

"Well...maybe not *old*." Marcus glanced over his shoulder, winking.

"Hey now." They both laughed, and Enver was pleased to note Marcus truly was as relaxed and casual as his choice of clothing for the night. He wasn't constantly surveilling his surroundings like he'd done the past few times they'd seen one another outside the club. "I didn't ask before, but if this isn't your thing, we can go to the movies or something."

Marcus spun in a slow circle, taking in the observatory's brightly lit atrium, his delighted gaze landing on Enver when he completed the turn. "Oh, no. This is totally my thing." He squeezed Enver's hand just as the guide called everyone over to the corner for an exhibit.

As the tour progressed, Enver found himself watching Marcus instead of listening to the information. Not that what the guide had to say wasn't interesting, but he couldn't stop the lingering glances each time Marcus was in his proximity. Each time Marcus lagged behind as the tour moved to the next exhibit, he caught up, his expression alight with delight. A warm glow settled inside Enver at the knowledge that he'd been the one responsible for that.

"Lots of science happening here, huh?" he teased.

Marcus nodded as enthusiastically as a child facing a decked-out tree on Christmas morning. "I used to spend summers at a camp. At night, I'd sneak out of my cabin and go down to the lake where there was a clearing. Stared at the stars for hours, daydreaming about going up there someday. Never made it, obviously."

"Is that why you came up with BLINC?"

"At first, yes," Marcus said. "It was a way to escape and be somewhere else. I could visit another universe if I wanted to." His gaze slid to Enver. "Then I figured out a few more…practical uses."

The telling gleam in Marcus's gaze made Enver want to muscle him against the nearest wall and kiss him. Devour his mouth again. Feel the weight of his cock in his hand for real instead of inside the constraints of the virtual world.

Instead, he curled his hand into a fist and put some distance between them. He remained quiet the rest of the tour, aware of the glances Marcus shot his way. The agitated Marcus was back, and Enver knew he was the cause. He pretended to be wholly focused on the tour guide even though his body was screaming to give in to his base impulses. Everything about this man screamed at him.

His willpower was being chipped away one damn glance at a time.

Dusk was starting to settle in as the tour ended and the guide directed them to freely explore the grounds, including the promise of a spectacular sunset at the top of the ridge, before meeting back at the main building for a peek at the night sky through the lens of the powerful telescope.

About half the group turned toward the well-worn path, but Enver headed to his car, retrieving the backpack he'd tossed into the backseat. "Hungry?" At Marcus's nod, Enver slung the bag over his shoulder and they made their way to the trailhead.

After a time, Enver signaled for Marcus to follow and they broke away from the rest of the group. The paved path wasn't as well used as the main route, with tufts of grass peeking between cracks in the concrete. The foliage wasn't as sparse either, causing the men to have to duck in a few places where the overgrowth had been allowed to freely grow.

"I thought we were going up to the summit to check out the view."

"Thought you'd like to see this instead," Enver said as they broke through the line of trees.

Marcus whistled as he stepped to the railing. "It's like the sky is on fire."

Enver concurred. Golden rays gave way to vivid orange, red, and pink, melting upward into purple and deep blue that would act as a canvas for the stars.

He pulled a wrinkled tablecloth from the side pocket of the bag. "Figured we could look at some gorgeous scenery while we grab something to eat."

He did his best to smother the answering heat that flooded his groin at the double meaning.

Marcus looked over the spread Enver had brought. "Should have let me know and I would have brought something."

Enver sat on one corner of the cloth, leaning on his hip while he propped up one leg. "Just some stuff I threw together at the last minute."

Marcus burst out laughing at the elaborate arrangement of pumpernickel bread sandwiches. The containers of fruit, nuts, dip, cheese and crackers. The obviously homemade brownies, and a bottle of wine. "If this is last minute, hate to see when you actually put a plan into motion." He accepted the sandwich Enver offered him, feeling his stomach rumble. "Forgot to eat lunch today."

"Drowning yourself in work again?"

Marcus tried to ignore the tone of disappointment ringing through the question. "Grae stopped by earlier and we hammered out the issue I kept having with the pixel resolutions."

Enver handed him a can of soda. "Sounds like good progress."

"Have some tedious work ahead of me now, but I'm excited about it. One of my contacts is loaning me his laser scanning equipment. It's going to greatly increase my pace." He opened a nearby paper bag, pleased to find a handful of chocolate chip cookies. "No more taking measurements by hand."

Enver waved off his offer of one of the treats, using the backpack as a pillow as he lay down. "Glad to hear it."

Marcus fell silent again, much like he had during the tour. As he examined Enver's face, he wondered if it was something he'd done or said, but playing over the night, he couldn't think of anything. Maybe it was talk of his work. He had a tendency to be so consumed he forgot the rest of the world existed. Forgot there were people out in the world he cared about. He'd done a piss-poor job at expressing how much he cared for them in return.

"Everything all right, Enver? You seem…pensive. Thought that was supposed to be my shtick."

Enver folded his arms back, propping up his head as he gazed up into the darkening sky. A cute smile turned up the edges of his lips. "Contemplating the number forty-two."

"'The answer to the ultimate question of life, the universe, and everything,'" they said at the same time.

It was insanely sexy to hear the phrase from *The Hitchhiker's Guide to the Galaxy* tumble out of Enver's mouth. Not something Marcus had expected, either. Giving in to the urge that had plagued him since the date had started, he leaned forward and brushed his lips against the rough stubble dotting Enver's jaw, delighting in the tremble that trickled through Enver before he went completely still. A soft, almost surprised sound drifted in the sliver of air between them as he glided upward. Their faces were so close, it was as though they were sharing the same breath.

He waited for Enver to tell him to stop, to back away and laugh off the advance so they could finish dinner and the tour like they were just two friends enjoying each other's company. But he didn't. A second later, he laid his lips against Enver's, watching his pupils blow wide as their mouths met.

Heat pulsed through his dick, screaming against the restriction of denim encasing him. Enver's eyes fluttered closed as Marcus slanted his mouth and deepened the kiss. It was powerful and potent. Everything he could have ever hoped for. Every suppressed base desire clawed inside him to get free.

Enver opened to him, cupping his hand around the back of Marcus's head as their tongues tangled. He angled Marcus's mouth, plundering deeper, drawing him closer. In the space of two heartbeats, he was laid out on top of Enver.

At the new angle, every inch of Enver was pressed again him. The hard planes of his chest, abdomen, thigh. The unmistakable steel ridge of his cock making an impression against Marcus's thigh. This wasn't a computer simulation. This was a real, live—damn fine specimen—male body against his. He unconsciously moved his hips, earning a ragged groan from Enver that vibrated his lips.

Pull away before you get any deeper, Holly.

But he couldn't.

Wouldn't.

Soul-deep arousal slammed into him with hurricane force. Before long, they were moving as one, grinding together as the kiss grew brutal, Enver's thick cock digging into Marcus's abdomen. Control shifted as the kiss quickly turned voracious and made sparks dance behind Marcus's eyes. He freely surrendered the power to the other man, allowing his aggression and force to dominate.

The intensity of their connection shook Marcus to his core as he pulled away. Looking at Enver's kiss-swollen lips, his bright eyes, the flush of excitement to his cheeks, it took Marcus a full minute to find his voice again to say, "We should get going if we want to catch the rest of the tour."

"If that's really what you want to do right now."

The husky tone made Marcus's blood race with heady speed through his veins, pulse in his brain like his head was going to explode. He burrowed against Enver, tucking his face against his neck.

"No," he whispered, sucking in a deep breath. "It's not."

In truth, he wanted naked flesh, and stiff dicks in full contact. He wanted to be in Enver's ropes for real, experience the high of subspace at the hands of a skilled Dom like the man beneath him. Most of all, he wanted to feel what he knew would be the glorious slide of Enver's dick in his ass.

Enver tilted Marcus's face back and brushed their lips together with a soft caress. "Neither do I." He studied his face, shaking his head as though dazed. "How are you so fucking sexy and sweet and…incredible all at the same time?"

The response died when Marcus's cell phone chimed loudly, signaling an incoming text message. His throat tightened as tentacles of fear constricted around his midsection, zapping his building arousal.

The phone chimed again.

Please don't let it be him.

A cold bead of sweat trickled down Marcus's spine. Drawing back, he scooped up his phone and shoved it into his pocket without looking. The cheery electronic tone was enough to remind him he didn't have the luxury of making out with the insanely sexy man looking up at him.

Breathe. Just breathe.

Another chime.

Shiiiiiit.

Concern flashed in Enver's eyes. "You need to get that?"

Marcus shook his head as a band tightened around his chest. "I should get going." The confusion mapping Enver's face punched him in the chest. *Christ, I can't do this to him.* The emotional blow, the reality that Marcus had fucked up, was too much. He had to get out of there.

He turned away, unable to stand knowing he couldn't lay the pieces of his past on Enver. Couldn't force someone to deal with his baggage when he still managed to fail at rational decisions over it.

Another chime broke through his thoughts.

Maybe it was Zoie with news.

No, she would have called him outright. Though she would be persistent, he'd told her he was going on a date with Enver. The zombie apocalypse would have to be in full swing for her to interrupt.

Five chimes in quick succession made him shove his hand into his pocket. Bile churned in his gut as he powered down his phone without extracting it and silencing another notification from an incoming message. Whatever was going on, whoever was blowing up his phone, he would have to figure it out completely on his own.

He grimaced as the denim pulled tight across his still

semi-hard dick. Minutes ago, Enver had been touching him. Kissing him like he was branding him with a mark of ownership. Making him feel alive and excited about their future together. And then…

His heart beat fast as he stared at the last traces of the amazing sunset that were fading, the blue-black sky filled with tiny pinpricks of light. The perfect night he was about to ruin with his next words.

"The new scanning program is generating the medical examination room for scenes while I am gone. Figured it wouldn't need me to stare at it while it churned." He held up his phone, forcing a smile. "It's letting me know there's a problem."

Enver sat up, gathering the trash from their meal. "Well, let's go then."

"No," Marcus said automatically as Enver started to rise. "Stay. Enjoy the rest of the night. I'm really sorry about this."

"Go on and take care of what you need to, I'll handle this." Enver shook out the tablecloth, folding it neatly into a tight square. "I get it. Really. Past my bedtime anyway," he said with a grin.

Marcus gave a tight laugh, but he didn't dare make eye contact with Enver again as he spun on his heel. He managed to throw a quick "Thanks." and "Goodbye." over his shoulder as he escaped down the path, heart racing so fast, he was certain it was going to explode.

As he reached the parking area, he realized he'd bailed like a specter in the night, fleeing with such speed, he was convinced he'd screwed up a shot at building anything substantial with Enver. He didn't want to think it was over, but how could he not after that kind of odd behavior?

He studied the parked cars as he made his way through the lot, taking inventory to compare the notes in his head. A few were gone, but he recognized every vehicle. By the time he'd made it to his car, his arousal had been replaced with a vile hatred that left a bad taste in his mouth. Everything looked right, but something was out of place. Perhaps not physically, but the overwhelming sense of dread that had followed him since the text message four weeks ago sat like a lead weight in his chest.

Inside his car, he gunned the engine and shot out of the space. He drove for several minutes before pulling into a gas station where he parked, but kept the motor running. Finally, he powered up his phone and watched a string of text messages and images appear on his screen.

You should really think about dressing up for a date more. Even for just a stupid place like an observatory, Mr. Holly.

An image followed, showing the instant when Marcus had squeezed Enver's hand. They were both smiling, looking at one another as though they didn't have a care in the world. Several more shots from the tour. He'd kept a critical eye on the crowd as they'd moved through the building, convinced he'd only recognized Enver. From the various angles, Davis had either hacked the other patrons' phones and stolen the images or had used a lackey to capture the pictures for him.

How dare you subject all those innocent people to your vile, disgusting depravity? And those innocent children. They didn't ask to see that kind of filth. Have a little respect for those around you.

A series of five pictures followed, these from outside the observatory. The elevated angle made Marcus think the snapshots had been taken from above. It would certainly explain why they hadn't been aware they were being watched.

His skin erupted in a cold sweat as he scrolled through the series of images. The first and second showed them departing the parking lot for the trail to the telescope. The third and fourth, as they'd broken off from the group to take the other trail. Finally, a shot of the kiss they'd shared high on the ridge, the sunset lighting the sky in flame. Under normal circumstances, Marcus would have admired the image of two men enjoying each other's company in such an intimate way.

God, could the two of you be any more pathetic? Two grown men fawning all over each other and can't keep it in their pants.

Another text arrived and he braced himself as he opened it. His heart froze as he stared at the image in disbelief. The black and white picture was different from the rest, with a grainy quality from a lower resolution camera. It was an overhead shot from the convention as he handed Enver one of his informational flyers, his phone number scrawled across the top in his messy handwriting.

Marcus closed his eyes and swore. *Son of a mother fuckin' bitch.*

Chapter Thirteen

For the first time since he'd invested his life savings in Noble House, Enver hadn't just thrown on any pair of pants and shirt before heading to the club for the night. After all, he was never the focus of a session. His attention was always entirely on the submissive. They were always more concerned with what he could do to them instead of what he wore while doing it. Functional and comfortable had always been his goal. But tonight, he'd taken care in selecting the perfect outfit. Tight-fitting black jeans, deep green shirt and heavy-duty boots.

Though his annoyance hadn't faded completely in the three days since Marcus had bolted through the tree line at the observatory, he still felt the burn of it churning in his gut. He'd been busy filling customer orders, so he hadn't taken the time to deal with the incident— or with Marcus. Of course, in that time, Marcus had done a hell of a job avoiding him. He understood crap came up that people sometimes didn't have any control over, but he bet Marcus's reasons had nothing to do with BLINC and everything to do with whatever he always kept looking over his shoulder for. For a good deal of that night, Marcus had been completely at ease. Then his cell phone had spooked him.

Enver was anxious to get to the bottom of it, which was one of the reasons why he'd agreed to another virtual scene inside Marcus's program when he'd received the text message inquiry. He was prepared to do whatever necessary because it was clear, in a short time, Marcus had made Enver do things he hadn't taken the time for in years. The whole clothing deal fascinated him as much as it pissed him off. Enver wasn't the type of Dom to get all googly eyed about a sub no matter what. He arrived, did his job to the best of his ability, gave them the scene of their life, and called it a day.

With Marcus, he wanted more.

Now if he would just stop running off whenever things got sideways.

"Hey, stranger."

Enver blinked, startled by the familiar voice. His former submissive's face came into focus as she approached, her long brown hair plaited into a fishtail braid that hung over one shoulder. As always, her beauty caught him off guard. Even as many times as they'd been together, he was still awed by the fact he'd gotten to know her so well. It pained him that things hadn't worked out for them as Dom and sub. Not only was she exceptionally receptive, but her quick wit had always kept him on his toes.

"Bracey." He stepped closer, pulling her into a friendly hug. "So good to see you." The familiarity of her lithe athletic form, the playfully fresh and feminine scent of her favorite perfume, brought back a flood of memories of their sessions. A tightness clenched around his heart as he remembered he'd been the one to end things.

As she pulled away, she gave him a half smile and set her hands on his jaw. "You look tired, Hercules."

He chuckled at the nickname she'd given him after a particularly intense session. While he'd been cuddling her during her aftercare, she'd wanted to watch a movie. He'd simply hit play on this DVD player and discovered his niece and nephew had loaded up their favorite Disney movie the last time they'd been to his house.

"Working too much, as always," he said with a shrug.

"You never work too much." She tilted her head, examining him as she brushed her thumb against his stubble. "Or too hard. You're efficient to a fault."

He grimaced at the reminder. "It's a wonder I'm not a masochist."

She stayed quiet for a long moment before speaking. "In a way, you are. You may not enjoy torturing others, but you sure as hell enjoy doing it to yourself."

He studied her without seeing her. Pieces clicked into place. He thought about how he'd gone out to the car after the initial session with Marcus. Ultimately, he'd thought he'd been trying to burn away his frustrations with his hand, but pain hadn't been one of those things he'd sought. In fact, he'd welcomed the burning, raw, intense ache that had blossomed. Used it to push himself further. He'd drained himself dry that night, and would have continued if he'd been physically capable.

"I'm sorry I wasn't…" *Fuck.* "Couldn't be what you needed, Bracey." An ache sat as heavy as lead in his gut, weighing him with a pain he would never be able to express.

"Look at me, Enver." She paused, waiting out his silence. She curled her fingers against his jaw, forcing him to look directly at her. "You were there when I needed you to be, were patient and kind when I needed. Harsh when I needed that too. You taught me so much. I will always be eternally grateful to you for that." She curled her hand around his forearm, her touch warming his skin. "Whatever it is that is hurting you right now? You need to deal with it."

"I don't have anything to give him." He hadn't realized he'd spoken aloud until she dug her fingernails into his skin.

"Give him you." She pressed a sweet kiss to his cheek. "Everything else is just noise."

He reined in a burst of panic at his confession, studying her. She had come a long way on her journey, blooming from a shy, inexperienced newbie into the expressive woman who stood in front of him. It had taken a while—months, in fact—but she'd learned how to ask for what she needed when he couldn't recognize it. He'd seen the inevitable long before she'd come to him with her concerns. She was a strong-headed submissive who had outgrown her Dom. It wasn't the first time it had happened, but it had been the first time he was remorseful about the fact he hadn't been able to give her what she needed.

Sure, he knew it was for the best to step to the side, but that didn't make the sting any less painful. It had been the right decision for them both, if her outfit selection for the night was any indication. She was clearly on the prowl. A fluffy pink skirt barely covered her ass and the matching skintight top clearly displayed the silver barbells through her nipples.

"Have a hot date?"

Though she nodded, her mouth twisted. "Haven't

found anyone that shared the kind of connection we do. Did," she corrected with a grimace. "Sorry."

"I wanted it to work out with us. Give you everything you needed."

"I know." She wrapped her arms around his waist, pulling him against her.

Bracey was easy to love. A good person, worthy of his trust and someone he should have envisioned a future with. But as much as he'd tried to think of having a normal life, she wasn't the one he saw standing next to him through thick and thin. Someday, she was going to make a lucky person very happy.

Sadly, it wasn't him.

"You go have some fun, all right?"

"Don't I always?" Bracey wiggled her hips. "And if I can't find someone, there's always Bob."

Enver smirked. They'd had a few interesting sessions with her battery-operated boyfriend. A sudden thought struck him. "Hey, you aren't the one stealing batteries from the supply closet, are you?"

She shot him a sly smile, but didn't respond.

"Kochran gets wind of that, you know he'll punish you."

"That's the idea, Hercules." She blew him a kiss as she disappeared around the corner.

For the first time since they'd discussed parting ways, a sense of peace overwhelmed Enver. He truly felt as though Bracey was going to be okay without him.

Enver was still standing there long after Bracey left, insides coiled tight as Marcus stepped beside him. He hadn't realized he'd been daydreaming and it hadn't been about Bracey. He glanced over to see Marcus had gone back to his normal attire of slacks, loafers and a pressed shirt. His glasses were also in place, as was every hair on his head. Either version of Marcus was everything Enver needed right now.

He wasn't interested in getting into things in the hallway. At the club at all, really. Despite his predilection for performing in public, airing his dirty laundry where anyone could hear was considered poor form.

"Don't all you nerd types wear a watch so you're never late?"

Marcus snorted loudly. "No one wears a watch anymore."

"Try telling that to Kochran," Enver said as he thought about the owner's habit of always being behind the tech curve. He followed Marcus into the room, trying his best and failing miserably not to stare at the way Marcus's ass moved as he led Enver to the room.

He remained quiet as Marcus unlocked the door, slid inside and immediately went to his station. The tension that had taken hold of Marcus that night at the observatory was absent as he moved with a swift grace, popping open the latches on the long rectangular cases housing the lenses.

"I was able to upgrade the HUDs last week, so no more bulky glasses and wires." Marcus held up a curving slice of clear plastic. The sleek set caught Enver's interest, but not enough to erase the confusion swirling through him. Had he imagined the entire date at the observatory? The heat and passion they'd shared with the kiss? Conjured it out of some fucked up masturbatory fantasy living inside his head?

"Ready?" Marcus wiggled his outstretched hand, obviously ready to test the setup.

"Sorry." Enver took the item, surprised by the lack of weight. "Distracted."

"We can shelve this for another time if there's somewhere else you need to be."

"Why did you really bail?" Enver blurted. He'd promised himself he'd shelve the conversation for another time, but the incident stuck with him. Better to clear the air anyway so it didn't clog up the scene once they were plugged in. "I know it's none of my business."

"No. It's not." Marcus dropped his hands to his sides, his set of lenses dangling from his fingers. "But it wasn't fair of me to bolt the way I did with some bullshit excuse even I didn't believe. I had some family stuff that came up and needed to be dealt with. I'm sorry if it seemed like I was avoiding you since then. You could have called or texted—never mind," Marcus added with a tight smile.

Enver scolded himself for believing the worst. He wasn't used to considering the fact other people had lives outside of the club. "Is everything all right?"

"Won't be for a long time. But it is what it is. We deal and we move on best as we can. Right now, we have new toys to play around with." Marcus obviously had something weighing heavily on his mind, but didn't want to discuss it.

"You shouldn't notice any differences in the display you see on your end." Marcus set the glasses in place, obviously pleased with the change. "You'll feel a difference in the weight of the unit on your face."

As soon as Enver dropped into the virtual world, he stalked over to Marcus's avatar and pushed hard against him.

"How flexible are you?"

* * *

Marcus's blood flashed hot. The demanding tone of the questions paired with the proprietary gleam in Enver's gaze caused Marcus's cock to harden, both in and out of the program. "In here, as much as you need me to be."

"Excellent." Enver stepped back, stripping away his shirt. "Out of your clothes and on your knees." As he popped open the top button of his jeans, a small pile of dark green ropes appeared near his foot.

"Glad to see you've finally gotten comfortable enough to work that out." Marcus swallowed when Enver shot a glare his way. "Clothes. Gone. Got it." He quickly stripped away his pants and shirt, his boxer briefs following. This time he left the clothing wherever it landed, not interested in making the effort to order the code string to run.

He dropped, noting the smooth surface of the floor under his shins and the immediate strain in his knees. Not knowing what to do with his hands, he mimicked the pose he'd seen the submissive adopt in the scene Enver had assisted with in Court.

"Go ahead and lean forward. Put most of your weight on your forearms." Enver crouched beside Marcus as he followed instructions. "Just going to do a rope ladder around your thigh and shin. Let me know if anything pinches or hurts."

Marcus balanced his weight forward, feeling the burn in his forearms fade off as Enver wound a length of rope around his bent leg and moved around, repeating the process on the second leg, binding Marcus's legs in the position.

"Relax and let me reposition you." Enver grasped him under the arms, shifting Marcus backward as he took all his weight. Upright again, Marcus's shins pressed against the coils of ropes, his butt cradled by his angled feet.

"Should have enough room to shift your knees apart, probably about shoulder width." Enver paused for a moment. "Maybe a little wider."

Marcus found he did have the ability to move his legs in a wide vee.

"Palms flat on the floor behind you."

He expelled a slow breath as he settled into the pose. The ache in his knees was so acute it felt real. It eased as time ticked away until it finally diminished.

"Never gets old," Enver murmured.

"What?"

"Watching a sub slip into the right headspace. Opening themselves up as they prepare for whatever they're about to face."

"Means I've nailed the programming in that aspect at least."

Enver touched his chin. "How about we not worry about the system for a bit and you just relax?"

Marcus not focusing on his program while in the system was next to impossible. His mind was always trying to conceptualize the next steps. What needed to be adjusted. Replaced. Those things were what had kept him sane for the past three weeks while he'd buried himself in work.

He'd turned the string of text messages from Davis over to the police, who were actively searching for the fugitive. Turned out he'd skipped a meeting with his parole officer, and local authorities were on the lookout for him. There was nothing else for Marcus to do except live some semblance of a life, the persistent threat hanging over his head.

His thoughts evaporated when Enver's mouth closed over his. Though it lacked the actual physical connection they'd shared at the observatory, it was still just as potent. Heat burned up his chest and neck, suffusing his cheeks before surging straight down to his dick. Enver groaned, slashing his mouth over Marcus's in a way that scraped and hurt, but Marcus knew they both needed that kind of pleasurable pain right now. When a sharp, metallic bite of blood assaulted his taste buds, a hoarse noise that barely registered as human escaped from his throat. He took a steadying breath as Enver drew back.

"There. You've done an excellent job, Marcus. Now just enjoy it. Nothing wrong with focusing on yourself for once. We can break things down when we're done if we need to, but I think you've got it this time."

If Marcus was still having difficulties concentrating, his brain ceased to function the instant Enver looped a section of rope around his wrist. Enver repeated the action on the other side, and then joined them together. "I need you focused."

"Sorry," Marcus muttered.

"Don't be sorry. Just do."

"There is no try," Marcus said with a laugh.

Enver smirked. "We can role play another time if you enjoy dressing up as a little green alien."

"Yoda kicks ass."

"And I'm going to kick yours if you don't relax." Enver stood, moving behind him, and touched the side of Marcus's face, causing Marcus to shiver against the contact. "Just going to do another simple harness around your torso, secure it all with the arm ladders to keep you in this position. No suspension this time. Sort of a modified mummification."

By the time Enver had completed the tie around his torso, all Marcus knew was that in the modified back bend, he was going to end up completely exposed. Already his cock jutted up from between his spread thighs, flushed an angry red to show just how aroused this was making him.

Outside, in the real world, he was just as excited.

Enver set to work, his brow furrowing as he concentrated on the task. Since first watching Enver help Oz with the submissive on the wood beam, Marcus found he liked watching Enver set himself to task. He managed to find a way to balance his skill with ropes with his care of the submissive he was winding the ropes around.

Marcus sank as each knot and cinch tightened against his body, connecting with that cottony headspace where everything felt thick and heavy. The sensations Enver made him experience inside BLINC were so addictive, he wondered what it would be like to do something like this in real life with him.

He looked down the intricate weaving of the rope harness and discovered Enver was wrapping a length of thin, bright neon-green cord around his shaft. Though Enver still wore a mask of seriousness to show he was concentrating, the edges of his mouth were curled up.

"You're enjoying this."

Enver's gaze flicked upward, the curl of his lips increasing. "Wouldn't do this if I didn't." He turned his attention back to finishing off the last of the tie, anchoring the rope ladder constricting Marcus's cock so it stood perpendicular to his body. The visual he must have made was intensely obscene and astoundingly erotic.

Enver stood, shoving his hands into his pockets as he looked down at Marcus. "Now *this* I'd like a photograph of."

Marcus was glad the program didn't have that capability, but it gave him an idea to add that feature for future use.

"Ah. You're thinking again. That's my fault." Enver crouched again, and hot, wet suction closed around the exposed tip of Marcus's cock. The warmth of Enver's mouth vanished, replaced seconds later by his hand. "My apologies."

It was maddening thanks to the rope Enver had expertly woven around Marcus's dick at intervals. His touch was there one second, gone the next. Touch. Deny. His mouth came back, his tongue playing over the smooth crown, dipping inside the slit to gather the precome leaking from the tip.

"You've very good at your work, Marcus. But you're about to find out how good I am at mine."

A wicked gleam darkened those eyes as he slid his slightly parted lips over the dark pink head, painting his bottom lip with fluid. The wet heat of Enver's mouth enveloped Marcus for a split second before withdrawing. Enver gave the tip a tender kiss before he closed his lips around the sensitive crown and sucked.

Sparks lit behind Marcus's eyes as Enver pushed down, taking the entire length—cock and cord together—in one swallow. Marcus whimpered as Enver began to move, taking him with long, slow pulls, manipulating the velvet steel skin. Enver's eyes fluttered shut, blissed out on the feel of the cock filling his mouth.

Marcus groaned when Enver pulled off, but the sound morphed into a whimper when Enver starting licking and kissing the underside of his cock and the heavy weight of his testicles. The press of the ropes against him was too much. Not enough. Everything and nothing. A maddening mix that was as intoxicating as it was infuriating. He felt it from the roots of his hair to his toenails.

Enver chuckled softly.

Marcus growled.

"What I could do to you if I had you in my ropes for real." Combined with the deep timbre of his voice, Enver's touch against his waist caused Marcus to shiver. "The members would love someone like you. Freely giving yourself, but still demanding more."

Marcus's hips moved as he fought against the ropes, fought to get deep inside Enver's throat again. Enver took his time working his mouth and tongue up the length, playing with the cord. Just before he reached the crown, he switched directions, moving lower until he pressed his tongue flat against the sensitive skin behind Marcus's balls. When he changed directions yet again, Marcus's cock flexed under his tongue, a drop of clear fluid forming on the tip.

Enver kept his gaze locked on Marcus as he lapped the bead off the crown. "Salty and sweet at the same time." He sucked the entire length into his mouth once more. He swallowed Marcus again, and retreated, working with a brutal pace Marcus couldn't keep up with.

Within seconds, everything went white hot. "Fuck… fuck…*fuuuuuuck*." Marcus's body went tight beneath the ropes, his hips bucking uncontrollably against the restriction. With a loud roar, he jetted into Enver's throat, coming harder and longer than he had in ages, jerking and twitching against the ropes binding him in supplication.

As the intense scent of sweat and sex wrapped around them, Enver milked him dry, chasing the last flawless jolt of pleasure as it rippled through them both. When he finally found the strength to open his eyes again, Enver was looking up at him, grinning, his back moving as he struggled to take a full breath.

Enver adjusted his position, coming up on one knee as he grabbed the back of Marcus's head. He ground their mouths together in a greedy kiss. Marcus tasted himself on Enver's tongue and moaned softly. Gradually, the power of the release faded, turning the kiss into something different altogether.

Something real.

Marcus blinked, startled at the sudden change in his vision. His eyes couldn't focus on any one thing other than the buzz racing through his system. What he did know was that he was staring at the ceiling of the room. He realized belatedly his body felt like it was soaring. That his head felt as though it wasn't screwed on to his body, floating freely somewhere in the clouds. Subspace wasn't a foreign concept to him, but it had never been like this before. And never after a virtual session. He'd take time to marvel at the phenomenon later, for now he was just going to bask in the luxurious sensation.

The ceiling blurred as Enver's face came into focus. He stood over Marcus, cradling the back of his head, just like he had inside BLINC, holding the lenses he'd taken off Marcus's face. "You all right?"

"I'm good," Marcus said slowly, as though his brain and mouth weren't communicating. "You?"

There was a flash of something in Enver's eyes. Regret? Discomfort? "Good. Looks like you got all of the kinks out."

"Well...not *out* per se."

"Not out of it enough to stop making jokes. That's a good sign." Enver gave him a half-hearted smile, making no move to sever their connection.

"What's a good sign?"

"Ropespace hasn't quite worn off even though we've unplugged."

"Explains why I can't feel my body. Like, I know it's there, but it's not at the same time."

It was Enver's turn to frown. He crouched, checking over Marcus's form. "Deeper than I was expecting. Probably have another good hour or two of the endorphin rush before you crash. On your feet. Let's get you somewhere more comfortable before you fall out of your chair."

Enver held his hand, fitting his shoulder under Marcus's arm when he swayed. The scent of arousal and pent-up sexual energy overwhelmed Marcus's already charged senses, spinning him higher. The room blurred a few times as a heavy weight settled into his limbs. He had no idea how it was possible to feel so wonderful and so fatigued at the same time. It was as though time had sped up all around him, leaving him to think he'd invented a time machine instead of a virtual reality program.

All he was missing was the DeLorean.

His head rolled against Enver's shoulder. "Are you my density?"

Enver snorted. "All right, McFly. One foot in front of the other. Come on now."

It took effort, but Marcus managed to get his feet to cooperate. Enver helped him lie down just as the world started spinning.

Sometime later, Marcus opened his eyes again to find his head in Enver's lap. There was no clock nearby to let him know how long he'd been out, but at least some of the fuzziness had faded and he didn't feel as though he was wrapped in cotton anymore. He glanced up, looking at the man's strong profile. His eyes were closed, his breathing a slow pattern in and out that indicated sleep. But the tense set of the thigh muscles under Marcus's head gave away the fact Enver was still fully engaged with the submissive on his lap.

Marcus cleared his throat, unsurprised that Enver didn't jump at the sudden noise. "Sorry about keeping you longer than intended. I should have warned you I can get a little…weird coming down from subspace."

"Aftercare is all part of the deal, Marcus." Enver brushed his hand against his forehead, pushing back the hair that had fallen into his eyes. "Don't apologize for enjoying yourself."

Marcus wondered what the hell else he'd done, but he was too afraid to ask. "Guess it's ready for full-on beta testing."

"No guessing." Enver grabbed Marcus's arm when he tried to sit up. "You did an excellent job. I think Kochran, and the rest of the members, are going to be clamoring for their chance once this is fully up and running. Certainly has my seal of approval. Now just relax. I'll watch over you."

With the promise echoing in his head, Marcus closed his eyes and slept.

Chapter Fourteen

Enver woke to a loud pounding. He groaned, pulling the sheets over his head. The noise continued. For a moment, he thought the hammering was due to a hangover. But the uneven cadence was external and getting louder. He groaned again, debating between ignoring his persistent visitor in the hopes they'd go away or retrieving his handgun from the safe to add a peephole to the front door.

Decisions, decisions.

"All right, all right. Christ." He tugged open the door and narrowed his gaze at Oz. "World better be fucking ending and you need a fresh supply of blades to fight off the zombies."

"You look like death warmed over."

"Feel like it." Enver stretched as he led Oz to the kitchen, running his hands through his messy hair as he walked. Joints and muscles ached as though he'd completed a hard workout. In some ways he had, at least virtually. How in the hell was it possible that all he'd truly done was sit in a chair and wear some crazy headgear but physically felt as though he'd participated in a sexual marathon?

"Don't you ever clean?"

"Just going to get dirty again." Enver eyed a nearby mug, trying to remember the last time he'd used it. "Seems like a wasted effort."

Oz grimaced as he snatched the cup up. "And here I thought you were a grown up." Before long, hot, soapy water filled the sink and Oz was methodically working his way through a pile. Then another. Another. Enver grew bored watching, his burning eyes drooping as he propped his chin up with his palms.

He snapped awake when Oz slammed a cabinet. "Do you mind?"

Oz slid a steaming cup of coffee toward Enver then sat at the small wood table across from him. "You still look like shit." Oz sipped and winced. "Tastes like swill."

Enver didn't much care how it tasted. It was hot and caffeinated. "Why are you here?"

"Question really is—why are you dropping?"

Enver rolled his eyes. "Yeah, right."

Oz set his mug down, folding his fingers around it as he leaned forward. "While you are your normal grouchy self, you're also out of sorts and lethargic. I may have never seen it on you before, but I know the signs well enough. Even experienced them a time or two myself. You, my friend, are Domdropping."

Enver hadn't dropped in years. As much as Enver wanted to deny the accusation, he knew Oz was right about the alteration in his emotional state. He didn't want to admit the truth about the unease he couldn't quite pin down because it meant Marcus's damn program was just as effective as real life. After seeing Marcus lost in subspace for a few hours immediately after the session, he should have expected the drop.

Fucking geeks and their toys.

"Who's the lucky sub?"

Enver waved off Oz's question, not interested in sharing the particulars. "Why are you bothering me again?"

"Kochran has been trying to get ahold of you. When he called to see if I'd heard from you, I volunteered to check up on you since I was out this way."

"That plug you custom-ordered is up on the mountain. Not quite ready yet." Enver refilled their mugs and the men fell silent as they drank.

"Who is it?" Oz repeated after a few minutes.

Enver rubbed at his temple. He wanted to believe the ache was due to his unfamiliarity with the programming, but he knew better. Just like he knew Oz would pester him until the end of days.

"Marcus." Enver buried his face in the mug so he didn't have to face Oz's scrutiny.

"The new kid at the club with all the virtual reality stuff?"

Enver winced at the "kid" comment. The disparity in their ages wasn't huge, but it wasn't close either. Yeah, he'd affectionately used the term toward Marcus a time or two, but hearing it from Oz exacerbated the issue. "Giving him a hand for a few days."

"Looks like you're giving him more than that."

Enver caught the trace of a smile, the gleam of mischief in Oz's gaze. "Fuck you."

"Sure I'm not too old for you?" Oz smirked as he stood, refilling both their mugs again. "He doesn't seem like your type either."

"He's not. Kochran volunteered me to help him set up the new virtual reality system at Noble House. They both thought I was a good candidate because I have the least amount of experience with technology. Why are you looking at me like that?"

Oz shrugged. "You going to be able to pull yourself together enough to get to the club?"

"What's the rush?"

"Dunno. Kochran was insistent you needed to be there. Told me to drag your ass in if I had to. Not really my thing, but…"

Enver stood, taking care to wash the mug since Oz had cleaned up. "Fuck you and your damn smug-ass grin really hard, Oscar. Get out of my house before I charge you double for that plug just on principle."

Two hours later, Enver strolled through the doorway of Kochran's office. Given Kochran's urgency, he expected a room full of people. Instead, he found Saint sprawled on the couch, his arms draped across the back.

Saint tilted his head in greeting. "Calls us for a meeting and he doesn't show."

"When have you ever known him to be early? Man's going to be late to his own wedding."

Enver took the hand Saint offered. "Speaking of nuptials, how are the newlyweds?"

"Grae's pregnant," Saint blurted.

Enver stopped, hovering over the seat he'd been lowering himself into. "Judging by your panicked expression, I take it this is a surprise development."

"She just told us this morning. I'm still trying to process the news." Saint ran a trembling hand over his face. "I don't know the first damn thing about being a father."

Enver finally sat, crossing his ankles. "Looks like you're going to get a crash course." He held back a laugh when Saint glared at him, thinking about how annoyed he was with Oz earlier. "What does your husband think?"

"Acting like he won the lottery."

In some way, Saint was right. Boyce was lucky to be alive thanks to an attack on his unit's camp overseas, and had PTSD to deal with. Though Enver enjoyed seeing his normally even-keeled friend frazzled, Saint needed support. "Think he's prepared for the additional stress?"

Saint nodded. "He's already making adjustments so he can be ready for the changes. Don't think I've ever seen him so excited."

An expanding family *was* a gift. "I have no doubt the three of you will have it all figured out by delivery day."

"And if they don't, they have an excellent support network." Kochran stepped through his office door looking relaxed in slacks and a thin sweater. "Congratulations, Saint. Sorry for the short notice for this. We're in a bit of a time crunch."

"Not sorry for sending your watchdog after me," Enver said without humor. "What's so damn important?"

"A few things now that I have you both here." Kochran tapped his lip a few times as he moved behind his desk. "I'm interested in knowing how each of you would feel about serving as witnesses for my coming out party. It's a formality, really, but I'd like for my two best friends to be there to mark the occasion."

"Same thing I said to you when I found out you're a switch—about damn time. I'd be honored," Enver added. "I take it what else you have to talk to us isn't as pleasant?"

Kochran forced a grim smile. "No, it isn't." He stood, pushing his hands into his pockets. "Noble House has experienced some hiccups the past few years that are more than growing pains. I'm trying to manage all this the best that I can, but I know my limits. I recognized that when Maddy forced her way through Ezra's coding to illegally access the website. We've implemented new security software and I've been told our protocols have been strengthened to prevent incidents where members feel unsafe."

Saint snorted. "Careful, Kochran, your two lovers' geek is rubbing off on you."

A genuine smile from Kochran this time. "I may not grasp their technology fetish, but I'm kinky enough to exploit the hell out of it." He gestured to Enver. "Speaking of tech, how is it going with Marcus?"

"You didn't call me in here to talk about Marcus either." Enver shifted forward in his seat, setting his elbows on his knees. "Get to the point, Kochran."

"Fair enough." Kochran held up his hands. "I'm interested in hearing your thoughts about adding some new blood I think can help us further expand."

"We can always benefit from a growing membership pool," Saint said carefully, his caution about the topic obvious.

"I was thinking more in the terms of venturing into areas none of us are proficient with. To do that, I believe we'll need someone invested in the club as much as we are."

Kochran's news hammered Enver in the center of his chest even though he'd known this sort of thing would be coming eventually. "Expansion isn't unheard of and certainly warranted to keep things fresh. But do you think bringing in a new partner is how it should be done?"

"I'm not equipped to handle the technology parts of this business, which are growing faster than I can keep up. I'm not interested in learning it either, but I like the direction we're heading. I think we should keep going, but I don't believe I'm the right man for that job. Are either of you willing to lead this?"

"I doubt either of us want that level of responsibility." Enver glanced at Saint who confirmed the statement with a shrug.

"I would never ask either of you to jeopardize your current workload, or your lives for the sake of the club. But I needed to extend the opportunity."

"You have someone in mind already," Enver stated, picking up on Kochran's tone and the way he kept dancing around the issue. That wasn't characteristic for him.

"I do." Kochran sighed. "And that's what I really brought you here to discuss." He crossed the office, shutting the door. Heavy silence settled in the air. "You both know my current situation."

Saint narrowed his eyes. "You're not doing this because you still think the members can't handle the news that you submit to Ezra, are you? We keep telling you the members aren't going to care if you suck dick while you're on your knees. Or spank a sub's ass while she's on hers."

"No." Kochran dismissed the suggestion with a wave. "But I ran into someone from my past recently who fully understands my precarious situation as well."

"Someone from your—please tell me you're not about to suggest who I think you are." Enver's blood heated as Kochran nodded. His tone of voice meant only one man. "You can't seriously be suggesting that you want to make that asshole a partner in the club."

"I am," Kochran said evenly. "On a personal level, I don't hold anything against Miles. What I did with him in my twenties, I did consensually. He only took advantage of the opportunity offered to him. From a business aspect, he has taken several companies into new territory with astounding results. I'm looking to tap in to that expertise."

"You've already spoken to him about it." The accusation in Saint's tone rang loud. Enver was glad to know he wasn't the only one bothered by the idea of inviting Kochran's former Master into the fold.

"No, I haven't," Kochran said carefully. "We ran into one another quite unexpectedly last week while Ezra, Maddy and I were out to dinner in Los Angeles. He was in town from New York on business." A shadow crossed Kochran's face, a signal that the meeting hadn't been easy. Facing your past rarely was, especially when it slapped you unexpectedly and forced you to deal with it. "I can't speak to his personal life, but as far as professionally, he has an astounding resume, one I think the club can benefit from. I wanted to discuss it with you both first before I went to him. And I want you both to be there when I present the offer."

"Good, we won't have to pretend to have a conversation where Saint and I accompanying you is up for debate." Enver knew little about Kochran's past with Miles since it wasn't something he talked about, but given Kochran's caution about taking his place as Ezra's slave, it wasn't too difficult to connect the dots. Enver had his own secrets to bear, knew the weight of them could be crushing. But sometimes…confronting the issue head on was the best medicine.

"I can't say I fully agree with this, but if you feel the

club, and the members, can benefit, I'm at least willing
to hear what he has to say. I have a stipulation that isn't
up for debate—either one of you disagree with what
I'm about to say, we table this and figure out something
else. I'm sure between the three of us we could come
up with some other way to expand." Enver paused as
he waited for confirmation from his business partners.
"Miles may own a stake of the club, but he doesn't play
here, or anywhere the Noble House name is present. No
negotiation. No compromise. Hard. Fucking. Limit."

"I knew there was a reason we're in business together. I have the same stipulation." Kochran turned.
"Saint?"

Saint's knuckles were white where he'd gripped the
arms of the chair. "First sign this guy is still a raging
asshole, I put my fist through his pie-hole."

"Deal." When the men rose, Kochran spoke again.
"Enver, do you have a few minutes to talk?"

Enver already had an idea what Kochran wanted to
discuss. "Yeah."

"Catch you guys later, I'm going to help Ezra and
Maddy with a patch they're installing so the system can
handle the new virtual reality implementation." Saint
left, closing the door behind him to close Enver and
Kochran off from the rest of the club again.

As Enver was trying to decide what to say to head
him off, Kochran broke the silence. "How is the work
with Marcus going?"

"Sure you should be asking me? I'm useless when it
comes to the tech. Or don't you remember telling him
to use me because I didn't know shit?"

"He'd give me a ten-minute diatribe I would need
Maddy or Ezra to decipher. I want an honest, non-

technical opinion. The members aren't going to care about the stuff the geek side of Noble House looks after. They do care about how it will benefit them during a scene. It's exactly why I'm asking your opinion."

"An unbiased one."

"I think we both know that isn't possible. I've seen how much time you've been spending with him."

And now the real reason for Kochran's urgency. "Is that a problem?"

"Of course not. But if I've noticed, so have others."

"Really sounds like this is an issue."

"Stop being so damn defensive, Enver." Kochran rubbed his forehead. "All I'm trying to point out is that you're spending a lot of time with him. I'm not worried. In fact, I think it's good for you."

Enver narrowed his eyes. "You're meddling."

Kochran's eyebrows rose. "There's something wrong with wanting to see my friend happy?"

"You worry about Maddy and Ezra and I'll make sure Marcus has the system ready to go by the promised date. How are *you*?"

The abrupt subject change stalled the conversation as the mask Kochran wore for the rest of the world slipped away to expose a man beneath. He looked beaten and bruised despite the crisp press of his suit. "Better. Eight months since Tory died and it still feels like there's a big hole in the center of my chest when I think about her."

"She's not hurting anymore."

"I know. Ezra and Maddy have helped a lot. Keep my mind occupied when I get buried under it all." The edges of his mouth turned up slightly, a sign he was thinking about something private. "Been there when I needed to talk."

"Got yourself a pair of keepers. About damn time." Enver remembered saying that exact same thing shortly after Kochran's sister Tory's death. It had been the first time he'd seen the three of them together, and he'd known Kochran had discovered the happily ever after he didn't feel he deserved.

"I've finally stopped questioning why they love me." Kochran absently spun the silver band Maddy and Ezra had given him during their collaring ceremony in a secluded area of the building.

"All about steps, man." Enver had walked similar steps himself. Though the struggle had become more acute since he'd met Marcus. Made him feel as though he needed to backtrack and revisit every one of those teachings to reinforce his strength. "Back to your original question. The system is going fine. Based on what I know, the members are going to love it. Marcus is a hard worker. It's clear he's poured his heart and soul into the project. I'm not aware of the terms of his contract, but is there some kind of incentive bonus involved?"

"No, but based on the reports Ezra, Maddy and you have been giving me, I'll make sure he receives proper compensation."

"Good." Enver was pleased that Kochran was willing to reward hard work. "He's more than competent to run the virtual leg of the club once it's up and running."

Kochran gave him an odd look. "He won't."

Enver wondered if he'd heard him wrong. "What?"

Kochran turned to his desk, rifling through a drawer full of files before he pulled out an unmarked file. He set it on the desk, flipping it open and scanning down a page until he found what he was looking for. "Here. Marcus is only contracted to set up the system. According to this, once it's running he'll then turn it over. In this case, Maddy and Ezra will take over the day-to-day operations and Marcus will only provide support if it's something they can't resolve. Ezra has already expressed concerns about the staff being able to handle the workload and wants to hire a few more geeks to his arsenal."

"So he's not permanent."

"No. He didn't tell you?" Kochran paused for an answer, but Enver had none to give. "Obviously not. Why do I have a feeling there is a hell of a lot more going on between you two than I'm thinking?"

"No," Enver said tightly. "He just fits in well at the club. I made assumptions, that's all. Let me know when that meeting is with Miles and I'll be there." Enver left the office before Kochran could say anything else. A tight knot had formed in his chest, one that he didn't know how to untangle.

Chapter Fifteen

Testing of the system had gone better than expected. Maybe too good. Marcus hadn't expected the bonus of actually experiencing subspace out of the program. It was certainly going to prove to be an excellent selling point to the members when the system went live. Though he hoped his reaction wasn't typical. Coming out of the state had proven more difficult than he imagined, far more than any time he'd experienced it before. He suspected what had made everything so powerful had something to do with the direct neural connection with BLINC.

"You all set?"

Enver's sudden question was nearly enough to make him jump. Instead, he snapped the lock open on the storage case for the visors and turned, immediately knowing something was wrong by the set of Enver's body and the narrow slits of his eyes.

"You okay?" he asked, genuinely concerned about Enver's well-being. They hadn't spoken since they'd left the club last night, but if he had to guess, Enver had been just as affected by the last session. He, of course, had never experienced Domspace, but watching his former Doms had taught him to recognize the signs. Power exchanges weren't one sided, as most of the general public seemed to believe.

Enver's lips thinned into a pale line as he closed the door behind him, stepping fully into the room. "Yeah."

Despite the fact it was only a single word, there was a story in that response. Dozens of questions that didn't make sense punched at Marcus's throat, fighting for freedom. Instead, he bit them back, and kept his tone even. Professional. Enver had simply been doing his job. No reason to read more into it.

"I've lined up a session of beta testing starting on Monday." Marcus tapped the power button on his workstation. "Ezra and Maddy are going to help with stress testing the system, so we can run several simulations at once. So far it's only been us."

A long stretch of silence filled the air. Swirls of too many emotions—uncertainty, fear, suspicion and hints of desperate hope—warred in his gut. He knew he was being stupid, but Enver wasn't giving him much to work with.

"Why—" Huskiness coated Enver's voice, a sign he was dealing with his own barrage of emotions. He cleared his throat and tried again, furrow lines appearing on his brow. "Why didn't you tell me?"

Fear iced his blood. Had Enver found out about the text messages from Davis? "Tell you what?"

"That you're not sticking around. You could have said your contract terms were only to set up the programming." Enver's voice turned cold as his posture changed. Anger visibly vibrated the air around him. "That the real reason why you took off at the observatory?"

I don't know what to say or do to express how grateful I am I met you, that's all.

Those words stayed locked in his throat. Marcus fought the tingle in his hands to touch this man. Feel the solidness of his frame. All the hard lines and angles from head to toe. He hadn't been able to get Enver out of his head since that first awkward meeting at the convention. Though he wanted to pursue something further with Enver, discover if the intense connection they shared was more than instant attraction, he knew the threat of Davis would hang over his life like a dark cloud. He wasn't willing to subject the object of his desires to that special version of hell.

If you want a future with him, you have to trust him with your secrets.

"Like I said, just a family issue that I had to take care of." The lie burned its way down his throat to his stomach, leaving a perforation a mile wide.

"I thought... Never mind." Enver fell quiet again. His gaze shifted, taking on a cloudy cast.

A crushing wave of loss bore down on Marcus, suffocating him, leaving him with a sick emptiness inside. He'd never experienced this kind of debilitating pain in his life.

"I can't do this, Enver," he whispered.

"I won't take up any more of your time then." Enver turned.

"No, that's—" Marcus's legs went weak. "Stop. Enver, don't go."

Oh God. Please don't leave.

For a few heart-stopping seconds, Marcus wasn't sure if Enver had heard him. But as Enver drew close to the door, his shoulders fell and he turned to face Marcus. A half dozen feet away, he stood, his body rigid, and Marcus could only think about how much he needed for this man to remain in his life—whatever the cost.

"My life is…complicated at best. I've got some shit going on that I'm trying to deal with. Failing miserably at it too." Marcus licked his lips, closing the distance between them. "You're one of those things."

Enver grimaced. "Sorry I'm such a complication for you."

"That…didn't come out like I meant it to. Nothing I'm trying to say is coming out right. Jesus. What I mean to say is that there are some things about my life that I'm not ready to talk about. With anyone," he added hastily. "And I know I've been letting it affect whatever it is that is between you and me. That was never my intent."

"You're not the only one dealing with demons."

"Yeah."

"I want… I mean, I think—*shit*. Now I'm the one who can't speak." Enver looked around the room, as though he wanted to find anything else but Marcus. Giving up, their gazes finally collided. "I just want you to know that you can talk to me whenever you want. May not have the answers, but I'm a pretty good sounding board."

"Thanks." The single word nearly broke something inside of him. He refused to allow Enver to get tangled up in the shit show that his life had become. But he knew he could trust this man more than anyone else. Maybe even more than Zoie. That truth scraped over already raw nerves. He'd be a fool to throw away their chemistry. Blood rushed with ridiculous speed through his veins.

He could do this.

They could do this. He just needed to be exceptionally careful.

As he closed the distance between them, he gave in to the beckoning need to touch Enver. He set his hand on Enver's chiseled jaw, feeling him relax against the contact of warm, firm skin. No matter how hard he tried, he would never be able to get this man out of system.

"Look at me."

Marcus felt Enver's breath caress his palm as he spoke. The gentle breeze pushed at the needs he'd been fighting from day one. The desires that Enver had awakened. When Enver touched Marcus's hip, Marcus had an instant flash of what it would be like to be held and slowly fucked by the man. An avalanche of want crashed against him so hard, he nearly stumbled.

But Enver pushed against him, offering him support. "Tell me why you didn't let me know you didn't intend to stick around."

"We were just two colleagues working on a short-term project. I assumed you'd figure out that I wasn't staying." Marcus's cheeks heated when Enver narrowed his eyes to glare at him. "Fine. Because I want you, all right?" Marcus tried to twist out of Enver's grip, but the other man held on. "God help me, I want you."

"It's going to take some work, but I'd like to…try. Us," Enver added. "I want *us* to try. I'm not the easiest man to get to know because I'm so used to closing down. Keeping to myself." Enver ran his hand down the line of Marcus's spine, the fabric of his shirt tickling his skin so he couldn't contain the shudder that racked his body. "But it seems like you've got the same kind of issues. Makes us quite the pair."

Marcus's cock jumped to full staff as terror raced through him, his hands starting to shake.

"One thing." He studied Enver's face, looking for traces of hesitation. "Something doesn't seem right? Just in general, like you feel like you're being followed or watched...let me know right away. Told you my life is complicated," he added with a forced smile.

"Answer one question and we won't discuss this again until you're ready." Marcus was the one who nodded this time. "You feel like *you're* being followed or watched, you let *me* know right away so we can deal with it. You heard that? *We.*"

Marcus knew there were questions Enver wanted to ask, but instead of offering, he nodded again. "Got it."

"Good," Enver continued. "Are you in any immediate danger now?"

"Not with you."

The affirmation was a boon to his soul, and he leaned forward, slashing his lips across Enver's. Losing himself, he crushed and bit and licked Enver's mouth, hungry and rough, but unable to contain all the pent-up desire. The smoky undercurrent of Enver that Marcus had come to adore filled his senses as he sank into the heat of the kiss.

Enver pushed closer, grabbed the front of his shirt and muscled him around so Marcus's back was pressed against the door. Though Enver had the physical superiority, Marcus still controlled the kiss. When Enver flicked his tongue against his, Marcus was convinced he was going to erupt in flames.

Oh, fuck, yes. Yes.

Enver yanked Marcus against him, running his hands up and down Marcus's back, inching up the fabric. When his hot palms connected with skin, a shudder trembled through Marcus. He tore his mouth away, breathing heavily, his sight blurring as he stared at Enver. Blood rushed to his cock and balls as Enver ground his hips against Marcus's pelvis. When Marcus tried to adjust himself, Enver simply grinned.

He covered Marcus's hand, following as he moved. Marcus sucked in an audible breath, pushing against the firm connection. Heat arced between them as their gazes collided again. Enver was the one who claimed Marcus's mouth this time, the contact searing through the haze filling Marcus's brain. Enver tilted his head, eating at Marcus's mouth.

That woodsy flavor mainlined straight to Marcus's bloodstream.

"Sorry," Enver muttered against Marcus's lips.

Marcus responded with a tight, high moan, pushing against Enver's fingers. "Thought it was pretty clear I like you being in control."

"Wasn't positive that was just for testing with BLINC."

Marcus leaned his head back until it contacted with the wall. "Wow. I realize we've got a lot of shit between us, but the bullshit factor is high right now." Enver gave him a level look that only caused Marcus to want him even more. The power coursing from him defied any fantasy he'd ever had about a power exchange. Thoughts of what he wanted them to do together filled every space of his thoughts. "Tell you what—let me show you what I really like, not just for testing purposes."

"Inside BLINC?"

"Of course." Marcus pointed to himself. "Geek, remember?"

Chapter Sixteen

The digital replication of Court greeted Enver as soon as he dropped into the program. Unlike last time they had jacked in for a round of testing, the room was empty except for a single leather overstuffed chair. A small pedestal table was positioned in front of the chair and Marcus knelt nearby.

A hot zing lashed at Enver as he thought about how intoxicating Marcus looked, waiting patiently for direction from his Dom. *That's the real Marcus.* Wise or not, he wanted Marcus with a passion far different from anything else he'd ever experienced. He had no idea where this was going to take them, but for the first time, he didn't care. This kind of power and passion wasn't something that could be tamed.

Marcus only wore a pair of jeans, his chest and feet bare. Enver smiled at the small detail. He could have easily gone without clothing, but the fact he'd decided not to meant more.

As Enver drew closer, he noticed a bottle of bourbon, a short glass and a cigar. "What's this?"

"Cigar service, Sir."

Enver stopped mid-stride. He had more than a few ideas what that meant, and could make more assumptions, but so far that had only brought trouble. Marcus clearly had a goal in mind and Enver was interested in seeing it play out. "Seems you have me at a disadvantage. I have no idea what that is."

Marcus's gaze dropped to the floor. "I didn't mean—"

"Tell me what your devious mind is working on now, gorgeous. I like when you're proud of your accomplishments and want to show off."

Bright spots appeared on Marcus's cheeks as he lifted his face. "I know you like to smoke. So I thought this would be a good test of the system. Cigar service is when a sub kneels next to his Dom while he prepares the cigar to his owner's liking."

There had to be more to this setup than that. Enver approached, picking up the telling heavy notes of arousal. As much as it fascinated him that a computer program could allow his brain to imagine the scent perfectly, he knew whatever else Marcus intended wasn't just sitting there watching him smoking. Could be, though. People got off on just about anything.

Enver sat, situating himself in the chair with Marcus between his spread legs. From this angle, Enver saw he'd been right. The ridge of Marcus's erection was pressing hard against the zipper. Enver's cock stirred in response. The visceral reaction he achieved inside BLINC still fascinated him.

He was flirting with danger. At some point, he knew he was going to end up pulling his safe word to put an end to this. Marcus had gotten under his skin, so he damn well knew why it was such a bad idea for them to keep doing this.

Yet he wanted to do it anyway.

Marcus placed the cigar in his palm and lifted it for

Enver's approval. Enver took it, the tight weave of the leaves feeling firm, but loose enough to allow for oxygen to reach the flame. Once more he was surprised by the minute details he could pick up through the virtual reality connection. At how much work Marcus put into something he clearly loved.

"You've pleased me. Go on."

Marcus took a cutter and snipped the tip of the cigar off to the shoulder. Enver watched in fascination as Marcus picked up a silver lighter, used his denim-clad thigh to ignite it and work on building a cherry.

"Clearly you've done this before."

Marcus gave a noncommittal shrug. "One of my first steady relationships was with a guy who liked cigars. We never exchanged power, but it gave me quite an education about the process. First Dom I was with liked this, but I wasn't trained enough for his tastes. I'd watch instead, learn. You can pick up a lot observing." He paused, checking his progress before he continued. "One couple we were always around were into some heavy stuff."

The way Marcus's voice changed in tone told Enver the situation he mentioned had made Marcus uncomfortable. "They pushed your limits."

"For the most part, I ignored them. Focused solely on my Dom and the other sub attending him to make sure she did her job correctly. I didn't mind sharing him non-sexually, but I wasn't going to allow anyone to displease him."

Enver smiled. "Such admirable loyalty."

Marcus dropped the lighter on the table, curled his fingers around the cigar and offered it. Enver accepted with a nod. As he set the cigar to his lips, the flavor of

Marcus danced across his tongue. The first few pulls were an intoxicating combination of smoke and Marcus.

He understood the appeal now.

"One night was a little much for me, and I asked for permission to step away even though I was abandoning my Dom. I couldn't...watch. Couldn't push it out of my mind enough to focus on him. I think it was too much for him as well because he came up with some excuse why we needed to leave."

"What happened?"

Marcus's throat visibly worked as he swallowed, and Enver could almost see the shame curling around his kneeling form. "With this, there are levels of service, just as with everything else in the lifestyle. That includes ashing. This particular couple enjoyed the full works."

"Did he put it out on her?" Enver could understand how someone with Marcus's background could have issues with a Dom marking his sub in such a way. He bore marks that forced him to face the unthinkable every day. "Mark her as his in some way?"

A noticeable shiver rippled down Marcus's body and he spoke quietly. "He used her mouth as an ashtray. She would come every time he did it. It was...too much." His voice dropped off at the last words. "I never stuck around to find out what else they did, but considering they were both into S&M, it isn't hard to imagine."

Though Enver wasn't interested in either practice, something told him Marcus would do it if Enver ordered him to. At least the ashing part. He deliberately rolled the cigar on the rim of the glass filled with two fingers of top-shelf bourbon so the ashes fell into the amber liquid.

"Sir." Marcus cupped his hands together, offering them to Enver. "You can use me."

Enver touched the top of Marcus's head, ruffling the fine hair and noting how the red strands sparked gold in the spotlight. "You're not my ashtray, Marcus. Ever. Even in a constructed world like this. Though the thought of you dirty is appealing, I want to be the one who makes you a sweaty, filthy mess. Fetch two glasses, please. I don't particularly care to drink alone." Despite the command, Marcus remained on his knees. "Is there a problem?"

"Sir, I…no." Marcus started to rise.

Enver caught his shoulder and forced him to stay. "What is it?"

Marcus's gaze flicked to the side, then back to the floor as though he wasn't sure where to look, but anywhere that wasn't Enver's face. "I would like to serve you while you enjoy your cigar." That gaze flicked to Enver's crotch. "If you'll allow it."

Even though Enver's cock gave a twitch in response, he knew he couldn't put off the inevitable any longer. What they shared didn't deserve this.

He dropped the cigar into the filled glass to extinguish it, leaned forward and cupped Marcus's jaw. Those gorgeous eyes studied him as Enver set his lips against Marcus's. He gently kissed him, his gut clenching at the thought that this could very well be the last time he touched Marcus. He held a secret that could be a deal breaker, effectively killing this relationship just as it was getting started.

"Monster."

Enver found himself staring into darkness. He blinked a few times as the sudden transition, impressed with the reaction of the program to the safe-word trigger. He hadn't meant to test the feature Marcus had told him about in the early days, but it had worked perfectly. As he removed the visor, he found Marcus staring at him, annoyance twisting his lips.

"What the fuck was that?" Marcus tossed his headset to the desk. "I offer you a blowjob and you sever the connection?"

"We need to talk." The look that ghosted over Marcus's face was exactly what Enver had been hoping to avoid. "*I* need to talk," he amended.

Though the panic didn't disappear from Marcus's expression, he relaxed. "All right."

Enver sighed as he stood, shoving his hands into his pockets. Talking about his issues was never easy. Even though he was comfortable with it, exposing something that deeply personal left him feeling vulnerable and exposed.

Much like the photo hanging on the second floor of the club.

"There's something important you should—need—to know about me before we go down this road together," Enver said carefully. "I thought I could avoid it, but...yeah. You need to know what kind of monster you're offering yourself to."

"What are you talking about?"

"I'm not the sweet and innocent man you think I am."

Marcus snorted. "Those are two things I would never use to describe you, Enver."

Good. Enver needed the levity. Needed Marcus relaxed because explaining the situation was just as difficult as hearing it.

"Everyone wonders why I never have sex at the club.

Why it is so rare for me to participate sexually—full-blown intercourse—in a scene."

"Always giving your sub pleasure, never taking any of your own. I haven't been here long, but I've heard."

Those rumors were exactly why Enver had safed out of the scene. He needed to set the record straight. "Speculation is that I don't enjoy intercourse. Couldn't be further from the truth. I enjoy it immensely, and that's the problem."

Marcus's brow furrowed. "What are you trying to say?"

"I'm a recovering sex addict." Enver paused, waiting for the information to sink in. When Marcus remained silent, he wondered if he'd made a mistake, but there was no turning back now. "When I started getting into the lifestyle, I already had a problem. The inherent nature of BDSM just meant that I was around people who recognized it. Before I realized it was an issue, I took risks. But the reward was never enough. I always had to have one more. I knew nothing else would compare. In that moment, nothing existed. Work, family, even my partner. There was just that pure, physical pleasure. Then it was jacking off in the bathroom at work. A lunchtime quickie in the car. It was leaving work, finding a hooker. Then that wasn't enough. So I picked one up at lunch, one after work, another after dinner. I did anything and everything I could to get off. I didn't even care if my partner did or not. I took what I needed and I was done. Sex for me was a drug, and I grabbed a hit whenever and wherever I could. Bottom line... I possessed a dangerous lack of self-awareness."

"Does Kochran know?"

"That's not what you want to know." Enver brushed his thumb down the side of Marcus's face. "Go on. Ask."

The question danced on Marcus's lips for several minutes before he finally spoke. "Did you ever…hurt anyone?"

"No. I never hurt or forced anyone to satisfy my needs. Ever. I was pretty fucked up, but I never crossed that line. I never will either. Violence is my hard limit." Enver paused. "To answer your other question, Kochran knows I struggled in the past with an addiction and that I choose not to engage in sexual activity. I provided him with paperwork from my therapist certifying that I wasn't a danger to anyone, but that's it. If you're concerned, my therapist is my first contact on my phone and I still see him if things get out of control. This is the only vice I have now." Enver pulled out a pack of cigarettes and tossed it on the desk. "Only using myself."

"I…saw you. In your car. Since we're confessing…" Marcus's head lifted, his cheeks bright with flushed patches. "The night I did the body scan. I came to give you the mineral oil 'cause you left it, and I found you…"

"Jacking off?" Enver finished.

"Yeah," Marcus responded quietly. "I'm sorry. I know I was intruding on a private moment, but I couldn't help it. You were just so…gorgeous."

Enver remembered the desperation that had clawed at him. The aching need he hadn't been able to rid himself of. "Rubbed myself raw trying to get you out of my system. Hadn't allowed myself to do that in ages."

Marcus licked his lips. "Why are you telling me this? Like I said, earlier, you could have just said you weren't interested in me and we could have moved on."

"Because we both know that's not the right answer

either." Enver stroked the strands of Marcus's hair, enjoying the silky feel between his fingers. "Besides, I spent almost an hour trying to get you out of my system and all I succeeded in doing was making me want you more."

"An hour?" Marcus asked, clearly dumbfounded. "You masturbated for *an hour*? Not sure if I should commend you or ask if you still have a dick."

"Both?" Enver sobered. "Sex won't be easy. There will be times that I want to, but I can't. That's why you needed to know. I'm not trying to push you away. I'm trying to keep myself—my addiction—under control. The safe word is just as important to me as it is to you. I'll honor it if you agree to do the same."

Marcus stood, inching into Enver's space. "Thank you for being willing to share that piece of you with me. I'm honored. And humbled." He slanted his mouth over Enver's, giving him a slow and easy kiss. For a long minute, Enver allowed Marcus to explore as he pleased. When Marcus's body trembled against his, Enver took over, plowing over Marcus's defenses and taking full control of the moment.

He broke away, panting. "Why don't we duplicate the setup in BLINC out here? Then you can suck my dick in appreciation."

Chapter Seventeen

Though the room Marcus entered was smaller than Court, the atmosphere was identical. The Keep, as Enver had referred to it when doling out instructions, was a private area free of outside distractions. No windows. A single entrance/exit point.

More importantly—no cameras.

A raised platform to Marcus's left took up over a quarter of the room, and held a single chair. Though *chair* was not descriptive enough. The fucking throne dominated the room with unspoken power. The kind of supremacy emitting from that side of the room told Marcus that chair was reserved for special occasions. That same twinge told Marcus that Enver had never used it, so it wasn't appropriate for what he had in mind.

Instead, he dragged over a vintage Craftsman-inspired lounge chair with oversized rolled arms. The masculine feel of it somehow offset the buttery softness of the leather. Perfect for Enver to sit in for what Marcus had envisioned.

As Marcus set his duffle on the floor, Enver's confession came to mind. Thanks to Marcus's own sessions with a therapist, he wasn't freaked out by the sex addiction news. Being in the lifestyle didn't exclude someone from having personal demons. He wasn't worried, but he understood Enver's caution, and appreciated it. It was definitely not a showstopper, and he was glad they were moving forward.

Marcus pulled a cigar out of the bag, along with his cutter and lighter. Then he set the bottle of bourbon and glass beside it. He'd forgotten to grab some ice from the lounge, but he knew Enver didn't intend to drink during their scene. It served as nothing more than a prop due to the strict rules at Noble House about combining alcohol and play—at least in real life. The virtual reality machine had no such rules. Though Marcus imagined even if those policies weren't in place, given Enver's history with addiction, alcohol still wouldn't come into play.

Unlike inside BLINC, Marcus stripped, shoving his clothes into the duffle. Just as he settled to his knees on the plush rug, the door opened. He didn't need to look to know it was Enver. The man's power and energy were astounding, pressing against Marcus's skin. No wonder he was usually the talk of the club, and not because of his unusual practices when it came to sexual contact. Marcus had felt his prowess knock against him as soon as he'd laid eyes on Enver for the first time, but he didn't fully understand it until this exact moment.

Some would consider their attempt at normalcy unhealthy. Two scarred souls seeking solace in one another. But Marcus had stopped listening, or caring, about those opinions long ago.

His focus snapped to Enver when he slid into the chair. Marcus risked lifting his gaze. The handsome beauty of Enver's features was breathtaking. Dark hair touched with gray at the temples. Blue-green eyes that constantly changed color, and were as sharp as a hawk, never missing a trick. The strong jaw etched from a granite slab.

That gorgeousness made it hard to think rationally, frying Marcus's synapses. Made the deliciously wicked moment all the more sinful. Marcus wanted to capture all the ruthless energy. In some way, he had inside the virtual reality machine. But out here it was wild and free.

Enver was risking a lot. Everyone had demons, but Enver had willingly unlocked the iron cage he usually kept his past confined with and let Marcus in. Enver was a man used to denial. Giving in this way, releasing himself of the deprivation, providing a connection they both craved.

"I'm here for your pleasure, Sir."

"Looking at you like this gives me pleasure." Enver leaned forward, curling his fingers around Marcus's shaft, pushing down to the root, and then moved under to tug on his nuts. Marcus moaned and jerked, lifting his face to meet Enver's gaze.

"I want to know what your mouth feels like on my cock inside your program," Enver said. He moved in until their lips were centimeters apart, and whispered roughly, "But right now, let me feel it during a scene for real." Marcus started to reach for the cigar and lighter, but Enver tugged him closer, claiming his mouth with a violent kiss. He slashed his lips across Marcus's and sank his tongue inside, owning him with a possessive dominance that had Marcus opening wider and keening for more.

Enver yanked his head back and to the side, tearing their mouths apart. He sat back with a huff, his chest moving rapidly as he fought to catch his breath. "Show me your skill with the cigar."

Marcus's body buzzed from head to feet, his grip on reality slipping. Enver was entirely too potent, coaxing him into compliance with nothing more than a heated glance and a single order. He kept his gaze locked on Enver's as he went through the motions of prepping the cigar the same way he had in the simulator.

He handed Enver the cigar, flicking the wheel on his lighter to spark a flame. Enver's cheeks hollowed as he sucked in a few times, until the cherry had a nice color. Marcus closed the lighter, returning it to the table, and sat back on his heels again.

Enver settled into the chair, rolling the lit cigar between two of his fingers.

"Sir, may I?" His mouth was even with Enver's thigh even as he asked.

"You may," Enver said around the cigar at the corner of his mouth.

Given the freedom, Marcus leaned forward to press his mouth against the denim straining over Enver's cock. He didn't open the zipper right away, wanting to prolong the moment unless Enver ordered him to. He breathed Enver in, creating pressure against the ridge, feeling the erection jump under the tight denim. He drew down the zipper and peeled back the two sides. Somehow, it didn't surprise him to learn that Enver had gone commando. The dark red flush of Enver's cock was beautifully framed by the cornflower-blue denim.

"You have an amazing dick." Even though he'd already seen it a few times in the simulator, he hadn't been this close for a while. "I've been wanting to tell you that since you let me do the full-body scan."

"Is that so?"

"Yeah." Marcus swallowed. "Couldn't stop thinking about how I could feed off it all night." He glanced up, certain that his own dick was going to snap off at the sight of the wicked heat dancing in Enver's gaze. Unimaginable warmth swirled to every corner of his body at the unguarded longing staring back at him.

"You're remarkably cute on your knees, dancing around the words to ask if you can suck my cock." Enver smirked, taking a few pulls on the cigar. He reached down, lifting himself free of the fabric and angling the shaft toward Marcus's mouth. "Suck me."

Marcus locked in on Enver's intense stare as he darted out his tongue. Warm, salty essence flooded his taste buds, saturating his system. Without thinking, he leaned forward and licked, enjoying the way Enver's thighs and abdomen tightened. He closed his lips over the crown, a warm tendril of pleasure arcing through him at the grunt Enver gave. He tasted a musky saltiness that told him Enver had been aroused at some point tonight. Inhaling the pungent, heady male fragrance of sex and sweat, Marcus tongued the indention pressing against his tongue, lifting his gaze when Enver inhaled sharply.

"Fuck." Enver's throaty murmur arrowed straight to Marcus's cock. The sound combined with the image Enver made caused Marcus's blood to riot. Enver titled his head back, took a long pull on the cigar and blew it out in a stream. Marcus wasn't sure why he found having Enver smoke while he sucked him off so insanely hot, but dammit, this was so fucking irresistible.

A cloud of smoke hung in the air, curling up toward the single light shining down on them. This time, when

Enver started to blow another stream, Marcus slid down to take him all the way to the root.

Enver's thighs jerked under Marcus's palms, another satisfied groan echoing through the room, saturating the already charged air. He didn't want to take his gaze off Enver, but he wanted to get completely lost in the man. Drown in him. Crawl inside him and lose himself. That authoritative way he still controlled the moment even though Marcus had his cock down his throat.

Enver's low sound of hunger spurred Marcus on. He breathed him in, scenting the sensual blend of male and smoke. Marcus yearned for more, wishing he would heal Enver with a snap of his fingers. It if was possible, he would. He felt safe with Enver, as though they could take on the world together.

Inside this safe space, his troubles with Davis didn't exist.

"Take it all." Enver's hand cupped the back of Marcus's neck, the clench of his fingers electrifying Marcus's skin. The tight grip and commanding tone signaled that Enver had allowed Marcus to play for long enough.

He gladly surrendered, loving the smell, feel, and taste of every hot inch down his throat. Aggression and lust mingled inside him, taking over his mind and body with the need to make this man come. Enver made deep, vibrating noises that almost sounded like an animal in agony as he started churning his hips.

Suddenly, he yanked Marcus's mouth off his cock, wrapping his hand around his well-lubricated shaft. As Marcus watched, Enver stroked himself with one hand, dropped the stub of his cigar into the nearby glass and wrapped his other hand around the back of Marcus's neck to pin him in the kneeling position between his spread legs.

He drove his hand up and down with piston-fast strokes, his penetrating gaze locked on Marcus. Within the space of a few long breaths, he shuddered and came, spurting seed onto Marcus's chest. Marcus gasped as the first jetting stream of hot semen hit his skin. He moaned as another splash marked him, fiery lust flickering through his core as Enver continued to orgasm.

Enver's gaze roved over Marcus as his strokes slowed. "Sexiest damn thing I've ever seen, kneeling there covered with my come." He tugged Marcus's mouth to his, kissing him with a brutal strength that told Marcus the orgasm hadn't flagged Enver's arousal. "How are you so fucking sexy and sweet and incredible all at the same time?" He shook his head, dazed as he grazed his knuckles up Marcus's jaw, over his cheek, and into his hair.

There was so much tenderness in his expression, Marcus feared he might cry. This man gave him a bizarre sense of belonging he couldn't explain. "It's hard to control myself around you—in or out of BLINC. I just…want you so much. Every time you touch me, I swear I feel it all the way to my goddamn soul. I could present myself on my knees for you forever," he admitted quietly.

"Sounds like a good way to spend time to me," Enver said in a soft voice as he folded over Marcus, holding him, breathing together as they sat still for long minutes.

"Sir, please." Marcus bit back a string of curses as the power of the moment washed over him.

"Christ, that desperate sound never gets old."

Marcus's heart pounded as though he'd just run a

marathon, every muscle limp. Enver reached between them, his gaze locked on Marcus's as he brushed his fingers against Marcus's thighs. Electricity jolted through Marcus at the contact, causing him to arch his back, his breath catching in his throat.

Sanity snapped. "Please…son of a bitch…shit… Sir. I can't…"

"God, Marcus—" Enver's voice was strangled, a quiet snarl brushing against Marcus's lips as he wrapped his hand around Marcus's cock.

"Shit," Marcus breathed out as he squeezed his eyes shut.

"Don't come until I say so," Enver ordered, his voice rumbly and gruff and all those things that made it so Marcus couldn't think coherently.

He tilted his head back and uttered a soft curse before he answered, "Yeah."

Enver stilled his head, gripping Marcus's shaft tightly. "Yeah?"

Marcus moaned. "Oh my God…fucking hell. Yes." He paused, struggling to maintain control. "Yes, all right?"

"Watching you obey me even though all you want to do is blow your wad turns me on. Love seeing you in my ropes, but this…" Enver squeezed the dick pulsing against his palm. "I can't fucking wait to watch you lose your shit while still covered with my come."

"Holy shit…yes. Please. Yes. I can't fucking wait anymore."

The echoed words hung in the air between them.

"You can, gorgeous." Enver nipped Marcus's bottom lip. "And you will."

Time ceased to function as Enver continued to hold

him, his grip tight and unmoving as that frustratingly wicked grin curled up the edge of his smug mouth. That beautifully sexy smug mouth.

"You're fucking amazing, Marcus."

As the benediction washed over Marcus, Enver slid his hand up the length of Marcus's dick. The movement was enough to cause Marcus to lose his composure. He gave a sudden shudder that quickly morphed into a convulsion as he began thrusting his hips furiously, hard rasping moans vibrating his throat.

The orgasm didn't just shoot through his cock, but seized his whole body to bring him to a violent pinnacle. He fucked into Enver's tight grasp, luxuriating in that sensational grip stroking him as his groans became a roar, unable to control his response. His seed exploded from him, the hot stream of his need spilling over the Persian rug rubbing his shins raw.

"You're so beautiful to watch." Enver rested his brow against Marcus's. "So fucking beautiful."

"Thank you, Sir." It came out thick, his chest weighted with far more than just the energy he'd exerted. He closed his eyes as Enver's arms wound around his shoulders. His breath left him a long expulsion. "Can I hold you?"

Enver pulled Marcus to his feet, standing with him, and stripped away his shirt, rubbing it over Marcus's chest to remove any ejaculate that hadn't already dried. He tossed it to the side and pulled Marcus closer, pressing his mouth against his ear as he guided him to a nearby couch. "I love that you smell like me now." He dropped, pulling Marcus down on top of him, arranging their bodies so their chests were pressed together, their legs tangled.

Overwhelmed, his body weak with exhaustion, Marcus sighed as he rested his cheek to Enver's chest, enjoying the sound of the strong heartbeat as he snuggled against him. "I'll add that little detail to the program."

Enver huffed out a laugh as he slid his hand down Marcus's back, the muscles trembling under his touch. "Later. Right now, you're going to not think about work and let me take care of you and tell you how much you've pleased me."

Pleasing a Dom had once given him a bright, needy edge. Now, with Enver, it was a deep, gut-aching need that involved his heart as much as his loins. "I could stay this way forever."

"So could I."

Chapter Eighteen

Marcus wrapped his hands around a mug, absorbing some of the heat as he scanned the coffeehouse. The first few hours after group session was always tough, leaving him feeling as though he'd been scraped raw, his past quickly seeping through the scars of the attack. Ground Hogs in Sacramento had always been a good place to decompress afterward. He'd found the trendy café's sister store in San Francisco while attending the Fordham Street Fair. The once-a-year kink-centric festival was always a good way to let loose and relax with people of similar interests.

"Mind if I join you?"

The familiar voice pulled him out of his thoughts. "Hey, cupcake. Always room at the booth, my gorgeous best friend."

In the twenty minutes since group, Zoie had pulled her long cascade of wavy chestnut hair into a high ponytail. Though her eyes were dry, the delicate skin around them was still red from where she'd been crying.

He gave her an understanding smile. "I see you've brought snacks."

She adjusted the plate of bite-sized pastries she'd arrived with as she sipped her coffee. "We both had a tough session tonight, so I thought we deserved chocolate."

The harsh sound of her voice grabbed Marcus's heart, twisting it hard. No one else in his life understood the kind of pain he lived with daily. "I keep waiting for it to get easier."

"It will. Someday."

He hoped she was right. Every day was a struggle, but at least it wasn't as prevalent as it had once been. He wanted to point out that Zoie was still attending group too despite the fact she considered herself past the tangle of emotions related to her own trauma. Though their situations were remarkably different.

"I know you don't believe me," she began. "But it really will. You'll be able to bury your anger over the ordeal and make peace with it."

A level Zoie herself hadn't achieved yet. Not if tonight's session of waterworks was any indication. "Thanks for meeting me. I know you're busy."

"Are you doing all right?"

Marcus shrugged. He hadn't felt all right since Zoie had called to report about Davis's parole months ago. "Do you know where he is now?"

"You know I shouldn't be talking to you about this."

"Then you wouldn't have come."

Zoie smirked. "Yeah, I know. Just thought you needed a friend. And that you would feel better if you knew everything is normal. No trace of him. It's like he's disappeared off the face of the Earth."

"He was a good student in high school. Just never had the motivation to apply himself. All it would take is the right contacts. You've said it yourself, contraband flows pretty readily despite all the controls you guys have in place."

"As much as the system tries to stop it from happening…you're right. He contacted you so soon after his release, he had to have set about obtaining information while he was still inside. I'll see if I can't find out more."

Words couldn't express how grateful Marcus was for Zoie's continued involvement. She'd worked his case as a rookie cop. One of her first. It had been an open and shut case, with video evidence of the attack thanks to the high school's foresight to install security cameras throughout the classrooms. Though she'd quietly moved up the ranks to detective, she'd maintained contact with Marcus so much that he now considered her his best friend.

"Been staying busy?"

"Trying to. Have a new client I'm installing a system for."

"You and your geek shit."

Despite himself, Marcus smiled. "Been hearing that a lot lately."

"Oh boy." She set her mug down and touched the back of his hand. "You've met someone."

"How in the hell do you do that?" Zoie's uncanny knack for uncovering something always amazed Marcus. It was a quirk that made her such a damn good police officer. "But yeah, I have. Nothing serious."

Zoie's eyes sparkled as she leaned forward on her elbows. As her sleeves slipped, Marcus caught sight of the faint lines along both of her forearms. She quickly adjusted the sleeves of her sweater, hiding the scars, as was her habit. "You don't do casual, Marcus. If some guy has your interest, I know he's something special."

Because this was Zoie, Marcus leaned forward. "Tall, dark and fucking gorgeous doesn't even begin to describe him." He spread his hands about a foot apart. "Monster cock. Nothing like I've ever seen."

She narrowed her eyes as she sipped her tea. "Ass."

He was glad to see amusement sparkling in her eyes, a nice change from the cloudy cast they'd been earlier during group when she'd been exposing her heart. He knew talking about the scars she'd self-inflicted as a young teen were still difficult to discuss, but also the best therapy because each one had a story that needed to be told.

"Oh yeah. He has a spectacular ass too. Sincerely, though. He's a nice guy. Older. Smoker, which I'm finding exciting for some reason. Hates technology. Shuns a lot of modern-day shit."

Her eyebrows rose. "That's a change."

"I know, right?" Certainly not the typical Dom he usually went for, but Zoie didn't know about that part of his life. He usually preferred someone who could meet him toe for toe in terms of computers and technology, but Enver was a refreshing change, both as a lover and a companion.

Marcus suddenly sat back, cursing softly. "Fuck me."

Zoie looked around, her sharp gaze assessing and searching for an immediate threat. "What's wrong?"

He waved off her alarm. "Sorry. Just had a revelation about Enver."

She visibly relaxed, but Marcus knew he'd set her on edge now. "Your beau, I take it?"

"Yeah," Marcus said slowly. "I realized that he's the first one I've had this kind of connection with in years."

Her face brightened with a wide smile. "Oh, Marcus,

that's wonderful! I'm so excited for you. Which means I need to meet him. Immediately. How does next Thursday sound?" She extracted her ringing phone. "Crap. It's the precinct."

"Need to go?"

She held up a finger as she answered and then listened. As she hung up, she stood. "Incident a few blocks from here. I'm serious about meeting this guy."

"You want to see if he checks out."

She glared at him in mock horror. "I resemble that remark."

He stood, pulling out a card he'd forgotten about until he saw her fidgeting with her sleeves again. "This is the guy I was telling you about, Constantine Volkov."

She eyed the bright artwork filling most of the card. "Does he look like the demon-fighting Constantine we both know and love?"

"I wish. But he's the artist I told you about when you asked if I knew anyone who did good work. I don't know him personally, but I've seen his art first hand." Marcus gestured to her forearms and the reminder of the cuts she'd self-inflicted as a teen. "Didn't think I'd forgotten about our conversation about doing something about those, did you?"

Her eyes clouded again for a second before clearing. She shoved the card into a slender pocket affixed to the back of her phone. He'd have to remind her about it again in six months, as was his habit.

A few years back she'd casually mentioned covering her scars as a way to move on. He would remind her of it until she finally bucked up the strength to talk to a tattoo artist about what she had in mind.

Zoie set her hand over his and squeezed. "Call me later?"

He nodded and she disappeared in a blur. Though he hated seeing how many hours she worked, he knew it kept her mind occupied. Allowed her to control a compulsion she would live with for the rest of her life.

He stepped out of the café and into the evening air, inhaling deeply as he thought back to his revelation about Enver. The last man he would have ever expected to take to the virtual reality machine as well as he had. Beta testing was progressing seamlessly, with the handful of testers blown away by their experience. There were adjustments to be made…there always were, but BLINC was close to completion. And Marcus would be free to move on.

Only he didn't want to.

His steps faltered as he drew closer to the dimly lit parking lot where he'd left his car before group. He blinked a few times, trying to process the sight of someone taking a sledgehammer to the driver's side door. Glass sprinkled the concrete where the headlights had already been shattered. A heavy bang reverberated through the night air as something heavy connected loudly with the sheet metal hood.

"Hey!" Anger propelled him forward. "Stop! That's my car." His words were drowned out by the vandal striking his car again. Too late he heard the scuff of a boot against gravel behind him. He knew better than to let his guard down, but the sight of someone working his car over had fuzzed his brain stupid.

He turned to face his attacker. Recognition clicked seconds before the first hit came. Pain exploded on the undamaged side of his face, taking him down in the blink of an eye. White and black spots danced before his eyes as he blinked, trying to process what was happening.

"Get up or I'll shove my fist up your asshole, you dickless faggot." Davis Connelly's face came into view, the gently sloping lines of youth gone thanks to ten years of jail. "Or maybe you'd like that, filthy pervert."

Marcus rolled to his side, struggling to make his body and his muscles work. He made it to one knee, but paused, his vision canting wildly. Davis took advantage of the position and Marcus heard the sweep of his leg an instant before it connected with his ribs. He waited for the explosion of pain, but he'd passed the point where he could even register the wrenching agony.

That was bad. Real bad. He'd been to this place before. Where the body was injured beyond the point it could process damage. Where everything shut down as self-preservation mode kicked in. He felt the crack as bones reacted to the kick, his lungs screaming as all the air was pushed out with brutal force.

"Do you have any idea how much I've thought about finishing what I started that day in the classroom?" Davis touched the ridges on Marcus's face, caressing them almost lovingly. As though he was admiring his handiwork. "Days upon endless fucking day in a ten-by-ten cell. Every day started and ended with the memory of how I didn't successfully rid this world of you."

Marcus collapsed, his breathing labored as he struggled to pull in enough oxygen. His brain was screaming for him to stand, to defend himself, but his body betrayed him, refusing to work. Most of all, he wanted sleep. To check out and finally, finally be free of the torment that he lived with every day. The hate and brutality would be gone. If he just lay there and let Davis finish the job he'd started, he would finally have that peace.

"Jeff, bring me the sledgehammer. I want to show this pansy ass how a real man fucks."

No. No. No.

Just as he gathered his strength and started to rise again, Davis grabbed the back of his shirt and shoved him down, pinning him with his foot. Marcus tried to roll to dislodge Davis, but his attacker's foothold was too strong. Cool air brushed against his skin, and Marcus realized belatedly that Davis had stripped his pants to his knees, fully intent on following through with his threat.

Adrenaline coursed through Marcus's veins as he struggled, fighting even though all he wanted to do was give up and end the madness. Somewhere through the haze, sirens pierced the air.

"Fuck, man. The cops. I thought you took care of them." The ground under Marcus's cheek vibrated as Davis's companion dropped the sledgehammer. "I'm gettin' outta here." Footsteps faded into the dark as he ran away.

Davis growled, pinning him in place with his knee now as he leaned close, put his mouth against Marcus's ear. "Mark my words, I'm going finish what I started ten years ago. Even if I have to take myself out with you to get the job done right, I will rid this world of your filthy, disgusting queer ass." The pressure against Marcus's neck vanished, and the rush of cold wind was replaced by a warm wetness on his exposed skin.

Frozen with fear, Marcus waited for Davis to deliver his end.

But minutes later as the sirens drew closer, he realized he was now alone.

He tried to get up, but collapsed against the ground, exhausted and spent as the last of his energy bled away. The pain that had been absent during the attack rushed forth, slamming into him with the force of a violent hurricane. He willed the darkness to come so he couldn't feel anything at all. But, stubbornly, he stayed fully cognizant and awake, feeling every bruise and scrape as they bloomed.

Blue splashed everything around him, a macabre dance of light against the concrete jungle that jutted up toward the sky. His body went immediately tense as a hand touched his shoulder.

"Marcus?"

His breath gusted from his lungs when he recognized the friendly voice. "Zoie." Thank god it was her and not some faceless uniform that would see him like this.

"Don't talk. I've got medical on the way."

"No." A slash of pain cut off what he was about to say. He groaned as he rolled up to his knees, forearm wrapped around his midsection as if that would somehow alleviate the ache. He fought with the waistband of his pants as he took stock now that the immediate shock had started to wear off. "Don't call the EMTs."

"Marcus—"

"No, Zoie," he barked out, his voice catching on a cough. "I've had enough of hospitals. You know that. I'll be all right." He accepted her assistance standing, held on with a tight grip as the world tilted wildly a few times. He fumbled with his pants, grateful when Zoie tugged up the fabric and buttoned them in place.

"What the hell happened?" She frowned when Marcus remained tight-lipped. "Off the record, promise."

"Get me out of here and we'll talk."

She studied his face, clearly torn between the oath she'd sworn when she'd earned her badge and loyalty to her best friend.

He knew her well enough to know she wasn't going to budge until he gave her something. "It was Davis."

That information seemed to cut loose her choice. She guided Marcus's arm over her shoulder, patiently supporting him. She looked to the uniforms that had just arrived. "Waller, I'm going to take him to the hospital myself. Ambulance is tied up with a crash over on Montez. They've got their hands full."

"What about the scene?"

"Just do the best you can until I get back. Call in CSI to start processing." She steered Marcus toward her cruiser, arm braced across his upper back, her hand buried in his armpit to help her balance the weight. "I hope to hell this is worth it to you, Marcus."

He leaned heavily against her car as she opened the door. "Thank you, Zoie." When she fired a caustic glance his way, he wondered if he'd made a mistake refusing the ambulance. She was risking a career that she loved and was good at to help him leave the scene of a hate crime without an official report. He already owed her so much he wasn't sure how he could repay her after this.

"Thought you were responding to another call?" He pressed his hand against his side as pain lanced up his ribcage.

"I was halfway there when dispatch radioed about this." She nodded to his damaged car. "Someone walk-

ing by called in a fight between a couple of men. Had
no idea it was you at first, but something—I don't know.
Just knew I needed to be here. Had someone else take
the other call, and here I am."

He sat without waiting for her help. "Christ al-
mighty." He was still swearing as she slid behind the
wheel, fired up the engine and gunned it away from the
curb. Marcus wrapped his arm around his midsection.
"Can't get a good breath in. Jesus, he packed a punch."

She gave him the side-eye. "I'm taking you to the
hospital."

"Zoie," he warned. "You're taking me to my house.
I just need to take a shower. Sleep it off. I'll be fine in
the morning."

"And you'll sleep away the stench of his urine on
you too?"

He remained tight-lipped, eyes forward as she wove
around a slow-moving car. He'd hoped he'd imagined
that. Or that his bladder had let loose during the attack.

"Fuck you, Marcus Holly," she said suddenly. "Fuck
you and the high horse you ride on because you think
you're too good for anyone's help." Passing headlights
highlighted her face as she drove, the determined set of
her jaw signaling she wasn't a pushover. "You aren't in
a position to tell me no, so you're at least going to get
someone to look to verify nothing is broken. Tell them
whatever you want about how this happened, I don't
care." When she pulled up to a red light, she turned to
face him. "If nothing else, as your friend, it will make
me feel better."

"I can tell them you kicked my ass during a sparring
match." He chuckled at the searing glare of impatience
she aimed at him. He'd forgotten she'd mastered that

expression. "Fine. Let them look me over. But they're not admitting me. I've spent too much damn time in hospitals as it is. I can't do it again."

"I can't keep this off police record, Marcus." Worry lines formed on her forehead. "Maybe if I'd been the only one there, the first one to arrive, but Waller and his partner...it's their scene."

"I know I'm putting you in a difficult situation, Zoie." He appreciated her understanding his fear. Davis had clearly shown an aptitude for skirting the law since his release. If the cops showed up at his door to arrest him, he'd just con his way out of the accusation with some bullshit excuse. Marcus had another idea in order to bring an end to this mess.

Fifteen minutes later, Zoie parked the car. She came around the side, offering him a hand he knew better than to dismiss after her outburst. As he stood, he saw her expression had softened. Gone was the hard-nosed cop, replaced with the face of his best friend and confidant. "I'm sorry I wasn't there to protect you, Marcus. Sorry I can't do anything to make this all go away."

Despite the pain lacing through him, he pulled her close and kissed the top of her head. "You've protected me in ways you can't even begin to imagine, Zoie." He continued to hold her as he realized he was going to have to cancel the contract with Noble House. The safety of those around him was now in jeopardy and ensuring it was more important than the money contract fulfillment would bring. More important than any connection he'd discovered with Enver.

Bullshit.

The echo of the word followed him into the hospital.

Chapter Nineteen

Enver couldn't stop thinking about how fucking gorgeous Marcus was every time he was on his knees, waiting patiently for further instructions. Deliciously submissive and ready for a well-earned orgasm. Enver intended to give him quite a few of those tonight during their session, in and out of BLINC.

His enthusiasm cracked as he opened the door, shattering completely as he looked over the empty room. The table Marcus kept his stuff set up on had been wiped clean. Not even a speck of dust, though Marcus was too meticulous and protective of his equipment to allow dust to collect.

Enver stormed through Kochran's door without knocking, stalking directly over to the desk where Kochran and Adelita Husk, the club's accountant, were working. Both were dressed in corporate attire better suited for a nine-to-five job in a high-rise full of cubicles instead of hunkered down in an office at a bondage and kink club.

"Where is he?" For a brief second, Enver hated the possessive nature of the demand. He had no claim over Marcus.

Adelita blinked, clearly not comfortable with the sudden tension charging the atmosphere. He winced as he remembered she was one of the few employees at Noble House who didn't partake in the kinky lifestyle. Plus, she was still mourning the death of her girlfriend less than a year ago. Her lifelong partner—and Kochran's sister—Tory had finally succumbed to the heart condition that had plagued her since childhood. She was fortunate to have lived as long as she had, and gotten to experience a love few people in the world were capable of.

"Afternoon to you too," Kochran responded without looking up, clearly not impressed with the intrusion.

Adelita stood, her posture rigid as she started gathering paperwork. "I can take care of this in my office."

Kochran handed her a stack of folders. "I'll come by and sign the rest of these when I'm done here."

Enver waited until the door closed behind Adelita then leaned forward, balancing his weight on his hands. "Where the fuck is Marcus?"

Kochran stared at him over the rim of his reading glasses. "I don't keep tabs on everyone, despite the rumors."

Enver's gaze flicked to the elaborate workstation set up on the desk behind Kochran. A grid of squares showed on the monitors that contradicted Kochran's statement. The goddamn King of Noble House knew everything going on in his club.

"His stuff is gone from the room. Where did he go?" Enver repeated with more force.

Kochran's brow furrowed as he removed his glasses. "I have no idea." He picked up the receiver on the desk phone, tapped a button and waited. "You have a second?" He hung up without responding to the person he'd called.

Kochran stood, vanishing from the office. He reappeared a minute later with several bottles of water and Saint in tow.

"What's up?" Saint settled on the closest chair, slinging one arm over the back and crossing his legs.

Enver remained tight-lipped as Kochran spoke. "Have you seen or spoken to Marcus today?"

Saint looked concerned. "Haven't seen him in a few days. Figured he was just busy with the program or something." His gaze flicked to Enver for the last part. "Why? Something wrong with the system? We're set to go live in a week from what Ezra and Maddy are telling me. Customers are going to love BLINC if the session Boyce and I had with Grae in there is any indication."

Enver knew that pleased look of satisfaction that hazed Saint's light green eyes. He still remembered pushing Marcus, seeing his partner's glassy gaze desperately trying to focus on him. He forced back the lump forming in his throat. No time to get all mushy now.

"His stuff is gone. Whole setup cleared out of the room."

"Maybe Ezra had him relocate. Moving closer to launch, he would need a more central location than where he's been set up. Give me a second." Saint pulled out his cell phone as he stepped out.

Kochran licked his lips. "When was the last time you saw him?"

"Last week. I was helping him with a scene." If Kochran found the truth in that lie, he didn't indicate, so Enver pushed on. "He said he had a meeting last night in Sacramento and would be back today." Enver swallowed against the tightness drawing his throat closed. He shouldn't have been that demanding, but damn if he could help it. He needed answers and he needed them fast.

I've got some shit going on that I'm trying to deal with.

The words echoed in his head, reminding him that he should have pressed Marcus on the issue. Forced him to give him more than a few vague details. He knew perhaps better than anyone that stuff like that—whatever *it* was—would only come forth when Marcus was comfortable enough to share. Enver had a sick feeling that those details had something to do with Marcus's sudden disappearance.

"Ezra hasn't seen him either," Saint offered as he stepped back into the office. He crossed the room with a few quick strides and leaned over Kochran's computer. The screens went blank as he worked.

Unable to remain stationary, Enver shoved his hands wrist deep into his pockets and tried not to imagine all the horrible possibilities. He wasn't someone prone to such nervousness, but something had been off with Marcus since that first night he'd introduced Enver to the VR world. The first night they'd kissed. It all seemed to have melted away by the time they'd taken things out of virtual reality and into the real world. Even as the pieces had been falling into place, there had been an undercurrent Enver couldn't put his finger on. He'd thought it had been his own worries about his addiction, but this was something else entirely.

"Hey, Thumper, you want to stop before you shake the club apart?"

"What?" Enver glanced down and realized he'd picked back up his nervous habit of tapping his foot rapidly. "Sorry."

"Bingo," Saint said triumphantly. "Got him. He moved his stuff out of the room at around three this morning. Club was just shutting down for the night. You here then?" he asked as he glanced toward the owner.

Kochran shook his head. "Had a gig at Screwdriver with the band. Tuesday nights are typically a slow night at the club, so it's entirely possible he could have left without being seen as the staff closed up."

Entirely possible given the lack of observation from the front door staff. Damn. Enver had neglected to inform Kochran of Rosen's screw-up that night. As much as he didn't want to admit it, he needed to accept the one thing he couldn't ignore: whatever had happened to Marcus, Enver had played a small part. If he'd mentioned Rosen's lapse in attention to Kochran after the incident, he would have corrected the issue. Then the staff watching the front door may have gotten suspicious of Marcus removing all of his equipment without notice.

Saint pointed to the screens, gesturing to the small row of numbers across the top of each freeze-frame. "Outside cameras have him and a woman loading up a white truck with the equipment. They pulled out of the lot about three-fifty."

"Truck?" Enver thought that was strange. "Sure he wasn't in a car?"

"Nope. Take a look." Saint queued up the video.

The image was grainy, but Enver recognized Marcus's form as he loaded his equipment cases into the bed of the sleek truck. "He has a piece-of-shit beater Firebird that he always hauls stuff around in." He leaned closer, trying to see if he could make out Marcus's face or recognize the woman helping him. "Something's going on."

"Any idea what?"

"Doesn't talk much about himself." Enver thought back to the first time Marcus had introduced him to the virtual reality world. "There was a family issue he mentioned a few weeks after he started. Almost left then." But Enver had convinced him to stay. Shit. Had that been a mistake?

"So maybe that's the case again. Maybe it's his sister."

The woman helping him could have very well been related to him. The grainy night-vision of the security cameras made it impossible to tell.

Kochran cleared his throat. "Regardless of what happened, we need to face the reality that we very well could be out of luck with the club's new expansion." He gestured to the screen. "We'll need to confirm, but to me it looks like he's taken everything he's been working on. If that's the case, Noble House is up the creek without a paddle in terms of virtual reality."

"I don't think so." Saint sat back, folding his arms across his chest. "I've been working with him on and off since we hired him. Ezra and Maddy too. Neither of them mentioned anything suspicious. Yeah, his behavior is a little odd at times, but that's typical for a code grinder. I don't think he's trying to screw us over, and Enver's right about something else going on."

"I'll keep in touch." Enver left without further explanation. He had no idea what to do or even where to look, but he had to do something instead of staring at a stupid computer monitor. Problem was, for the first time since he'd admitted his sex addition, he felt helpless.

* * *

It had been four days since the attack, and Marcus swore he could still catch the stench of urine on his skin. Still feel the press of Davis's hands pinning him to the ground, holding him immobile, threatening bodily harm. He was convinced no matter how hot the water, how much soap he used, he wouldn't ever be able to rid himself of the putrid aroma. He hadn't slept a full night since. Every time he closed his eyes, his vivid imagination carried him to a place where Davis had followed through with his threat.

Once the hospital had released him, instead of sleeping, he'd hopped himself up on energy drinks, shoved every bit of his equipment at the club into the truck borrowed from Zoie, and spent hours driving as far as he could away from California. Zoie had offered him cash, but he'd declined. He wanted a paper trail—the wider the better. He'd make one as extensive as the Grand Canyon if he had to if that's what it took to keep those he loved safe.

Still, he didn't have unlimited funds and had to be smart or this impromptu road trip would be over before it began. Road trip, hell. He was fleeing. When the money started to dwindle, he'd have to resort to selling the equipment they'd piled into the back. Better in the long run, really. It would be easier to run without all the baggage.

The other thing he had accepted from Zoie was a disposable phone. It sat charging on the dashboard, the red light beckoning for him to send a message or make the phone call he desperately wanted to make.

She'd surprised him when she'd handed it to him, convincing him that he needed a way to contact her if he thought he was in danger again. Though she hadn't said as much, Marcus was convinced she had the untraceable phone because she might someday do exactly what he'd done.

The temptation to make contact with Enver was a powerful force he had fought against since he'd pulled out of the Noble House parking lot. But he couldn't risk putting Enver in danger. Couldn't live with himself if something happened to him. Maybe leaving this way wasn't the smartest idea, but it was the only option Marcus could think of where everyone he cared about remained safe.

Spotting a truck stop in the middle of nowhere, he pulled into the lot. Aches and pains erupted through his body as he exited the vehicle.

When he stepped out of the bathroom, he came face to face with Davis. A monstrous sneer nearly split the man's face in two.

Marcus blinked, and the man before him gave him a curious glance. "You all right, son?"

Not Davis. Not even close.

Panic nearly caused his knees to collapse from under him. He burst through the glass doors, swallowing the bile burning the back of his throat. Long hours on the road had notched his paranoia to an all-time high. As he fast-walked to the truck, cold sweat erupted over his body.

Fuck. No. Fuck.

He would not break down in the middle of Nowheresville in the state of Clusterfuck.

He. Would. Not.

In the safety of the truck, he ignored the ringing phone as he clutched at the wheel, setting his hands against his forehead. Inhaled deeply and counted to ten. Exhaled. Stared at the rumbling semitrucks jockeying for position at the pumps in the hopes that it would soothe him.

The persistent ringing of the phone finally made him snatch it up. Zoie's name was displayed on the screen, and Marcus let out a slow breath as his heart rate settled. "Hey, cupcake."

"You all right? Took a bit for you to answer."

"Just had to pull over to take your call. Too tired to try to focus on driving and talk to you at the same time." The lie slid easily off his tongue. Though, in reality, it wasn't total fabrication. He exited the truck, leaning back against the bed as he tilted his head back to look at the sky. "You doing okay?"

"More importantly, are you? Sounds like you need some sleep."

"Planning on stopping tonight for a few hours," he lied again.

"Where are you—wait, never mind. Better I don't know."

Which was good since he didn't know himself.

She sighed heavily. "We're closing the case on the attack. Told the sarge we chalked it up to some kids out trying to cause havoc by vandalizing an abandoned car because they were bored. He laughed it off as boys will be boys."

Which meant she'd buried the truth. "Thank you."

"I still don't agree that you've painted a big target on your back." She paused. Marcus imagined her sitting at her desk, hunched over as she rubbed at the headache she'd probably been fighting since she'd found him in the parking lot. "But I understand. Just promise

me you'll stay safe and contact me if you suspect anything. Anything at all even if it turns out to be a sloth
winning a marathon."

"I promise, cupcake, as long as you do the same."
Which was absurd. Zoie didn't have anyone chasing
after her.

"I haven't seen him. No one has, even his parole officer. He seems to think Davis crossed the border and
we'll never hear from him again." She sighed heavily.
"Know I'm not supposed to, but I hope that's the case."

"No," Marcus spat out. "He's going to crawl out of
the woodwork again at some point. Could be tomorrow.
Could be five years from now. Davis is patient. And
calculating. He'll wait however long he needs to especially because he fucked up the other night. Didn't get
to finish the job." That single-minded focus also meant
Davis wasn't going to stop until he had Marcus's blood
on his hands. Which meant it was Marcus's duty to keep
everyone else out of Davis's crosshairs by getting as far
away from California as he could, however wrong that
line of thinking was.

"I know," she said quietly. "You didn't ask, but...
I've got eyes on your man."

"Zoie." He colored his voice with a touch of anger,
though he wasn't upset to hear her confession. Not truly.
That connection to Enver, however minute, was all he
had left.

"I knew you'd eventually ask me anyway, so I
thought I'd head you off. Normal stuff. House. Store.
The social club."

He tensed at the mention of Noble House, remembering he hadn't explained anything to her even as she'd
helped him flee. "Uh, about that."

"Did you forget I helped you move your equipment out of there? Can't walk into a place like that and not know. I already knew about your tastes when it came to sex, Marcus. Beyond you being gay. Can't know you as well as I do and not figure it out. Anyway, I lost track of him yesterday when he left in the middle of the night, but I located him at a cabin on top of a mountain on the outskirts of Eldorado National Forest. Been there ever since. Don't have to know him to know he's hurting without you. Like he's trying to hide from something too. He's got some demons of his own."

The ache he'd tried so hard to keep at bay flared anew. The update only poked harder at the need to hear Enver's voice again. It took a few minutes before he had the strength to answer without his voice cracking. "Thank you for keeping him safe, cupcake."

"I'll do what I can. You just…take care of you. I have to go." She ended the call abruptly.

Marcus stared at the wispy clouds, tapping the phone against his thigh. It beeped softly, signaling a text message had arrived. Out of habit, he tensed. When he glanced at the screen, the tension filtered off as he read Zoie's demand to contact Enver. Girl would just not give up. He wanted to reach out to the man who meant so much to him. God, how he wanted to. But hearing Enver's soothing whiskey-smoke voice would gut him.

He stared at the phone screen, his fingers hovering over the keys as he debated sending him a text. What would he say? Warn him about Davis? Beg for forgiveness? Profess his love?

There was no right answer. No solution where he didn't look like an ass.

The sky started to take on the powerful, rich reds of

sunset, casting crimson and violet hues on the mountains off in the distance. He hadn't realized he'd gotten so lost in his thoughts that so much time had passed. For the first time since the attack, he'd been able to check out. Not give any fucks. The reality was that he couldn't afford such a luxury. He also couldn't afford to contact Enver no matter how much he couldn't stop thinking about all the ways he wanted Enver to touch him, fuck him. All the ways he wanted to serve Enver, make him come.

Watch him. Lick him.

Love him.

"Fuck you for making me love you, bastard." With another vicious curse, he slid back behind the wheel, tossing the phone into the passenger seat. The engine roared to life and he pulled back onto the two-lane highway to nowhere.

Chapter Twenty

Enver stood on the deck attached to his workshop, watching angry storm clouds close in as the sun set. A splash of lightning ricocheted off the dark clouds, glinting off the windshield of the car sitting farther down the mountain. The same vehicle had been tailing him since the day after Marcus's disappearance.

He blew out a plume of smoke into the quickly darkening sky. Thanks to the Noble House security footage and a little old-fashioned boots-to-the-ground surveillance work of his own, he knew his stalker was the same woman who had helped Marcus remove his gear from the club. He'd struggled with confronting her to demand to know what had happened, but he'd kept his distance so far. Strangely, he was comforted by her presence because she was the only remaining connection he had to Marcus. As long as she was there, Enver knew deep down inside Marcus was okay.

He scented the reek of cop even across the distance. Thanks to an encounter with a less-than-law-abiding police officer in his late teens, he still had a healthy distrust of police who took advantage of their authority. Though he doubted this woman was one of those that kind of power corrupted, he still had his guard up.

The timer he'd set beeped and he pushed away from the railing, extinguished the cigarette and stepped back inside just as the first drops of rain started to fall. He pulled the casserole dish out of the oven, filled a large Thermos, grabbed his raincoat and set off down the road.

The drops had turned into a deluge just as he arrived at the car and crouched down next to the driver's side door. She'd left the window open before she'd fallen asleep, her camera still perched on the sill. Her head was tilted back against the headrest, her face relaxed in sleep.

Dark circles smudged the fine skin under her eyes, her hair dull and limp, as though she hadn't taken a shower for a few days. Since she'd fallen asleep during her watch, Enver imagined she was pushing herself to the limit trying to keep tabs on him and juggle the rest of her responsibilities.

He tapped the door lightly, noting she didn't stir at the noise. "In deep, aren't you, sweetie? Push yourself to the limit just like he does." He ran a hand over his unshaven face, feeling the scrape of a week's growth against his palm. Leaving her here wasn't an option. His need to care for people was too ingrained, and she may not have thought so, but someone needed to look out for her too.

He knocked his knuckles against door a bit harder, the sound thudding deeply off the nearby trees. Her eyes opened slowly, her gaze landing on him but not truly seeing him as she was caught somewhere between sleep and wake.

He set the Thermos of coffee on the sill. "No, you're not dreaming. Yes, I'm your guardian angel. Just like you've been mine for the past week. Except I have fresh hot cocoa."

Her eyes widened suddenly. "What the hell?"

"Relax." He wiggled the container toward her. "Just thought you could use something to drink. From the looks of it, you could use a shower and some sleep too. Real sleep."

"Yeah." She visibly relaxed as she set the now unnecessary camera to the side, adjusting in the seat so she was upright again. She didn't seem bothered by the rain streaming in rivulets off the protective shield at the top of the window.

"Where is he?" He held her gaze without offering further clarification.

"It's better if you don't know."

"Where. Is. He." He put as much force behind the words as he could, as though he was instructing a new subbie for the first time.

She shook her head. "He doesn't want you to come after him. It's too—"

"What?"

"Dangerous," she finished. "Don't you think I would be with him if he'd let me? I tried to reason with him, but he's stubborn and hardheaded. Wouldn't listen. But you probably already know that."

"You helped him fill up the truck with his equipment," Enver pointed out with a wry smile.

"It's my truck. He couldn't go anywhere in that piece of shit he has, but you already know that too. When I couldn't reason with him, I gave him what I could to help. Least I could do to keep him safe."

"Where is he?" he repeated calmly. He growled when she remained stubbornly silent. Pushing her was like trying to topple a cinderblock wall with his bare hands. "Fine. Is he safe?"

She licked her lips, studying him for a minute before answering. "For now, yes."

"The 'for now' part is what bothers me." There was more he wanted to ask, but the tight fist that had taken up residence in his chest since Marcus disappeared eased. For now, it was enough to know Marcus was okay.

He wiggled the Thermos at her until she accepted it. "You get tired of playing clandestine cop and want to dry out, there's an extra cot in my workshop you're welcome to use. Lasagna on the stove. Forecasters are saying this storm is going to hang around for a few days. May produce a few flash floods. Rather not have to worry about you down here by yourself, but if you're going to stay, expect regular checkups from me. And more hot chocolate." He stood and spun on his heel, shoving his hands into his pockets as he started to trek back up the gravel roadway.

His intent had been to let her know he was aware of her presence, but he'd felt an instant kinship toward her, threads of their friendships with Marcus intertwining even though they'd just met. His connection with Marcus had been just as instant. Given the fact she'd helped him abscond, she was obviously an important fixture in Marcus's life.

Halfway up, he heard the engine fire to life, tires cracking rocks as she followed him. She pulled in next to his car just as he mounted the staircase leading to the workshop. He waited under a small overhang that protected him from the driving rain, holding the door open.

He lifted his brow when she hesitated. "If you prefer to be soaked, by all means, stand there."

"I just…um."

"You're uncomfortable, I get it. You're not my type, if you're concerned I have ulterior motives."

"Oh, right, 'cause I have tits instead of the dangly bits?" she scoffed.

He rolled his eyes. "You're vanilla."

"How do you… Never mind. I really don't want to know." She heaved out a breath, staring at him for a few more seconds before ducking under his arm.

"Christ," he muttered as he followed. He hung his coat to dry and toed off his wet shoes. "Shower is through the door over there if you want to wash up first."

"I'm good."

He eyed her, noting the puddles forming on the concrete around her. Stubborn. "Suit yourself." Lighting up the stove hadn't been on his list of things to do tonight since he could take the cold, but considering the fact his unexpected company was dripping all over his workshop, he changed plans. Within a few minutes, he had coaxed the flames and turned on the fan so the heat would vent into the room.

"This cocoa tastes like dirt." Despite her statement, she drank again and even refilled the lid she was using for a cup.

"It's hot, which is more than you had down there." He left her, moving to the tiny kitchenette area he rarely used to dole out two helpings of lasagna. She eyed him when he returned and offered her a plate. "When's the last time you ate?" When she continued to refuse, he crouched next to the chair she'd climbed into and set the plate on her knee. "You can't help him if you keep refusing to take care of yourself. And you can't live on hot chocolate."

"Why hot chocolate anyway? Usual stakeout fare is strong coffee."

He ate a forkful of lasagna before replying, "You don't seem like the coffee type. But every woman I know is a chocolate freak."

"That's some stereotyping you have going there."

"Well, am I wrong?" he asked around a mouthful of lasagna.

The corner of her mouth lifted for a split second before smoothing as she accepted the fork, and dug in to the food. They ate in silence, watching the flames lick the top of the cast-iron stove a few feet away. When they had both finished, he cleared the plates, dropping them into the minuscule sink to clean later.

"Enver Furst," he offered as he crouched by the chair again, feeling it was important they were on eye level given her caution. Though she'd tailed him, gotten used to his patterns, she didn't truly know him and was clearly wary of his motives. "Though you probably already knew that, didn't you?"

She confirmed his suspicions with a nod. "Detective Zoie Landry."

Indicating her rank clearly meant she didn't intend to keep this friendly despite his hospitality. Fine by him. He didn't intend to revoke his invitation given her shuttered expression, but he knew asking her the questions gnawing at his gut wouldn't find the answers he wanted. At least not tonight.

He retrieved a thick blanket and a soft flat sheet from a shelf in the bathroom. "It's not much, but you can use the cot since it's close to the fire. I'll take the chair over in the corner."

"Little early for bed."

"When was the last time you slept?" Her silence was answer enough. "Thought so."

She remained silent as he killed the overhead light, the flames of the fire casting a golden glow that gave him enough light to direct him to the far corner. The wood popped and hissed, the only sound in the room as he settled in the recliner he usually slept in since the workshop didn't have a formal bedroom. The springs creaked as they took his weight, the leather groaning as he engaged the latch to lower the back to a reclining position.

He listened to her move around and situate herself, then her breathing. When it grew shallow and even to indicate she'd fallen asleep, he allowed himself to follow.

He woke a few hours later, the glow of the fire dulled as it had gone through all the wood he'd fed it earlier. He rose, quietly padding over to the cast-iron stove to drop a few more logs into the pile of glowing ashes. In a few minutes, he had stoked the flames high enough that he could grab another few hours of sleep.

As he turned, he found Zoie's gaze on him. "Didn't mean to wake you."

"I wasn't asleep." She sat up, curling her legs underneath her. "Haven't slept well for a week or so."

"You aren't the only one." Sleep had come in fits and starts since he'd discovered that Marcus had disappeared. Some of the questions he'd had wouldn't wait until morning after all. "You said he's safe. Is he all right?"

"He's—I wish there was more that I could tell you,

Enver, but it's not because I want to keep the information from you. I just don't know. He's not being very up front with me, so I can only go off what little information I have." Weariness etched her pretty face, aging her many more years than the lines should have. "He *is* safe, that much I do know. I'm doing what I can to keep him that way."

"By keeping tabs on me?" Enver bit back the venom leeching through his tone. The agony he felt was going to squeeze the life out of him. "I'm the last one you need to worry about."

"Don't you see?" Her voice cracked on the last word.

He drew in a breath as he met her gaze, recognizing the sorrow and anger and utter devotion in her eyes.

"He loves you. I've known him a long time and I've never seen him act or talk about someone the way he does about you. He's out there somewhere, doing what he feels he needs to do to protect you because some asshole—"

She abruptly stopped herself, chewing on her lip as her gaze darted away. Though Enver's blood started to boil at the thought of someone hurting Marcus, he held his tongue. She'd obviously slipped, not intending to disclose what she knew about the reason Marcus had left.

"Does this have anything to do with his scars?" Her tight-lipped response spoke volumes. He cursed his ineptness with computers, his lack of skills when it came to seeking out information during this age of technology everyone else had latched on to. He should have paid more attention when Maddy had tried to show him the finer points of Google-fu. That was a maze of information he wasn't interested in exploring. Gentle fingers against his jaw brought his focus back to Zoie.

"You are the one who has the power to break him emotionally, Enver." She sniffed, lifting her pointed chin as she held his gaze. "Which means you're exactly the one I need to worry about. If something happened to you...he'd be devastated. Yes, I was looking out for you."

"Stalking me," he corrected.

"Okay...yes, stalking you, I just... I won't apologize." A protective fierceness filled her expression, giving him a glimpse of the unconditional love she had for Marcus. The brightness in her eyes indicative of the tears she was holding back. He also noted the way she was shivering despite the heat churning from the fire.

Marcus would never forgive him if something happened to her either.

Enver shifted to the cot, gesturing her closer. She came willingly, sighing against his body heat as he wrapped an arm around her shoulders to tuck her against his body.

"You can't help him if you're lying in a hospital bed with pneumonia. When is the last time you had a full night of sleep?"

"He didn't tell me you were a nursemaid."

"When?" he said sternly, weighting his words with the aching loneliness clawing at him, exposing a side of himself he'd only previously showed Marcus.

Her whole body gave a hard shiver that he knew wasn't because she was still cold. "Wow. I get what he sees in you now. I mean, I saw it before when he talked about you, but in living color, I get it." She paused, playing with the corner of the blanket. "I know he's being a cunty potatohead, all right? Don't think I haven't tried to reason with him." The determined set of her jaw indicated she wasn't the type to back down easily.

"Cunty potatohead?" he said slowly, wondering if he'd heard correctly.

"We call each other that when we're being unreasonable."

"Well, next time you talk to him, tell him I think he's being a weaselhead fucknugget."

"Sounds like him." She huffed out a laugh. "He's doing this because he truly believes he has no other choice." She drew her hand out from under the blanket, held something out toward him. "Call him," she said in a low voice, the earlier hint of amusement gone. "He's got a burner. Untraceable."

Enver took the phone, turning it over and over in his hand. He wanted to call. Needed to. But the vague bits of information Zoie had given him indicated Marcus believed his life was in danger. Enver couldn't be responsible for further adding to that precarious situation by doing something stupid. If Marcus truly wanted to contact him, he would have done so already.

He returned the phone. "As I said before, knowing he's safe is enough."

"You're just as stubborn as he is."

He looked down, found her gaze on him still. Her color had returned, her eyes not as bloodshot as when he'd confronted her at the car. The fierceness with which she loved Marcus touched something deep in Enver's soul. He swore softly. "I love him too, Zoie."

Her fingers tightened on his shirtsleeve. "He needs to hear that."

"Will it bring him back?" he countered. "If I take

that phone, call him and tell him how I truly feel, how monumentally stupid I think he's being for not letting me choose my own fate, will he come back to me?" The sorrow darkening her eyes answered his questions. "Get some sleep," he repeated. "We'll figure out a way to get him home to us."

Chapter Twenty-One

"Davis is dead," Zoie announced without preamble.

Marcus was so jostled by the news, he felt light-headed. Oh hell no, he wasn't going to faint. Zoie would never let him live it down. Thankfully he hadn't been driving when he'd answered the phone.

"What?" His voice came out as a hoarse croak, unaccustomed to use after eleven days of silence. He sat up, gaze automatically scanning the lot of the shopping center he'd parked in a few hours ago to catch a bit of sleep. The ringing phone had startled him out of a dream he couldn't remember but still felt the lingering traces of.

"Had the nibble of a lead yesterday that I didn't think would amount to much. Got a good bite about four this morning."

Which meant she's been working around the clock. He was prepared to issue a stern warning when she rushed on.

"I was right about Mexico. The *federales* weren't very cooperative, but you know I'm damn persistent. Wasn't going to give up on my gut. Hounded a wet-behind-the-ears rookie who didn't know any better and he finally slipped." She paused, her muffled voice sounding as she covered the mouthpiece. "Sorry. Chief wants a report. Anyway, Davis Connelly was arrested three days ago on bullshit charges he was smuggling drugs across the border. But toss in resisting arrest and the fact he's American, and they threw him into *Cereso Las Cruces*."

Marcus knew almost next to nothing about Mexico, but he remembered catching a news report earlier in the year about the state of the prisons in the country. Overcrowded, understaffed and unsafe.

"That particular prison in Acapulco is known for rampant violence. We hear about it all the time up here, especially since the California's jail population is so high. Authorities can normally keep it contained, but something sparked a riot between two rival gangs. Twenty-eight deaths, and the death toll is still climbing. Positive identification for Davis arrived ten minutes ago."

It took him several moments to process everything Zoie had said. After two weeks of operating on high alert as he zigzagged around the country, he wasn't sure what to say or do. He'd been convinced he was going to have to spend the rest of his life on the run. Now he had a freedom he hadn't known since before the attack that had disfigured him.

"You there?" She hesitated. "Marcus?"

"Yeah," he managed to croak out. "I'm right here, Zoie." Even though he truly had no idea where *here* even was. His body ached as though he'd been stabbed repeatedly in the gut and was now bleeding all over the floorboard of the truck.

Some of his anxiety eased as he realized the weight of his demons were no longer sitting on his shoulders. Leaving may not have been the best decision, but that chapter of his life had finally found a resolution. He could move on. Wouldn't have to spend his days constantly looking over his shoulder. Wouldn't feel his bowels liquefy every time his phone signaled an incoming text message. No more phantom images superimposing over real life where he'd kept inserting Davis.

"He misses you."

Marcus didn't need clarification of who Zoie meant. His hand curled, the sudden need to reach out and touch something that was so far away vibrating through his limbs. "Do you know where he is right now?"

"Still up on the mountain, as far as I know. I'll send you the address. Text me when you two untangle yourselves."

It had taken everything in Marcus not to abandon Zoie's vehicle and locate the nearest airport. Instead, he'd gone into the store, and discovered he was in Osage, a rural town just outside of Thunder Basin in Wyoming.

The trek back to California took three days. Three long days where he chewed up the mileage by driving as much as he possibly could, once again hopped up on energy drinks, and catching short naps when his eyes started to burn.

This time, instead of the fear of Davis finding him again, the terror biting at him was that Enver would dismiss him. Wouldn't let him explain. By the time he pulled the truck next to Enver's vintage muscle car, he was exhausted. But a burst of energy lit a fire inside him with the knowledge Enver was steps away.

As he shut the truck's door, he caught a glimpse of himself in the window and swore as he ran his hand over the facial hair that had grown in. His clothes were

wrinkled, his hair windblown from his habit of driving with the windows down. He'd bypassed his house
completely in favor of coming directly to the address
Zoie had texted him. Nothing he could do about it all
now because he wasn't interested in stalling.

An apology sat on the end of Marcus's tongue as he
stepped inside the workshop. Whatever Marcus had
envisioned, it wasn't that of a smith, despite the fact
he knew Enver made most of the metal implements for
Noble House. It furthered Marcus's belief that Enver
had an old soul. In an age full of technology, instant access to the world and everyone in it, Enver had a forge
nestled near the Eldorado National Forest.

The workspace was utilitarian, clearly a location
where hard work and determination poured free like
droplets of sweat. The walls were packed with shelves
and pegboards holding various tools, bins of screws,
nails, bolts, earplugs and safety goggles without any sort
of organization. Stacks of scrap metal, toothy blades
and power grinders all crowded every available hori-
zontal space. This kind of disarray made him wonder
how anything got built.

Then his gaze landed on the man who owned it all.

A wall of emotion slammed into Marcus, flickering through him as a sign of a coming storm set to rav-
age everything. A golden glow originated from a box
perched on top of a stack of cinder blocks. Enver stood
near the makeshift oven, a denim-blue long-sleeve shirt
plastered to his frame as he beat some kind of hammer
against a glowing brick of metal.

He stopped, examined the quickly cooling item, set
down the hammer and slid the brick into the oven. He
used his shirtsleeve to wipe at the sweat drenching his

brow, but it had little effect since he was covered with perspiration. Frowning, he grabbed a bottle of water and chugged half of it. The other half he upended over his head in an effort to cool his body temperature.

Marcus half expected tendrils of smoke to waft up from Enver's body. Some guys got all bothered and spun up at the idea of their lover all done up in a suit and tie. Not Marcus. Seeing Enver hot and sweaty with his shirt covered in a fine layer of soot and hard work made his tongue wag.

Enver looked capable and dangerous even in ordinary long sleeves and jeans.

Marcus shivered. Both from the cold pressing against his back and the sight Enver made while he worked hard. Enver discarded the bottle, snagged another and checked on the item in the oven. His gaze briefly flicked toward where Marcus stood waiting, then back to the oven. He pulled the block out and set it on the anvil. Without a word, he picked up the hammer and started working on the piece again. Loud bangs filled the space, obliterating any opportunity to hold a discussion.

Message received loud and clear. Marcus had fucked up. He was lucky Enver hadn't ordered him to leave. But maybe ignoring him was worse. A silent punishment. Fine by him. He was more than willing to wait out Enver just so he could say his piece.

Marcus pulled up the collar of his down-lined jacket and leaned against the doorframe. At least the view was gorgeous. He didn't even mind the fact Enver was covered so completely, though the reason for that became clear as sparks arced away from each pounding hit Enver delivered. Safety was always at the forefront of Enver's mind. Even during the virtual scenes with

Marcus, Enver had checked and rechecked the rigging that had cradled Marcus's avatar.

The same arms that Marcus and Grae had spent so many hours sculpting for the virtual realm bunched and flexed as Enver hit the piece over and over again. It quickly became apparent that Enver wasn't just working on his craft. He was also taking out his frustrations. The thought of what could happen if Enver lost focus haunted Marcus.

The blows stopped, as did the noise.

"Snow's gonna hit soon."

Marcus had expected pushback for what he'd done. Had been prepared in the event Enver wanted nothing to do with him, not a comment about the weather. "Just need to say a few things and I'll leave."

Enver's gaze passed over Marcus all the way to the floor, then back up again. The way Marcus's cock responded to Enver's perusal should have disturbed him, but instead, it fueled all the reasons he'd come back. All the reasons he should have never left in the first place. He had no idea he could react so viscerally to another person, but all these feelings and sensations went beyond the physical. The knot of the hard-yearning ache bloomed in his already agitated stomach.

"Say whatever the hell you want." Enver turned his back to Marcus. "Doesn't mean anyone is gonna listen."

Marcus knew he deserved Enver's reaction. He cleared his throat as though it would help Enver hear him somehow. "Doesn't mean I'm not going to talk anyway." He rubbed his nose as he gathered his courage. "I told you I used to teach high school. Computer science, specifically, but I never said why I left."

Enver grunted, but Marcus pushed on. "I quit teaching because of these." Marcus gestured to his face, throat and shoulder. "Different time even ten years ago. Very different place. Gay men stayed in the closet for their entire lives. Especially there. Small town doesn't even begin to describe it, but I wasn't going to let them control how I decided to live my life. I didn't make it a secret that I chose to date men, but I didn't flaunt it either. It was just my life, you know?

"One of my students wasn't very accepting of life in general. Davis ran into me on a date at a park. He was nice enough at the time, but there was a large crowd gathered for movie night. Most of the town, really. Probably wasn't interested in making a scene. Few days later, he asked for some extra help after school. He wasn't a very good student, and as a teacher, I never wanted any of my kids to fail. I was there to help them succeed.

"He showed up for the lesson, waited until I came to help him with the coding in a program and dumped the entire contents of a container full of chemicals he'd brought with him. Hurled a few vicious insults I don't remember because I passed out from the pain. He never made it a secret he did it. Even waited for the police to show up and arrest him. Always thought he called them himself, but no one ever told me. So fucking proud of his accomplishment. Pleaded not guilty all through the trial just to put me through hell, drag everything out. Force me to relive that day over and over."

Marcus sighed as the weight of everything settled on his shoulders. He'd been foolish enough to believe he'd put it all behind him. "A couple of months ago, Davis was paroled."

Lines formed around Enver's mouth. "The first night we went to Boylesque." At Marcus's nod, he continued.

"I could tell you were distracted, but I just thought you were stressed out about the program."

"The texts trickled in occasionally. Just long enough for me to think he'd moved on, accepted his new life out of prison, and then *bam!* Right in my face again." Marcus pressed on. "Our date at the observatory? String of texts and images of us. One of which was when I gave you my number at the convention. He used a drone to track me. Not as much of a good-behavior-in-prison type that everyone thought. It shook me. Put a fear of God inside me that I've not experienced since the initial attack. Until two weeks ago."

Enver's fingers went white as he gripped the hammer.

The pain of that night flashed through Marcus, a reminder of the vicious agony Davis had delivered. "After group therapy, my car was vandalized and I was attacked. It was Davis. He got in a few cheap shots that took me down. Threatened to rape me with the handle of the sledgehammer his buddy had used to destroy my car."

Enver swore quietly.

"When that didn't happen, when he realized the cops were coming, he emptied his bladder."

Enver's expression twisted.

"Please, just let me say this."

Enver nodded even though Marcus knew it took immense effort for him not to lash out. "He made it clear he wanted to finish the job. I panicked, made Zoie promise to bury it all because I didn't want to go through everything again. I've been down that road, and it's exhausting. I took my shit and left because I don't want some fuckwad from my past to ruin everyone else's life. Hurt those I love. Locking Davis up again would just deepen his anger. At least on the road, making him track me down, I kept him busy. Didn't make a lot of sense, but at the time, it was all I could think of."

Realization flashed in Enver's eyes as he set down his tool. "Running away doesn't solve anything. Never has."

"You don't think I know that?" Marcus bit back the flare of anger that sparked in his gut. Enver wasn't at fault for any of this. "I wanted there to be a different alternative, but I couldn't see past the worry something would happen to you. That Davis would come *for* you. I figured if I could keep him focused, he'd go after me. Leave you alone."

"I'm not angry you left, Marcus," Enver said with a voice laced with bitter resentment despite the calm and even tone. "I understand acting on impulse, probably better than anyone else. God knows I do. I'm angry you took it upon yourself to remove my choice, my say, in a matter that affected you. You didn't offer me the opportunity to protect you like I promised I would."

Marcus lost himself so quickly in Enver's steely glare he was dizzy. "So...you missed me?"

Enver hooked his fingers through the loop on the back of Marcus's jeans, hauled their bodies together and slashed his mouth over Marcus's. They came together in a raw explosion of energy and heat, unleashing a brutal clash of two out of control male bodies.

Marcus grunted when Enver backed him against a workbench, feeling the true strength of the man as he pinned him in place. The steel length of Enver's cock pressed against his thigh. He was so focused on the slide of Enver's tongue against his, he gasped when Enver closed his hand around his cock, groaned when the hold constricted to the point of blinding pain.

"What I missed, gorgeous, is hearing that sound from you when I don't give you a choice but to surrender. I missed seeing you look at me with these damn puppy-dog eyes. Missed seeing them focused on me while I'm sliding my dick between your lips." Enver drew his hand along Marcus's length, palming the crown before releasing him. "Most of all, I missed seeing you geek out and have a nerdgasm whenever something goes right with your system."

"Nerdgasm?"

Enver set his hands on either side of Marcus's hips, lowering his head as he shook it. "I despise the fact you made me interested in your tech shit."

Marcus grinned as he pressed a kiss to the top of Enver's head. "I don't despise the fact you like old shit."

"That's because I *am* old shit."

Marcus laughed lightly. "Yeah, you are."

"Speaking of your tech shit—your actions and your words contradict one another. You're not truly okay with these." Enver paused, taking a few minutes to trace the discolorations mapping Marcus's skin. "You never told me why you leave these out of the simulations."

Panic nearly stopped Marcus's heart, heat flushing his skin. He knew they were overdue to have this conversation. Knew he owed Enver an explanation.

"Hey, it's all right." Enver pressed a kiss to Marcus's forehead as he grabbed his trembling hands. "You don't have to tell me if you don't want to. Doesn't change what I'm about to say."

"I need to," Marcus said slowly as he turned his head to brush his lips against Enver's knuckles. "It's detrimental to a relationship when there are times I can't even look at myself, so I owe you an explanation. I— shit, this is harder than I thought."

He squared his shoulders. "I thought you should have a perfect submissive. Someone who wasn't flawed or broken. Out here, in the real world, I can't control what people say or do or think. I can't be...normal. In BLINC, I can give you what you deserve." He buried his face against Enver's neck, muffling his next words. "Yeah, I know. Sounds even stupider saying all that out loud."

"I don't know whether to be touched or pissed, Marcus. But thank you for telling me."

"Thanks for not giving up on me."

"As much as I hate knowing the truth behind them, don't use BLINC to take them away again. Next time we're in there, you're the same as you are out here. I want to see every perfect flaw on this gorgeous face. Deal?"

Marcus blew out a long breath. "Deal."

Chapter Twenty-Two

A hard, yearning ache he wanted to never end surged inside Marcus as he touched Enver's collarbone, his jaw. Lifted Enver's face so he could look into his eyes and feel the heat of the man he'd grown so close to. Saw that same heat glint in Enver's gaze when Marcus stirred the challenge as he continued to touch Enver, trace his face. The relaxed curve of his mouth. The slope of cheekbone.

This close, he saw every illicit thought running through Enver's mind. Thoughts that made Marcus glad he'd swallowed his pride and come back. He saw the fury still simmering under the surface. The barely restrained anger and violence. Perhaps he craved the fight and violence himself. It would give them an outlet for everything churning in the volatile air between them. All the unspoken things they hadn't gotten around to saying to one another yet.

In a sudden explosion of movement, Enver clamped down on Marcus's wrist, yanking it around behind him to pin it between his shoulder blades. Using the subservient position to his advantage, he used his leverage to shove Marcus to the floor.

Enver followed him to the ground, shoving his hand into Marcus's underwear to wrap a possessive grip around Marcus's cock. Enver immobilized him by thrusting one of his legs between Marcus's and pushing his muscular thigh hard against the base of Marcus's testicles.

His rough touch made it clear he intended to jerk Marcus off for no other reason than to prove that he could. He relentlessly fisted Marcus's dick, the brutal touch rousing something primal inside Marcus. He released Marcus's wrist, wrapping his hand around the back of Marcus's neck and angling him backward.

Gazes locked together, Enver leaned forward to catch Marcus's lips as he gripped hard and fast so Marcus wouldn't move as Enver thrust his tongue deep inside. Marcus's hips jerked in response to the bruising kiss, silently pleading for more.

A ripple of energy radiated through Marcus, wanting Enver to stop as much as he wanted him to continue. The possessive touch won, however, and Marcus relaxed against him, allowing the man the freedom to do whatever he wanted.

Enver paused, holding Marcus's dick loosely against his fingers. "I need to know this is okay. After what you just told me happened with Davis—"

"You aren't him," Marcus interrupted. "Not in a million years. I need…we both need for you to be who you are, Enver." To savagely take whatever it was that he sought from Marcus. In so many ways, Marcus needed it too. "Don't let what he did change what you want to do."

"Oh, I won't. I just want to be clear about consent and safe words. Since I've got your permission, how about reminding me of that safe word so we're clear there, too?"

"Fucknuggets." Marcus barely managed to get the word out before Enver took full advantage of Marcus's surrender by stroking his knuckles up and down Marcus's length, down to the balls, gripping them firmly in his fist and squeezing a few times.

"Oh fuck," Marcus whispered as he gripped Enver's shoulder. "I didn't come here for this. I came to apologize and see if we could work through things. See if I'd fucked things up beyond all recognition."

"Since you're seconds away from blowing your wad in my hand, I'd say things aren't as fucked as you think."

Marcus tried to catch his breath as the truth swirled in the charged air. The handful of orgasms he'd experience before with Enver had been through the virtual connection. Brain waves manipulated to make Marcus believe Enver touched him.

In the Keep, when Enver had jerked him off, he'd been too lost to focus on the sensation. Too caught up in the madness of desperation to fully appreciate the act. But now, in Enver's overheated workshop, Marcus actually felt the frantic slide of flesh against flesh. Heard each of Enver's ragged breaths. Smelled the rich, tempting aroma of Enver's hard work and dedication to his craft.

"Your entire body is responding to my touch, my voice." Enver rubbed his thumb against the crown of Marcus's cock, slicking the fluid leaking from the tip as he rubbed the ridged head. Marcus swore quietly as he reached up and slapped a hand on the edge of the bench to keep from tearing off Enver's clothes.

"I'd say you're perilously close to begging me to fuck you, gorgeous." Enver leaned closer, sliding his tongue over his lower lip.

God, Marcus wanted that mouth. That fucking glorious mouth just inches away from his.

Enver's eyes flashed, brilliant and bright in triumph as Marcus started bucking his hips, his eyes nearly rolling out of his head at the magnificent slide of Enver's palm up and down his shaft. He wanted Enver to devour him. Eat him alive. Pin him to the floor and brand his ass with one of those irons hanging on the wall behind them. A hard shiver went through him, his blood hot and thick in his veins. His mind a jumble of thoughts as he tried to rationalize his need with the warped thoughts of being punished for his actions.

Enver twisted his wrist, sending a bolt of pleasure arcing through Marcus. Dark, humorless laughter sounded in Marcus's ears as Enver sped his pace. With a few quick beats, Marcus was moving his hips rhythmically with Enver's movements.

"Don't come." Enver nipped at Marcus's collarbone, the bright splash of pain adding a layer to Marcus's arousal. "Don't you fucking come, you hear me?"

"Yeah," Marcus managed to say around a few quick-fire breaths. There was more he needed to say, more he thought they needed to work out, but Enver was quickly stealing his ability to think rationally. Fuck it, they could talk later. Or not. He realized he didn't care when Enver released his dick, slipped a hand lower between his thighs and slipped a slickly coated finger into his ass.

"I don't—" Despite his words, he tightened his muscles, using what little leverage he'd been given to feel the glorious in and out slide of Enver's finger. Enver snarled in warning, but Marcus kept moving, unable to stop himself. "I know you can't…we can't…"

"It's all right, Marcus. *I'm* all right because you came back to me. We'll work out the rest later. Right now, I need to be inside you."

The violence that had saturated the air earlier had dissipated, leaving a naked hunger Enver wanted to take advantage of. His gaze roved over Marcus's body stretched taut in the assisted backbend. He greedily took in all the exposed flesh, prickles of heat moving across his lower abdomen as he looked at Marcus's cock, flushed dark red, jutting away from his body.

He'd never seen anything more beautiful in his life.

When Marcus began to tremble against him, Enver pressed his face into his hair, inhaling the fading scent of shampoo. He'd never felt this way before. Never wanted to drown in someone before, lose himself in the all-consuming power another person held over him.

Swamped with emotion, he released his hold, removed his finger and winced at Marcus's whimper. "Shh, just a second." With a few quick movements, he'd stripped them both and led Marcus to the cot still positioned near the stove. He was tempted to stand over Marcus's nude form, drink in how the dying flames of his forging oven played over the perfect ridges of Marcus's abdomen, the knot of scars across one pectoral muscle. But the pull to have all that hard flesh against his, unencumbered by clothing, was too much.

He settled his body over Marcus's, capturing his mouth in a slow, languorous kiss as he used his tongue to pull forth a deep groan. Marcus shifted under him, pulling Enver's hips down so they were groin-to-groin. Enver broke the kiss, trailing his lips along Marcus's collarbone, up his neck, along the soft edge of his hair-covered jaw. He rubbed his cheek against it, loving the raspy sound of the short hairs against his own unshaven face.

Marcus lifted his hips, dragging the length of his cock against Enver's. Enver took Marcus's mouth again as they ground their hips together, fluid leaking from them both to lubricate the gentle friction the motion created. They rocked together, slow then fast, teasing and taunting one another with equal amounts of vigor. Neither Enver nor Marcus were in control of the moment, their worlds in perfect balance and harmony.

Marcus gazed up at him through half-lidded eyes, lust burning between them that threatened to eviscerate rational thought. Enver was almost too dazed, too strung out on the power arcing between them to continue. He'd intended to keep this slow and easy, to make tender love to the man who had changed his world exponentially and convinced him love was possible. But Marcus was slowly peeling away each tenuous thread of control Enver had.

"Fuck me, Enver. Use me as hard as you need." Marcus touched his shoulder as his gaze landed squarely on Enver, his naked yearning shining in his eyes. "I need you to."

Enver hadn't thought it was possible for his cock to get any harder, but those words, those four words— *I need you to*—impossibly stiffened his dick. But as much as he wanted—needed—to punish him, make him understand how devastating his choice to leave had been…he couldn't give in to the request.

Emotion clogged his throat, tightened a fist around his heart as though it was going to burst out of his chest as he spoke. "Monster."

Chapter Twenty-Three

"Wha—what?" Marcus tensed beneath him, Enver's safe word robbing the air of sexual tension. "Is something wrong?"

Enver sat back on his heels, listening to the cot groan in protest at the change. He slipped one leg to the side, bracing his foot on the floor and shifting his weight.

Marcus grabbed his shoulder, fingers tightening to the point of pain. "Don't leave."

"I'm not. Just don't want to overbalance us." Who was he kidding? The scales were tipped far out of balance already. Enver closed his eyes, unable to stand the way Marcus's confused gaze lanced straight to his heart. Specters of anger and regret filled in the spaces where Marcus had laid him open with his quiet demand of surrender. He'd thought he'd understood the magnitude of his feelings for Marcus, but then he'd offered himself—*shit*.

Marcus laid his hands on either side of Enver's jaw, angling his face. "Look at me."

"Give me a minute." Enver closed his eyes, counting every breath, every heartbeat of those sixty seconds. Finally, he met Marcus's gaze. "Didn't expect that."

"Just tell me what's wrong. Please."

"I—" He fisted his hands, hating how torn up inside

the situation made him feel. "I thought I could sepa-rate my anger at you from everything else. Just shove it to the side and deal with all of this later so we could be together. But it…hurt. Damn it, I'm hurt. Know-ing you thought so little of what is between us tore me fucking apart." He let out a harsh laugh that held no trace of amusement. "God, I want nothing more than to bind you in ropes and punish you right now for being so damn stupid."

"Then do it," Marcus blurted.

Enver closed his eyes again, unable to stand looking at the open surrender Marcus offered. "I could. Right now, I know you would let me bend you over, take my belt and stripe your ass raw. And then I would fuck you so hard you wouldn't be able to walk tomorrow. But I can't. I don't trust myself to not take my anger out on you and that is the wrong fucking time to exchange power. Bottom line…you didn't trust me, Marcus," he said quietly. "You didn't believe me when I promised to keep you safe."

Enver winced as the sensation of a knife twist-ing in his stomach assaulted him all over again as the truth spilled between them. None of what he'd just said changed the heart and personality of the man he had somehow fallen in love with.

"Meeting you has been the most incredible experi-ence of my life," Enver said slowly, hating the shaking tone of his voice. "You need to know that. I don't… I don't know what—for the first time, I don't know how to handle what I'm feeling. Even with my addiction, I knew how to fix it. This… I—you own my heart and soul, Marcus, and I don't fucking know what to do. I want you so much, but I can't—I can't survive having my heart ripped out by you a second time."

In the Rough

Marcus's face crumpled, his voice cracking. "I am so sorry I hurt you. I know however many times I say that it will never be enough." He tugged on Enver's fingers, linking their hands. "I ran because of you. Whatever else you want to think, you have to know that I needed to keep you safe. Keep all my drama away from you. Stupid as it sounds, running was the only way I could think of." Marcus kissed his way up Enver's neck, stopping with his mouth at his ear. "I love you." His chest heaved unevenly as he said it. "I promise, and I don't see that ever changing." Husky thickness coated the words as he dragged Enver's face close.

Marcus grazed his mouth across Enver's, and then did it again and again. Enver squeezed the solid, warm flesh of Marcus's arm, and moaned at the first flick of their tongues. He tunneled his fingers into Marcus's hair and descended, taking his mouth roughly. What started with a nip increased in brutality as the deep kiss of complete ownership consumed Enver inside and out. Marcus kissed him back with equal fervor.

Finally, Enver drew back, his gaze coursing over Marcus's face. He kept his hand curled tightly around Marcus's nape, holding him in place. Marcus's hair stood up in rakish angles, his breathing uneven, his lips red from kissing, and his pupils blown wide.

"Still the most incredible thing I've ever seen. Christ, I love you, gorgeous." Eyes open, Enver brushed his lips against Marcus's. His heart fluttered. "I want you forever. And I'll keep you safe forever."

"I love it when you get all possessive." Emotion shined in Marcus's eyes.

Enver lost himself completely in the younger man's sincere eyes and sexy mouth, capturing Marcus's lips again as a bone-deep love he'd never thought he'd have flourished. As their bodies came together again there was nothing to mute the sharp sensation of contact between their cocks.

He pushed Marcus's knees apart, hooking one leg over his hip. "Call me old-fashioned—"

"Well, you *are* old."

Enver nipped at Marcus's bottom lip. "Hush. As I was saying, call me old-fashioned, but I want to take you the first time face-to-face." As he ran his hand down Marcus's spine, the man trembled and his opening contracted against Enver's finger when he touched it. "You good with that?"

"Yeah." Marcus made a needy little noise as Enver traced the pucker, toying with it and enjoying the sounds. Early ejaculate beaded up the tip of Marcus's cock, sliding down the side of the crown.

Unable to stop himself, Enver palmed the head, dragging his fist up and down the shaft. Marcus looked up at him, his stare filled with raw need. As Marcus tensed beneath him, his dick spit out another fat pearl of fluid. The salty essence filled Enver's senses as he swiped it up, rubbing it against the tip of a single finger. A deep, base hunger coiled around his cock, straining it toward the man whimpering underneath him.

Marcus shivered as one lubricated finger dipped inside his anus. "Jesus." Ragged desperation filled his voice, touching off new fires of need deep inside Enver. "Fuck."

"Always so eloquent with your language, aren't you, baby?"

As desperate as Enver was to get inside Marcus and put them both out of their misery, this was more than just slipping on a condom and pounding away the need.

He took his time, circling his finger around the opening. Teasing. Dipping inside so he could watch the expression of sheer joy wash over Marcus's face. He added a second finger, watching in fascination as Marcus's mouth went slack. The voice, the body, the eyes…the entire presence of this man lured Enver as if it were just the two of them in the world.

It was perfect, and nothing else mattered.

As he continued to use shallow strokes, never removing his fingers, but never burying them fully, Marcus gave a frustrated growl. The noise made Enver smile as he pressed a gentle kiss against Marcus's shoulder.

He wrapped his free hand around the back of Marcus's neck again, plunging his tongue between Marcus's lips to delve deep, their tongues sliding against one another. Christ, he'd forgotten how delectable Marcus's mouth was. How much he liked kissing him. How spectacular that skilled mouth felt wrapped around his cock.

When Marcus's muscles clenched around his fingers, Enver knew he was overwhelming him. Knew Marcus had to be screaming inside his head for Enver to just put him out of his misery. He understood that frustration well.

"That's it, gorgeous, take it." Enver slid deeper, using long, slow strokes with his fingers. He brushed Marcus's prostate and held him tighter as his entire body seized.

"Fuck. Fuck. Fuck."

Enver chose that moment to add another finger. A few seconds later, another. When Marcus went lax, Enver was dizzy as hell, spun up in the headiness of the moment. Of feeling Marcus under him and so fucking responsive.

Suddenly, Marcus clamped around his fingers, his

hips bucking wildly out of control as though someone had sent a shot of pure adrenaline straight to his cock.

Enver set a steadying hand on his hip. "Easy, I can go all night."

"Not sure I can if you keep this up." Marcus trembled, letting out a breath.

"Yeah…you can. Relax for me," Enver said as he nudged the tip of his now condom-covered penis oh-so-carefully against Marcus's pucker. He spread Marcus's cheeks, the charged atmosphere snapping as he held himself poised at Marcus's entrance. He eased in, taking his time to enjoy the slowness.

They both sighed loudly as Enver's cock fully breeched Marcus's ass.

As he rocked deeper, Marcus started to chant, "Shit. Damn. Motherfucker."

Enver went still as unfathomable pleasure ripped through him in one fiery swoop and then raced back to his dick buried in Marcus ass. He set his face in the crook of Marcus's neck, his own chant of singular words flashing in his head.

Hot. Tight. More. Hot. Tight. More.

He obeyed his need, driving his length forward and didn't stop until he buried himself balls-deep. Scorching heat and clenching walls surrounded every inch of his cock, killing him with mind-altering pleasure. He pulled all the way out and thrust back into the heaven of Marcus's ass again, needing to move.

He moaned as he pushed into the tightness again, liking the feeling of Marcus trembling around him. He rocked again, enjoying the quiet curses spilling free each time he thrust particularly deep. "I love fucking your ass. Love feeling you flex, hearing you groan every time I bottom out."

"So damn good." Marcus sucked in a breath, screwing up his eyes. "Can't get enough."

Enver knew the feeling well. They moved together, finding the same rhythm. Kept it as the cot groaned beneath them. "The sweetest fucking ass."

He lost himself in that flushed face, the hair standing up at wild angles. He rocked his hips, the cot giving a loud creak in protest. But he didn't stop, easing his slick cock in and out until those fathomless eyes lost focus. The cot could break for all he cared—he only wanted to keep fucking Marcus.

"I need you like this." He kissed Marcus's shoulder. "Just like this."

"You've got me."

"No. Every night, like this. Tender. Slow. Exploring and learning."

Marcus's eyebrows lifted. "No kink?"

He drove hard into Marcus, earning a gasp. "Doesn't matter if I have you in ropes, give you a blowjob or we make love." Enver dropped down for a kiss, his spine tingling at the way Marcus felt moving under him. Marcus encouraged it, rocking his hips, offering more of himself even though Enver didn't think it was possible to slip deeper.

"Do you know why I can't stop wanting you?" Marcus only moaned in answer, a harsh, guttural sound that speared Enver. "Can't stop needing you." Marcus shuddered when the head of Enver's cock grazed that sensitive bundle of nerves. "Can't stop thinking about how sexy you are." Enver brushed a kiss between Marcus's eyebrows.

Marcus opened his eyes slowly, his pupils blown wide in the blissed-out state Enver was keeping them both balanced on. "So fucking hungry for you, Enver." The words arrowed straight down to the point where they were joined. "Could...ah, God... I hate you as much as I love you."

Enver almost shattered at the surge of passion and desperation warring inside that sentence. The pain and longing trapped under the urgency. The specters of regret still circled despite their earlier talk. They could forgive each other temporarily, but this connection with one another exposed a weakness that had the power to destroy them both.

When Enver feathered his fingers over his face, Marcus gave a sudden groan, his body seizing. His release came quick and hot, spurting scorching fluid that flooded the narrow space between their abdomens. Marcus's muscles clamped around Enver, putting a stranglehold on his dick. He sucked in a breath. Held it. Let go with a strangled cry bordering on a sob as everything inside him released and he blew into the condom. The climax shattered through him, forcing him deeper while his cock pulsed inside Marcus as stark pleasure ripped through him.

Exhaustion swamped him as he collapsed against Marcus. For long minutes afterward, he remained, pulling in cleansing air until he could breathe without his entire body heaving. He still had his cock resting inside Marcus, still had his fingers locked in a bruising hold over Marcus's hands. He knew he needed to get up, to give Marcus the freedom to move, but holy hell, he didn't want to separate from him.

In any way.

Chapter Twenty-Four

Enver switched the mug of coffee to his other hand as he slid the glass door closed behind him. The storm had moved out overnight, leaving a fresh layer of snow that would sparkle when the sun rose over the mountains. It would melt by midafternoon, leaving rivulets of ice by midnight. Right now, early dawn colored everything dove-gray.

He sipped his hot drink as he kicked at a pile of powdery snow near the steps. A twinge shot up his calf and thigh, radiating hot needles around his hip. Wincing, he rubbed at the pain, thinking about how much being forty-three sucked sometimes. His mind might have been on board to fuck all night, but his body was reminding him he needed to recharge.

Enver glanced over his shoulder. He'd left Marcus in a tangle of sheets and blankets on the ancient cot he was sure they'd break with their combined weight. But it had held steady through all three hours they'd gone at one another. He set his coffee down, pulling his lighter and a cigarette out of a nearly empty pack. Watched the first tendrils of smoke waft up from the end as he lit it, inhaling that first morning drag.

After spending years worried about how he'd react

the first time he buried himself balls-deep inside someone again, it felt good to finally have the answer. His
head doctor had assured him the world wouldn't end,
but a slice of his soul hadn't been convinced. Marcus
had been the first person he'd wanted to tempt fate for.

Even though their previously explored roles in power
exchange hadn't been in play last night, he was open
to every sensation, every emotion and feeling that had
passed between them. He often felt that way after an
intense scene with a submissive, but this was the first
time he'd experienced that total clarity after baring
himself so utterly. His shields were down, making him
vulnerable—naked and afraid. He'd lost it years ago, so
intent on the euphoric high of sexual release that he'd
forgotten the beauty of connecting with another human
being on an emotional level.

Marcus had given him that gift once again.

"Holy fuckballs, it's freezing out here."

Enver turned, somehow unsurprised to see Marcus
hadn't gotten dressed before joining him on the deck.
Marcus folded his arms in front of him as he switched
his weight between his bare feet. Enver offered him the
last of his coffee as he took another drag.

Marcus waved him off. "Aren't you cold?"

Enver shrugged, dropping the spent filter into the remaining liquid. "You're the one not wearing any shoes."
He popped a mint, chewing it as he watched Marcus
continue to shift back and forth. "Or clothes."

"Can I have one of those?" Enver handed him a mint,
which Marcus studied before slipping between his lips.
"You're like Willy Wonka with your never-ending supply of candy. Or Houdini, 'cause I'm still wondering
where the hell you came up with a handful of con-

doms out of thin air." Marcus danced around a little, clearly unprepared for just how cold it was outside. "Guy spends time living on top of a mountain by himself, has a supply of condoms and you gotta wonder."

"It's the Boy Scout in me," Enver said as he set the dirty mug on the nearby glass-topped table and tugged Marcus against him, wrapping his hands around Marcus's thighs so he could take his weight as he lifted him. Instant warmth enveloped him as he wrapped Marcus's legs around his waist. Marcus shivered, but Enver wasn't convinced it was entirely because of the temperature or the snow. "Haven't always been alone up here either."

Marcus narrowed his eyes. "Go on."

"Had a dog once." He nipped at Marcus's lip. "When he made a bolt for the door, I knew I had to let him go."

"Bolt for the…" Marcus trailed off as the joke sank in. "That has got to be the lamest—" He broke off when Enver pushed him against the glass door. Instead of protesting, Marcus went limp.

Enver skimmed his fingers between the cleft of Marcus's ass, enjoying the way the muscles trembled under his touch. He delved deeper, slowly exploring and enjoying the way Marcus started shaking against him.

Marcus jerked when Enver skimmed his fingers over his opening. Teasing and tracing the rim with slow, circular patterns. Despite the cold and the snow, Marcus's cock stirred against Enver's abdomen.

"Someone's eager this morning." Enver wiggled his finger, pleased when Marcus relaxed, accepting him. As he slipped deeper, Marcus whined briefly before it turned into a lust-filled groan. He'd expected the resistance given the hours they'd spent wrapped around one another. Loved that it evaporated so quickly as Marcus surrendered.

"Fuck. Fuck. Fuck," Marcus chanted, his thighs clenching tight around Enver's waist. "I can't. I can't again. Too much. *Sooooo* much."

A band formed around Enver's chest from hearing Marcus's broken words. Marcus released another harsh moan as Enver pushed his finger to the last knuckle. He whimpered when Enver stroked the pad of his finger over the sensitive bundle of nerves.

"You're going to promise me something, Marcus. Right here, right now, while I have my finger buried in your ass."

Marcus's eyes flared open, his body stiffening. The morning sunlight filtered over Enver's shoulder, playing over the ridges and valleys of the scars that defined Marcus. Coloring the ravaged skin in a way that was both horrific and beautiful at the same time.

The first attack would never stop haunting Marcus.

Enver would never forgive himself for not being there to prevent the second.

Satisfied he had Marcus's full attention, he continued. "No more secrets between us. We know the ugliness. Have been through a lot of shit and have the scars to prove it. You get even the slightest inkling you're in some kind of trouble—from anyone, even your neighbor's cat, I don't care—you let me know. You give me the choice from now on. You got that?"

When Marcus remained silent, Enver hit the wood panel next to the patio door, holding his breath for the shock of cold that followed seconds later. Snow rained down, causing Marcus to loudly curse. The shock of cold had the intended effect and Marcus's erection flagged slightly. But that didn't bring a halt to Marcus's string of vicious insults.

"Jesus Christ, you're a sadistic fucker." Marcus laughed around the words, breathing hard as Enver continued to work his fingers in and out. Flecks of water dotted Marcus's skin as the snowflakes melted, glistening in the sunlight rising behind Enver. He sucked in breath after breath, but his erection didn't lose strength again.

"Yeah, I am. Get used to it, 'cause you've unleashed him." Enver surged forward, slashing his mouth over Marcus's in a hard, biting kiss that drew blood. He twisted his finger, loving the way Marcus moaned each time he plunged into the hole again and again, wreaking havoc.

Pleasure rushed through every part of his body as Marcus's muscles clenched around him in shallow, fast pulses as he stimulated ultrasensitive nerve endings.

"We have an understanding now?" Enver was ready to keep Marcus on the edge like this, snow melting between them for as long as necessary.

Marcus dropped his head back against the glass, his eyes going half lidded in a blissed-out state. "Yeah. We do." Marcus's cock stirred again despite the snow that had gotten caught between them. Because of the angle, Enver could see the deep red flushed tip peeking up through the ice crystals. Fascinated with the sight, he brushed some away, exposing a few inches, while still leaving the rest buried beneath the snow.

Sensation play like this could be replicated in Marcus's virtual machine, but elements of the real world had always been missing. Almost there, but never quite the same. No matter how sophisticated Marcus's program became, there was no way it could get the dichotomy of the moment this flawless. The heat of body temperature perfect. The snow. The air. The sunrise.

The desire.

Fueled by the realness of their encounter, no com-plicated computer equipment between them, and the promise hanging in the air between them, Enver drove deeper. Marcus groaned loudly, his muscles relaxing as he accepted Enver's fingers. A surge of need and want tangled with other emotions Enver wasn't afraid of thanks to the man writhing against him. A tighten-ing of every muscle in his body as his desire ratcheted higher with a savagery he couldn't explain.

He gripped Marcus's ass, feeling the muscles bunch and flex as he worked him higher. He knew he could utter a single command that would yank Marcus over the edge. He wanted to weep for the beauty of the man writhing against him. Wanted to roar that this man was his. Utterly and completely his. He wanted to tear at Mar-cus's flesh, get inside him in a way few had. Possess him.

Marcus pushed against Enver's intrusion as much as he could in the position he was in, hips tilting up, quiet curses spilling from his lips in the same cadence at Enver's thrusts. Suddenly, Marcus snarled, his body going still. Enver shoved his fingers deeper, knowing Marcus was about to spill.

Enver could have stopped him, he knew. Could have relentlessly tortured Marcus, edging him over and over while the snow melted between the heat of their bodies. But the need to watch Marcus lose utter control clearly in the light of day was too great.

Marcus shouted, spurting fluid over his chest, ab-domen and the remnants of snow between their bodies as he came. Enver continued to work his fingers, spurring Marcus's orgasm on, drawing it out until Marcus was bucking against him again, dry humping the air.

Marcus shivered against him, but it wasn't because of the cold.

"Sure as hell beats the VR system."

Pink colored Marcus's cheeks, giving him an even more youthful appearance. "Yeah."

Enver glanced down to the mess on Marcus's stomach, thinking how sexy a sight that was. "I'd say I'm sorry, but I'm not."

A slow sinful grin turned up the edge of Marcus's mouth. "Since we both know you're a sadistic son-of-a-bitch—no, you're not."

"Still the sweetest ass in the world."

"Still the biggest cock in the world." A soft huskiness sounded in Marcus's voice as he wiggled his ass against Enver's crotch. "One I want down my throat again. But for fuck's sake, let's go back inside." He squirmed free, darting back into the workshop. By the time Enver followed him inside, he was examining the cast-iron oven with a critical eye. "How the hell do you turn this thing on?"

Enver grabbed a few towels and a heavy blanket from a chest. "May I suggest an alternative means?" He handed a wet washcloth to Marcus before sitting on the ancient couch and draping the blanket over his lap.

"You're wet."

"So are you." Enver waved his finger at Marcus's torso and abdomen, now glistening from where he'd wiped himself down. "Now get over here before I drag you over by your semi-hard dick."

Marcus gestured toward Enver. "Sure your old man lap can handle it?"

Enver growled. "One more comment like that and this *old man* will show you just how much of a sadist he can be."

He dragged Marcus on top of his thighs, tugging the thick blanket so it covered them both. Marcus shivered once, and buried his face against Enver's neck. For a long time, Enver simply sat there with Marcus straddling his lap, enjoying the serenity of the moment.

He'd spent so much time working Marcus over last night he'd exhausted himself in the process. He'd missed that, though he hadn't realized how much until earlier. After a scene with a sub, he'd tend to whatever aftercare they'd required and that was it. He usually walked away with a lot of fond memories and his feelings intact. But the connection he shared with Marcus was something else entirely.

He ran his fingers over Marcus's face, a tightness clenching his chest as he touched the ridges and valleys. The specter of the past Marcus had lived resided in the scars. They were the reason Enver didn't feel the necessity to mark Marcus further despite his words to the contrary last night.

"My best friend wants to meet you."

"The friend test so soon?" Enver thought it best for the moment not to mention the fact Zoie had spent the rest of that night curled up in Enver's arms and cried herself to sleep right there on the same couch because she'd been worried.

Marcus shrugged. "You don't have to if you don't want. Zoie's schedule is a little crazy sometimes, depending on her caseload. She's a cop," he added.

"I know. I can tell she's important to you and meeting her is equally as important, which makes it important to me. Just name the date and time and I'll be there. Now, didn't you say something about my cock and your throat?"

"This spectacular cock?" Marcus nudged the organ in question with his inner thigh. "I believe I did."

"Tell me more," Enver ordered in a harsh voice.

"You know those two veins that run up the underside of your cock?" Enver nodded, watching as Marcus fondled his zipper, drawing it down as he spoke. "I want to lick them. Slowly trace them with my tongue. Use my mouth to suck you until you're hard and beautiful." He parted the flaps, wrapping his fingers around the already hard shaft. "I want to hear you order me to take you deep. Give you so much pleasure I don't know where you stop and I begin."

Enver's muscles tensed as Marcus began to move his hand, the first drops of precome lubricated his palm.

"I want to taste you everywhere. Touch you over and over. I need you in my ass. Digging so deep inside me." He twisted his wrist, speeding the pace. "You tempt me and entice me and inspire me like no one ever has before, Enver."

"Flatterer," Enver managed around a strangled breath, trembling at the depth of emotion shining in the eyes staring back at him.

"Feel like I've been waiting for you forever." Marcus eagerly tugged on Enver's cock. "Nobody makes me feel the way you do. Makes me think the things I do. The dirty, filthy things."

Enver's vision went white as Marcus took him deep into his mouth, sucking him from root to tip in one full, mind-blowing drag.

Chapter Twenty-Five

Marcus shoved his hands into his jacket as he waited outside the restaurant. Since his car had been trashed during the altercation with Davis, and Zoie had taken back the truck he'd fled in, he'd been forced to walk everywhere, take public transit or rely on other people to get him where he needed to go. He could have ducked inside, but he wanted to see who showed up first.

Five minutes later Enver arrived, strolling across the street from where he'd parked looking every bit the man Marcus had fallen in love with.

"You made it," Enver said as he stepped onto the sidewalk.

"Afraid I wasn't going to show up?"

Enver took a drag on his cigarette as he eyed him. "You do have a habit of splitting."

Marcus knew it was said in jest, but he still regretted bailing. No matter how much he assured Enver he was sorry for fucking up, how often he promised Enver he was there to stay, nothing but time would heal the hurt. They'd get past it, he was confident of that.

He recognized Zoie's truck as she pulled into the parking lot. A minute later, she mounted the sidewalk, hugging Marcus as she came close. She released him, then immediately embraced Enver. Marcus covered his amusement as Zoie spoke quietly to Enver. He wondered what they were saying as Enver responded in the same hushed tones. He glanced quizzically at Zoie as she patted him on the chest as she passed and disappeared into the restaurant. Enver squeezed the cherry out of his cigarette, discarded the filter in a nearby ashtray and popped a mint while Marcus wondered what the hell was going on.

"Do you guys secretly know each other?"

"Let's just say we had a long, intimate evening together sitting in front of the fire and discussed the finer points of cunty potatoheads." Enver smirked, leaning over to give Marcus a quick peck. "Quite an interesting woman. Telling me I'm good for you one second, then swearing to cut off my balls if I break your heart the next."

Marcus glared at Enver's back as he stepped into the restaurant. Every time he thought he had his life figured out, something happened to toss him off balance.

A wall of noise hit Marcus in the noisy bar area. Though it was festive, it didn't capture one's attention in the same manner as the lounge at Noble House. At the club, at any moment members could spontaneously start fucking. He had serious doubts that would happen here.

Marcus made his way through the crowd, locating Zoie at the far end of the bar with a cocktail already in her hand. "That kind of night, huh?"

"Hell of a day." She paused long enough to take a long sip.

"Everything all right?"

She waved her hand. "I just need to kick back a few of these, get my rocks off and sleep for three days. In no particular order, of course. Though the fucking would be better while I was still awake." She signaled the bartender for another round. "Or if I had a guy."

Of course, just as Zoie wrapped up her confession Enver arrived, but he didn't seem fazed by her honest statement. Clearly amused, he offered Marcus a beer while he took a sip of his own. "Should only be about ten minutes. Couple of parties haven't cleared out like expected." He paused while they watched Zoie as she pounded the first drink and pulled the second closer. "Is everything all right?"

"She'll be fine. Probably have to drive her home tonight. She's not usually like this," Marcus explained, though he had no idea why he needed to justify his friend's drinking habits. He didn't push for her to elaborate. She either couldn't tell him or chose not to discuss whatever case was dragging her through the mud.

"I get it." Enver touched his chin, turning his focus away from her as she engaged in a conversation with the man beside her. "You care about her. A lot."

"We have a long history." Marcus frowned at Enver's knowing glance. "Not like that. She worked my original case. Went above and beyond her civic duty. Helped me after the trial and our friendship just grew from there. You know, typical straight girl/gay best friend."

"You also share something that I suspect has bonded you even more." Enver pressed his palm to the side of Marcus's face. "I saw the marks on her arms when she came to my workshop. Is she a cutter?"

"Once upon a time." Marcus lowered his voice. "We both attend the same support group. She doesn't talk much about why anymore and that's hers to share, but I suggested she contact Constantine because she's mentioned covering the scars with some elaborate tattoo work."

"You're a good friend for wanting to help." Enver's expression softened. "She deserves ten more drinks in thanks for helping you." He set his hand on Marcus's hip, brought their bodies together so that Marcus felt the tight ridge of his erection. "And you are anything but typical."

Marcus opened for Enver as soon as their lips touched, tongues and teeth scraping together. Emboldened, he slid his hand between their bodies to cup Enver's hard cock. Enver severed the kiss with a soft curse. Marcus simply grinned as he withdrew his hand, snagged his beer and took a long swig. The beer didn't taste as good as Enver. Nothing tasted as good as Enver.

"Fucking-A, you two are hot."

Enver chuckled. "I see she shares your gift with vocabulary."

"What can I say?" Marcus shrugged. "The Padawan learns well."

Enver rolled his eyes. "And your *Star Wars* love too."

Zoie grinned. "Trained in the ways of the Force, he is."

"Dear Lord." Though Enver rubbed the lines between his eyebrows, the amusement sparking in his eyes gave away the truth. Marcus felt a bone-deep possessiveness at the sight, possibly more than ever before. Something fundamental had changed between them in Enver's workshop last week.

He truly did love Enver. The ache burning in his gut signaled that. He'd exposed himself at the workshop. Left himself cold and as naked as their encounter outside the morning after. It had left his soul defenseless as well, but Enver was there to guard it.

The hostess appeared and guided them to their table. Enver excused himself after they'd ordered.

"Holy shit, man." Zoie tapped her fist on the table a few times. "I have to say, I'm jealous."

Marcus gave her a cheesy smile. "You'll have to clarify that envy."

"Him. You. What you have together. For someone you haven't known that long, you've fallen pretty deep already." She leaned back, raising her arms and locking her hands behind her head. "I've seen a few of the guys you've dated, but never anyone like him. I'm proud of you, you know."

"Why's that?"

"You could have taken off. Hid away after all the shit in Sacramento."

"I did," he reminded her.

"But you're with him now. Me. Having dinner. Being…normal."

"I tried to run, but I came back. For him."

Zoie grinned, springing up and coming around the table to embrace him. "It's about damn fucking time. Oh my God, I'm so excited for you." She squealed loud enough to turn a few nearby heads.

Marcus turned serious despite Zoie's exuberance. "He can break me, Zoie. I'm not certain I'll be able to put myself together again when he does. And he will— at some point I'm going to fuck things up again just because that's my nature, and the force that keeps pulling us together is going to shatter us both."

"Yeah." She tilted her head. "You will 'cause that's how love works. But for once, take the risk of getting your heart broken by someone you love. Someone who loves you in return because that's the best damn heart-break of all."

"Sometimes I worry about you, Zoie."

Enver returned to the table, sneaking a kiss with Mar-cus as he sat.

"Monumentally. Not. Fair."

Enver arched an eyebrow in Zoie's direction, elicit-ing a laugh from Marcus. She tossed back the last of her martini, blinking at Enver with glassy eyes. Though he didn't know her well enough to determine if this was a nightly occurrence, Marcus didn't appear bothered by her drinking.

Sometimes a person just needed to let loose.

"You're prettier than he is." Her words came out slurred.

Marcus snorted, smoothing it ineffectively behind his fist. "She's talking about you."

"I think she's talking to the waiter she's waving over for a refill." Enver watched her for a time, concerned for her state. "Sure she's going to be all right?"

"Just needs to forget something. Only does this when jobs get bad, which isn't often. She's got a lot of pent-up frustration she isn't the best at dealing with." Marcus held up a set of keys. "Besides, I've made sure she can't go anywhere without us."

"You guys can stop talking over my head. I'm tipsy, not incapable of talking." She reached over and touched Enver's face, her clumsy fingers brushing against the side of his nose. "Marcus is so lucky."

Her face was suffused with pink, a sign the alcohol was truly getting the best of her. Enver snatched the martini glass from in front of her when she reached for it next. He sniffed, frowning. "It's soda water."

"Mine." She yanked it away, licking her lips as she swallowed the last of the liquid. As their waiter passed, she raised the glass. "Can I get another one of these?"

Marcus eyed the waiter, silently communicating their earlier arrangement. "We know it's water, she doesn't. I had them switch it out when we got the table. I suspect some of this behavior is exhaustion, so the little bit of alcohol she's had is hitting her hard." The food was delivered and the table fell silent as they ate. Conversation started up again about midway through with Marcus picking up the trailing ends of their conversation. "Zoie has a tendency to overwork herself. She's good at her job, but…fiercely dedicated. Doesn't know when to call it quits."

"You're a good friend to her." Enver watched as Zoie pushed the remaining food around on her plate. He signaled for a passing waiter. "Can we get a bag for her food and the check, please?"

"I owe her a lot," Marcus responded after the waiter left.

"Something tells me you'll spend the rest of your life attempting to make it up to her."

"Yeah." Marcus reached over, tangling his fingers with Enver's. "This was nice, thank you. We'll have to do it again when it's a better night for her. She's going to be pissed at herself for drinking herself stupid."

"I can hear you."

Both men fell silent.

"Can't believe how adorable you guys are together. You two ever want to add a dysfunctional female to your sexual adventures, give me a call sometime." She touched Enver's face again. "So. Fucking. Pretty."

"Let's get her home." Enver handed Marcus his keys. "Take my car. I'll follow in her truck. At least she doesn't have her cruiser."

"Can't imagine you in a cop car."

Enver spun the keyring around his finger. "Care for a full-body cavity search?" Zoie chose that exact moment to groan. She slapped her hand over her mouth, her upper body jerking with a few dry heaves. "She throws up in my car, you'll find out how it feels to get dry-fucked outside of your VR machine."

"Promises, promises," Marcus responded with a grin. "If it's all right, I don't think she should be alone tonight. Okay if we take her to my place?"

"Going to stop for a carton and I'll meet you there."

"Fess up. You're upset it isn't her cop car." Marcus spun his finger in a circle. "You wanted to hear the noisy siren go woo-woo."

"Guilty as charged." Enver cut the kiss with Marcus short when Zoie groaned loudly. "Get her home." He slid behind the wheel of Zoie's truck, noting how strange it felt to sit in a vehicle that wasn't his. Despite Marcus's accusation, he was relieved it wasn't Zoie's work vehicle. The last time he'd been in one, he'd been watching EMTs roll his mother into the back of an ambulance. Her assailant had been shoved into the back of another cruiser, his fellow officers shaking their head in disbelief at the level of violence in his mother's injuries.

As he shook off the threads of that night, he pulled out of the lot and thought about the evening. He had instantly liked Zoie, feeling a kinship with her that went above and beyond their mutual connection with Marcus, despite his wariness of cops. She'd been through something in her life that caused her to push so hard at her job. Given the information Marcus had confessed about how they knew each other, Enver didn't doubt that she gave her all to each and every case she was assigned. Zoie was a permanent fixture in Marcus's life, and to love him was to love her as well.

He belatedly realized the light he'd stopped at had turned green at some point. He held up a hand in apology to the car behind him, wondering why they hadn't honked to alert him.

After stopping for a carton, he pulled up to Marcus's house. The driveway was empty and the house was still dark. Odd. Marcus should have beaten him here by ten minutes. Unless, of course, he'd needed to stop while Zoie dumped the contents of her stomach on the side of the road. Ah, youth. He'd had a few of those benders under his belt when he'd been that age.

Once inside, he settled on the couch and kicked back, turning on the television for some background noise while he waited.

Chapter Twenty-Six

"Think I'm gonna barf." Zoie followed the statement with a groan as she fidgeted in the passenger seat.

Marcus pulled the car into a parking lot, and killed the engine. When he glanced over and saw Zoie was clutching her stomach and mouth, he leaned over and pushed the door open. Enver would have his ass if his spotless interior was coated with a layer of vomit.

"Out," he ordered, pushing on her shoulder to aim her a different direction.

She groaned again as she leaned to the side. Seconds later, her body gave a sudden lurch. He winced, setting a hand on her back and rubbing small circles to soothe her. Best thing was just to let her get it out.

Zoie moaned as she dragged herself upright and slumped against the bench seat. "Oh God. I think I'm gonna die." She winced as she wiped her mouth with the back of her hand.

Marcus fired up the engine again, pulling back out onto the deserted street. "Promise you're going to live. Won't like it much for the next twelve hours or so, but you'll survive."

"He loves you."

The seatbelt suddenly felt too tight against his chest.

He tugged, realizing it wasn't the restraint at all, but a heavy feeling right in the center. As he turned onto Main, the line of stores dark because of the late hour, he decided to downplay her statement. "Alcohol's talking, Zo."

"I'm drunk, not blind." Her head rolled to the side, her tongue darting between her lips as she stuck it out at him. "Neither are you, because you love him too. I've known you a long time, Marcus. Never seen you this head over ass about someone, and I don't want you to lose something so good for you." She gave him a sleepy smile. "You deserve it."

"I know. I've thought about—holy shit!" Marcus swerved to avoid a car that had appeared from nowhere. He overcorrected, feeling the backend of the heavy vehicle start to fishtail. He jerked the wheel in the other direction, realizing too late that they were headed right for one of the storefronts.

Marcus jammed on the brakes, the pedal connecting with the floorboard as the system failed. They vaulted the curb and an instant later smashed through a bench on the sidewalk, followed by a sickening thud as the car slammed into the building and came to an abrupt halt.

He blinked, trying to process what had just happened. He took immediate stock, noting a few bruises and scrapes, but no significant damage as he disengaged his seatbelt. "You okay, Zoie?"

"Yeah." She coughed once, tugged off her seatbelt and threw up all over Enver's once-pristine dashboard.

He tried the door, but it was pinned by a large metal trashcan he'd sideswiped. "Going to make sure I didn't hit anyone. Sure you're okay?" After she nodded, he pulled himself through the window, noting the starburst pattern on the windshield where it had cracked from the force of the crash.

As he stepped away from the ruined car, he noticed he'd destroyed the ancient bench outside Three Mile Bookstore. The right front of Enver's car was folded accordion style thanks to the solid brick storefront. Steam and smoke billowed from the busted radiator.

"He's going to kill me." Marcus whistled as he continued to tally the rest of the damages. Shattered headlights. Crumpled front quarter panel. Crushed steel bumper. The list went on. Thankfully, the sturdily built car looked to have sustained the brunt of the damage, which had saved them from more significant injuries.

"You all right, buddy?"

"I think so." Marcus started to turn toward the voice, but felt a sharp jab in his neck. "What the—" Everything immediately whirled before his eyes, a pinwheel of shapes and colors. He stumbled, a strong hand capturing his.

"Easy there."

"I don't feel good." As the shadowed figure stepped into the puddle of light cast from the nearby streetlight, Marcus went down on one knee. The last thing he saw was Davis Connelly's maniacal grin.

Golden sunlight and unfamiliar voices caused Enver to wince as he surfaced from sleep. He must have left his light-blocking blinds open before falling asleep. Moving to stretch, he realized he wasn't in his bed. Rubbing at his eyes, he groaned as he sat up, his back protesting loudly with a sharp twinge right down his spine. His vision took a few seconds to adjust, but when it cleared he realized the television was the source of the noise.

Someone screamed as the camera panned up to show a tornado chewing up the ground.

The room fell silent as he shut off the action movie. Looking around, he realized this wasn't his living room, or even his house. Marcus. He was in Marcus's house. He'd fallen asleep on the couch waiting for Marcus and Zoie to arrive. He must have been so out of it they hadn't wanted to wake him.

Enver stood, shrugging off his jacket, suddenly feeling overheated. He prepped a pot of coffee, knowing they would all need some fuel. Enver made his way to the bedroom, noting the closed door of the second bedroom where Zoie was probably sleeping off the last of her bender. She wouldn't want anything to eat, but they'd force some water and protein into her.

First, he needed a shower. And maybe a little alone time with Marcus. They'd hadn't yet explored the power exchange aspect of their relationship to full capacity outside of the virtual reality world, and he was looking forward to uttering commands that would bring Marcus to his knees.

Marcus's bedroom was empty as Enver glanced in. The bed was a tangle of sheets, but Enver knew that didn't mean anything as Marcus never made the bed. He listened for the sound of the shower, noting only the still silence that indicated he was alone. A check through the other rooms showed they were just as empty.

Worry started to churn his empty stomach. He snatched his coat off the couch as he passed, glancing through the front window, frowning when he saw the driveway was empty. Zoie's truck sat at the curb where he'd parked it.

"Shit."

How could he have been irresponsible enough to fall asleep before they'd arrived? He glanced at his cell phone, blowing out a relieved breath when he saw a message from Marcus. When he swiped the screen to accept, there was no text, but instead an image that stole his breath, clenched a tight fist of panic around his heart and made his vision sheet red.

Zoie was bound and gagged, mascara streaked in thick trails down her cheeks. Panic shone clearly in her eyes as she stared directly at the camera. Beside her, Marcus was bound and gagged as well, his eyes closed and his face relaxed in unconsciousness. His wrists were chained to a column that held him upright.

The timestamp indicated the image had been sent two hours ago.

Enver already had the phone to his ear as he snapped up Zoie's car keys and ran out the door. He didn't know who had taken the picture, but he could easily guess Davis was responsible. The bastard had taken them both in one shot. The information Zoie had been fed about Davis's death had been bogus. Another instance of corruption that deepened Enver's apprehension of the law and those who said they upheld it.

Too goddamn easy.

Enver should have never let Marcus drive home alone. He should have just piled everyone into Zoie's truck when they'd left the restaurant and retrieved his car the next day. Simple. He would report the situation to the authorities, but his first priority was getting to Marcus and Zoie, not filling out a pile of paperwork or answering a shit-ton of questions.

The horrific image spoke for how little time he had to locate them. Every second counted.

"Better be good, Enver." Saint's voice was husky, as though he'd been awakened or had been in the middle of something. Like fucking his wife or husband. Perhaps both. Enver didn't care if Saint had been screwing the governor of California—he needed some dependable geek power. And he needed it fast.

"Can you track a cell phone? Find out its current location or where it was when a message was sent?"

"Sure. How many laws am I going to break?"

The knot around Enver's heart tightened. He hated vocalizing his worse fear. "Marcus and his best friend have been kidnapped."

"Kochran's place." All traces of huskiness had vanished from Saint's voice. "Fifteen minutes."

Chapter Twenty-Seven

"Wakey, wakey."

The gentle crooning was as melodious as a lullaby. In half consciousness, painful tension pulled at Marcus's shoulders and upper back. A hard pressure wrapped his wrists, and through his hazy vision, he spotted the dull glint of metal.

For a few confusing minutes, he assumed Enver was retaliating for his wrecked car and had bound him to make good on that threat about dry fucking him. But then the horrific memories of the accident and the seconds afterward rushed in and brought him to full consciousness like a cold spike shoved through the top of his head.

"Time to rise and shine."

Marcus heard the layer of hatred under the words that sent ice skittering down his spine. He lifted his head, his gaze meeting the madman who had irrevocably altered his life.

"Ah, there you are." Davis tilted his head as though examining Marcus. "Better if you're awake for this next part."

A lash struck the center of Marcus's back. He screamed as fire erupted in a trail from neck to waist.

Hooked with barbed tips, the lash took his flesh with it when it was yanked away. As it struck again and again, Marcus tried on concentrate on their surroundings to give his brain something else to focus on. There was nothing he recognized because the lighting was low, but he could make out basic architecture indicative of a house.

"You made me this way." Davis's voice stayed whisper-soft as he walked around Marcus in a circle. "You turned me into a horrifying monster."

He heard movement as Davis drew his arm back for another strike. He tried to stay relaxed as the fiery lash came again, just inches away from the first, but the pain was overwhelming. More flesh peeled off his back in strips. Pain jolted through his body, subsequent strikes merging into one vibrating field of pain. Unlike the adrenaline rush that came with introducing pain play during a scene, the pure, raw, unbelievable agony almost caused him to pass out a few times. But Davis knew when to pull back, when to draw out his torture. Under different circumstances, he would have been revered as an exceptional sadist at Noble House.

The intense pain overrode Marcus's fear so the only thing that was left was anger. Davis didn't deserve his anxiety anymore. He tried not to think about Enver, about how much he loved him because he didn't want to taint what they shared, but the memories of their time together were the only thing keeping Marcus tethered to consciousness.

The lashes stopped, finally, and thirty tension-filled seconds passed before Davis spoke again. "You'll be dead shortly, because I'm going to finish the job I started ten years ago. I would have finished it that night in the parking lot, but this stupid bitch and her cavalry interrupted us. That's twice you won, cunt. It won't happen again."

Zoie only grunted in response.

"They'll throw you back in jail," Marcus managed weakly, pressing his cheek against the column as though it would give him strength.

"Don't you understand? I'm going to kill us all," Davis said impassively, the corner of one side of his mouth lifting.

Marcus had never seen such abject evil staring at him. Ten years ago, during the initial attack, youth had dominated Davis's features. The man staring at him now was a monster far larger than the body housing it. The distorted facial expressions were an obscene aberration of hell on Earth. Above all, Marcus believed Davis's vow to kill.

The truth of the situation tightened cold hands around Marcus's guts. He snarled and pulled at the chains with as much force as he could muster. He was not going to die here. Not today. He shouted, trying to get through to Zoie. Warn her. He fought with the chains, feeling his skin tear underneath the rough metal, but the lingering effects of the drug and the blood loss made him dizzy. The smell of his own blood, the sickening pain of the wound across his shoulders, back and wrists made him nauseous.

He refused to pass out.

It was impossible to control his thoughts as Enver raced toward Kochran's house, breaking every California traffic law by taking advantage of the fact he was driving a truck with a turbo engine. Terror and fear warred with desperation. He wasn't the type to automatically assume the worst while hoping for the best, but the images from the text had been burned into his brain.

"Shouldn't have left him alone."

He slammed his hand against the wheel, grinding his teeth as he sped around a sharp curve. Damn them all for letting their guard down. Logic told him Davis would have kidnapped Marcus without the elaborate misdirection. But at least he would have been there with them. Maybe been able to stop it.

Or put his hands around Davis's throat and personally choked the life from him.

His headlights splashed against the stone walls of Noble House as he turned down the dirt road leading to Kochran's place. A pang clenched his gut as he passed the club, a reminder of all the memories stuffed inside the walls.

About a half mile from the club, he parked alongside a row of cars at the perimeter of a field, noting Saint had already arrived. Field grass swayed in the light breeze, a soft rustling of sound as Enver made his way down the path. The door to Kochran's hidden house opened as he approached, a sign somewhere along the way, security cameras had been installed and he was being watched. He descended the long, circular staircase of the converted missile silo, forcing himself not to race down the stairs lest he break his neck.

Voices on the second to last floor prevented him from going all the way to the bottom where Kochran's living space was. He found a knot of people hunched over, working diligently with the computer screen's glow lighting their concerned faces. No one spared him a glance as he joined Kochran and Boyce off to one side.

"Any luck?"

Kochran set his hand on Enver's shoulder and squeezed. "Nothing yet. Ezra and Saint are listening to the police scanners, looking for any usual activity. You were pretty insistent about keeping the cops out of this. You sure about that?"

Enver nodded. "It's obvious Zoie was fed bogus intel. No way to know who to trust at this point. I appreciate the concern, but let's just keep it with us for now. Things get too hot, we'll bring them in."

"Act first, ask for forgiveness later. Got it. Maddy fired up her masked unit and is trying to run a trace."

"Going to be hard if he turned off the phone after sending the images," Maddy tossed over her shoulder. "Not impossible to track a cell that's shut down, but it'll take some work."

"Have you tried searching cell towers?" Saint stretched out his fingers for a split second before continuing.

"Working on that right now." She fell quiet for a few moments, her focus shifting to the task.

Enver noticed a few red marks above the collar of her shirt. A pang of regret stabbed at him. He'd obviously interrupted a private moment, but he hadn't known who else to call.

"Mothertrucker," Maddy swore loudly. "Signals bouncing all over the place. I can't get a good lock."

Enver didn't want to consider what that meant. His fingers itched to do something—anything—but the computer experts were already hard at work. He'd just be in the way.

"Let's get everyone some fuel," Boyce offered as he tapped Enver on the arm. "Watched pot never boils and all that. Come on."

Enver gratefully accepted the escape and followed Boyce downstairs to the kitchen. Boyce headed straight for the pot and went about making coffee.

A sense of fragility and uncertainty swamped Enver, causing his knees to weaken and his heart to hammer solidly against his rib cage. He stumbled to the table, clutching the edge of it, slowly lowering himself into the seat as he tried to keep his breathing calm and even, tried his damnedest not to freak out. Thought he'd succeeded until a sheen of cold sweat erupted across his forehead and his hands started to shake. He pressed his fingers against the table, using the force in an effort to quell the trembling. A wave of emotion crashed against him as powerful as a tsunami colliding with the shoreline.

A glass filled with several fingers of amber liquid slid between his splayed hands. "Take the edge off."

Enver downed the entire contents without a second thought. The burn down his throat stole his breath and broke through the sense of utter defeat threatening to drown him. "Thanks." He hated the fact his voice broke and paused until he was certain he had everything under control again. "Thank you, Boyce. I'm just…out of sorts."

"Long as you don't beat yourself up about it. Happens again, let me know. Love to put a few dents in Kochran's top-shelf bourbon. Alcohol isn't the best thing for a panic attack, but this isn't exactly normal." Boyce tapped the table, his gaze searching Enver's. "Need a few more minutes?"

"No, I'm good." Feeling more settled, Enver rose and set the empty glass in the sink. "I'm just…helpless." A twinge of panic started to creep in again, but he muscled it back, determined he was not going to succumb to another wave of panic. Instead, he fell into the simple task of preparing several carafes full of coffee for the crew working upstairs while Boyce starting pulling together items from the fridge for sandwiches.

In a few minutes, they had a hearty spread that they started stacking on several trays Boyce found in one of the cabinets. Pleased with their efforts, they hefted the trays and were halfway up the stairs when a surge of yells erupted on the next level.

Grae appeared, her green eyes wild as she tried to snatch the tray from Enver. "Maddy found them in Richvale. Small farming community about two hours north of here. House was recently purchased by a bogus corporation." She muscled the tray away from him, shooing him as she passed. "Go. I've got this." When he hesitated, she narrowed her eyes. "I'm pregnant, Enver, my arms and legs aren't broken. Go. Now."

"Text me the address," he demanded over his shoulder as he passed the flurry of activity.

Any sort of rational thought about contacting the local authorities like he'd promised Kochran never even crossed his mind as he vaulted the stairs, taking them three at a time. His priority was to find the house and stop a madman.

He sped up as he neared the door, bursting through it at a full run. A distant storm splashed lightning across the horizon as he reached the truck. He cursed the fact Zoie hadn't driven her cruiser last night. He would have looked forward to hearing that noisy siren go *woo-woo* after all.

Everything inside Marcus went cold as Davis touched Zoie on the top of her head. She yelled, jerking away from his touch. But with her restricted movement, there was only so far that she could go.

"Do you have any idea how hard it was to decide who to take out first? The high school teacher who flaunted his immoral lifestyle on his students, or the rookie bitch who couldn't leave well enough alone?" Davis crouched, touching Zoie on the shoulder. She growled at him, but the noise only seemed to feed Davis's hatred. "I had to be patient. So, so patient. Prison taught me that. Taught me how to use that time wisely to plan. But when I saw you together that night in Sacramento, I almost fucked up. I listened to Jeff's taunts that I should kill Marcus right then and there. But that wasn't part of the plan. So he had to go first. Then I could focus on what really mattered."

"You killed him." The knowledge was like a lead weight in Marcus's stomach. Lighting flickered outside, splashing everything white for a split second. A loud boom followed several minutes later.

"No," Davis insisted with a shake of his head. "I set him free. Just as I'm going to do with both of you."

He touched the side of Zoie's face with an almost tender caress.

Consciousness seemed to fully take hold of her then. She screamed, bucking and pulling at the chains wrapped around her body. The noise twisted Davis's face into a mask of something Marcus's couldn't recognize.

"You are just as vile as he is. Filthy. Disgusting." Davis backhanded Zoie, her head jerking to the side as she absorbed the blow.

"Leave her alone, Davis. It's me you want."

"This repulsive gash kept me away from my family."

"You dug your own grave, asshole." Zoie spit blood,

growling softly. "Be a man and own your shit. You're going back to prison, you know that, right? Or maybe playing with the boys again is what you want."

"Shut up, bitch."

But Marcus knew that Zoie wasn't going to be swayed.

"I saw your files." She lowered her voice. "Your parole officer was more than happy to share your records with me when they were trying to find you. You're not telling Marcus the whole story. The same one I didn't tell him to spare him the details about what you've been up to. Seems like you made a special friend a few months after your sentence. Ink was barely dry on the paperwork and Dante Esposito had already made you his bitch."

"I said shut *up*." Davis reeled back with his fist, but Zoie tipped herself over so he instead connected hard with the column she was still secured to. His howl of pain echoed through the empty house. He shifted, turning so he was at a better angle to where she was now writhing on the floor in an effort to get away.

Zoie grunted when Davis's foot connected with her midsection.

"Stop!" Marcus shouted, desperation racing through his blood stream. "Leave her alone, Davis. I know what you're going through. You're confused. Maybe scared and angry too. I can help you with your feelings. I can help you sort it out."

Davis looked up, his body strung tight and clearly ready to continue the beating. "Can you make me straight? Fix me so I don't want a guy's dick shoved up my ass?"

Marcus closed his eyes for a moment, convinced the situation couldn't get any worse.

"You don't need to be fixed, Davis. Just let Zoie go and I'll stay. I'll help you." Marcus's blood ran cold when he noticed a shadow darkening the doorway behind Davis's shoulder. He'd been wrong.

This whole scenario could get monumentally worse.

A flash of lightning from the approaching storm illuminated the planes of Enver's face. Marcus needed to keep Davis talking because damn it if he was going to let this fuckwad get the better of him again. Enver may have promised to keep him safe, but Marcus had brought this all down on all of their heads. He couldn't live knowing he'd been the one responsible for any more death and destruction.

He risked a glance directly at Enver as he approached, but the older man just held his stare, clearly ignoring Marcus's silent pleas to go away. *Fuck. Fuck. Fuck.* He recognized that determined set of Enver's eyes. Knew there was nothing he could say or do that would sway Enver's mission. Maybe he could distract Davis. Give Enver some kind of advantage.

"Please let me help you, Davis." Marcus turned his focus solely on his attacker. "There are programs out there to help you deal with whatever emotions you're trying to deal with. They'll even help you accept yourself."

"I will never accept this." Davis gave an inhumane howl as a boom of thunder split the air. "I need to be fixed. Make it so I'm not an abomination like you. Some freak. You need release, Marcus. Release from the ugly monster that makes you angry about the way you are."

Davis was projecting, but as long as it kept his attention on Marcus, he wouldn't notice Enver slowly creeping up behind him.

"Do it," Marcus urged. "End this all for us right now so we can be free of our pain."

"No," Enver snapped with thunderous force. "You know better than to give orders, gorgeous."

Son of a mother-lovin' bitch.

He should have known Enver wasn't going to make this easy. The sick wave of nausea swelled, but he did not have time for this shit. A new sort of panic expanded inside Marcus, worse than everything he'd experienced with the initial attack and the beating weeks ago. That had all just been him. Davis couldn't kill Enver or Zoie—Marcus wouldn't allow it.

Davis spun, clearly unsurprised to find they had a guest. He spit on the floor, growling at Enver. "You're both disgusting creatures."

"That's where you're wrong," Enver countered. "We're normal, average people who wash dishes, mow the lawn, yell at the television during Monday Night Football." Enver's fury-laced gaze cut to Marcus for a split second. "We have careers and wake up next to each other."

Davis balled his hands into tight fists that shook from the force of his contained rage. "You fuck him."

"I do. Quite well, I might add. He's there for me just like I'm there for him. We love each other and there isn't anything you or anyone else can do to keep us apart." For a split second, Enver and Marcus were the only ones in the room.

Then Davis began to laugh maniacally and brought the horror of the situation back into focus.

Listening to Marcus negotiate with a madman had stilled Enver's heart, turned his stomach inside out.

But he recognized the technique. Marcus had been desperately trying to save the unredeemable. Davis aimed his unholy gaze directly at Enver. Good. If his focus wasn't on Marcus, he couldn't do any more damage.

Marcus wrenched at his bonds, metal scraping over stone. Any other time, that kind of sound would have been music to Enver's ears.

Davis shot Marcus a stony glare. "Give up trying to escape, you pathetic excuse for a human. I knew he would find us. I didn't make it hard to find us because I wanted him to come. I'm going to eliminate him too."

With Davis distracted, Enver lunged, ramming into him with so much force they tumbled over the back of a sofa. They fell in a tangle of arms and legs. Davis rolled to his feet, spread his legs wide and tackled Enver before he stood upright.

Enver kicked out, blocking a punch. Undeterred, Davis came at Enver with a second blow, this one landing squarely on the jaw. Pain doubled Enver's vision, but he shoved his elbow into Davis's stomach, effectively pushing the other man away.

Davis stumbled, went to one knee, and sprang back up to slam his body into Enver's. Both men fell hard to the floor, the pitifully thin carpet absorbing none of the shock. Enver rolled up, his back connecting hard with the column Marcus was chained to. Enver started to turn toward him, but a chilling scream wrenched his attention back to Davis.

He'd gotten Zoie in a chokehold, her pretty face a mask of terror now as he severed her air supply. Enver roared to life, using the animalistic sound to propel him forward. He aimed for Davis, but with his hold, Enver knew he was going to take them both down. No help for

it. He drove into Davis with all the force he could muster, driving his fist hard into the attacker's chest. Zoie
rolled off at an angle, breaking free of the strong grip.

Davis's breath came in short, wheezing gasps as he
tried to get in a lungful of air. Enver struck, punching
the man hard in the kidney. Davis stumbled, flailing
his arms out to retaliate, but Enver followed with an
uppercut that caused his eyes to roll back.

Hours of pent-up fury propelled Enver to yank Davis's shirt collar to keep him from falling to the ground.
The man swayed, but stayed upright thanks to Enver's
forceful grip. Enver drove his knee hard into the asshole's groin once. Again. Once more just because it was
so damn satisfying to feel and hear.

Enver landed another uppercut. Then another, the
shocks of pain fueling his rage to hit harder and stron-
ger. There was no finesse to the blows, nothing but brute
strength as he pounded on the man who had tried to
take so much from him.

"Stop, stop!" Zoie's desperate, hoarse plea broke
through the haze. "Killing him won't make him pay. It's
too good for him." She coughed a few times. "Too easy."

"I'm not, but he deserves to pay for trying to take
you both away." Enver drew back his fist to strike again.

"Enver, stop." The raspy plea from Marcus was the
only thing that prevented Enver's fist from making contact again.

Alarmed, Enver looked over to see the clear gaze of
his lover through swollen eyes. Enver growled, knowing that if he went too far, Marcus would never forgive
him. He wouldn't be able to forgive himself either.

He tugged Davis closer, putting their faces inches
apart. He shook him a few times to guarantee he had

his full attention. "I will do everything I can to make certain you are put in a cell with the most sadistic son of a bitch at the prison, who is going to make your life a living hell."

Despite his better judgment, Enver released Davis and stepped away. He started toward Marcus, but he waved Enver off with a jerk of his head. "Check on Zoie first. I'm all right."

Everything inside him called to Marcus, but he knew his lover would just argue with him to tend to his best friend. The last thing any of them needed was more tension. Enver crouched beside her. "Thank you," he said quietly.

Zoie said nothing in response, clearly understanding the meaning of Enver's appreciation.

"You gonna be okay?" he asked as he freed her.

She nodded, licking her lip. "I will be in a few. Go. I'll take care of Davis." She waved him off as she rolled to her back, sprawling out as she inhaled and exhaled a few times. "Need to contact dispatch."

He handed over his phone. "Call it in." Thankfully, she didn't mention the fact that he should have called it in himself instead of blowing through like Hurricane Enver. He'd made a promise and the cops would have just gotten in his way.

Enver crossed to Marcus, his heart nearly stopping when he finally spotted the damage done to his back. More scarring he'd have to live with for the rest of his life. At least he wouldn't have to look at those marks every minute of the day. Instead, Enver vowed to kiss every single one of them for the rest of *his* life in order to alleviate the painful reminders. He dug out the key he'd confiscated from Davis, but something else needed his attention first.

He stepped against Marcus, finally breathing easy for the first time since he'd discovered Marcus and Zoie had never made it to the house. Marcus leaned his forehead against Enver's shoulder and exhaled. Enver held him, careful of the fresh wounds as he popped the lock.

"I need to sit down," Marcus insisted breathlessly. "I'm going to be sick."

Enver guided him to the floor, giving him support as he groaned. A sudden commotion over his shoulder had him glancing back. The sight that greeted him stopped his heart. Davis had tossed Zoie off and was struggling to stand.

"He's got a gun!" Zoie yelled.

Enver threw himself over Marcus, turning his face just as a shot was fired. A hot streak of pain erupted across his back as the noise of someone fighting battled with the sudden ringing in his ears.

Another shot echoed through the space, and everything fell silent.

A few seconds later something surged underneath him and he realized he was crushing Marcus. He tried to move, but found his arms and legs were sluggish. Fuck, he hurt everywhere. Sick waves of pain ebbed and flowed through him. He finally managed to roll off, grunting as he sprawled on his back and stared at the ceiling. He told himself not being able to feel the floor under him wasn't a bad thing.

Marcus's face appeared overhead. "You shouldn't have come."

"Don't make me slap you." Enver's head lolled to the side as he tried to see if Zoie was all right. "Need to help Zoie. Davis is going to hurt her too." Gray edged his vision, taking up more and more of his eyesight.

"Zoie's fine. She turned the gun on him."

Enver felt a chill moving through his shoulders and back, radiating around to his chest.

"Enver. Enver!"

He blinked, but couldn't focus.

"Don't die on me, you fucker."

"Won't." Despite the hazy vision, Enver saw Marcus's face was wet with tears. He tried not to think about what that meant. Instead, he focused on something happier. "Who else is going to marry your stubborn, geeky ass?"

Shock registered in Marcus's eyes. An instant later, Enver passed out.

Chapter Twenty-Eight

Three days later, heart still in his throat, Marcus couldn't stop pacing.

"You're going to wear a pattern into the linoleum." Enver growled when Marcus paused, shot both his middle fingers toward the bed and continued. Enver grumbled a few more times as Marcus made a full circuit of the room.

Marcus didn't care. He hadn't been able to sit still since they'd arrived at the hospital. Too much pent-up energy. Too much worry about things he had no control over. Too many what-ifs playing over and over in his head. Thanks to Zoie's quick actions, Davis was no longer a threat to anyone. He truly was dead now. But that didn't make this whole situation any easier.

Of course, Enver had been Mr. Calm and Cool the whole time, insisting he was perfectly fine and didn't need medical attention as they'd been loading him into the back of an ambulance.

As Marcus shoved his way into the ambulance, he'd snapped at Enver to be quiet, which had promptly shut the obstinate Dom up.

A nurse appeared in the doorway, and Marcus's heart leapt into his throat. "Did you need something, Mr. Furst?"

Enver pointed to Marcus, a scowl darkening his features. "Give him those sedatives you keep trying to shove down my throat every four hours."

She smiled as she noted Enver's vitals on a slip of paper she'd removed from her pocket.

"How is he?" Marcus asked, trying not to let his anxiety show. The nurse's glare signaled he was doing a piss-poor job.

"Perfectly fine, just as I told you two hours ago. And two hours before that." She folded her arms over her generous midsection, looking every bit the authority figure. "You know, the cafeteria is serving chicken noodle soup today as the special. It's one of the more popular menu items. You should give it a try." She huffed at his scowl and drew herself up to her full height, which was several inches above Marcus's. "Strapping young boy like yourself needs to keep his strength up."

Marcus recognized the not-so-subtle order to get out of the room. "I'll be back in a little bit." His stomach growled as he realized he hadn't eaten today. He'd been too busy worried about Enver to consider the need for food.

As he made his way to the first floor, he remembered pacing the halls as Enver had been in surgery. Remembered the terror that had nearly choked him every time the doors to the surgical ward had opened. Davis had gotten in a clean shot, so the bullet had still ended up lodged in Enver's upper back just inches from his spine. The skilled doctors had been able to remove the slug with minimal damage, allowing the wound to heal cleanly with little scarring.

Marcus's phone rang and he drew it out of his pocket right away, worried something had happened in the few minutes he'd been gone. He was already making his way back to the elevator bank when he saw who it was.

"Hey, cupcake." He relaxed, slowing his pace and detoured away from the elevators. "How are you feeling?"

"Marginally human again thanks to several scalding hot showers and my marvelous room-darkening blinds." She yawned, the sound of sheets rustling coming over the speaker. "I may even leave the house today."

Marcus smiled. He already owed Zoie his thanks for ten years' worth of guidance and friendship, but now he knew he could never repay her for being the one to save Enver's life. Without her quick thinking, the bullet could have hit dead center and made mincemeat out of Enver's insides. Then he'd be pacing the halls of a funeral home instead.

"How's your man?" she asked around another yawn.

"Grumbly as ever. Doctors say he should be able to go home soon." Marcus leaned against a wall and noticed he was outside the hospital chapel.

"Best place for him to recover is at home and being cared for by the love of his life. Think of all the sponge baths." She groaned. "Wait, scratch that, now I'm thinking of them."

"Need a nurse of your own?"

"No. I'm thinking about the two of you," she mumbled. "Monumentally not fair."

"I'm sure that could be arranged when Enver is feeling better." Marcus smiled again as she swore loudly. Teasing her was a cherished moment. If things with Davis had taken a different turn…

"Now that *that* image is burned into my brain, how are you, Marcus? Really?"

He let his guard down because it was Zoie. At least

partially. "Barely holding it together. But I'll be all right. Each day gets better as he does."

"That's not what I meant."

"I know." Marcus paused. "As strange as it sounds, it helped me get closure. Davis won't be able to hurt anyone else. I never wished for him to die even though I hated him for everything he did to me, but—"

"I get it," she interrupted. "No reason to explain the details. You're not going to flake out of group now that this is all over, are you?"

"Fuck no." Just because Davis was dead didn't mean the process of healing from the original attack was over. He was certain he'd get better a little each day, but also convinced it would always hang over him.

"I'm glad he's okay. That you're going to be okay, too. You deserve it. And him. We should all be so lucky." She cleared her throat, clearly caught up in the emotion of the moment. "I need to go. Call in so I can let Sarge know when I'm coming back to work. I'll stop by the hospital tomorrow on my way in."

"Don't rush it, okay?" Marcus knew she would. Zoie's personality wouldn't allow her to sit for too long on one thing. She needed to feel useful and productive. Do something with her hands or she became restless. "Could always take another few days and come give Enver a few of those sponge baths."

"Fucker." She laughed. "I love you."

Marcus eyed the chapel doors as he ended the call with Zoie, walking forward and entering the room. Couldn't hurt to say a few more prayers.

The soft knock on the door caused Enver to tense for a split second. He hated that sensation. Though he knew it would go away eventually, that uneasy feeling kept him on edge. Now he was the one looking over his shoulder.

"Come in." He cleared his throat, tried again.

Zoie peeked in. "Not interrupting you guys, am I?"

He gestured her forward as he readjusted the angle of the bed. "I was just enjoying a few moments of peace and quiet."

She snapped her fingers as she stepped inside. "Well, damn, I must have missed the orgy."

"That was at three." He glanced to the display on the muted television set. "But if you stick around, I'm sure I can call a few friends who would be really happy to put on a show for you."

Her bright peal of laughter was just the medicine he needed. As much as he loved Marcus, the man had gotten downright morose since Enver had taken the bullet. Marcus had finally conceded to going home the night before, after a rousing argument that had left Enver exhausted. Something was still off that he couldn't put his finger on.

She set her hand over his. "You look tired."

"They keep waking me up every few hours to poke and prod at me. Makes no damn sense 'cause all they keep telling me is to get some rest. Ready to get out of here," he added with a heavy sigh.

She shook her head. "Surprised they haven't discharged you yet."

"Supposed to break out of here tomorrow. Be nice to sleep in my own bed." Eat whenever he wanted. Shit whenever he felt like it instead of when they told him to in those absurdly tiny cups they kept bringing.

"Marcus actually left you alone for a few minutes?"

Not without a struggle. "I managed to convince

him to go home to sleep, take a shower and get a fresh change of clothes. Pretty sure the nurses were ready to throw him out if he didn't leave. He went, but reluctantly. First night of good sleep I've managed since they checked me in." As much as he hated to admit, it was the truth.

Her eyebrows drew together. "I'm monopolizing your alone time. I'll stop by when you're settled at home."

He caught her hand, tugging her back to the bed when she tried to leave. "Sit." He put force behind the single word, knowing she could be just as stubborn as her best friend and would need the push.

"Well." She blinked, bright spots of color dotting her cheeks as she sat. "Certainly didn't affect that part of your personality, did it?"

He gave her a wicked grin that made her blush deepen. "I need you to do something for me."

"As long as it's not connected to that look you're giving me," she challenged, skepticism ripe in her tone. "The one I'm sure has made countless lovers throw themselves at your feet."

"Stop blaming yourself." He waited a beat before continuing. "I've only met you a few times, but that's long enough to let me know how you feel about Marcus. How much you love him. To know you would do anything for him."

She angled her chin up, her expression growing hard. "I fucked up, Enver. Big time."

"No," he corrected. "You were trying to help a friend."

She deflated before his eyes, but he wrapped his fingers through hers to give her strength she desperately needed. "I should have...done better. For both of you. I missed the drone purchase when I was digging through his finances. Everything. I should have looked into how he got information before his release, but I caught another case and got—that's just an excuse. I got fed bad intel. Rookie fucking mistake. Followed it through just like I knew I shouldn't have and I believed every word I was told."

"Like he knew you would. I don't believe Davis Connelly was a stupid man, Zoie. I think he spent years in that jail cell plotting and calculating every possible scenario. There is no way you could have predicted how dedicated he was. Predicted the lengths he was prepared to go to in order to follow through."

"It's my job to." Tears spilled over and tracked down her cheeks. "It makes me…gah. I feel like such a tool. A stupid rookie tool who doesn't know her ass from her badge. I failed Marcus on a monumental level. Both as a cop and as his friend. Hell, I don't even deserve to be called that anymore."

"Oh, honey. That can't be further from the truth. Right now you've got so much guilt and frustration filling you up that I can almost see it leeching from your pores. You sacrificed a big chunk of your life to dedicate it to helping others." He gripped her hand tighter, commanding her attention with the gesture. "But I also see a strong, vibrant young woman who is willing to work her fingers to the bone, no matter how tough the job, in order to do her best. I see a woman who not only saved the man I love, but who also saved herself. Focus on that, 'cause I'm not going anywhere anytime soon."

"Neither am I," Marcus added as he stepped into the room.

Enver's heart seized for a split second the way it did

each time he saw Marcus. That sensation would never get old, and he was grateful he was still around to experience it. Zoie tugged on his hand to let go, but he held strong, unwilling to let her go just yet. "So, what do you say, cunty potatohead?"

She giggled at the nickname, squeezing Enver's hand. "Guess I'm stuck with you guys if you're going to tie me down and force me."

"I think there's a little kink underneath all that Zoie-vanilla." He burst out laughing at the horrified expression she shot his way, leaning forward to poke her in the side. A shooting pain erupted across his back and down his shoulders, reminding him why he was in the hospital in the first place. "Ah, that was a bad move."

Marcus's face grew tight with concern as he stepped toward the bed. "You all right?"

"Yeah, just moved too fast." His stomach gurgled, bile stacking up into his throat. No matter how many times he tried, he couldn't swallow it back. He jammed his thumb down on the button to lower the incline of the bed, sighing when the pain ebbed.

As he willed his stomach to settle, he listened to their murmured voices, losing focus a few times as he drifted in and out of sleep. God, he was tired. So, so tired.

When he opened his eyes sometime later, he discovered he was alone with Marcus. He glanced around the room, noticing the angle of the sunlight filtering through the blinds had changed.

"How long was I out?"

Marcus shrugged. "An hour or so."

From the tone of his voice, Enver knew it had been longer. "Zoie head off?"

"She's decided to take a much deserved, and needed,

vacation. Don't think she's ever taken one. A real one at least. Her boss told her to take all the time she needed."

"Good. She's strung tighter than a coil." Enver finally took stock of Marcus's clothes, pleased to note they weren't the same as when he'd left. His body language was still off. Though he wasn't looking over his shoulder or flinching at every shadow, he was still agitated. "You get some rest?"

"If you can call it that." Marcus stood, shoving his hands into his pockets. "I've been meaning to talk to you."

Enver didn't care for the tone of that statement, but he had a feeling he was about to be educated as to what had Marcus strung so tight. "Got all the time in the world."

Marcus avoided eye contact, his gaze darting around the room even though he'd been there enough to memorize everything. "Do you remember what you said before the ambulance showed up?"

"I'm old, not senile."

"I'm just… I'm not the right fit for you, Enver. You deserve to have someone who doesn't come with all the fucking baggage I do. I almost got you killed."

"What is it with you people?" Enver swore loudly, pushing back the pain stabbing between his shoulder blades as he shot up to a full sitting position. Even though he was weakened by the injury, he found the strength to grab the front of Marcus's shirt in his hands and haul him onto the bed.

"News flash—I almost got *myself* killed. Wasn't like anyone twisted my arm to shield you because it was the right thing to do." Enver paused for a second, feeling the pain ebb for a split second as another emotion swamped him. That was a feeling he could handle and snagged it, allowing it to flourish. "I'd do it again in a heartbeat for you, Marcus. Over and over again if that's what it takes to convince you how damn much I love you."

Marcus remained frustratingly silent. Volatile emotion swirled between them, a building tempest that would soon combust if something didn't break. Enver breathed heavily, feeling Marcus's chest expand and contract against his. Each inhale and exhale caused the fire erupting across his back to wrap around his torso and made his shoulders tingle, his fingers buzzing with the familiar numbness that crept in when he'd spent too long working a piece at the forge. The agony firing across his back was almost too much to take. He'd always considered himself on the high scale for pain tolerance, but it seemed his body had reached the limit.

For long minutes, a stalemate hung in the air.

Finally, pissed, at his wit's end and knowing he wouldn't last too much longer, Enver spoke. "I get you need some time after everything you just went through. You have my permission to wallow and beat yourself up for as long as it takes to get BLINC up and running. Then…we're going to have a long talk that will start with me revoking that permission. After that, it will be done. Over. And you will not wallow a second past that." He paused for a second, allowing the words and tone to sink in. "Are we clear?"

Marcus nodded, his throat working as he swallowed.

"Good," Enver forced out, muscling through the blinding pain trying to consume him. "Now, remember this, you stubborn, frustrating weaselhead fuck-nugget, I love you. I don't love you despite your scars. I love you *because* of them. Because they are your life. And I want to be a part of your life forever. One day I hope you'll be able to fully drop those walls that are re-stricting you from happiness and live like you deserve to." Enver stared up at Marcus, not hiding the love and passion filling him. "I love you," he repeated softly as blackness edged his vision.

He finally let go of Marcus's shirt and succumbed to the pain.

Seconds after watching Enver's head roll to the side, Marcus recognized the loud alarm filling the room. Just as he started to react, someone burst into the room and yanked him off the bed.

"What's happening?" Marcus demanded as he stumbled backward, heart in his throat.

The nurse ignored him, checking the heart monitor that had a thin green line running along the bottom of the screen. She jammed her finger on the call button. "Code blue. Room four. Code blue STAT."

Marcus couldn't process the flurry of activity that swarmed into the room. White coats, wheeled medical equipment. Shouting. They all kaleidoscoped around him in a dizzying array as he focused on the never-ending flat line. The pixels and lights that visually indicated his lover's heart had stopped.

He hadn't gotten to tell him. To swear his love in return. To confess how grateful he was that Enver had swept into that horrific situation with Davis and saved the day like some modern day superhero. He knew he shouldn't have hesitated at Enver's marriage proposal. Should have answered him as soon as he'd woken up from surgery. Maybe hearing the confirmation would have given him the strength to recover.

He'd been convinced he couldn't give himself to

someone because he couldn't get over all the bad shit that had happened in his life. Didn't want to wish that on anyone. But getting over it sounded so damn easy. Years and years of therapy, group and solo, had taught him that even if he wanted to, he couldn't crack open his skull, scoop out the bad parts and light them on fucking fire. If a cure for his mental state was that easy, he would gladly watch the shitty remains of his life burn to the ground.

The question wasn't if he loved Enver. He did in that truly, madly way others always talked about. He was honored to be gifted with those words and now he would never be able to return them. And Enver had loved him completely and honestly. Loved him with a passion and ardor that Marcus had no idea love like that existed. Never believed that kind of future was meant for him. And now it had slipped through his fingers…

"We've got a problem."

Marcus's head snapped up, his heart beating so hard against his rib cage, he was convinced it would shatter from the brutal force. He closed his eyes, waiting to hear the inevitable. That he would never be the same because Enver wasn't there anymore. They'd shared a bond that transcended definition, and now…

When the scattering of soft chuckles filtered through the roaring in his ears, his eyes popped open. The doctor stood next to the bed, a wry smile turning up one side of her mouth as the bundle of wires plugged into the monitor dangled over her finger.

"Contacts got dislodged." She eyed Marcus. "Must have come loose when he shifted around."

When he'd dragged Marcus on top of him and declared his undying devotion.

The instant she reconnected the clamps to the diodes, the room was filled with the reassuring cadence of Enver's heartbeat. Relief flooded Marcus, a cleansing rush of emotion that brought tears to his eyes. He sagged against the wall, grateful it was there to support him because he couldn't keep himself upright.

Everyone filed out of the room except for the doctor. She made note of Enver's vitals, nodding as everything returned to normal. She crossed to Marcus, touching his elbow. "Do you need to sit down, dear?"

Even though he shook his head, he sat. He dropped his face into his hands, breathing in and out a few times before he calmed down. His gaze met the doctor's, finally noticing the astonishing contrast between her ice-blue eyes and her dark skin.

"Thank you." He licked his lips, foolish emotion causing him to snort. "Still a little on edge."

She set her hand on his shoulder, a comforting touch when he didn't know he needed one. "He's going to be fine."

"Not sure I will."

"You'll both be fine." She squeezed again before crouching down to bring herself eye level with him. A knowing glint shined in her eyes. "Just be careful not to dislodge them again when you're…roughhousing. Also going to suggest holding off on any more of *that*." She paused to clear her throat and level a look at him that clearly indicated she knew they were more than friends. "Until he's healed. Going to be a few weeks."

"It's funny. We met because of those." He gestured to the patches dotting Enver's still exposed torso. "Not those exactly, of course, but I use similar units in my work." He decided to forgo the aspect of his machinery that would probably make the woman's toes curl.

"You're a doctor?"

"Close. Programmer." He gave her a brief rundown of BLINC and its capabilities, though he didn't know why he felt the need to dump the information on her. Maybe it served as a distraction to keep his mind off the terror that had gripped his bowels minutes ago.

She crossed her arms, tapping her finger against her bottom lip as she stood. "Could something like that be used in an educational capacity? Give surgical students time with a virtual model of a human or specific organ while they're still in med school? Might up their confidence level quickly."

He immediately began thinking of the various applications the program could be adapted to. The original intention of the system hadn't been to service people's pleasures and kinks. In the beginning, he'd envisioned adapting it to immerse gamers for a true four-dimensional experience. Now he imagined users practicing extensive and complicated surgeries before they got near a patient with a blade.

"I don't see why not. The technology is designed to fit the user's needs."

She pulled out a business card from her pocket, scribbled something on the back and then handed it to him. "Once your schedule clears, give me a call so we can talk more. I'm interested in investigating this further and explore the avenues I can use for my students."

He'd forgotten the facility was also a teaching hospital. "I should be finished up with my current project in a few weeks."

He paused to glance at Enver. He'd always believed

he'd pack up and leave after he was done with the Noble House program. But now...his life was spread out before him with endless possibilities. However, now one commonality was in play.

Enver waited at the end of them all.

Chapter Twenty-Nine

Marcus folded his hands in front of him and leaned over, pressing his knuckles to his forehead. The force did nothing to distract him from the reality that was about to happen. *Nothing to it. You've already done this thousands of times.* He breathed in and out a few times, pushing aside the various aromas that were starting to give the room its shape.

To make it his.

As the launch date for BLINC had approached, Kochran relocated the system to a dedicated room that Marcus had dubbed the Sanctum. Beta testing had been completed last week. Tonight, he would usher in a new phase for Noble House and welcome virtual reality to the list of services available for members. He'd already finished the scans of the first clients at around five that morning, and in just thirty minutes, they would arrive for the first full-scale run of the system.

His baby was finally, finally going public.

A familiar hand wrapped his nape. Another hand slipped between his hand and his forehead, giving him more cushioning. He forced out a quick breath, relieved to have someone there who knew him so well.

He sat back, tipping his head upward to stare into those gorgeous multi-colored eyes. "Hey."

Enver leaned over, pressing a quick peck to his lips, wincing only slightly from the position change. "Ready?"

"No," Marcus blurted as his stomach lurched. "I think I'm going to throw up."

"You're going to be fine." Enver rubbed his thumb against the side of Marcus's neck, the slow movement having the intended calming influence.

Marcus wasn't convinced despite Enver's reassurance. "No way I can just shut it all down and walk away, is there?"

Enver's gaze grew hard. "Do we need to have a little session by ourselves first to convince you everything is going to be fine?"

The tone of the question added a husky thickness to the air, immediately calming him. And also reminded him that since the encounter with Davis, their sex life had been relegated to the virtual scenes inside BLINC. He longed to feel Enver's skin against his, and more than just actually sleeping together, since that was all Enver was capable of during his recovery. With Marcus's work schedule, there hadn't been much sleeping either. But now that the program was set to debut, a whole lot of his time was set to be free. And he intended to make up for all his late nights, missed meals and delayed conversations.

"No," Marcus responded, already thinking about how being tied in Enver's ropes for real would feel. "We still need to talk."

Enver stood, stretching his arms out slightly and turning his torso to loosen his muscles. "And like I told you at the hospital, get past all this first. Then we'll finish that talk."

A heavy knock sounded, indicating the time for BLINC's debut had arrived.

Marcus huffed out a breath, willing his heart to settle.

As the door opened and Enver ushered the first customers in, he set his hand on Marcus's shoulder. "Believe me, I haven't forgotten I want to shower you with everything you deserve. Fill in the missing pieces of your heart with my love. My attention." He leaned over again, pressing his warm lips against Marcus's ear. "My come."

Marcus's cock pushed against his pants.

Enver was clearly eyeing the bulge. "Mmm…going to take care of that later. For long, long hours. Until you're writhing and pleading and screaming my name."

Marcus went impossibly harder.

Enver licked his ear. "Done freaking out now?"

"Ass." Marcus chuckled at Enver's deep laugh. "Yes. Thank you."

Wearing a pleased grin, Enver turned to face the two club members who had come in and were nervously looking around. "Come on over so Marcus can take good care of you." As they made their way farther into the room, he directed his attention to Marcus again, all business this time. "I've got a meeting to get to. You going to be at Kochran's soiree later?"

"Sure, I'll meet you there." Marcus stood, popping open the latches on the storage cases. "Let's get you guys hooked up and started."

Enver stepped out of the way, shoving his hands into his pockets as he settled in to watch Marcus as he smoothly switched into proud papa mode with the first official customers. The meeting he needed to attend was taking place in Kochran's office downstairs in an hour. Plenty of time for Enver to kick back and observe for a little bit.

A dull ache made him roll his shoulders. Like Marcus, he'd been putting in long hours. The work had been exhausting but fulfilling—he'd been on a mission and pushed himself to continue until the task was finished. The results of that hard work weighed heavy in his pocket, waiting for the right time to present the item to Marcus.

A high, tittering laugh drew Enver's focus back to the other occupants of the room.

The setup Kochran had constructed for the program was impressive. He'd dedicated an entire section on the second floor of the club to it, closing down several popular rooms in an obvious statement that the new technology was going to be a hit with the members.

Enver had enough firsthand experience to know Kochran was right.

Along one wall of Sanctum, a row of open cubicles with floor-to-ceiling partitions had been erected. Every surface inside the cube space had been painted various dark colors. Aesthetics weren't particularly necessary since participants would be plugging into the computer system, but Kochran had worked with Marcus to create a functional but entertaining space.

A handful of larger spaces had been partitioned off along the back wall. Half of them had curtains pinned back against the outer walls that could be closed for privacy. During the testing phase, Enver had been present when they'd run a scenario where a couple could put on the visors and be intimate with one another both virtually and physically. Though that portion of the system wasn't ready for public consumption yet, Marcus and Kochran had put some serious thought into where they believed the project would go and had allotted space for expansion.

The last section took almost the entire length of the room and was intended for multiple partners to interact as they chose. Saint, Boyce and Grae had extensively tested that part of the system, and from what Enver understood, it worked just as flawless as the rest of BLINC. Not that he'd ever doubted for a moment that Marcus wasn't capable of delivering on his promises.

Enver smiled as he watched Marcus work at what he'd dubbed the command post for the entire operation. His focus was razor sharp as he introduced his first customers to the basic functionality. The love he had for the system he'd developed hadn't waned a bit.

With that on his mind, Enver slipped from the room, leaving Marcus to work. He had business of his own to handle. Not in a rush, he took his time making his way downstairs. Belatedly, he realized his route had taken him to the lounge area he used to spend a great deal of his time in. Since Marcus had come to the club and monopolized his attention, he couldn't remember when he'd last been through, let alone stopped to pay attention.

The black and white floor-to-ceiling photo still hung in the same spot. Bracey was still in his arms, rope marks decorating her skin. Unlike last time, Enver looked at it with a new appreciation. He no longer hated the photo or that it showed how vulnerable he could be. In fact, he loved that about the image because it reminded him that it was okay to show that side of himself.

He owed that revelation to Marcus. Hopefully he felt the same way and the conversation they were going to have later had a much different outcome than at the hospital. Enver touched the protective pouch for the item in his pocket, hoping that the rest of the night went smoothly. The meeting Kochran had been trying to arrange was finally going to take place, and if things went well, Noble House was set to move off in yet another direction.

So many things were changing. For someone so set in his ways, it was sometimes hard to keep up. But with each new change brought new experiences and new people into Enver's life. Without those changes, he would have never met Marcus.

His cell phone vibrated against his thigh, reminding him he was now late for the meeting. With one last glance at the photo, he made his way downstairs and knocked on the office door.

Kochran's muffled voice filtered through the solid wood. "Come in."

Enver steeled himself with a deep breath and entered. Saint sat in his usual place on the couch, arms spread wide with his legs kicked out and ankles crossed. Kochran sat perched on the corner of his desk, wearing his usual three-piece suit.

The other occupant was a man Enver didn't recognize but knew a great deal about thanks to a few recent late night conversations with Kochran. As he closed the door behind him and stepped fully into the room, the man stood. "You must be Enver. Miles Stormare. It's a pleasure to finally meet you."

Enver accepted his offered hand, noting the firm but still friendly handshake. The man was nothing like he'd pictured based on Kochran's descriptions. He'd expected tailored suits, power ties, crisply pressed shirts and an attitude of impassivity to match that polished packaging.

Instead, Miles wore a cranberry flannel shirt rolled to the elbows, exposing the black and red ink covering both his forearms. Cream-colored suspenders that were obviously there only for fashion's sake buttoned into the waistband of well-worn jeans. Shiny loafers showed a bit of age along the toe. His dark hair was pulled back into a short ponytail at his nape and his full beard was neatly clipped. His expression was open and honest, clearly prepared to make a good impression.

"Kochran and Saint were just telling me about the newest technology the club is debuting tonight. I'd love to see it in action." Miles held up his hands, his posture relaxed despite the fact he was clearly on trial. "On a purely observational level, of course."

Enver eyed Kochran, who was swirling his glass so the ice cubes clinked against the glass.

"Miles and I have already spoken about the, ah… terms you and Saint expressed concerns about. And he's agreed to them all." Kochran shifted, leaning to one side to see around Enver as he held up a closed fist, his lips twitching in amusement. "Even yours, Saint."

"I want to assure you both that I'm not the same man I was when Kochran and I were together. He and I have talked extensively about what happened between us and come to an understanding that suits us both." Miles rocked forward on his feet, the shine in his loafers glinting in the office lighting as he continued. "But at any time, if either of you—or even you, Kochran— are uncomfortable with my work methods, I expect my

partnership to be terminated." The blunt words weren't
accompanied by a snide smile. No arrogant cock of the
head. No fidgeting to indicate a lie. "I'll even tear up
the contract myself."

Jesus. This guy was so damn charming it was difficult not to like him, not to mention he had a charismatic
sensuality that couldn't be learned or bought. Exactly
the kind of person who would normally be welcomed
with open arms at Noble House.

As much as Enver wanted to dislike the man based
solely on Kochran's history with him, he got the sense
Miles was the kind of man he could have deep, exis-
tential conversations with at a bar over cigars and a
few drinks. In a matter of a few minutes, he'd been
disarmed by a perfectly normal, genuine man who was
sincerely interested in Noble House and what he could
offer the club.

Enver understood why, and how, a young and im-
pressionable Kochran had fallen under the man's spell.
Miles had put Kochran through the ringer, taking him
as a full slave for a month before disappearing, never to
be seen again—until now. Looking at the men standing
side by side, despite their remarkably different attire,
Enver saw similarities in their personalities. Though
he knew Kochran was fully committed to Ezra and
Maddy—a bond that would be sealed during the party
later—he wondered how much Miles had unknowingly
shaped Kochran into the man he'd become today.

Miles glanced at each of the men, a wry smile tipping one corner of his mouth. "Look, I know I'm coming into an already established partnership that works
just fine. You're happy with that, I get it. I'm not looking to change things, but I *am* looking to make what

you have even better. From what I've seen Noble House is one of a kind. I want to seize that potential and use it to make something even more special. I believe the club is just the beginning."

"How so?" Saint asked, a touch of skepticism coloring his voice. "What kind of markets do you see us expanding into that we can't do without you?"

"Ah, that's the multimillion-dollar question we're going to discuss in depth." Miles rubbed his hands together, his brown eyes shining with excitement. He pulled a slender tie clip he'd had pinned to his shirt placket and wiggled it. "This is a USB full of ideas I've got for expansion that I believe will take Noble House further than the three of you have ever imagined. I'm ready to start laying down the details and get rolling with whatever we come up with. I understand there's a party later you need to get to so I suggest we get the ball rolling."

The three men looked at one another.

"Sorry to say," Enver said dryly, "he sells a good game and I'm interested in playing along to see what the four of us are capable of." He glanced over at Saint, and then at Kochran. "Don't think we have anything to lose at this point since he sounds way more capable at this kind of thing than the three of us. Game if you guys are."

Kochran drew himself to his full height and smiled. "Let's do this."

Chapter Thirty

The once-dark, relatively unused basement of Noble House had been transformed into a glittering display of chrome, glass and black leather. Members filled every inch of available space, eager to find out what Master Kochran intended to announce.

"I will."

Enver turned his focus back to the handful of people he stood with in the corner under an arch of black, white and silver balloons. He'd missed what the officiant had said that garnered the response from Ezra, but most of these commitment ceremonies were all the same.

He hated the monkey suit he'd been required to wear, but Kochran had insisted the collaring ceremony be a formal affair. Enver had to admit, it was a nice change of pace from the usual yards and yards of leather that usually dominated the member's wardrobes.

The trio had performed their first collaring ceremony in secret, held in the Keep with only a few select members present. Enver had been to that event as well, but the atmosphere had been remarkably different. The full triad relationship between Kochran, Maddy and Ezra was out in the open now, so there was no need to be clandestine.

Kochran went to one knee in front of Ezra. He bowed his head in supplication, and whispered, "I accept you as my Master."

Enver's thoughts and attention drifted again as Maddy stepped forward to add her vow, his gaze scanning over the sea of familiar faces. Not that he wasn't interested in the ceremony, he simply had other things on his mind. A vow of his own to make.

Just as disappointment was starting to well in his stomach, he spotted Marcus sitting all the way in the rear with his head tilted back and his eyes closed. From the even movement of his chest, it was clear he was asleep. He'd been pushing himself too hard the past few weeks, determined to make the second deadline for BLINC since he'd missed the first thanks to the kidnapping.

A loud eruption of applause snapped Enver's attention back to the trio. Their curious gazes made him realize he'd been staring at Marcus longer than intended. Instead of offering his hand, he embraced each of them, saving the last for one of his closest friends.

"About damn time," he said to Kochran, glad that this time he'd said it the words weren't darkened by the death of Kochran's sister.

"Quit your gloating, asshole." Despite the statement, Kochran's voice lacked any heat. "You know this isn't the end of your duties, right? Need you to stand up as my best man in the spring."

"Nothing better I'd like to do." Enver had something else he needed to say to Kochran. "Listen, I never got a chance to say thanks for your help tracking down Marcus and Zoie. I'm... I couldn't-—I think if you guys hadn't stepped up, I wouldn't be standing here having this conversation." Enver noted the crowd pushing around them, eager to offer their congratulations. "I'm going to get out of the way and stop monopolizing all your time. We'll catch up later and talk."

He turned away, intent on convincing Marcus to get some sleep, but his gaze landed on Oz. He looked tired as well, but Enver knew it wasn't due to lack of sleep. If anything, Oz usually slept too much. There weren't many things that came between Oz and his bed.

Enver detoured to where his friend sat at a table. "Hey, got a second?"

"Sure."

"Finished your custom job." Enver set a second velvet bag he'd had in his jacket pocket on the table. Given Oz's enthusiasm when he'd placed the order, he expected him to pounce. Instead, the other man just blinked a few times as though he'd forgotten he'd placed the order in the first place. "You all right?"

"I…no. I'm not." Oz snatched the bag and stood in a rush. "I'm outta here."

Enver clamped his hand on Oz's shoulder. "Sit."

Oz grumbled something under his breath, but complied. Enver snagged a couple glasses of champagne from a passing sub dispensing refreshments. The ceremony was one of the few occasions Kochran had allowed alcohol in the club, but he'd also ordered an edict that no play was allowed by anyone who chose to drink.

"Yes, I know. I'm an overbearing asshole. Something is eating at you, my friend."

"Leave it alone, Enver." Oz downed one of the glasses and reached for the other.

"No, I won't." Enver pushed the flute to him, knowing he didn't intend to drink if the rest of his night went according to plan. "You've been moping around like a toddler who lost his favorite toy for the past month. What's the deal?"

"Fuck my life," Oz said succinctly.

Enver glared, waiting for further explanation.

"Forgot how fucking annoying you are sometimes, Furst." Oz fell quiet as he slumped back in the chair, his hands falling to his lap. "You ever think about what if the scene isn't enough for you? All this sex and sin and debauchery. What if it…what if it isn't enough?"

Enver didn't think he'd ever seen Oz looking so dejected. "I take it this has something to do with that custom plug?"

Oz stared at the bag for a bit before nodding. "Yeah. Wish to hell it didn't, though."

"What are you talking about?"

Oz's lips turned white as he pressed them together. Clearly he had something to say, but was hesitant.

"Christ, Oz, you look like you're going to burst a blood vessel or two." Enver leaned forward. "Are you okay?"

"Yeah," Oz said tightly. He looked like he wanted to say more, but clamped his mouth shut when a group of submissives walked by, giggling as they waved at the men.

"One of the subs?"

"I wish." He ran his hands over his freshly shaved head. "Be less fucking complicated if it was. You ever thought about what you'd do if you were interested in someone not into all this?"

Enver sat up, taken aback by the question. "Depends on the person, I suppose. You telling me you had me make that for someone not in the lifestyle?"

Oz dipped his head and muttered, "Yeah."

Considering how much time Oz spent at the club, it was hard to imagine him with someone who wasn't interested in exploring power exchanges. It wasn't unheard of, but for someone so dedicated to D/s and the club, it was uncharacteristic.

As Enver shooed away another eager submissive approaching Oz, he spotted Marcus on the other side of the room. He was no longer asleep. Instead, he was surrounded by a group of members. Judging by the hand gestures and the delight glowing on his face, the discussion revolved around BLINC.

As Marcus spread his arms, demonstrating something about the program, he made eye contact with Enver. He gave a lopsided smile and a wink that warmed Enver through. In an instant, the truth hit him squarely between the solar plexus.

"Yes, I would give it all up for love." He turned back to Oz. "A thousand times over. Whoever it is, you should tell them how you feel. They may surprise you."

"It's…complicated. He's unlike anyone I've ever known."

Enver swore he saw a pink tinge flushing Oz's cheeks. He couldn't recall a time he'd seen him so spun up about someone. "All the more reason to talk to him."

"And I can think of a hundred different reasons why I shouldn't." Oz fiddled with the bag, stroking his finger over the shape through the velvet. "It's stupid, really. I guess I'm just not used to feeling a connection with someone outside of this place. Can't muster the courage to even ask him for his phone number, but I can have you make him a custom plug." He growled. "I'm an idiot."

"It's not stupid," Enver countered with a frown. "And you're not an idiot. You just need to get past your own head, man."

Oz scowled, scooping up the plug as he stood. "I don't have time to get all googly eyed about someone anyway. Better off alone."

As Enver watched Oz weave through the crowd, he remembered thinking the same thing not so long ago.

Despite the surge of people partying on the dance floor, Marcus sat alone at a table in the farthest corner of the expansive room in a much-needed moment of peace. Though he should relax and have a good time to celebrate the successful launch of BLINC, he was too much of an observer to fully enjoy himself. It was also the first time he'd had a moment to himself since the program had gone live to the members. Once Louis and Rachel had gotten done with their session, they'd immediately told their friends. The system had only been up and running for six hours and already Marcus had a client list a mile long.

"I can tell by the look on your face, you're thinking about work. Do you ever take a break?" Enver set a glass of champagne down and slipped into the seat beside Marcus. "It's Kochran's coming out party, for Pete's sake. He's announcing to the world he's a bisexual switch with a soon-to-be husband *and* wife. You're supposed to get drunk and disorderly by this shocking news."

Though Marcus didn't share Enver's enthusiasm since he hadn't known the trio all that long, he did have reason to celebrate. The past ten years living with fear and constantly looking over his shoulder were finished. All the work and dedication he'd thrown at BLINC had paid off with a long-term contract with Noble House. Not to mention the added bonus of the meeting he'd had last week with the doctor who'd ordered twenty licenses to use the program on the hospital campus. Marcus was going to have to hire an honest-to-god staff to help him.

He truly did have reason to celebrate, but he wasn't interested in drinking. Instead, he eyed Enver. Kochran had insisted on making the event a formal affair and the members had delivered, dressing in their absolute finest to mark the occasion. Kochran had asked Saint and Enver to stand as witness for his announcements, showing their unwavering support for their friend and business partner. Which meant Enver was dressed in a tux.

Enver hadn't lasted long in his, though, as Marcus had suspected. His flawlessly pressed white shirt was unbuttoned at the throat, his bowtie hanging loose around his neck. At some point, he'd ditched the formal jacket. Half dressed, he still looked damn handsome in Marcus's eyes.

His attention snapped back when he heard a *thunk* on the table. He blinked at the square bag the size of his fist sitting in front of him. His gaze darted to Enver, who wore the ghost of a smile that made Marcus's pulse race. He ordered himself to calm down as he eyed Enver. "You've got that look again."

"Which one?" Enver asked as he casually sat back, obviously trying to feign ignorance. His expression went blank as he nudged the bag closer. "Go on." He leaned in, brushing his lips against the collar of Marcus's shirt then skimming up his throat to his ear. "Or I will have you slip on that cock ring I gave you last night and make a mess of your perfectly pressed slacks with an exceptionally long, exceptionally thorough hand job right here at the table."

Marcus's fingers trembled as the explicit image of Enver doing just that flashed behind his eyes. "This isn't a matching plug, is it?"

Enver's eyes glinted. Those fucking gorgeous eyes that were filled with emotion. "No, but I'm absolutely going to make one for you now."

"Of course you are," Marcus muttered as he pulled on the ties. The idea wasn't a poor one. He'd wear anything Enver made for him. Anything at all. He shook the bag, inhaling sharply when the heavy weight spilled across his palm. He stared at the item for what seemed like forever, his mind blanking of coherent thought and speech.

He turned the highly polished metal over, the light from the candle centerpiece catching on the smooth surface. The last thing he expected to find was a simple analog watch. The silver band contrasted starkly with the cobalt-blue face and the mother-of-pearl hands and indicator dots used to read the time.

"I picked up the mechanical insides from a jeweler in San Francisco who dabbles in making custom jewelry for some of our members. The outer casing of the face and entire band are my handiwork, though. Much smaller than what I'm used to working with, so it's not perfect."

But it was, in so many ways. "It's gorgeous, Enver."

"I know you wanted to finish that talk, but I couldn't wait to give it to you." Enver took it from him, unlatched the catch and flipped over the back, holding it up so Marcus could see the simple block letter engraving.

From your one and only weaselhead fucknugget.

Marcus burst out laughing. When he calmed, he noticed Enver looking at him expectantly. "Is this what I think it is?"

"It's a collar, yes. Meant to be worn at all times. Everyone else will think it's just a thoughtful present from your boyfriend, but you and I will both know better." Energy crackled in the air around them, the kind that heralded an approaching storm. "I wasn't so out of it that I didn't see how you reacted at the hospital to my commands, Marcus. Or remember that time in the snow on my deck at the workshop. You don't have to wear it until we've had a chance to go over some things, but I want you to have it."

"Enver, I don't…don't. Shit." Marcus swallowed the emotions clogging his throat as the rest of the world dropped away. The man he loved had just given him— *made him*—the most gorgeous, heartfelt present. "I don't know what to say."

"Whatever your heart tells you."

"It says yes." Marcus shot Enver a boyishly playful grin.

"About damn fucking time." Enver took his mouth with a brute force that caused Marcus to shiver. "What do you say we celebrate with some play in Court?"

Marcus froze. "Enver. You don't have to do this for me. Just because I'm—"

"It's time, Marcus." Enver kept his eyes trained on Marcus as he gently kissed him. "Everything with you is easy. Natural. I don't have to fight for control with you. I did in the beginning because I didn't know how to handle you. I didn't expect this—expect you."

"You just needed to find someone younger who could match your sex drive." Marcus could spend all day with

Enver, making love or fucking away the desperate need that clawed at them both. Marcus understood exactly what Enver meant because, for him, loving Enver was as natural as breathing. And now he had Enver's collar.

"So, about that talk we've been meaning to have."

"Yeah." Marcus swallowed carefully. His body felt strung out and empty, aching with a need he knew only one person could fulfill. "What I've actually wanted to talk to you about is that I said a lot of things in that hospital room that I've changed my mind about. Then I was still the man who was always on the run, constantly looking over his shoulder. The fact I didn't need to do that anymore was so new I didn't know any better. For once, I'm on a different path. That's because of you. You're the difference, Enver. The person who makes me want to stand my ground. I feel like a different person."

"But you're not," Enver countered. "You're the same man you've always been, Marcus. You're just not afraid anymore."

Marcus agreed, lacing his fingers together with Enver's. "There's never been any doubt we have a physical connection. From the second I spilled my papers all over you at the convention, I knew our link was overwhelming. I also know that love isn't easy or kind. It cuts us to the quick when we're at our most vulnerable. Leaves us bleeding in bright crimson splashes against a dull world. It skews our moral compasses, and robs us of our ability to choose between right and wrong. All so we can be with the person we're convinced we're destined to be with."

Warm happiness settled in the center of his chest. Life was damn good. "I'm ready to spend the rest of my life with you, Enver. If you'll still have me—"

"Still have you?" Enver interrupted. "I just gave you a collar that I made *for* you. What makes you think I don't want you?"

"A collar and a marriage are two different things," Marcus said carefully, his heart racing as trepidation slid through his midsection. "You may want me only as your submissive, but not your husband."

Enver touched the side of Marcus face. "For us, gorgeous, they're one and the same."

Marcus blew out a relieved breath as he offered the watch to Enver, shaking his wrist until Enver fastened it in place. "Who knew you were so romantic?"

The glint that had been lighting Enver's uniquely colored eyes shifted to something darker. "Nothing romantic about what I want to do to you."

Marcus sucked in a sharp breath. "Well."

Enver tilted his head toward Marcus's, their foreheads meeting. "Been needing you all night."

"Why didn't you find me sooner? We're in a sex club. Plenty of dark corners and private rooms. Hell, we could have had a quickie right here and no one would have noticed."

"Oh, they'd notice. And they'd hear. And knowing the perverts we're surrounded by, they'd watch every last second of it. But I don't want a quick fuck. I want you in my ropes. For real. In Court. *Now.*"

"Keep talking like that and I'll come before we even get started."

Enver's eyes flared. "No fun in that."

Marcus shook his head. "Didn't think so."

Celebration still going on around them, Enver curved a hand around the back of Marcus's neck tilting his head to deepen the kiss. Marcus was aware of the noise of the crowd, the raucous cheers of the party, but he didn't care. After what felt like an eon, Enver pulled back.

A chill rippled through Marcus. "I can't believe I almost lost you."

"Fuck you all to fucking hell, Marcus Holly." Enver drew in a deep, shuddering breath as he pulled Marcus into his arms. "You're my miracle, Marcus. You know that, right? You have helped me in ways you can't even imagine. In ways I can never express. You helped me— we helped each other become the best we both could be. Now will you just fucking marry me already and let me love and protect you?"

"Yes, Enver. Yes, I accept your collar and your marriage proposal."

"Let's get out of here." Enver stood, shifting his tux pants to hide his obvious erection.

"I was wondering why we weren't already gone."

Chapter Thirty-One

Marcus inhaled sharply as Enver guided him through the double doors that led to Court. The vibrations from the party downstairs caused the concrete under his feet to tremble as his gaze swept over the room. He'd spent plenty of time in Court taking measurements for BLINC, but now he was able to look at it with a less critical eye.

The usual heavy red drapes had been replaced with lighter panels composed of celadon, sky blue and charcoal gray. Not only did the muted cool tones seem to float, they transformed the room into something softer, blunting the harsh edges the space was known for. Further adding to the changes, the center of the room was dominated by a king-size bed with soaring metal posts and a metal canopy frame composed of bold black scrolls. The overhead framework was ornate and sturdy looking, clearly intended to support more weight than a simple decorative drape. Four long lengths of rope hung from the canopy bars, holding a large square of heavy-duty fabric that had been stretched to form a bed.

It was a masterpiece designed for sin.

And it had Enver's craftsmanship stamped all over it.

Marcus turned, giving Enver a conspiratorial smile. "That bed is not made to be slept in."

"Sleeping is at the bottom of a very long list of things I want to do with you right now." Enver tugged on his hand. "Consider this an engagement present."

Marcus was too stunned to be annoyed. "How did you know I would accept?"

Enver kissed his hand. "Because I know you, gorgeous."

For a long moment they stayed quiet and still. The comforting feeling whenever Enver called him that blossomed inside Marcus. Said in that whiskey- and smoke-laced voice...magic.

Will I ever get used to how he melts my insides?

The answer was a hard no.

The gift was presumptuous, but Marcus didn't mind. In fact, it added to the warmth swirling through him as he stepped closer, marveling at the skill that had gone into crafting the piece of furniture. "Is this what you've been doing all those nights I was working on the system?"

Enver bounced on the balls of his feet. "Had to do something with that junk heap you left me after the crash."

"Wait. What?" Unable to help himself, Marcus touched one of the columns. "This was your car?"

"Didn't feel right to try to rebuild her. Decided I had other plans for her." Enver touched the nearest support post and a panel popped open to expose several eye-bolts. "Thought I'd welcome you to my brand of the dark side."

"It's amazing." Marcus didn't bothering restraining the emotion clogging his throat. No one had ever taken such a horrible memory and turned it into something amazing. "Thank you."

"Care to test it out?" Enver nudged a bag with his foot as he sat on the edge of the mattress, pushing with his feet to cause it to swing slightly.

Marcus eyed him, trying not to let his skepticism show. He didn't want to spoil the mood Enver was building. "Only if…if you're sure about this."

"I used sex as a fix-it-all. A way to make me feel something. Anything. I don't need sex now for the physical release. I need it because I need you. So, I've never been more certain of anything in my life." Enver tugged Marcus into his lap, snuggling their bodies together. He ran his fingers up Marcus's side, the touch equally ticklish and arousing through the cotton. He nipped at Marcus's collarbone then did it again and again until Marcus shivered and uttered a soft curse.

"Besides, everyone else is busy with the party downstairs. Figure they can go another few hours before it breaks up," Enver continued. "Think of Court as our own personal dungeon for the night."

Enver dragged over the bag he'd set on the mattress, extracting a few bundles of rope and positioning them over Marcus's spread thighs. "Since we're not inside your fancy toy now, we need to discuss some boundaries."

Marcus traced the line of Enver's collarbone. "I'll do anything you want me to."

"Anything?" Enver asked, one of his brows lifting in that sexy way that caused Marcus to think dirty, naughty thoughts.

"The limits we discussed that first day haven't changed. Neither has my safe word." Marcus tapped the watch he vowed to wear. "Plus, I always have a reminder, thanks to you."

Enver unwound one of the bundles, looping the rope on itself to negotiate the first tie. "So willing and trusting. You want nothing more than to please me. I like that." He kissed Marcus lightly before finishing. "I like that a lot."

Marcus shivered in anticipation, a line of goose bumps rising up the length of his spine as he thought about all the ways Enver could possibly tease and torment him. "What do you have in mind for me?"

Enver eyed him as he continued to thread the length of rope together. "Whatever I tell you to do."

Marcus blew out a breath, his heart racing as he squirmed against Enver's thighs. "Where have you been all my life?"

Enver set the section he'd been working on to the side, captured Marcus's jaw between his hands and positioned their faces inches apart. He whispered, "Waiting for you."

The room spun. Marcus's hands started to shake, his heart thumping so hard it was difficult to hear over the roar in his ears.

"And just so we're clear... I fully intend to spend the rest of our lives making up for it. But we've got a few things to cover since this is our first official rope scene. I need you to promise that you'll safe word if you're uncomfortable. If something pinches or doesn't feel right. If you feel any sort of numbness or tingling. The rope is intended to cradle you, not hurt. Understood?"

"Yes, Sir."

Enver's eyes glazed over for a split second before clearing. He leaned forward, touching his lips to Marcus's. "Like how that sounds." He set the section he'd been manipulating and wrapped his hands around Marcus's waist. He untucked the shirt and slid his fingers against Marcus's abdomen before digging the tips into Marcus's sides. Watching Enver do his set up work was almost as mesmerizing as actually being bound in his ropes.

Marcus gasped at the intense sensations flooding his system as his muscles trembled under Enver's touch. In a blink, he was staring at the ceiling of Court. Enver hovered over him, rucking up his shirt higher so he could lean down and press a soft kiss between his pecs. He levered up and forward, grinding his pelvis against Marcus's so their cocks were pressed together through the fabric of their pants.

Their mouths met again, a grinding assault on all five senses as Enver took him over. A breeze brushed over his abdomen as Marcus belatedly realized that Enver had undone Marcus's shirt and was currently working on the waistband of his pants.

"You need to be naked too." Caught up in the heat swirling around them, Marcus's voice had gone husky. But he didn't care. The only thing that mattered at the moment was how consumed he was.

"All in due time, gorgeous."

Enver stripped him between kisses, cursing softly when the pant leg and sock tangled. Marcus couldn't help but laugh. Enver shot him a stern look, but Marcus knew there was no heat behind the glance.

"I can't stop thinking about you being inside me."

"All in due time, gorgeous," Enver repeated, this time with a gleam in his eyes and a smile tilting up the corners of his mouth. He kept that gaze honed on Marcus as he reached for the first bundle of rope. "Right now, I just need you to relax and let me make you even more of a treasure."

Marcus nodded, lifting his wrists in offering. "Please."

As Enver bound Marcus's wrists individually, the rest of the world grayed around the edges and went fuzzy. His elbows followed with just enough strain to cause some tension, but not to make him uncomfortable. Enver looped a band around Marcus's chest, circling the ropes over his shoulders so it connected with the bands at his elbows. Similar networks wrapped his legs and waist.

Marcus fell into a trancelike state as Enver worked. He wanted to admire Enver's diligence and attention to detail, but he was finding it hard to concentrate on anything except how wonderful everything felt. He lost track of time, the room, the bed and even the texture of the rope being wrapped around his body. The only thing he was conscious of was how he didn't care about anything at all and how freeing the sensation was.

Marcus realized Enver was talking to him, and opened eyes he hadn't even been aware of closing. "What?"

"I said," Enver responded, "I didn't think it was possible for you to get any more beautiful, but turns out I was wrong." He dipped his head, pressing his mouth against Marcus's ear. "I think I love you a little more after seeing you truly bound by my ropes."

Marcus sighed as Enver's lips met his, their movement unhurried and careful, as though it was possible to break the spell. As Marcus opened for him, Enver slipped inside his mouth, taking his time to thoroughly taste him.

Marcus felt like a kid in a playground, having the time of his life on his favorite apparatus. He wanted Enver to do all the things to him at once. Suck him. Fuck him. He moaned around Enver's tongue, overwhelmed by the power of his desire.

After what seemed like forever Enver stood to toss up a few long lengths of rope over the sturdy canopy. When he started attaching each of those dangling ropes to the sections tied to key points on Marcus's body, he saw where this was going.

Enver crouched, bringing his gaze level with Marcus's. "I know that sound. That slight inhalation as you realize what I'm going to do to you."

A bolt of hot lust shot through Marcus. "Yes, Sir."

"And what is that?" Enver asked with a telling grin worthy of the Cheshire cat. His cheeks were flushed, his lips slick and swollen from the kisses they'd shared.

"You're going to play with me."

Enver's eyes glinted. "Indeed I am, gorgeous."

Enver checked and rechecked the pulleys he'd threaded the ropes through. Satisfied, he took up the loose end and tugged hard. Marcus's eyes flared wide as his weight became fully supported by the rope.

"Comfortable?"

It took a few beats before Marcus answered. "More than, Sir."

Enver loved the way that sounded, slightly slurred, as though Marcus was drunk. Enver notched the rope higher, wrapping the loose end around his fist securely. Gaze on Marcus's, he touched Marcus's knee with his bare foot. The gentle swinging motion caused Marcus to inhale and moan softly.

"Almost perfect." Enver pulled hard on the rope, ratcheting Marcus higher. Satisfied, he tied off the free end, securing it so that the knot wouldn't come undone until he was ready to untie Marcus. But that would only happen after he'd made him a warm pool of thoroughly fucked male.

Marcus was on his hands and knees, suspended over the mattress. Enver was tempted to look at him this way but the throbbing of Marcus's too-hard cock was too much. Gaze on his sub, Enver peeled open his pants and freed his erection.

He suddenly threw back his head and laughed. "I swear you're salivating, Marcus."

"Yeah, I am." Marcus licked his lips. He had never passed up a chance to show off his skills when it came to giving Enver a blowjob. He was too addicted to the rush of power that came from holding Enver's cock in his mouth. Truth was, Enver got off on watching and feeling the man he loved do it too.

Marcus nuzzled Enver's already hard shaft, struggling with the ropes as though he wished his hands were free to assist. He finally gave up when he realized it was futile, and played his tongue across the center seam, tracing the prominent vein on the underside of the shaft.

"You're too good at this." Enver buried his fingers in Marcus's rumpled hair, tugging on the strands. Because of the way he was bound, Marcus's body moved forward. Enver drew him back, and this time, Marcus tongued the slit.

Enver continued to feed Marcus his cock, watching in fascination as his shaft disappeared between Marcus's lips. Marcus took the treatment, begging for more through the use of his mouth and tongue and teeth.

Enver growled, tugging Marcus forward so he took more dick into his mouth in one long slurp. Marcus sucked and sucked, using his tongue to cradle the thick shaft nestled deep in his throat.

Marcus had the sexiest damn mouth Enver had ever felt around his dick. He stretched wide, working strong, mind-altering pulls from root to tip. Every time Enver pulled back, Marcus swirled his tongue around the tip and slit, moaning and groaning his pleasure as he opened wide to take more when Enver would push forward.

"Gonna blow soon if you're not careful."

Marcus's gaze flicked upward, those pleading, unguarded eyes looking up as he practically purred.

"Like that idea, don't you? My seed coating your throat? Lingering on your tongue while I take your ass and fuck it hard."

Marcus sucked in so solidly, his cheeks hollowed.

"*Fuck.* Fucking-A." Enver drew back his hips, ramming them forward as Marcus took him all the way again. They were suspended there, as though someone had hit pause. The need to come vibrated through Enver, an irresistible force that marked him in every way possible.

Unable to stop himself, he released suddenly, his dick pulsing hard a few times as Marcus continued to enthusiastically suck, drinking every drop Enver gave. When Enver finally pulled free, a ghost of a smile played over Marcus's lips.

"Quite satisfied with that, aren't you?"

Marcus's smile vanished. "No, Sir." His gaze fell to Enver's semi-erect cock. "I still need you inside me."

Enver crouched, folding his hands in front of him to

rob Marcus of the view. "I dunno. Not sure I'll be able to get it up again. Me being an old man and all."

Marcus snorted and rolled his eyes. "*Puh-leeze.* You have stamina a college frat boy would be jealous of. I'm going to wear out long before you do."

Enver touched the corner of Marcus's mouth, wiping away a few drops of fluid. "Have a problem with that?"

"Not in the least." Marcus grinned widely. "I'm one lucky son-of-a-bitch."

"I'm the lucky one." Enver moved his mouth to Marcus's, almost whimpering at the intimacy swirling between them. He bit and tugged, and then licked and soothed away the sting. He wanted to shove his way into Marcus's mouth and devour him whole, but as Enver drew back, the sight of that playful half smile hit him with an unexpected wave of emotion and punched him right in the center of the chest. But this time, it was even more powerful given Marcus's vulnerable position and the trust he continually offered Enver as their relationship grew. Unconditional love and acceptance rushed through him, filling in all the remaining spaces to make him whole. Enver could fall for this man over and over and over again.

He had the rest of his life to love Marcus.

Marcus glanced between Enver's spread thighs, snorting softly when he spotted the telling signs of a growing cock. "See? I knew it."

"Yeah, yeah. Quit gloating." Enver's dick twitched in response to that hungry gaze, eyelids half-closed already. So fucking gorgeous, all that need and want and hopeless longing showing clearly in Marcus's blissed-out expression. It was similar to how he looked when he was creating endless strings of the stupid code that got him all spun up sometimes. Enver wasn't complaining. He'd never get tired of seeing Marcus look that way.

Never got tired of being the cause.

"Christ, Marcus," Enver murmured as he tugged him closer. "Think I've switched out one addiction for another." Their mouths met in a messy kiss. Everything slowed again as the desperate urgency morphed to a languid build of pleasure. He'd never expected that kind of intimacy to exist for him.

Never in his wildest fantasies had he imagined someone like Marcus Holly.

Enver kissed the top of Marcus's head, breathing in the warm, comforting scent of shampoo and knowing he had to be inside him soon. He stood, shifting beside Marcus to allow room for the instructions he was about to give.

"Push with your feet, and lift up just like you're going to stand without the ropes binding you." He wrapped his hand around Marcus's elbow, guiding him as he changed position. Marcus made the transition smoothly, a testament to his agility in the ropes and Enver's skill level as a rigger. Still suspended in Enver's complicated maze of ropes, Marcus was now in a reclined seated position, his legs spread slightly to allow unimpeded access to his ass and his cock.

Unable to help himself, Enver touched the straining tip, spreading the pearl of precome that had gathered there. Their gazes locked, dark and hungry for one another as he lifted his finger to his mouth. Emotion hung in the air between them so thick, Enver swore he could see it. The intensity would have frightened him if it was someone other than Marcus. He saw the acceptance of a man who loved him despite his flaws.

"Enver."

The desperate sound of his name tripping past Marcus's lips shattered the moment and propelled Enver into motion. He stripped completely in a matter of a few heartbeats, tossing his clothes away haphazardly.

One hand on his fully recovered cock, he tore open the condom foil with his teeth and discarded the package. Gaze locked on Marcus, Enver rolled on the rubber, making a show of the task just to watch Marcus's expression go all hard and ravenous again. And just because he could fuck with him, he took his time slicking on a thick coat of lube.

Marcus started fidgeting in the ropes.

"Comfortable?"

"Yeah." At Enver's raised brow, Marcus cleared his throat and tried again. "Yes. Just...need..."

"Go on."

He took a few breaths, slow and steady as though he was trying to calm his system. "Need you."

Enver didn't need clarification, but fucking with Marcus was too decadent. "To do what?"

"Anything. Anything at all. Anything you want."

"Ah, all good answers." He added additional lube to two of his fingers before tossing the packet to the side. He paused, momentarily mesmerized by the sight of Marcus straining against the ropes, flushed red cock so hard it was perpendicular to the rest of his body. "It just so happens, I want to fuck you."

Tension bled from Marcus as he relaxed against the ropes, allowing them to cradle him. His eyes. God, his eyes went all heavy-lidded and distant as he tumbled into the right headspace. "I'm all yours, Sir."

Enver could spend hours teasing him, listening to

those hushed words of absolute surrender. He pressed lubed fingers against the pucker, pleased with the answering hiss. Marcus tensed for a split second and then exhaled as Enver slipped inside. He was tempted to take himself in hand to stroke himself while he slowly fucked Marcus. But the enticing display spread out before him was too gorgeous. He spread his fingers slightly against the clench, working those muscles to open Marcus even more, prepare him so Enver could slide right inside.

Satisfied with his work after a few minutes of mercilessly teasing, he went to one knee and rolled down onto his back so he lay on the mattress with Marcus suspended above him. Though he was no longer eye-to-eye with Marcus, the view was just as exquisite—the elegant slopes and curves of his shoulders and back all bound up with Enver's rope. He dragged the tip of his cock along Marcus's ass crack, enjoying the way the two firm globes separated by his ropes kept Marcus wide and ready for him.

Despite the roaring in his ears to drive up into Marcus, Enver took a few steadying breaths and spoke. "I'd love to keep you like this. Ready and waiting for me to come fuck you at my leisure. New art for the club, maybe."

"Please." Marcus gasped. "Sir."

"What part?"

"All of it. I just… I need you inside me."

The desperate tone of the words triggered something inside Enver. He yearned to give Marcus everything he wanted and more for the rest of his life. "And I need to be inside you, Marcus. Stretching your ass, making it sore so you feel the ache days and days later. Knowing the man you love was the one who gave you that pleasure."

Marcus only moaned in answer.

Enver wrapped his hands around the two handholds he'd created for himself while encasing Marcus in the ropes. They creaked, but he was confident in his abilities to know they would take the additional weight.

Muscles and veins stood out on Marcus's arms as he patiently waited. His breathing was uneven, vacillating between shallow and deep. Everything about him—the heady smell of his arousal, the sight of him poised for what Enver had in store—was unspeakably sexy.

Unable to restrain himself any longer, Enver positioned his dick at Marcus's entrance and thrust upward. Marcus's muscles clamped around him as he cried out, then immediately relaxed as Enver drove deeper, powering into him.

"Fuck." The word tumbled past Marcus's lips as a ragged sob.

A delightful, tortured, trembling little sob.

Enver understood—he couldn't concentrate on anything except fucking him. He levered his hips back against the mattress and thrust up. Deliciously, endlessly fucking Marcus with insane slowness and punishing power.

When he glanced down, watching his dick slide in and out of that delectable ass, he ran out of breath. His lungs burned from the lack of oxygen, but he powered through it, loving the way his muscles trembled from the effort. Never wanting it to end.

He tightened his hold on the makeshift handles, squeezed his eyes shut and rode Marcus good and hard. Each time his hips impacted with Marcus's ass, his lover's whole body jolted and quivered in the bondage. The force of their lovemaking also shook the bed frame, driving home the fact Marcus was at Enver's utter mercy.

A low, throaty moan sounded above him. The noise wrapped around Enver's cock and heart, connecting them in a way he'd never thought possible. He was hungry and desperate and ah, God...*yes*.

Marcus's ass went impossibly tight around Enver's cock, forcibly hauling him over the edge so he had no choice but to career out of control right along with him. Enver pumped fast a few times as he chased his climax then buried himself to the hilt, trying to get as deep inside Marcus as he could. Even still, it was never enough.

It would never be enough.

"Oh...ah, fuck!" Marcus shouted, a sound that didn't even sound human.

The whole world went supernova, everything pulsing and vibrating as they came together in a symphony of curses and shouts. Enver was certain he could go for hours like this, hanging in that decadent state of nirvana that made him feel as though he was soaring.

Everything burned in that oh-so-good way as his body sagged back against the mattress. Just the tip of his already softening cock was nestled inside Marcus's ass, as though Marcus wasn't ready to let him go. He was tempted to stay like this for as long as it took for him to get hard again, but Marcus had already been suspended in his bondage for longer than comfortable for a novice.

Enver took a few minutes to regain his bearings, knowing his job wasn't complete despite the heaviness trying to settle into his bones. He still had a submissive to attend. When his vision cleared and he felt steady enough, he discarded the condom and released the ties he'd set to secure Marcus in the suspended position. He lowered the rigging slowly, relaxing his grip only when Marcus was flat on the mattress.

As their gazes met, Marcus whispered, "Thank you."

Enver pressed a gentle kiss to his knee as he unwound the rope. "You don't have to thank me, but you're welcome."

"I don't think I could ever thank you enough."

"You already have, gorgeous." He continued freeing Marcus, checking any pressure points to confirm he hadn't pinched any veins, rubbed skin raw or broken any blood vessels. Satisfied the red marks were the result of Marcus's movement while he'd been restrained, he dropped the last of the rope into a pile on the floor he would clean up later.

"Feel all right?" Enver asked as he settled beside Marcus, pulling him close as he tugged a soft sheet up to cover them from the waist down.

"Good," Marcus responded with a lopsided smile as his eyes slid closed. "Fucking fantastic."

Enver caressed Marcus's cheek, loving the way his fingertips slid against the fine sheen of drying sweat and enjoying the heat of their skin pressed together. Marcus held his gaze, his eyes not as glassy or dilated now. Without a word, he offered his mouth.

Though every bone in Enver's body felt as though it had been reduced to rubber, he kissed Marcus long and slow, pushing against his lips with the tip of his tongue. Marcus opened, groaning softly as Enver slipped inside. Thoughts of what they'd done, what he wanted to do to him in the future, evaporated as his focus became how damn satisfying it was having Marcus against him.

Panting, he broke the kiss. He pulled in a breath, ready to settle down for Marcus's aftercare—and maybe a little of his own—but forced it out in a rush when he saw those eyes with the blown pupils gazing up at him with love and pleasure written all over his striking face.

"You're a walking, talking threat to my sanity, you know that, gorgeous?" He chuckled softly as Marcus's limp cock stirred against his thigh. "Always ready to go."

Marcus curled his arm around Enver's torso, lifting his knee to nudge against Enver's testicles. "Look who's talking."

"Is that good or bad?"

"It's a very good thing," Marcus said against Enver's neck as he nuzzled closer.

This had always been one of Enver's favorite parts of a session. Before it had been about letting the dust settle after an intense scene. But with Marcus, it was about reconnecting on a deeper, emotional level. Though Enver had always been careful to shower a sub with his affection and appreciation, with Marcus he felt the need to be especially demonstrative with his thanks. He'd demanded so much of Marcus, overwhelming him in every way possible and he'd taken it all and given back tenfold.

In the span of a few heartbeats, Marcus's breathing fell into an even pattern and his body grew heavy as his exhaustion finally got the better of him. Enver lay there with the man he loved cradled in his arms, wondering how the night could possibly get any more perfect.

A soft noise caught his attention, and he finally noticed they weren't as alone as he'd thought. He turned his head, looking out over the handful of people who'd gathered in the room at some point. The surge of anxiety he expected didn't arrive.

In fact, he felt more settled than ever before.

He pushed out a breath, waiting for the panic that had once accompanied the idea of having sex in public. He had no idea how long any of them had been there, but he found he didn't care. In fact, that warm glow that had taken up residence in the center of his chest since Marcus had accepted his proposal was back. Something told him there would be a lot of public play for them in Court—a paradise for exhibitionists and voyeurs alike—from this point forward. He had a beautiful, loving and willing submissive at his side.

What more could he ask for?

Drifting along on that post-amazing-sex high, he made eye contact with Kochran and Saint, searching for some kind of reprimand in his friends' gazes. Instead, he found nothing but total acceptance. Their respective lovers stood with them, an unlikely grouping of six that none of them could have ever imagined.

Now the group would be eight strong because of Marcus.

"About damn time, Furst," Kochran murmured as he pulled his soon-to-be wife against him and kissed her forehead. Ezra stepped against Maddy's other side, kissing her shoulder as he touched Kochran's face.

Saint and Boyce flanked Grae, their hands clasped together over her midsection.

And now Enver had Marcus. They'd come together in the most unlikely of ways, but they'd made it work. He couldn't have asked for anything better than the group of people he had with him in this room right now. He knew, even though the Noble House owners had found those they wanted to spend the rest of their kinky lives with, the best was yet to come.

* * * * *

To find out about other books by Sara Brookes or to be alerted to new releases, sign up for her announcement list at http://eepurl.com/mbG31.

This wasn't the first time Maddy had hacked into a kinky website. Porn sites weren't the easiest to weasel into, but certainly the most fun. Oddly, the task brought her a sense of accomplishment her day job didn't fulfill. It also provided hours of amusement on an otherwise boring Thursday night.

She adjusted the boom microphone on her headset as she waited for her business partner to accept the audio chat request. While she sat idle, she noticed a heavy layer of dust along one end of the long dining table she used as a desk for her dual computer setup. The fine particles' perfection was marred by a line of paw prints courtesy of her cat, Samoa.

"Hey, Maddy." Steve's baritone voice rescued her from her debate about the merits of attaching dusting pads to Samoa's paws. "I was just chatting about you to a potential client who insists his site is secure enough without our 'extremely expensive services'."

"If it truly is, he wouldn't be talking to you," she replied. "Send me the details and I'll show him just how much he desperately needs us." Maddy tried not to sound eager about the idea of schooling some unsuspecting *n00b* who doubted her skills.

"That's my girl." A soft ding sounded over the line as Steve received an email. "And another satisfied customer who can't stop praising your work. You make this too easy sometimes, Maddy."

Fact of the matter was, most of the time this job *was* too easy. "Got a live one for you, if you've got the time."

"I always have the time for you. Finished up work for the night already?"

"You mean the exceptionally boring list of client websites I was given to intentionally break into? Pfft. Please don't insult me. Packets are already on the way, along with my billable hours."

She wouldn't have to mention how bored she'd been with the tasks. How the work lacked challenge. Steve would know their job of rooting around an assigned website for glitches and then putting together a solution package for the customer was work she could execute blindfolded. Even though the responsibility didn't give her the same exhilarating rush of infiltrating unsuspecting sites, it certainly paid the bills.

"Just grabbing a snack between meetings." He paused, a sign he was ingesting his go-to snack of Funyuns. No doubt there was a can of Dr. Pepper nearby. "Go ahead and educate me, wise master."

She verified they were the only ones on the private network he'd set up before she tapped a button on her keyboard to share her desktop screen. While she didn't doubt Steve's skill in the least, in their line of work it paid to double and sometimes triple check before execution.

"Holy shit." Surprise filtered through her earphones as Steve got an eyeful of her latest discovery. "Warn a guy next time."

Maddy winced. The XXX-rated splash page that displayed a nude woman bound with ropes of pink LED lights had probably shocked Steve's vanilla mind. She'd forgotten not everyone was as comfortable with deviant behavior as she was. Risks had been a part of her everyday world since the age of twelve, when she'd stolen her father's car and taken a joyride to Disneyland.

"Sorry." She drummed her fingers on her desk as she waited for him to get over his surprise. She didn't feel bad about scandalizing him. Steve O'Doyle wasn't just the co-owner of Devtag, working out of the East Coast bureau while she provided support out of her home office in California—he was also her ex-boyfriend. As far as a kick-ass gaming companion and business partner, Steve was the man. However, when it came to the matter of sex, the poor guy had "clueless" stamped across his forehead. Too married to his work to have normal, healthy relationships.

"Take a look at what I just ran across." She right-clicked to open a window for the source code, effectively covering the explicit image to preserve Steve's sensibilities. While he wouldn't care what the website was peddling, he would be interested in the strings of code used to construct the site.

"This is…whoa." Quiet whispers sounded as Steve read through the lines populating his screen. "I think you hit the motherlode."

She sat up straighter as Steve fell quiet. "Biggest steaming pile of shit you've ever seen, right? You'd think a sex website would have stricter security protocols."

Steve's loud snort came through her headphones. "My skills aren't top-notch, but even I know better. Whoever coded this drivel should have their geek license revoked. No one codes like this."

"Except for maybe some pimple-faced junior high school dweeb working on a WYSIWYG interface," she responded as she wrinkled her nose at a string of characters she recognized from her basic computer classes freshman year of college, which had indeed had what-you-see-is-what-you-get software. She'd never seen programming code this disorganized and simplistic. It had been too easy to crack, and Maddy hated easy. Easy meant a loss of revenue. "They're just giving away their porn. Quality sex videos should never be free. Fucking amateurs."

"School 'em, Maddy-girl."

"You going to stick around to watch?" she asked as she pulled up a search on her second desktop computer. The one with the unmasked, fully legal IP address she used for her everyday browsing. As she read the extensive background on the About tab of the website, she recognized the name of the owner, Kochran Duke. "Hey, I know of this guy."

"Former beau?"

"Didn't you know I have lovers all over the country?" Maddy giggled at Steve's snort. "I didn't say I knew him, just that I know *of* him. The Duke family owned most of downtown San Francisco when I was in high school. Think my mom mentioned chatting with Kochran's parents a few times at the country club when she took tennis lessons Dad gifted her one Christmas. Also called them stuck-up prudes, if I recall correctly."

"Which is saying a lot coming from your mother."

Steve hadn't needed to point out the obvious. Her mom got along with everyone, and found the tiniest detail to like about the meanest, rudest person in the world. For her to express her aversion to the Duke family said a lot about how they conducted themselves.

The knowledge that Kochran owned the club wouldn't stop Maddy's intrusion of the website. He might have connections and nothing better to do with his parents' millions, but she had megaskills that trumped bored millionaires.

She cleared her throat, antsy to get started. "You never said if you're going to hang."

"I've got a meeting with a new client based in Japan at ten, but I can stick around for a few more minutes. Always a joy to watch Maddy Zane, badass hacker extraordinaire, work."

Maddy smirked. "All right. Let's see what this place is really all about."

A few keystrokes got her back to the front page of the website for a fetish organization near Sacramento called Noble House. According to the scrolling marquee across the top, it was a hybrid kink club with a physical location to serve members as well as the website.

"Unique concept, I'll give it that much," Steve said around a mouthful of snacks. "Odd name for a BDSM club, though. Not that I'm well-versed in that department."

Maddy had seen and heard plenty of BDSM club names, but nothing like this. As though Kochran equated his business to some modern-day fairy tale of sin where he probably saw himself as the ruler. Given her mother's description of his parents, it wouldn't surprise her to hear. "Think I'm going to snoop around a bit more. See just how lax things are."

She focused on her custom-built secure desktop with its high-level encryption that allowed her to surf without anyone tracking her geolocation and quickly added a bunch of random information to the membership database. When it came time to complete a sexual interest list, she blindly filled out a few pertinent details. Thankfully Steve couldn't see the screen of that computer, but no reason to tick off boxes for stuff she *actually* liked.

Once that was done, she had the system generate a random password. When a generic confirmation email arrived, she snorted loud enough to disturb the cat now sleeping on the corner of her desk. She glanced to the computer's clock. "Accessed and joined without spending a dime in forty-one seconds."

Mothertruckers.

"Looks like we've got another idiot playing with a toy he has no right to own." Steve's short burst of laughter signaled his amusement. While Maddy knew Steve wasn't into kinky sexual practices, she did know he got a thrill from illegally accessing websites. That shared interest was why they'd started a legitimate business together even after their relationship had fallen apart.

"Time to find out just how far down this rabbit hole we can go," Maddy stated as she assigned herself a screen name, choosing something she would have never dreamed of in real life. She pulled up a blank email and shared the username and password with Steve. "Just use this account for right now. No reason for both of us to be there if it's not necessary."

"Trixy Malone?" Steve asked a minute later.

The mocking tone of Steve's voice made her roll her eyes. "Just poke around a bit to see if you can figure out busiest sections so we can avoid them."

Though she could find out the information in a few minutes, it would keep Steve occupied while she hunted for the best spot to drop in a beauty of a program she'd written to allow her to return to the site undetected whenever she wanted. Most of the time the websites she hacked weren't worth a revisit, but who was she to pass up a free ticket to unrestricted porn?

"Based on the webstats, the video archive is the most visited area," Steve offered a few minutes later. "Members' message boards come in a close second. The archives would be the easiest place to drop in a virus, but also too predictable. Even with the rudimentary code, the website admin would quickly find the intruder. Then again, if it was the same coder responsible for this junk heap, maybe not. Taking the chance isn't worth it. Better to find someplace more secure."

Samoa jumped off the desk and wound between her legs, meowing loudly that it was well past dinnertime. "Yeah, yeah. Demanding fat cat, aren't you?"

"Hey!" Steve exclaimed, clearly offended. "I know I've let time get away from me, but no reason to insult a guy for a few extra pounds."

"My roommate is reminding me it's well past dinner time." Maddy scooped up Samoa and scratched between her ears. "Didn't you say you had a meeting? I've got this from here."

"Yeah," Steve said with a sigh. His reluctance to leave came through the line. Like her, he clearly wanted to explore further.

"I doubt we're the first ones to discover the hole, Steve. Not even sure it's large enough to notify Kochran. Probably just a fluke." Anomalies weren't uncommon on the internet, but she didn't believe that was the case. Something told her this couldn't be written off as a simple glitch.

"Could be a potential client," Steve noted. "All right with you if I stick around?"

That was the beauty of their partnership. Steve saw dollar signs and a possible new contract that would further expand their business. Maddy saw ways to pad her hacker resume. It was a win-win for them both. "Of course. Be back in about ten minutes."

She tossed her headphones to the desk as she rose. The brief break in the action would let her clear her head, concoct a game plan, and get some much-needed fuel. She made her way to the kitchen to grab a can of tuna for Samoa and a container of soup for herself. Not her preferred dinner, but certainly the easiest and quickest. And according to the note stuck to the cabinet, her only choice. She leaned a hip against the counter and noticed a second note affixed to her refrigerator. A third and a fourth on her coffee pot. All bright little slips of neon-colored paper reminding her she hadn't been grocery shopping in three weeks.

Restocking her cabinets took time, and now that she'd discovered a weakness, she didn't *have* time. With full access to the website, she wanted to exploit the flaw that called to her, as addicting as any drug. Groceries be damned.

If she'd found the way in, so could someone else. She wasn't about to let some jerkoff swoop in and claim this victory. Not when she'd rightfully done so. Steve wouldn't want that to happen either.

Some people found pleasure in whips and chains. Madeline Zane got off on skirting the law. Laws were more like guidelines anyway. A line drawn in the sand just begging to be crossed. Maddy hadn't yet found a single line she hadn't been willing to leap over.

Samoa had already curled up in her worn office chair by the time she arrived at her desk again. Maddy gently nudged the cat away, settling down in front of her setup. Samoa strutted across her desk, leaving another line of tracks through the dust before settling in one corner. The cat's lemon-yellow eyes flashed, clearly annoyed plans for a nap in the comfort of the chair had been interrupted.

Pissing off her cat was the least of Maddy's concern. As she settled her headphones into place, she saw Steve was still logged in. She'd hope he hadn't been able to get out of the meeting he'd mentioned earlier, but it didn't appear so. "Find anything?"

"Despite the ease we got in with, everything looks well organized," he offered.

"At least something around here is done right."

She wasn't looking for anything in particular. Just a place where she could settle down for a bit and innocently interact with legal, paying members of the site. Sure, she'd broken countless federal privacy laws, but she had to entertain herself somehow. If she hadn't gotten out of San Francisco, her life would have been the typical upper-middle class life her parents had settled into. A brick rancher with a white-picket fence and a pool in the backyard. Days spent shuttling two-point-five kids to karate and ballet lessons. Nights entertaining the neighbors and gossiping about the same thing day after day. Rituals of civilized social interactions where she'd be expected to mask her truest desires. Nothing wrong with that sort of lifestyle, but Maddy had known at a young age she'd been destined for something else.

Shaking off the phantom threads of the life she didn't

want, Maddy focused on the website. While everything looked interesting, she was especially intrigued by the four tiny blue letters in the top right of the window.

"Hey, Steve, you see the beta-testing section?"

"Logging in now."

She followed without hesitation. User-level testing meant that section wasn't fully functional yet, but the developer welcomed feedback from users. It also meant glitches that were prime for exploitation. Bugs that could be manipulated, as Steve would say.

Though the graphically intense section took a few minutes to load, the speed still surprised her. "Someone spent a lot of time constructing this. Reminds me a little of SimLife."

Steve laughed. "You know, it does."

SimLife was a quirky computer game she'd played as a teen where she'd spent hours meticulously developing a computer-generated character. The game hadn't kept her attention long, as the personality parameters she'd given the character had caused it to set fire to the house in a fit of paranoia and perish.

A towering building that resembled a fortress stood off to her left. Thanks to a quick round of Google-fu that displayed images of the actual building, she knew it was the BDSM club in virtual glory.

Thick, lush forest surrounded the building, the summer-green leaves blowing gently in a computer-generated breeze. It was a nice effect that added a layer of authenticity to the world.

"Guess we'll see just how close it truly is. Let me whip something up for us." The controls were easy enough to quickly figure out. She put together a character truly fitting of the handle Trixy Malone. Red flowing locks. Big boobs. Shapely legs that went on for miles. After a few adjustments—and the addition of a low-cut, tight fitting outfit she would have never selected in real life—she saved the character. Steve's wolf whistle confirmed she'd chosen wisely.

She dropped her newly minted avatar in the center of a pixelated cobblestone street. She used the arrow keys on her keyboard to steer toward a signpost at an intersection. Three arrows directed the flow of vehicular and pedestrian traffic. To her left was the club. To her right, a city center bustling with activity.

"Interesting," she said, tapping her fingers again the desk again. "Wasn't expecting there to be anything beyond the club in here."

"How about we split up?" Steve offered, "You can check out the town and I'll take a look at club."

Maddy glanced through the coding before asking, "Can we do that?"

"You're not the only one with skills, Zane." A second later a duplicate of her Trixy avatar appeared on the screen. "Simple enough to drop a loop into the code to trick the program into allowing us two av's of the same character. Go forth and explore. Let me know what you find."

She watched Steve guide the dupe of her sim toward the club building before she headed to the right. As she drew closer, she noticed mixed-use buildings that housed a variety of businesses. Strange for a fetish club website. She wandered around for a time, making small talk with the other simulated people through simple chat bubbles. She wasn't looking for anything in particular in this secondary world, just somewhere to settle into comfortably and put her observation skills to work. Steve hadn't said anything for a few minutes, so she assumed he was busy exploring the club. Or getting his mind blown.

She approached a pair of sims who were obviously not inhibited by the public setting. The female avatar sat on an ornate park bench, her legs spread. A man kneeled between her thighs, his face buried deep as he worshipped her. Just as Maddy passed, the woman grabbed the man's head and gave off a high, keening wail according to the little chat bubble that appeared over the sim's head. Of course simulated public sex would be allowed in an explicit virtual theme park.

When she noticed a yellow blinking light at the corner of her screen, she remembered her old computer game's need to be fed at regular intervals. "You getting the same notification, Steve?"

"Yeah, I see it. I was just going to ask you about it. Health depletion, maybe?"

"I think so. Give me a second." She steered her sim to a frozen yogurt cart to purchase a small tub. She clicked "eat" and her sim gobbled up the sweet confection in record time. The yellow dot changed to a red heart, her sim content with her life not hanging in the balance.

"Well, isn't that clever? Think we're good to go now." Easy to see how hours upon hours could be lost inside with members dropping a few cool bills in a short span of time. It was more than just a way to interact sexually with the club and other members. They could also have entire lives. Families. Jobs, for fuck's sake, as she thought about the sim that had sold her the treat. "Looks like there are two settings. A single payment system for an allotted amount of time and another game mode like this. Either way, someone is going to make a fortune when this program clears beta testing."

"No shit," Steve responded.

"How are you making out?"

"This place is unreal, Maddy. Never seen anything like it."

"Not offending your virgin sensibilities, is it?" She hadn't thought of it before, but perhaps it would have been better for her to explore the club aspect of the sim instead of Steve.

"Very funny. I'm a grown boy who can handle— holy fucksticks. These two guys are in a wrestling ring doing some seriously impressive MMA moves. This is better than watching Conor McGregor in the cage… or maybe not."

"Okay?" Maddy asked, concerned Steve had gotten in over his head.

"Guy just came out of the crowd, grabbed the other guy's dick and started blowing him. They both took the first guy down. Time for me to move along."

Maddy giggled at the panic-tinged words from her friend. "Sure you don't want to switch?"

"No. Things can't get much worse than that. Let you know if I find anything else worth discussing."

She wanted to point out Steve was going to probably run into a lot he'd have questions about, but she left him alone for the time being. Instead, she angled toward a theater and decided to go inside to see what kind of moviegoers this place catered to. It wouldn't be hard to guess, given the atmosphere, but she wondered if the movies would be computer-generated as well. As she slipped through a pair of swinging doors, she found a darkened theater with most of the seats filled.

Up on the oversized screen, the images weren't simulated as she'd thought. Instead, it appeared to be a live feed from inside the real club. It was an odd mix of life and computer-generated simulator she found fascinating. Surprisingly, the video quality was remarkable. The decor of the room on the screen was impeccable and lush. The theater around her, though truly just an artful arrangement of pixels, had the same attention to detail.

A sign this place wasn't just some run-of-the-mill porn site managed by a bunch of sweaty, kinky people looking to make some money. This was how these people *lived*. They breathed bondage and domination.

Small conversation bubbles appeared over the heads of several members. Though they appeared interested in the video playing on the screen, the hot ticket for the night would be a session starring Kochran Duke himself. If the accolades were to be believed, Kochran wasn't just the owner of the club, but an active participant. The Hardcore King of Noble House had quite a reputation, and a number of fans judging by the chatter taking place among the theater patrons. Evidently, he was the best at what he did. The only person she knew who was *that* good at what he did was a comic book character, and she seriously doubted Kochran had an adamantium-coated skeleton or looked like Hugh Jackman.

While she didn't consider herself a prude by any means, that was a lot of naked flesh parading around as entertainment for the audience while they waited for the featured scene to begin. They'd taken a page straight out of *Rocky Horror*—the avatars on the stage acted out whatever was occurring on the screen. Right down to the orgy. Thighs and shoulders and breasts and butts

and cocks all came together in a pile of sinfully decadent human flesh. Loud moans and groans accompanied the sounds of flesh slapping together.

Outside of the sim, her body temperature rose. She
was alone in her house, Steve couldn't see her, but that
didn't stop her cheeks from heating as she watched the
people writhing on both screens. She shivered. Goose
bumps crawled up her arms, collected at the base of
her neck, shot down her spine and punched her in the
gut. She'd gone from world-class hacker to wanton sex
goddess in two seconds flat.

Now she understood why Noble House was considered one of the premier fetish sites on the internet.

Don't miss
Switch It Up *by Sara Brookes.*
Available now wherever
Carina Press ebooks are sold.
www.CarinaPress.com

Also available from Sara Brookes
Ragged Edge, *a Body Masters novel*

Dalton is no stranger to hitting rock bottom. He's worked hard to turn his life around. Now he has a quiet life, a successful business and a no-strings-attached arrangement for sex with Kincade. Everything is just as it should be. Then a late-night rendezvous is interrupted by a sexy newcomer, and Dalton realizes something is missing.

Caught up in the intense passion the men share, Erin finds herself fighting her desire to run or to get between these two hard bodies. She's convinced her attraction is wrong. However, a little persuasion from both Dalton and Cade convinces her she belongs with and between them.

Erin's surrender becomes Dalton's reawakening. A BDSM master, Dalton is in his element wielding command, and soon the threesome fill their nights with mind-blowing pleasure. But when a piece of Dalton's past resurfaces, it threatens the very foundation he's built and could put him back at the bottom.

To purchase and read this and other books by Sara Brookes, please visit Sara's website at sarabrookes.com.

About the Author

A native Virginian, Sara sold her first romance novel in 2009. Since that fateful day, she's published books in various sub-genres of romance, been generously honored with several awards, and saved the world from evil chocolate chip cookies.

She has won the PRISM Award from the RWA's Fantasy, Futuristic and Paranormal chapter for Best Futuristic Romance, and the HOLT Medallion award from RWA's Virginia Romance Writers chapter for Best Erotic Romance. She was also selected as a finalist for an RT Reviewer's Choice Award for Best Erotic Romance.

Though she may insist otherwise, Sara loves the places her mind conjures and has always been fascinated by the strange, the unusual, the twisted and the lost (tortured heroes are her personal favorite). She is an action movie junkie, addicted to coffee and has been known to stay up until the wee hours of the morning playing RPG video games. Despite all this geekiness, she is a romantic at heart and is always a sucker for an excellent love story.

You can find Sara on the web at www.sarabrookes. com, on Twitter at www.Twitter.com/Sara_Brookes, on Facebook at www.Facebook.com/brookesofbooks, her street team group at www.Facebook.com/groups/brookesbooktique and via her new release notification newsletter http://eepurl.com/mbG31.